PENGUIN CLASSICS

RUSSIAN ÉMIGRÉ SHORT STORIES
FROM BUNIN TO YANOVSKY

BRYAN KARETNYK is a Wolfson Scholar at University College London. He was awarded a degree in Russian and Japanese from the University of Edinburgh in 2008, having spent periods in Moscow, St Petersburg and Tokyo, and went on to serve in British Intelligence for a number of years before returning to academia. In recent years he has translated several novels by the émigré author Gaito Gazdanov, including *The Spectre of Alexander Wolf* (2013), *The Buddha's Return* (2014) and *The Flight* (2016). His work focuses on Vladimir Nabokov and the literature of the Russian diaspora.

T0200842

Russian Émigré Short Stories from Bunin to Yanovsky

Edited and with an Introduction and Notes by
BRYAN KARETNYK

PENGUIN BOOKS

IVAN JURITZ, *in memoriam*
1988–2015

PENGUIN CLASSICS

UK | USA | Canada | Ireland | Australia
India | New Zealand | South Africa

Penguin Books is part of the Penguin Random House group of companies
whose addresses can be found at global.penguinrandomhouse.com.

First published in Penguin Classics 2017
This edition published in 2019
001

Introduction and editorial material © Bryan Karetnyk, 2017
All translations copyright © the translator(s) concerned
The Acknowledgements on pp. 423–8 constitute an extension of this copyright page
All rights reserved

The moral right of the editor and the translators has been asserted

Set in 10.25/12.25 pt Adobe Sabon
Typeset by Jouve (UK), Milton Keynes
Printed and bound in Great Britain by Clays Ltd, Elcograf S.p.A.

ISBN: 978-0-241-29973-9

www.greenpenguin.co.uk

MIX
Paper from
responsible sources
FSC® C018179

Contents

RUSSIAN ÉMIGRÉ
SHORT STORIES

Chronology

Prior to January 1918, the Julian calendar was in use throughout Russia, lagging thirteen days behind the Gregorian one common in Europe at the time. All dates before 1918 are given in accordance with the Julian calendar ('Old Style') and thereafter with the Gregorian calendar ('New Style').

1914 *15 July*: Outbreak of the First World War.

1917 *23 February–3 March*: February Revolution.

2 March: Abdication of Nicholas II.

25–6 October: October Revolution. Leader of the Provisional Government Alexander Kerensky flees Petrograd as Lenin seizes power.

1918 *3 March*: Treaty of Brest-Litovsk signed, ending Russia's participation in the First World War. Russia descends into civil war.

March–November 1919: Allied intervention in the Russian Civil War.

July: Nicholas II and all immediate members of the royal family are executed at Ekaterinburg.

11 November: Armistice signed between the Allies and Germany, ending the First World War.

1919 *October*: General Anton Denikin's White Army is defeated at Oryol.

1920 *February*: General Evgeny Miller and 800 Russian refugees are evacuated from Arkhangelsk to Tromsø. Admiral Alexander Kolchak is executed by the Bolsheviks.

March: General Alexander Kutepov's Volunteer Army evacuated from Novorossiysk to the Crimea, where they join with General Baron Pyotr Wrangel's army.

November: First issue of *Sovremennye zapiski* published in Paris; first issue of *Rul'* published in Berlin.

December: Collapse of the Crimean defences. Baron Wrangel flees Russia. Remnants of the government and the White Army are evacuated to Gallipoli and Constantinople.

1921 *January*: More than 130 Russian émigré newspapers have been set up worldwide.

February: Last evacuations from the Crimea.

September: Norwegian explorer Fridtjof Nansen is appointed the League of Nations' High Commissioner for Refugees, his principal brief to assist the many Russians displaced during the Revolution and Civil War.

1922 *January*: More than 700,000 unnaturalized Russians are believed to be living in Europe and the Near East, approximately a third of whom reside in Germany, and a further 145,000 in the Far East, mostly in Harbin and Shanghai.

28 March: Vladimir Dmitrievich Nabokov (father of the author) is killed by ultra-right monarchists in Berlin in an attempt to assassinate the liberal politician Pavel Milyukov.

September: German ships SS *Oberbürgermeister Haken* and SS *Preussen* carry more than 160 expelled Russian intellectuals from Petrograd to Stettin, Germany (now Szczecin, Poland).

1923 *June*: Germany estimates that some 360,000 Russians are living in Berlin.

November: Hyperinflation peaks in the Weimar Republic.

December: Almost sixty émigré publishing houses have been founded in Berlin.

1924 *16 February*: In Paris Ivan Bunin gives a speech on the 'mission' of the Russian émigré community, promoting the notion that the Russian emigration is the true heir to Russia's cultural legacy following the Revolution.

6 June: First 'Day of Russian Culture' held in Estonia.

September: *Illiustrirovannaia Rossiia* begins publication in Paris. Baron Wrangel establishes the Russian All-Military Union (ROVS), an organization whose aim was to purge Russia of Bolshevism.

1928 *25 April*: Baron Wrangel dies in Brussels and is succeeded as leader of ROVS by General Kutepov.

1930 *January*: Around 175,000 Russians are thought to be living in Paris, while the figure in Germany has reduced to 90,000. General Kutepov is kidnapped in Paris by the OGPU (Soviet secret police) and is succeeded as leader of ROVS by General Miller.

March: *Chisla* begins publication in Paris.

1931 *October*: Final issue of *Rul´* published.

1932 *February*: Japanese forces occupy Harbin; many émigrés leave for Shanghai and Hong Kong.

6 May: At the Hôtel Salomon de Rothschild in Paris, Russian émigré poet Pavel Gorgulov assassinates French president Paul Doumer.

September: Founding member of the Eurasia Movement and member of the Communist Party of Great Britain Prince Dmitry Svyatopolk-Mirsky quits England for the Soviet Union.

1933 *January*: Hitler takes power in Germany.

November: Ivan Bunin becomes the first Russian to be awarded the Nobel Prize for Literature.

1934 *June*: Final publication of *Chisla*.

1936 *July–April 1939*: The Spanish Civil War.

1937 *February*: The centenary of Pushkin's death is marked around the Russian-speaking world.

June: In Leningrad Prince Mirsky is arrested by the NKVD on suspicion of being a British spy.

August: *Russkie zapiski* begins publication in Paris and Shanghai.

September: General Miller is kidnapped in Paris by the NKVD and smuggled back to the Soviet Union, where he is tortured and executed.

November: Japanese forces occupy Shanghai.

1938 *December*: Henri Troyat (b. Lev Aslanovich Tarasov) is awarded the Prix Goncourt for his novel *L'Araigne*.

1939 *6 June*: Prince Mirsky dies in a corrective labour camp near Magadan in Russia's Far East.

September: Final issue of *Russkie zapiski* is published. Britain declares war on Germany. In France, all 'undesirable foreigners' are rounded up for deportation.

1940 *April*: Final issue of *Sovremennye zapiski* is published.

May: Vladimir Nabokov and his family escape to America aboard the SS *Champlain*.

June: Paris is occupied by Nazi troops.

October: The extensive collections of the Turgenev Library in Paris, the world's largest Russian library in exile, are confiscated and transported to Germany, where they disappear.

Introduction

Some natural tears they dropped, but wiped them soon;
The world was all before them, where to choose
Their place of rest . . .

Milton, Paradise Lost

Exile has a long and distinguished literary pedigree. From the expulsion of Adam and Eve from the Garden of Eden to the Egyptian and Babylonian captivities of the Israelites, from Ovid's exile at Tomis to Dante's banishment from Florence, the loss and attendant grief wrought by these episodes have inspired one of the world's richest, most poignant and most powerful literatures, giving rise to histories, laments and prophecies. Yet it is also in moments of the most profound crisis that renewal and innovation are found. For all the trauma of deracination and the privations of a life lived under foreign skies, the salt bread of distant lands has often nourished artists and writers, giving many the strength if not to surmount, then at least to endure their exilic condition, and to create works of great pathos, tragedy and humanity. Such was the case for those great swathes of Russians who in the opening decades of the twentieth century fled their homeland in the wake of revolution and civil war: the literature they would write is inextricably linked with the history of their exile.

The October Revolution of 1917, when Lenin's Bolshevik forces seized power from the Provisional Government, found a number of Russian artists already living abroad, principally in Paris and various other cities throughout Europe. Artists such as Wassily Kandinsky and Naum Gabo, and avant-garde poets such as Valentin Parnakh, Serge Charchoune and Mark Talov, had quit Russia in order to immerse themselves in the new artistic movements storming Europe at the start of the twentieth century, from Dada and futurism to surrealism and expressionism. Their numbers were nevertheless relatively slight, and their relocation for the most part self-imposed. However, in the years immediately following the February and October Revolutions of 1917 and the ensuing Civil War in Russia, a deluge of White Russians escaping the 'Red terror' of the fledgling Bolshevik regime would inundate Europe and the rest of the world. Precise figures of these refugees are still disputed, although most recent estimates put their number somewhere between 800,000 and 2 million. While a disproportionate part of this 'first wave' of Russian emigration did come from the upper echelons of the political, social and cultural elites, all strata of society were accounted for in the exodus, which encompassed almost every nation, caste and creed from within the vast boundaries of Imperial Russia. As one critic noted:

> Contrary to popular fancy, the Russian emigration was more than a parade of ballerinas, operatic basses, grand dukes, and would-be Anastasias ... Thousands of Cossacks and soldiers from the defeated White armies imparted a military coloration. Politicians, journalists, lawyers, doctors, engineers, priests, professors, businessmen, and shopkeepers contributed a bourgeois flavor. Muzhiks fleeing famine added a peasant element, and a dash of *Lumpenproletariat* and criminal flotsam mingled with the general flow.[1]

The routes taken out of Russia were manifold, but three conduits came to be the most common: the Russian north via Finland or the Baltic region; the south through the Ukraine, the Crimea and the Caucasus; and the Far East, across the border into Manchuria. Civilians were often carried along with the general flow of military movement. As the Red Army gained territory throughout 1918 and 1919, the beleaguered soldiers of the White armies, along with many of their wives and children, were pushed out to Russia's extremities. The ordeal was a brutal one. Admiral Alexander Kolchak's army, the largest in Siberia, was driven eastwards from Ufa in the southern Urals, along the Trans-Siberian Railway through Omsk and Tomsk, eventually coming to a halt at Irkutsk, where in February 1920 the Bolsheviks ultimately executed Kolchak. The depleted army, now under the command of General Vladimir Kappel, fled farther east, across a frozen Lake Baikal and into Manchuria via Chita. Chill winds and extreme subarctic temperatures felled many during the retreat, leaving, according to contemporary accounts, a macabre tableau of frozen corpses on the ice. In the south the Volunteer Army, first under General Lavr Kornilov and later under General Anton Denikin, also suffered staggering losses: having been repelled from Rostov in February 1918, they retreated south into the frozen steppes of the Kuban – the infamous 'Kornilov Ice March' – where the troops, ravaged by losses and abject conditions, mounted an ill-fated attack on Ekaterinodar, the newly established capital of the North Caucasian Soviet Republic. Following Kornilov's death during shelling outside the city, Denikin led the army in one final assault on Moscow before it suffered a decisive defeat at Oryol. After retreating southwards once again to Novorossiysk, the remaining troops and civilians were evacuated to the Crimea.

For many émigré writers, the horror of the Civil War would become a recurring theme in their respective oeuvres, often more formative to their work than the experience of exile itself would ever be. The Crimea in particular took on a symbolic role as Old Russia's last stand. Many would see Russia for the last time as they were evacuated from the Tauric Peninsula after it was finally taken by the Bolsheviks in winter 1920. One hundred and twenty-six ships – British, French and Russian – carried more than 145,000 men, women and children across the Black Sea, mostly to Gallipoli and Constantinople. In her collection of short stories *Morning (Utro)*, Bunin's protégée Galina Kuznetsova would vividly recall the chaotic scenes as civilians and troops clamoured for space on board the departing ships, and the pathetic scenes as Cossacks were forced to abandon their horses. Later others, such as Ivan Lukash, would remember the haunting, dream-like atmosphere that pervaded those first days of exile in the partitioned Ottoman Empire.

With the evacuation of the Crimea, Russia's Civil War drew to a close. Those who had fled Bolshevism initially sought refuge on Russia's periphery, hoping that the instability of the regime would bring about its swift collapse. Constantinople, Sophia, Belgrade, Riga and Prague became the first centres of emigration in Europe, with Harbin and Shanghai serving similarly in the Far East. As the years progressed, however, and the situation became more entrenched, many of those European refugees would travel onwards to Western Europe, with large numbers resettling in Paris and Berlin, the two major European capitals of the emigration during the interwar years. By 1922, a conservative estimate placed some 250,000 Russian refugees living in the Weimar Republic, and up to 75,000 in France – a figure that by 1930 had increased to almost 200,000, according to a report prepared by the Sub-committee of Private Organizations for Refugees. Aside from Russia's historical and cultural ties with France and Germany, pragmatics also played a crucial role in these migratory trends: France's labour shortage in the wake of the First World War was an attractive factor for many Russians, and, similarly, the collapse of the German currency and rampant hyperinflation made living in the Weimar Republic a temptingly affordable prospect. Such was the initial draw of Berlin – in both economic and cultural terms – that even many of those Russians who had lived in Paris prior to the First World War would soon migrate eastwards to Berlin, 'to rejoin Russia'.[2]

While much of the old political and military elite headed for Paris and Brussels, Berlin – and in particular the districts of Wilmersdorf and Charlottenburg (or 'Charlottengrad', as it became known) – made its name as the first capital of Russian cultural life abroad, with masked balls, exhibitions, poetry evenings, cabarets and theatres, as well as the publication of newspapers and magazines catering to the new diaspora. Berlin, however, was a locus not only for White Russians. Throughout the early 1920s Russian émigrés and their Sovietized compatriots sojourning in Berlin mixed more freely than one might have expected: liberal policies governing the movement of people meant that the city temporarily played host to every sort of Russian, trenchant anti-Bolshevik and proud Soviet passport-holder alike, as well as every shade of grey in between. Of this

confluence of people and competing ideologies, the Soviet writer
Ilya Ehrenburg recalled:

> There was a place in Berlin that reminded one of Noah's Ark where
> the clean and unclean met peaceably; it was called the House of
> Arts and was just a common German café where Russian writers
> gathered on Fridays. Stories were read by Tolstoy, Remizov, Lidin,
> Pilnyak, Sokolov-Mikitov. Mayakovsky declaimed. Yesenin,
> Marina Tsvetayeva, Andrey Bely, Pasternak, Khodasevich recited
> poetry ... A storm broke out at a lecture by the painter Pougny;
> Arkhipenko, Altman, Shklovsky, Mayakovsky, Gabo, Lissitzky
> and I argued furiously.[3]

Come 1924, the Weimar Republic had been able to curb hyperinflation and stabilize its economy following the introduction
of the Rentenmark the previous year, driving up the cost of
living and forcing many émigrés to leave. Despite the considerable difficulty of obtaining work permits, many chose to join
their compatriots in Paris, where the sizeable Russian community
had established a similar enclave, situated predominantly on the
border of the Bois de Boulogne – in the 16th arrondissement in
Passy and Auteuil and in the suburb of Neuilly.

The Far East saw the influx of over 250,000 Russians between
1918 and 1922. More than half of these settled first in Manchuria
and at China's treaty ports such as Shanghai, Tientsin (Tianjin)
and Tsingtao (Qingdao), while others ventured farther afield, to
Hong Kong, Indochina, Japan and elsewhere. Railway enterprise at the turn of the twentieth century had given Russian
industrialists a lucrative way into Manchuria, and so by the time
the Revolution came, Harbin, one of Manchuria's largest cities,
already had a well-established Russian community of approximately 34,000, making it a natural destination for those fleeing
Bolshevism in the East. By 1922 Harbin's Russian population
had almost quadrupled, and the city had developed a vibrant
cultural scene that boasted a symphony orchestra, an opera,
three daily Russian newspapers and a variety of weekly magazines catering to its Russian inhabitants. It also hosted regular
visits from notable public figures, academics and international

performers. In fact, Harbin was one of the few destinations where the Russian émigré community largely fared better than the local population, who in this particular case lived in the cholera-infested *fangzi* by the wharf. In Shanghai, amid the tree-lined avenues of the French Concession, 'little Russia' with its three Orthodox churches also accommodated its fair share of Russian celebrities, including the singer Alexander Vertinsky and the artist Vladimir Tretchikoff. For many, however, the living in Shanghai was more arduous than in Harbin. Within many poverty-stricken families women in particular faced a difficult and dangerous time: a report prepared by the League of Nations estimated that in Shanghai some 22.5 per cent of Russian women between the ages of sixteen and forty-five were probably engaged in prostitution.

The headlong rush to escape the Red terror and its privations during and immediately after the Civil War meant that the majority of Russians fled between 1917 and 1922 – often in last-minute circumstances, often with few belongings. Personal accounts of the time are replete with stories of smugglers, jewels sewn into stuffed toys and even foreign currency hidden in umbrellas.[4] Despite this, funds often ran dry very quickly, and life abroad would be for many one of unrelenting hardship. The foreign press delighted in the romantic vision of aristocrats fallen on hard times – 'Princess as a Cow-Keeper: How Ruined Russians Earn a Living' ran one headline. There were indeed cases of noblemen becoming bakers, ice-cream vendors, even navvies; admirals turning their hands to millinery; generals becoming taxi-cab drivers; aristocrats turned restaurateurs. One account even told of an ex-colonel of the Imperial Russian army, now a dustman at Cannes, who was reputed to take *Tatler* merely to keep track of acquaintances;[5] while another gentleman only just managed to scrape a job as a cashier at a Russian restaurant in Constantinople by virtue of having been a professor of mathematics in former days.[6] Many also found occasional work in the burgeoning film industry: Countess Sumarokov-Elston spoke of 'the whole of Russian Nice . . . working as extras' for the director Rex Ingram and of the mountains above Cannes being transformed into a

Caucasian *aul* for the making of Alexandre Volkoff's *The White Devil* (1930), which starred the celebrated Russian actor Ivan Mosjoukine.[7] For many, however, the work was eminently bleaker. Gaito Gazdanov, for example, after a succession of menial jobs – loading and unloading barges on the Seine, washing locomotives, working at the Citroën factory – settled into the dismal routine of a night-time taxi-cab driver; Boris Butkevich, having landed at the port of Marseilles from the Far East, worked as a docker until his untimely death from tuberculosis, hastened by hunger and abject poverty. As Princess Zinaïda Schakovskoy summed up in her recollections of the period:

> The hardships incurred by the young émigré writers and poets should be realized by posterity. Heroes of literary passion, they were practically killing themselves not only by sleepless nights but also by hard work alien to their calling. There were the long years of bookkeeping for Smolensky, window-cleaning for Sofiev, house-painting for Alferov, night-watching for Zurov, graveyard shifts of heavy work at the station for Scott [Boldyrev], errand-boy jobs for Knut. Their existence was tragic; their past was the Civil War; their present, the cafés of Montparnasse; their future – there was no future.[8]

In the first years of emigration, the Russian expatriates lived as true refugees, preserving the hope that the Bolshevik regime would fall. As the years passed, however, and the fledgling Soviet state consolidated its power and gained international recognition, such hopes diminished until they were all but dashed by the mid-1920s, turning yesterday's political refugees, who had fled war and oppression, into émigrés *à l'ancien régime* and establishing them in their newfound status as exiles. Their legal status would nevertheless become increasingly insecure as a new wave of nationalism spread throughout Europe. The League of Nations, under the direction of Fridtjof Nansen in his role as High Commissioner for Refugees, introduced identity papers (the Nansen passport) to those Russians who had become de facto stateless persons; however, this document was severely limited in the powers it granted the bearer, and the continual pursuit of visas would become the bane of many émigrés' lives. Those who accepted Soviet passports, on the other hand, faced derision and scorn from all corners of the émigré community and were held by many to be traitors.

Whether for political reasons or for the sheer inability to contemplate a life lived beyond its borders, some Russian intellectuals did opt to return to their homeland: among major artists and writers, Andrei Bely, Marina Tsvetaeva, Maxim Gorky, Alexei Tolstoy, Yakov Protazanov and Sergei Prokofiev would ultimately find themselves back in the Soviet Union after periods abroad. Fuelled by a recognition of the loss of many of the country's most eminent artists and thinkers, the Soviet government actively sought to entice émigrés into returning. The Soviet author and agent Alexander Tarasov-Rodionov, for instance, once tried unsuccessfully to lure Nabokov back to sing the glories of 'farms, factories, forests in Fakistan', occasioning on the part of the émigré author only scorn and mirthful derision when he recalled the episode years later.[9] Astonishingly, even the Tsar's former military attaché in Paris, Count Alexei Ignatiev, returned and rose to the rank of lieutenant general in the Red Army; and another notable nobleman, the influential literary historian, critic and sometime politician Prince Dmitry Svyatopolk-Mirsky, also returned to the Soviet Union in 1932, having joined the Communist Party of Great Britain. One of the relatively few émigrés to have spent their exile in the United Kingdom, Mirsky numbered among his acquaintances much of the London literati. On the occasion of his departure Virginia Woolf noted in her diary: 'So hot yesterday – so hot, when Prince Mirsky came . . . now [he] returns to Russia "forever". I thought as I watched his eye brighten and fade – soon there'll be a bullet through your head.'[10] She was very nearly right. Mirsky fell under suspicion of spying for the British and was arrested by the NKVD in 1937, at the height of the Great Terror; he was convicted and sent to a corrective labour camp near Magadan in Russia's Far East, where he would die two years later. In an ironic twist of fate, Tarasov-Rodionov was also arrested during the Great

Terror on charges of spying; he was executed by firing squad in 1938.

The climate of emigration not only held a mirror to pre-existing political divides, but also ingrained them, driving the wedges deeper. Instead of uniting around their shared exilic condition, the Russian diaspora in fact became increasingly factionalized. In Europe, alongside liberals and staunch monarchists, there were also former Socialist Revolutionaries (SRs or *Esery*), Eurasianists (*Evraziytsy*), Young Russians (*Mladorossy*) and the Smenovekhovtsy.[11] In the Far East, pro-monarchist political adherence paved the way for the establishment of the Russian Fascist Party, which was headquartered in Harbin under the leadership of Konstantin Rodzaevsky. The experience of exile not only caused many to adopt a more entrenched political stance, but also polarized the diaspora with regard to its cultural aims and orientation – a distinction that would crystallize around the divide between the so-called 'older' and 'younger' generations.

As the Russian communities abroad began to see their status as refugees turn into that of exiles, the attendant psychological and intellectual reorientation brought the question of the émigré community's role in Europe into sharp relief. Harking back to the centuries-old notion of Russian messianism, the concept of the Russian 'mission' was given new impetus by the older generation of artists and writers, most notably in a speech of 1924, 'The Mission of the Russian Emigration', given in Paris by the writer and future Nobel laureate Ivan Bunin. The notion came to be encapsulated in the popular aphorism: 'We are not in exile, we are on a mission' (*my ne v izgnan'i, my v poslan'i*).[12] Thus many came to view the emigration's purpose, at least initially, as one of preservation and transmission: the preservation of the 'true' Russian heritage – that is, its culture as it was prior to its rupture in 1917, and in stark opposition to the emerging Soviet one – and its transmission, not only to their own children growing up in emigration, but also to the wider world. Of all the arts, literature was to prove the most divisive. For practitioners of music, dance and the visual arts, it was relatively easy to integrate into the cultural milieux of their

respective host countries. Diaghilev's Ballets Russes, composi-
tions by Rachmaninov and Stravinsky, works by Kandinsky,
Bakst, Somov, Larionov and Goncharova, to name but a few,
were immediately accessible to foreign audiences; yet the written word, by its very nature, was an altogether different matter.
Bound by its linguistic specificity, it was concrete, politicized,
inaccessible to outsiders. Indeed, for all the many Russian publishing houses that had been set up across Europe, émigré
writers, with few exceptions, experienced difficulty in finding
foreign markets for their work, since Western publishers were
more readily interested in the new literature emanating from
the Soviet Union.[13]

Nevertheless, the émigré press throughout Europe and Asia
was remarkably vibrant. By January 1921 over 130 Russian
newspapers had been set up worldwide. Berlin established itself
as the centre of émigré publishing on account of the cheap
labour and production costs resulting from hyperinflation,
although Paris, Riga, Prague, Harbin and Shanghai would also
remain significant publishing centres of the emigration until
well into the 1930s, when geopolitical events would gradually
but implacably halt their activity. Alongside newspapers, the
so-called 'thick journals' – a legacy of Russia's Silver Age –
were established broadly around the existing literary–political
groupings and reflected the splintered, often factional nature of
the arts in emigration. These several-hundred-page monthlies
and quarterlies contained poetry, short stories, excerpts of
novels, and reviews, as well as political, social and philosophical essays and criticism.

The pages of the liberal daily *Rul'* (*The Rudder*) in Berlin,
edited by Vladimir Dmitrievich Nabokov (the father of the
author), together with the left-leaning *Poslednie novosti* (*The
Latest News*) and right-leaning *Vozrozhdenie* (*The Rebirth*) in
Paris, offered the main loci for the politics of exile to be played
out. Even ostensibly trivial matters, such as spelling and orthography, took on the form of vehement public rhetoric within the
various publications' covers.[14] As the 'ark' of culture, the purity
of the Russian language was held as sacrosanct and many feared
its perversion through exposure not only to foreign languages,

but also to the influence of Soviet neologisms and jargon. While such fears were perhaps not entirely unfounded, instances of waning command over the Russian language would provide feuilletonists such as Teffi and Don Aminado with an abundance of grist to their satirical mills.

By far the most prestigious and long-standing of émigré journals in the interwar years was *Sovremennye zapiski* (*Contemporary Annals*). Founded in Paris in 1920 by a group of Socialist Revolutionaries including Mark Vishnyak and Vadim Rudnev, the first issue carried a statement from the editors, declaring their dedication 'first and foremost to the interests of Russian culture ... eschewing the question of any political affiliation held by the authors'. A bastion of the old guard, however, *Sovremennye zapiski* throughout much of the 1920s carried works penned by only the older generation – that is, those who had published in Russia before emigrating – and was initially reticent to include anything by the younger avant-garde and modernist writers and poets. Such was the reason that *Chisla* (*Numbers*) was launched. Despite its relatively short lifespan – ten issues in eight volumes over a period of five years – *Chisla* managed to make a name for itself as one of the most outspoken and controversial journals of the emigration. Under the general editorship of Nikolai Otsup, it opened its pages to the younger generation of writers, counting among its contributors the likes of Gaito Gazdanov, Yury Felsen, Irina Odoevtseva and Alexander Ginger, and the poets Boris Poplavsky, Anatoly Steiger and Serge Charchoune.

While the older generation of writers saw it as their duty to preserve and transmit their Russian cultural heritage, the younger generation was far more engaged in the literary trends of its European host countries. In Adamovich's satirical 'A Literary Studio', we see a group of writers collaborating on a new novel, conscious of avoiding any overlap with Soviet literature, yet caught between the Silver Age legacy of the emigration, the traditionalism of the older generation of writers and the influence of Proust and French modernism. Georgy Ivanov in his experimental 'The Atom Explodes' blends the traditions of classical Russian literature with French existentialism and the *document humain*,[15] while Yury Felsen's conscious reworking of Proust and Poplavsky's influence from the surrealists marked a distinct departure from the Russian tradition. Many authors on both sides of the generational divide also maintained close relations with leading figures of European letters: Ivan Shmelyov, for example, corresponded with and was highly esteemed by Thomas Mann; in the 1930s Nabokov frequently associated with leading Francophone literati including Jules Supervielle, Jean Paulhan and Franz Hellens; after emigrating to the United States, Vasily Yanovsky befriended W. H. Auden, who even wrote the introduction to Yanovsky's English-language debut *No Man's Time* (1967). Several among the younger generation would even leave Russian behind as their chosen literary language. The most famous among these is, of course, Nabokov's transition from Russian to English, but French was also the literary choice of Irène Némirovsky, Elsa Triolet, Joseph Kessel and Zinaïda Schakovskoy, to name only a few. Writing in French, the Russian-born Henri Troyat and Elsa Triolet would even go on to win the Prix Goncourt in 1938 and 1944, respectively. Literary groups such as the Studio Franco-Russe brought together leading figures of the French and Russian émigré worlds of belles-lettres to discuss topics ranging from Dostoevsky and the West to André Gide, Marcel Proust, René Descartes and Paul Valéry.

War would ring a death knell for much of émigré culture in Europe and Asia: the rise of Fascism throughout Europe and Japan's bid for empire in the Far East led to another wave of displacement for the émigrés. Although Russians had been trickling out of Berlin since 1924, Hitler's seizure of power in 1933 and its consolidation in the years after provided further impetus for many more to leave. Likewise, the Japanese occupation of Harbin and the establishment of the Manchukuo government in 1932 forced many Russian Harbinites to quit the city; many travelled south to join their compatriots in Shanghai (the so-called 'yellow Babylon') and Hong Kong, but as Japanese forces entered Shanghai in 1937 many would leave China altogether. As Europe and Asia yielded ever more to the grip of Fascism and imperialism, many émigrés would be compelled to pack their suitcases once more – this time fleeing to the Americas, if the funds were available – or else risk their fortunes amid the chaos of war.

The printed word suffered a fate similar to that of its authors: publishing houses and printing presses were forcibly closed, and many of their archives destroyed. For a time, at least, the Russian émigré community would fall silent. Its fate in the postwar years, however, looked very different. Those who had remained in Western Europe found that comparatively few publishing houses reopened – certainly nothing compared to the many that had been set up in the emigration's heyday – although a few outlets, such as *Novyi zhurnal* (*The New Review*), were launched in North America. Émigré culture was becoming more and more mistrusted in a progressively left-leaning Europe. Combined with the fact that the younger generation was growing up and had generally become much better integrated into its host cultures than the older generation had been, the vibrancy and individuality of the émigré enclaves waned. Their literature, banned in the Soviet Union until glasnost, would have to wait until the 1990s to receive the recognition it deserved.

The historian Marc Raeff notes that the privations of life in exile often led writers to undertake small projects: reviews, essays and short stories.[16] Compounded by the crisis of the novel in postwar Europe, the short story became the preferred creative vehicle for many émigré writers from the 1920s onwards. The novel in its traditional form was deemed by many European authors unable to reflect modernity and the postwar condition, and so the short story became a locus of creative innovation. Indeed, its vogue and distinction throughout this period was phenomenal: during the years of emigration the genre was raised to a prominence and level of sophistication that had never before been seen in Russia. Such is the rationale for this anthology, which presents a selection of stories by prose writers of the emigration. While the presentation of works is chronological according to author, the works themselves also reveal the history of the emigration, and the biographical notes on each author, as well as the editorial notes for the stories, provide additional historical and literary contextualization.

Throughout the collection readers will notice arabesques of recurring, contrasting and complementary themes, bridging writers of both the younger and older generations: from the hellish days of the Civil War and the agony of leaving Russia, to the tragicomedy of life in exile, plagued by the dream and nightmare of returning to Russia and those 'shadows of days' that haunted their memories. We see also an intimate portrait of the uncertain and shifting climate of *les années folles* and the Great Depression, the angst and anxiety of an age between two wars, one in which the polarizing ideologies of Fascism and Communism competed for supremacy. Beneath the surface of these stories simmer the various love affairs, rivalries and the very personal (and occasionally very public) vendettas of their authors; yet more importantly the stories reveal the bravery and courage of those writers, many of whom, having lost their homeland and everything dear to them, and endured such terrible hardship, found the strength to create and innovate.

The nature of an anthology is, of course, such that there is always more left out than it is possible to include. Regrettably, not every major writer on both sides of the generational divide is represented here: significant omissions include the authors Alexander Kuprin, Alexei Remizov and Boris Zaytsev; satirists Alexander Amfiteatrov and Arkady Averchenko; poets Marina Tsvetaeva, Anatoly Steiger, Boris Poplavsky and Valery Pereleshin, among many, many others.[17] Nor, in dealing with Russian émigrés, have we delved past the first wave of emigration that followed the revolutions of 1917 and the Civil War; the second and third waves, including the likes of Joseph Brodsky and Sergei Dovlatov, are beyond our scope: these tasks must fall to future anthologists. What is hoped for this anthology is in some measure a rediscovery of many authors long and unjustly forgotten by history. Most of the authors contained in this volume were banned from publication in the Soviet Union and have themselves only recently been rediscovered by their compatriots; compounding this neglect, reading tastes in the West have traditionally privileged Soviet literature as Russia's representative literature of the twentieth century. Yet, as we hope to demonstrate, these émigré authors and their works represent some of the most talented Russian writing of the last century, and moreover a unique confluence of European and Russian literary traditions. Their primary vehicle, born of necessity, was the short story, and it is for this reason that we present them here, with the aim of giving them a new lease of life, a new journey under foreign skies, in a new language.

B.S.K.

NOTES

1. John J. Stephan, *The Russian Fascists: Tragedy and Farce in Exile, 1925–1945* (London: Hamish Hamilton, 1978), pp. 1–2.
2. Annick Morard, *De l'émigré au déraciné: la 'jeune génération' des écrivains russes entre identité et esthétique (Paris, 1920–1940)* (Lausanne: L'Age d'homme, 2010), p. 58.
3. Ilya Ehrenburg, *Men, Years – Life. Volume III. Truce: 1921–33*, tr. Tatiana Shebunina in collaboration with Yvonne Kapp (London: MacGibbon and Kee, 1963), p. 20.
4. See, for example, the many personal histories contained in Part I of Michael Glenny and Norman Stone, eds., *The Other Russia* (London: Faber and Faber, 1990).
5. Ibid., p. 269.
6. Ibid., p. 231.
7. Ibid., p. 270.
8. Zinaïda Schakovskoy, 'Russian Montparnasse', *The Russian Review* xxxi/4 (1972), pp. 360–68 (p. 368).
9. Vladimir Nabokov, *Strong Opinions* (New York: Vintage, 1990), p. 98.
10. Virginia Woolf, *A Writer's Diary: Being Extracts from the Diary of Virginia Woolf*, ed. Leonard Woolf (London: Hogarth Press, 1953), pp. 181–2.
11. In exile, the Central Committee of the Party of Socialist Revolutionaries kept a 'foreign delegation' based in Prague, which operated between 1923 and 1940. The Eurasianists, Young Russians and Smenovekhovtsy were dubiously dubbed 'pro-Soviet patriots': in varying configurations they sought to square Russian Orthodoxy and monarchism with the fact of Soviet rule in Russia. The groups splintered and largely descended into factional bickering; none survived the Second World War.

12. The phrase is commonly attributed to Zinaida Hippius or Dmitri Merezhkovsky; however, Maria Rubins has pointed to the likely source being Nina Berberova's 'Lyric Poem' (*Liricheskaia poema*), which appeared in *Sovremennye zapiski* in 1927, containing the line: 'I'm not in exile, I'm on a mission' (*Ia ne v izgnan´i, ia – v poslan´i*). See Maria Rubins, *Russian Montparnasse: Transnational Writing in Interwar Paris* (London: Palgrave Macmillan, 2015), p. 236, n. 6.

13. Ivan Shmelyov, Alexei Remizov and Dmitri Merezhkovsky are three notable exceptions. Several major works from these authors' oeuvres were translated into English in the 1920s and 1930s.

14. On 1 January 1918 the Soviet Union implemented spelling reforms designed to simplify the old orthography. Despite the fact that these changes had in fact been prepared by the Academy of Sciences prior to the Revolution, émigré publications maintained, as a matter of principle, most aspects of the pre-Revolutionary orthography into the 1970s.

15. The *document humain* or 'human document' was first articulated by Émile Zola and Edmond de Goncourt. Growing out of the French Naturalist school, this confessional genre was seized upon by some émigré writers, merging with the extant Russian tradition of psychological sketches, and would draw a major polemical dividing line between Georgy Adamovich and his literary coterie on one side, and Vladislav Khodasevich and his own on the other.

16. Marc Raeff, *Russia Abroad: A Cultural History of the Russian Emigration, 1919–1939* (New York and Oxford: Oxford University Press, 1990), p. 81.

17. In a bid to mitigate these omissions, several of these and other émigré authors' works available in English translation are listed in the Further Reading section that follows.

Further Reading

Selected Russian Émigré Fiction
in English Translation

M. Ageyev, *A Romance with Cocaine*, tr. Hugh Aplin (London: Hesperus, 2008).

Mark Aldanov, *The Fifth Seal*, tr. Nicholas Wreden (London: Jonathan Cape, 1946).

Nina Berberova, *The Accompanist*, tr. Marian Schwartz (New York: New Directions, 2003).

—, *The Billancourt Tales*, tr. Marian Schwartz (New York: New Directions, 2001).

Ivan Bunin, *Dark Avenues*, tr. Hugh Aplin (London: Oneworld Classics, 2008).

—, *The Life of Arseniev*, ed. Andrew Wachtel, tr. Heidi Hillis et al. (Evanston, IL: Northwestern University Press, 1994).

Gaito Gazdanov, *The Buddha's Return*, tr. Bryan Karetnyk (London: Pushkin Press, 2014).

—, *The Flight*, tr. Bryan Karetnyk (London: Pushkin Press, 2016).

—, *Night Roads: A Novel*, tr. Justin Doherty, with an introduction by László Dienes (Evanston, IL: Northwestern University Press, 2009).

—, *The Spectre of Alexander Wolf*, tr. Bryan Karetnyk (London: Pushkin Press, 2013).

Simon Karlinsky and Alfred Appel, Jr, eds., *The Bitter Air of Exile: Russian Writers in the West, 1922–1972* (Berkeley: University of California Press, 1977).

Vladimir Nabokov, *Collected Stories* (London: Penguin, 2001).

Irène Némirovsky, *Suite Française*, tr. Sandra Smith (London: Vintage, 2007).

Temira Pachmuss, ed. and tr., *A Russian Cultural Revival: A Critical Anthology of Émigré Literature before 1937* (Knoxville: University of Tennessee Press, 1981).

Boris Poplavsky, *Apollon Bezobrazov*, tr. John Kopper (Bloomington, IN: Slavica, 2015).

Ivan Shmelov, *The Sun of the Dead*, tr. C. J. Hogarth (New York: E. P. Dutton & Co., 1927).

Teffi, *Subtly Worded*, tr. Robert Chandler et al. (London: Pushkin Press, 2014).

V. S. Yanovsky, 'Double Nelson', tr. Isabella L. Yanovsky, *Iowa Review* xlii/1 (2012), pp. 62–74.

Selected Russian Émigré Poetry and Drama in English Translation

Robert Chandler, Boris Dralyuk and Irina Mashinski, eds., *The Penguin Book of Russian Poetry* (London: Penguin, 2015).

Jerome Katsell and Stanislav Shvabrin, eds. and trs., *On the Border of Snow and Melt: Selected Poems of Georgy Ivanov* (Santa Monica: Perceval Press, 2011).

Vladislav Khodasevich, *Selected Poems*, tr. Peter Daniels (London: Angel Classics, 2013).

Vladimir Nabokov, *Collected Poems*, ed. Thomas Karshan, tr. Dmitri Nabokov (London: Penguin, 2012).

—, *The Man from the USSR and Other Plays*, tr. Dmitri Nabokov (San Diego: Harcourt Brace Jovanovich / Bruccoli Clark, 1985).

—, *Plays. Lolita: A Screenplay. The Tragedy of Mister Morn*, tr. Thomas Karshan and Anastasia Tolstoy (London: Penguin, 2012).

Marina Tsvetaeva, *Phaedra: A Drama in Verse*, tr. Angela Livingstone (London: Angel Classics, 2012).

—, *The Ratcatcher: A Lyrical Satire*, tr. Angela Livingstone (London: Angel Classics, 1999).

Autobiography, Diary, Letters and Memoir

Nina Berberova, *The Italics Are Mine*, tr. Philippe Radley (London: Vintage, 1993).
Ivan Bunin, *Cursed Days*, tr. Thomas Gaiton Marullo (London: Phoenix Press, 2000).
Vladimir Nabokov, *Letters to Véra*, ed. and tr. Olga Voronina and Brian Boyd (London: Penguin, 2014).
—, *Speak, Memory* (London: Penguin, 2000).
Teffi, *Memories: From Moscow to the Black Sea*, tr. Robert Chandler et al. (London: Pushkin Press, 2016).
V. S. Yanovsky, *Elysian Fields: A Book of Memory*, tr. Isabella Yanovsky and the author (DeKalb: Northern Illinois University Press, 1987).

Selected Reference Works

Olga Bakich, *Valerii Pereleshin: The Life of a Silkworm* (Toronto: University of Toronto Press, 2015).
David M. Bethea, *Khodasevich: His Life and Art* (Princeton: Princeton University Press, 1983).
Brian Boyd, *Vladimir Nabokov: The Russian Years* (Princeton: Princeton University Press, 1990).
Lesley Chamberlain, *Lenin's Private War: The Voyage of the Philosophy Steamer and the Exile of the Intelligentsia* (New York: St Martin's Press, 2007).
Michael Glenny and Norman Stone, eds., *The Other Russia* (London: Faber and Faber, 1990).
Leonid Livak, *How It Was Done in Paris: Russian Émigré Literature and French Modernism* (Madison: University of Wisconsin Press, 2003).
Thomas Gaiton Marullo, *Ivan Bunin. From the Other Shore, 1920–1933: A Portrait from Letters, Diaries, and Fiction* (Chicago: Ivan R. Dee, 1995).
—, *Ivan Bunin. The Twilight of Émigré Russia, 1934–1953: A Portrait from Letters, Diaries, and Memoirs* (Chicago: Ivan R. Dee, 2002).

Prince D. S. Mirsky, *Contemporary Russian Literature: 1881–1925* (London: Routledge, 1926).

Marc Raeff, *Russia Abroad: A Cultural History of the Russian Emigration, 1919–1939* (New York and Oxford: Oxford University Press, 1990).

Maria Rubins, *Russian Montparnasse: Transnational Writing in Interwar Paris* (London: Palgrave Macmillan, 2015).

Greta Slobin, *Russians Abroad: Literary and Cultural Politics of Diaspora (1919–1939)*, ed. Katerina Clark et al. (Brighton, MA: Academic Studies Press, 2013).

Films

L'Accompagniste [The Accompanist] (dir. Claude Miller, 1992).

Despair (dir. Rainer Werner Fassbinder, 1978).

Dnevnik ego zheny [His Wife's Diary] (dir. Alexei Uchitel, 2000).

Est–Ouest [East–West] (dir. Régis Wargnier, 1999).

Triple Agent [The Triple Agent] (dir. Éric Rohmer, 2004).

A Note on Transliteration

The very nature of the Russian emigration meant that many of the figures and works mentioned in this anthology underwent various reincarnations in foreign languages and scripts; as such, any transliteration system imposed on a collection of this type invariably requires that certain concessions be made.

For the reader's ease, a modified version of the simplified British Standard transliteration system has been used throughout this book. Names, places and Russian words have furthermore been rendered using the most commonly recognizable and readable style (e.g. Alexander rather than Aleksandr). Accepted and preferred spellings of names, where they exist, have been used (e.g. Chaliapin, Mosjoukine and Weidlé rather than Shalyapin, Mozzhukhin and Veidle). Bibliographical entries detailing the sources of original publications, however, have been rendered according to the more scholarly Library of Congress system.

A Note on Transliteration

Russian Émigré Short Stories
from Bunin to Yanovsky

What is your most memorable dream?
                                    —*Russia.*

VLADIMIR NABOKOV

In Paris

IVAN BUNIN

When he had his hat on – walking down the street or standing in the metro – and you couldn't see the silver in his short, reddish hair, it was possible to imagine, given the freshness of his thin shaven face and the upright bearing of this tall thin figure in a long, waterproof coat, that he was no more than forty. But his bright eyes had a look of dry sorrow, and he spoke and acted like a man who has been through a great deal. At one time he had rented a farm in Provence; he had heard any number of caustic Provençal jokes and he liked to drop them now and again, with a little smile, into his always clipped speech. Many people knew that his wife had left him long ago, back in Constantinople, and that ever since then he had lived with a wound in his soul. The secret of this wound was never revealed to anyone, but sometimes he couldn't help hinting at it, joking sourly if someone brought up the subject of women: *'Rien n'est plus difficile que de reconnaître un bon melon et une femme de bien.'*[1]

One damp, late autumn Paris evening he went into a small Russian restaurant on one of the dark side streets near Passy. Attached to the restaurant was some kind of a delicatessen, and he had inadvertently paused outside its wide window. On the shelf inside were cone-shaped pink bottles of rowanberry vodka and squat yellow bottles of zubrovka,[2] a plate of stale fried meat pasties, a plate of greying meat rissoles, a box of halva and a tin of sprats; farther back was a counter of hors d'œuvres, and behind that – the unfriendly Russian face of the woman who owned the establishment. There was light in the shop and, standing on the dark side street with its cold, greasy-looking cobblestones, he felt drawn to this light. He entered, nodded to the owner and made his way through to a more dimly lit room adjoining the shop; this was still empty and the paper tablecloths looked clean and white. There he unhurriedly hung his grey hat and long coat on the horns of a coat-stand, sat down at a little table in the far corner and, absentmindedly rubbing together hands covered in reddish hair, began to read an endless list of hors d'œuvres and main dishes, partly typed and partly written in violet ink which had smudged on the greasy paper. Suddenly a light went on in his corner, and he saw a woman of about thirty, with a look of distant politeness, coming towards him; she had black eyes and black hair parted in the centre, and she was wearing a white lace-bordered apron over a black dress.

'*Bonsoir, monsieur*,' she said pleasantly.

She looked so pretty that he felt flustered. '*Bonsoir* – but you're Russian, aren't you?' he answered awkwardly.

'Yes, I am. I'm sorry – I've got used to speaking French to our customers.'

'Oh – do you get a lot of French people here?'

'Quite a lot, and you can be sure they'll order zubrovka, bliny and even borscht. Have you decided what you want?'

'No, there's so much to choose from. Tell me what you recommend!'

In a mechanical tone she began listing the dishes, 'Today we have sailor's cabbage soup, Cossack meatballs . . . Then there are veal chops or, if you like, you could have a shashlyk à la Kars . . .'[3]

'Splendid. I'll have cabbage soup, please, and then the meatballs.'

She took the little pad that hung from her belt and wrote on it with a pencil stub. Her hands were very white, aristocratic looking. Her dress was a little worn, but clearly from a good shop.

'Would you like some vodka?'

'I'd love some. It's horribly raw out there.'

'What would you like with the vodka? There's some wonderful Danube herring, our red caviar's only just come in, we've got lightly pickled gherkins . . .'

He looked at her again: the white lacy apron looked good against her black dress, and beneath the dress he could make out the fine breasts of a strong young woman. She had no lipstick on her full, fresh lips, her black hair was coiled into a simple knot, but her white hands looked well cared for, the fingernails shining and slightly pink, obviously manicured.

'What would I like to start with?' he said with a smile. 'I'll just have the herring, if that's all right, with some boiled potato.'

'What wine would you like?'

'Red. Just your ordinary house wine.'

She noted this down on her pad and brought over a carafe of water from another table. He shook his head: 'No, *merci*, I never drink water, nor do I add water to wine. *L'eau gâte le vin comme la charrette le chemin et la femme – l'âme.*'[4]

'A fine opinion you have of us,' she observed calmly and went off for the vodka and herring. He followed her with his eyes, noticing how gracefully she held herself and the way her black dress swayed as she walked. Yes, she was polite and professional, and all her movements and gestures were those of a dignified, unassuming waitress. But what about her shoes? How could she afford those good-quality, expensive shoes? There must be some well-to-do, middle-aged *ami*. It was a long time since he had felt as animated as he did this evening – thanks to her – and the thought of this *ami* was rather annoying. Yes, from year to year, from day to day, in our heart of hearts there's only one thing we wait for – a meeting that will bring happiness and love. Really, this hope is all we live for – and how vain it is.

He came back again the following day and sat down at his little table. She was busy at first, taking an order from two Frenchmen, repeating out loud what she was noting on her pad: '*Caviar rouge, salade russe . . . Deux shashlyks.*'

She went out to the kitchen, came back in and went up to him with a slight smile of recognition.

'Good evening. I'm glad you liked it here.'

He stood up and said cheerfully: 'Good evening to you! I like it here very much. And may I ask your name?'

'Olga Alexandrovna. And may I know yours?'

'Nikolai Platonych.'

They shook hands; then she raised her notepad.

'We've got a wonderful soup today – *rassolnik*.[5] Our chef's quite remarkable, he used to work on the Grand Duke Alexander Mikhailovich's yacht.'

'Splendid, I'll have the *rassolnik* ... And have you been working here long?'

'It's my third month here.'

'Where were you before?'

'I was a saleswoman at Printemps.'

'Staff cuts, I suppose?'

'Yes, I'd have stayed if I could.'

He realized with pleasure that he was probably wrong about the *ami*.

'Are you married?' he asked.

'Yes.'

'What does your husband do?'

'He's working in Yugoslavia. He was in the White Army. I imagine you were too?'

'Yes, I fought in the Great War and in the Civil War.'

'I knew straight away. And I imagine you're a general,' she said with a smile.

'I was once. Now foreign publishing houses commission me to write histories of those wars ... But how come you're on your own?'

'I just am.'

The following evening he asked, 'Do you like the cinema?'

'It can be fun,' she replied as she placed his borsch on the table.

'They say there's a very good film showing at the Étoile. Would you like to come and see it with me? You do have days off, I assume?'

'*Merci*. I'm free on Mondays.'

'Well then, let's go on Monday. What's today? Saturday? The day after tomorrow, then. Is that all right?'

'Yes. So you won't be coming in tomorrow?'

'No, I'm going to see some people I know, out of town. But why do you ask?'

'I'm not sure . . . Somehow it'll feel strange not to be seeing you.'

He looked gratefully at her and blushed. 'Strange for me too. There are so few meetings in life that bring happiness.' And he quickly changed the subject. 'So, the day after tomorrow. Where shall we meet? Where do you live?'

'Near the Motte-Picquet metro.'

'Couldn't be better – the same line as the Étoile. I'll be waiting for you by the metro exit at eight-thirty precisely.'

'*Merci.*'

He bowed with mock exaggeration and said, '*C'est moi qui vous remercie.*[6] Put the children to bed,' he said with a smile, wanting to know whether or not she had any children, 'and jump on the metro.'

'I haven't been blessed with children, thank God,' she said, and glided away with the plates.

He felt moved as he walked home, but there was a frown on his face. 'It'll feel strange not to be seeing you . . .' Perhaps this really was the providential meeting he had so long been waiting for. Only it was so late, so late. *Le bon Dieu envoie toujours des culottes à ceux qui n'ont pas de derrière.*[7]

It was raining on Monday evening; the sky over Paris was a dark, murky red. Hoping she would go on to dine with him in Montparnasse, he skipped lunch, went into a café on the Chaussée de la Muette, had a ham sandwich and a glass of beer, lit a cigarette and got into a cab. When they reached the Étoile metro, he told the driver to stop and stepped out into the rain; the fat red-cheeked driver waited trustingly. The wind blowing from the station could have been from a Russian bath-house; dense, dark crowds of people were opening umbrellas as they climbed the stairs; a vendor beside him was calling out the names of evening newspapers in a low staccato quack. Suddenly she was there, among the people coming up. He walked joyfully towards her.

'Olga Alexandrovna!'

She was elegantly and fashionably dressed and her eyes, outlined in black, looked at him freely, not like in the restaurant, and she graciously extended one hand, a small umbrella dangling from the wrist, as she held up the hem of a long evening dress with the other hand. 'An evening dress,' he thought, feeling happier still, 'so she's expecting to go somewhere after the cinema too.' Turning back the cuff of her glove, he kissed her white wrist.

'You poor man, have you been waiting long?'

'No, I've only just arrived. Let's get into the taxi.'

And with an excitement he had not felt for a long time he followed her into the cab, which was half-dark and smelled of damp cloth. The cab swayed as they turned a corner, a street-lamp momentarily lit up the inside – and he instinctively put his arm round her waist, sensed the smell of powder from her cheek, saw her large knees under the black evening dress, the gleam of a black eye and her full lips with their red lipstick: this was a different woman.

In the dark hall, watching a white, shining screen where droning aeroplanes with wide wings were flying at oblique angles and dropping into the clouds, they quietly began to talk.

'Do you live on your own, or do you share with a girlfriend?' he asked.

'I'm on my own. It's awful, really. The *pension*'s clean and warm but, you know, it's the kind of place men bring girls to for the night, or even for an hour or two ... I'm on the fifth floor, there's no lift, of course, and the red stair carpet ends on the third floor ... If it rains in the night, I feel such ennui. I open the window and there's not a soul to be seen. The whole city's quite dead. Just one solitary streetlamp, somewhere or other down below in the rain ... And you're a bachelor, I suppose, and you live in a *pension*, too?'

'I've got a small apartment in Passy. I live on my own too. I've been in Paris a long time. For a while I lived in Provence, I rented a farm there. I wanted to get away from everyone and everything, and to live by the work of my own hands – but that proved too much for me. I hired a Cossack to help, but he turned out to be a drunkard – and a gloomy and frightening one at that. I tried breeding chickens and rabbits, but they all kept dying. Once I was nearly bitten to death by my mule – an extremely vicious and clever beast ... Worst of all was the

utter loneliness. My wife left me when we were still in Constantinople.'

'Are you joking?'

'Not in the least. It's a common enough story. *Qui se marie
par amour a bonnes nuits et mauvais jours.*[8] Though I didn't
have much of either myself. She left me during the second year
of our marriage.'

'Where is she now?'

'I don't know.'

She was silent for a long time. Some imitator of Charlie
Chaplin kept running stupidly about the screen, his bowler hat
cocked to one side and his feet splayed out in shoes that were
down-at-heel and far too large for him.

'Yes, you must feel very lonely,' she said.

'Yes, and what can I do but be patient? *Patience – médecine
des pauvres.*'[9]

'A very sad medicine.'

'It is indeed. So very sad,' he went on with a slight smile,
'that I've sometimes even glanced at *Illustrated Russia* – there's
a section, you know, where they print little personal notices
like: "Young Russian woman from Latvia feels lonely and would
like to correspond with sensitive Russian Parisian. Please include
photograph." Or "Serious lady, auburn hair, unsophisticated
but *sympathique*, widowed with nine-year-old son, wishes to
correspond, serious intentions, with sober gentleman at least
forty, financially secure, employed as chauffeur or similar,
enjoys home comforts. Intellectual interests not essential." I
quite understand her – they really aren't essential.'

'But don't you have friends and acquaintances?'

'I have no close friends. And acquaintances are poor
comfort.'

'Who keeps house for you?'

'There's not a lot of housekeeping to do. I make my morning
coffee myself, and I make lunch myself. A *femme de ménage*[10]
comes in the evening.'

'You poor thing,' she said, squeezing his hand.

And they sat like this for a long time, hand in hand, united
by the gloom and the closeness of their seats, pretending to be

watching a screen towards which, up above their heads, a beam of smoky, chalky-blue light was being shone from a little cabin on the back wall. The Chaplin imitator, whose battered bowler had risen off his head in horror, was hurtling, in the remains of an antediluvian automobile with a smoking samovar chimney for an exhaust pipe, straight at a telegraph pole. The loudspeaker let out a variety of musical roars while the smoke-filled pit down below – they themselves were in the balcony – resounded with thunderous applause and desperately joyous laughter. He leaned over towards her:

'You know what? Why don't we go somewhere like Montparnasse? It's terribly boring here and there's no air.'

She nodded her head and began pulling on her gloves.

After sitting down again in a half-dark cab and looking at the windows – which were sparkling from the rain, flaring up from time to time like diamonds of different colours in the glow of streetlamps or the reflections, now blood, now quicksilver, of advertisements up in the black height – he again turned down the cuff of her glove and gave her a long kiss on the hand. Her eyes too were strangely sparkling, their lashes thick and black as coal, as she sadly and tenderly leaned over towards him, till he could taste the sweetness of lipstick on her full lips.

At La Coupole they started with oysters and Anjou, then ordered partridge and claret. By the time they came to coffee and Yellow Chartreuse, they both felt a little tipsy. They smoked a lot; the ashtray was full of her blood-red cigarette ends. As they talked, he looked at her flushed face and thought that she was quite a beauty.

'But tell me the truth,' she said, picking tiny crumbs of tobacco off the tip of her tongue. 'You must have met some women during these years.'

'Yes. But you can guess what kind ... Nights in hotels ... And you?'

She was silent for a moment. 'There was one very painful story ... No, I don't want to talk about it. A boy, a pimp really ... But how did you and your wife separate?'

'I'm ashamed to say. She met a boy, too – a handsome young

Greek, extremely rich. And after a month or two there was
nothing left of that pure, touching young girl who had wor-
shipped the White Army and all of us in it. She began dining
with him in the most expensive bar in Pera and he would send
her enormous baskets of flowers. "I don't understand. Surely
you're not jealous, are you? You're busy all day long – and I
have such fun with him. As far as I'm concerned, he's just a
sweet boy – and nothing more." A sweet boy! And she was
only twenty herself. It wasn't easy to forget her, to forget the
girl I'd known back in Ekaterinodar.'

When the bill came, she checked carefully through it and
told him not to leave more than ten per cent as a tip. After that,
the thought of saying goodbye in half an hour seemed stranger
still – to both of them.

'Let's go to my apartment,' he said sadly. 'We can sit and talk
a bit longer . . .'

'Yes, yes,' she said, taking his arm and pressing it to her side.

A night taxi with a Russian driver took them to a lonely little side street, stopping in front of a tall building beside which,
in the metallic light of a gas lamp, light rain was falling on to
a rubbish bin. They entered a suddenly bright hall, squeezed
into the small lift and went slowly up, embracing and quietly
kissing one another. He managed to get the key into the lock
of his front door before the corridor light cut out and led her
first into a lobby, then into a small dining room where only one
bulb lit up in the chandelier, shining bleakly. Their faces were
already tired. He offered her more wine.

'No, my dear,' she said. 'I can't drink any more.'

He asked her again. 'Just a glass of white wine each. I've got
some excellent Pouilly Fumé on the window ledge.'

'You drink, my dear, but I'm going to wash and undress.
And to bed, to bed. We're not children and I'm sure you knew
very well, when I agreed to come back with you . . . And anyway, why shouldn't we stay together?'

Too overcome to answer, he quietly led her into the bedroom; from there an open door led into the bathroom and he
turned on the lights in both rooms. These lights were bright, it
was warm from the radiators and the rain was drumming

quickly and evenly against the roof. She immediately began to pull her long dress over her head.

He went out, drank two glasses of sharp, icy wine one after the other and, unable to wait any longer, went back into the bedroom. Opposite him, reflected in a large mirror on the wall, he could see the brightly lit bathroom. She was standing with her back to him, naked, white and strong, leaning over the basin and washing her neck and her breasts.

'No – keep out!' she said, and, throwing on a dressing gown yet not covering her full breasts, her strong white stomach or her taut white hips, she went up to him and embraced him as if she were his wife. And, as if she were his wife, he embraced her, all her cool body, kissing her still damp breasts that smelled of soap, her eyes, her lips from which she had wiped off the lipstick.

Two days later she left her job and moved in with him.

One day in winter he persuaded her to put all the money he had earned into a safe-deposit box in her own name at the Crédit Lyonnais. 'Just to be on the safe side,' he explained. '*L'amour fait danser les ânes*,[11] and I feel as if I'm twenty. But anything can happen . . .'

On the Tuesday before Easter he died in a carriage on the metro. As he was reading a newspaper, his eyes rolled back in his head and he slumped back against the seat . . .

As she returned in her mourning dress from the cemetery, it was a lovely spring day, spring clouds were floating here and there in a soft Paris sky and everything spoke of young, eternal life – and of how her own life was now finished.

Back at home, she began to tidy up the apartment. In the corridor, in a wall cupboard, she found his old summer great-coat, grey with a red lining. She took it off the peg, pressed it against her face and, still hugging it, sat down on the ground, her whole body convulsed by sobs, crying out, pleading with someone for mercy.

Three Short Stories

IVAN BUNIN

Un petit accident[1]

A winter sunset in Paris, with the enormous panel of sky covered in strokes of murky colours, mellow and many-hued, spreading over the Palais Bourbon, over the Seine, over the ballroom-like Place de la Concorde. Now the colours fade, and the Palais Bourbon looms dark and heavy, as the fairytale silhouettes of distant buildings rise behind it against the red murk of the sunset. Slim spikes of greenish gas flames are strewn throughout the pistachio haze of the city, which resounds endlessly with the many-pitched horns of automobiles speeding off in all directions, their headlights bright in the deepening twilight. Now darkness falls, and the candelabra of the Place de la Concorde cast their reflective silvery glow, while up in the black summits the lugubriously flowing lights of the invisible Eiffel Tower flicker like lightning. Over the Boulevards the darkness blazes with the crude opulence of advertisements, a fiery Babylon of celestial billboards, at times vitreously streaming, at others gorily flashing in the pitch black. The fast-moving headlights of the automobiles keep multiplying within their many-voiced torrent – someone's unseen hand is smoothly conducting this orchestra. But now it seems as if the hand has flinched; near La Madeleine there is gridlock, the sound of whistles and horns, the avalanche of cars is constricted as it is crammed closer together, slowing down the flow of an entire section of Paris. Someone within this tidal avalanche, someone who still managed to hit the brakes of his fast little auto, vividly yet softly lit inside, is slumped over his steering wheel. He is

wearing a white silk scarf and a matte top hat for a night out.
His eyes are closed and his young, tritely classical face is already
looking like a mask.

In the Alps

A dark, warm, humid night in late autumn. A late hour. A village in the Hautes-Alpes, quite dead, long asleep.

A motor car gathers speed, smoke-white pillars rushing hori-
zontally ahead. Illuminated by them, along the road glimmer
piles of gravel, the metallic copper needles of a stunted fir grove,
then a few derelict stone huts; beyond them, a solitary streetlamp on a little square, the gem-like eyes of a sleepless cat that
has leaped off the road – and the black figure of a man walking
with broad, sweeping steps, the hem of his cassock billowing, a
young curé in large, coarse boots ... He strides, tall, slightly
stooping, head bowed, the only person not asleep at such a late
hour in all this wild mountain back-country, doomed to spend
all his life there – where is he going, and why?

A square, a fountain, a melancholy streetlamp – as though the
only one in all the world and for some unknown reason lighting
up this whole long autumn night. The façade of a little stone
church. An old bare tree near the fountain, piles of fallen, blackened, damp leaves beneath it ... Beyond the square, darkness
again, a road past a wretched cemetery, whose crosses, arms
outstretched, almost seem to catch the streaks of light coming
from the motor cars.

'In such a night ...'

The environs of Odessa. A clear, balmy night at the end of
August. They were walking along the steep cliffs above the sea.
Gazing at its vast, radiant plain, he began, with mock solem-
nity, to recite:

The moon shines bright: in such a night as this ...[2]

She linked arms with him and continued:

> In such a night
> Did Thisbe fearfully o'ertrip the dew . . .

'Hang on, hang on: where did you come by such learning?'

'The same place you did. I wasn't always the virtuous wife, a simple woman of blessed Konotop. I finished the gymnasium in Kiev with the gold medal.'

'Well, you know, that was so long ago . . .'

'What's this? Sweet impertinence? You're wrong: it was twelve years ago, all told.'

He cast a sidelong glance at her tall, upright frame, her lively freckled face:

'Quite so. Just the day before yesterday, when I met you, I placed you around thirty. Though for a Ukrainian that's old age.'

'Leave my old age in peace. And I'm no Ukrainian: I'm a Cossack. Why don't you tell me who this Thisbe was, I've forgotten.'

'Lord knows. In any case, something marvellous comes next, if I remember rightly.'

'Quite marvellous':

> And saw the lion's shadow ere himself
> And ran dismay'd away . . .

He dolefully continued:

> In such a night
> Stood Dido with a willow in her hand
> Upon the wild sea banks . . .

She finished in the same tone:

> In such a night
> Medea gather'd the enchanted herbs
> That did renew old Æson . . .

'Heavens, how wonderful it is! Medea, the enchanted herbs . . . But still no one to love *me*.'

'So what am I doing here?'

'You're a cynic and a novelist: I need a poet. Anyway, what's the use? My fortnight's holiday will shoot past, and then I'll be back in Konotop.'

'No matter. Fleeting happiness is all that counts.'

How sweet the moonlight sleeps upon this bank!

'Not quite upon a bank, but upon this cliff. Let us sit awhile, Medea.'

'Let us sit, Æson . . .'

Turning off the path, they sat down on the parched grass atop the cliff.

'What I like about you, Dido, is your throaty Ukrainian voice. And then you're a clever girl, gay . . .'

She removed the Tatar bootee from her bare foot, shaking the dust out of it, and wiggled the toes on her slender foot, half dark from the sun.

'A marvellous foot. May I kiss it?'

'No, no, not on your life! "In such a night did sorrowful Medea . . ." What are you doing! At least let me finish! . . .'

They returned late, when the moon had already declined and the golden waters were gleaming duskily by the shore below, and it was so quiet that you could hear their sleepy ebb and flow.

Thou Shalt Not Covet

TEFFI

'Thou shalt not covet thy neighbour's visa, nor his cabin, nor his currency.'

This is the commandment of the new refugee.

The sole commandment, and a wise one.

For, verily, visas, cabins and currency are a source of great tribulation.

What did we, your average Russians, know in the old days about visas? Only that if you were travelling to Austria or through Austria, you had to do something or other to your passport. You took it to Sergievsky Street, where someone like a doorman slapped it with something like a stamp, and took something like three roubles for the privilege.

'What's that for?' you would ask.

'Austria is a poor country. Austrians are people, too. They need to eat.'

And that was that.

But now, visas have taken on a well-nigh mystical shape and significance, and this is why someone who works with visas is called a *vis-ionary*.

If you want a visa, you run around doing everything you can, you can get your right to entry and exit and all the rest of it, but still not get a visa. And nobody can tell why not: it's a mystery.

So you make inquiries.

And out of the mist, strange things begin emerge. For instance, you are told that if you want to go from London to Paris, it's best to go via Holland.

Why?

Because the *vis-ionary* sees what others are unable to see. The *vis-ionary* understands that certain people called Bolsheviks are known always to take the most direct route to reach their goal. Therefore, it stands to reason that if you, too, choose a direct route, then you, too, are a Bolshevik. And as France doesn't need any Bolsheviks, you won't be allowed into France. Now do you understand? There is no arguing with the iron logic of the visa, according to which those who travel by the same route are, in fact, exactly the same as one another.

You can tell a bird by its flight, as they say.

But if you go through Holland, that's another thing altogether. In Holland there are canals and fresh air. Good for blowing away the cobwebs. The Bolsheviks are afraid of air, they need to keep their revolutionary sentiments intact. So they avoid Holland.

There is another aspect of visa logic that is puzzling. Why is it just as difficult to get out of France as it is to come in?

I understand that France loves us very much and finds it difficult to part with us. That's why the French authorities make it so hard for us to leave. It's as if they were trying to talk us out of going. It's very good manners. Just what hosts are supposed to do:

'Why leave so soon? In any case, you're already too late for the last metro. No, we won't hear of it, and that's that! We'll lock the door and hide the key!'

It's rather nice, actually, isn't it? Flattering that they care so much about you.

But why should it be hard to get back into the country again? I fail to find a reassuring explanation for this. Why should a six-week absence transform somebody into an undesirable and unwanted person?

'To forget so soon, good God!'[1]

How fickle can they be?

Usually, in affairs of the heart, the harder it is to say goodbye, the more joyful the eventual reunion. But in this case . . .

Could it be that they just don't want people to 'circulate'?

Or perhaps they're afraid of draughts?

Whatever the case, it's important to get to the bottom of things.

And that means you have to 'take steps'.

This is something that Russians are extraordinarily good at doing. In fact there is a particular way of 'taking steps' that is unique to Russians. It's not something that foreigners can understand.

'Taking steps' in the Russian manner means running to the consulate before it is open and to the embassy after it is closed. It means sitting first in one place and then in another in a foyer on a hard wooden chair. Asking to make phone calls here, there and everywhere and not getting through anywhere. Going, on the advice of one person, to see the aunt of another person, to get her to put pressure on another person. Or, stopping people in the street, grabbing them by the coat buttons so they can't get away, telling them everything in great detail and asking for advice. Going into some bank and asking to speak to some Pyotr Ivanovich who has never worked there in his life. And then going into the newspaper office to complain what a scandal it all is when the office happens to be empty.

Meanwhile, as you do all this, it is also considered correct procedure to clap your arms against your sides in irritation, to lose your wallet and leave your briefcase with all your documents in it in every possible place: in the metro, on the bus, in taxis, restaurants and shops, in the embassy, the consulate and the bank, and to look for it in all the wrong places.

All this is called 'taking steps' – and only Russians do it. People from other countries simply travel around; Russians take steps merely in order to be able to leave a place. People from other countries study; Russians take steps in order to be able to study. People from other countries are treated for illness; Russians take steps to get treatment. And finally, people from other countries live, whereas Russians take steps to receive the right to exist.

Russians are so accustomed to all this that they won't even drink a cup of tea without taking steps to find out how much tea is considered correct.

And it isn't all plain sailing once you have your visa, either. A visa can be overstayed, or understayed; it can expire. There it sits, your visa, at the back of your wallet; it sits there and sits there and one day it suddenly expires. And then the whole business starts over again. You have to lose your briefcase, make phone calls, stop people in the street, run around here there and everywhere.

But while your visa is intact and in the prime of life, you have to find yourself a cabin on a ship. This is no easy matter. Nobody will take on a passenger. Or if they do, they insist on certain conditions: no food for twelve days. Then you have to start all over again, 'taking steps' once more.

The French won't take you, the English won't take you. The Italians won't take you. There is, apparently, some tribe from Southern Polynesia that is prepared to take you, but they don't have a ship to carry you on. Sometimes, for a hefty sum, the Greeks will sneak you on to an American steamer chugging away between Sebastopol and Constantinople under a Tahitian flag. No sooner do they get you on board than they begin to drag you from place to place. First to Odessa, so that you can be shot at. And then to somewhere like Berdyansk, where more steps have to be taken. They hang around there for twenty days and then take you back again. And they don't let you ashore when you need to go. They take you back home, and you have to start 'taking steps' all over again: losing wallets, leaving behind papers, calling people, buttonholing them, running here there and everywhere.

As for currency, don't get me started.

I will be criticized as it is for writing on gloomy subjects.

I shall say only one thing:

Thou shalt not covet!

Hedda Gabler

TEFFI

A card on the door read:

Madame Elise d'Ivanoff

Fantaisies

What did that mean, I wondered: 'Fantaisies'?

I rang the doorbell again.

There was a lengthy shuffling of slippers on the other side of the door. Then it stopped. Someone was standing there, quite still. I thought I could hear the sound of breathing.

It began to feel uncanny. I thought of the scene from *Crime and Punishment*. Suddenly the door opened.

'Ah! *Entrez, entrez!*'

'Madame Élise?' I asked.

'Yes,' she said. 'Well, actually, my name is Olga. But I prefer Élise. It has a ring to it. Olga doesn't have the same ring. I have a passion for sounds. *Élise d'Ivanoff.*'

She lifted her head proudly, and I had a good look at her.

Madame d'Ivanova was large and stout, with slippers on her bare feet. She was dressed in an extraordinary fur wrapper, so tattered and worn that it made her look like an animal that had escaped from a hunt, but not before the hounds had taken a sizeable hunk out of it.

Her hair fell in uncombed clumps, and a metal hatpin protruded from the back of her head.

'Anna Petrovna advised me to come to you,' I said, getting down to business. 'You see, I need . . .'

'Wait,' she stopped me suddenly. 'First I must show you a

portrait of my daughter. Now where did I put it? I had it just before you came in. I was standing before it, reciting Rubenstein's poem "Night".[1] Only eight years old, but what a talent! Quite extraordinary. Dances like Pavlova and writes poetry like Vladimir Solovyov.[2] I've sent her out to get some thread. Tell me, are you hounded by forms?'

'By forms?'

'Yes, by forms.'

'Well, I ha-haven't really n-noticed . . .'

I stole a quick glance at the door. Would I manage to get there in one leap before Madame d'Ivanova pounced on me?

'Now, as for me,' she said, 'I am hounded by forms. They give me no rest. The soul of Velázquez dwells within my breast. Oh, to take up a palette, a brush, and to mix, just to mix and mix . . .'

'So you're a painter, then?' I inquired.

'I am hounded by colours. Oh, if only I had a paintbrush!'

She threw back her head, narrowed her eyes and stood stockstill. I decided to take advantage of the lull in conversation.

'I've come to ask you to do an alteration. You see, this dress—'

'Just a minute,' she said. 'Now *you*, for instance. I would drape you in turquoise silk. And then at the front I would add a touch of ostrich. A *speaking* touch. Do you see?'

'Yes, of course I see,' I said. 'Nothing simpler.'

'And the back I would embroider with coloured imperial silks. Now, where are my silks?'

She turned abruptly. The movement sent a package flying from the sofa. The package rolled over and over, unwrapped itself, revealed itself as a piece of salami and stopped in the middle of the room.

Madame d'Ivanova, meanwhile, had bustled over to a table by the window.

'Now where are my silks?' she asked again.

On top of the table was a pile of crumpled newspapers. From beneath them protruded a dirty spoon and a felt slipper.

'Now,' she said. 'They're here somewhere, I know it.'

She rummaged confidently in the newspapers.

'Here we are. Oh, no. What is this? A herring? Where has this herring come from?'

I didn't know where the herring had come from either. I maintained a guilty silence.

Just then somebody rang at the door. Madame d'Ivanova froze and put a finger to her lips. The bell rang again. And again. And again. Then there was a knock at the door.

Then everything went quiet again.

Madame d'Ivanova tiptoed to the door and put her eye to the spyhole.

'She's gone now,' she said. 'The old fool! She dragged in some brown bombazette the other day. She wanted me to make her a house robe. Well, I mean, really! Just listen for a moment to the horror of it: the horror of those sounds: "bombazette", "brown house robe". And she's sixty years old into the bargain. Not for any price would I agree to make her a house robe. Tell me: you're an authoress, are you not?'

'Well, yes, in a manner of speaking,' I said.

'So you write day and night?'

'Well, no. Why paint such a gloomy picture of it? I write now and again.'

'But what if images throng your mind and give you no peace?'

'They don't, actually,' I said. 'They're fine. The images, that is. They give me peace.'

'I'm not sure I understand you,' she said.

Again, I tried to take advantage of the lull in conversation.

'The thing is, I've brought an old dress. I wondered if instead of these sleeves you cou—'

'Wait,' she said, interrupting me. 'Tell me, when you are engaged in the process of creation, when, forgetful of the world, you pursue elusive spirits as they flee; and when your hand feverishly seeks and grasps the pen, don't you feel at that moment a sense of sublime ecstasy?'

'Well,' I answered. 'I couldn't say. You see, I'm not really in the habit of grasping feverishly. What I was wondering was, how much crêpe de Chine would I need to make wide sleeves?'

'Oh. So you're still thinking about that, are you? It's remarkable. So many women come to see me, and all of them want to talk endlessly about alterations and crêpe de Chine and so on.

Just recently, for instance, I had a very famous singer here. I was elaborating on my theory of sounds to her. Sounds *pursue* me. Sounds give me no peace. A high C awakens in me a state of religious ecstasy, and B flat evokes memories of childhood, E sharp is our estate in Penza, before it was leased. Well, I spoke to this singer about my theory for a long time, I was in a state of ecstasy: my face was pale, only my eyes burned wildly. And do you know what she said? "When you finally shut your mouth," she said, "you can take my measurements." And this from a singer! A sacred guardian of the arts! Well, if she sends me tickets to one of her concerts I shall simply return them. Well, no, I shan't return them, I just shan't go. And if I *do* go, I shall smile quietly to myself all the way through the concert. Oh, she'll understand all right! She'll understand that uncanny smile . . . While she is on stage, singing, aglitter in her diamonds of vulgarity, I shall sit in the upper circle, modest and proud, and smile quietly to myself. And let history judge which of us is the true heroine. I have faith in history alone. History cannot be bought and sold.'

'I'm sorry,' I said, 'but I really must go now. Perhaps I'll leave my old dress with you, and if I could ask you just to take off . . .'

She smiled contemptuously.

'Yes, of course, I knew that was the way it would be. You're a fine one too, and a fancy one. But tell me, when you are among friends, brought together in an ardent circle about your humble lamp by feverish discussions of art that last till dawn, when the hovering shades of Nekrasov and Nadson[3] lean over you fondly, seeming to lend an ear to your discussions, and when the shadow of the great Tolstoy . . .'

I'm not quite sure how it happened. At first I didn't understand where the screaming was coming from. Later, of course, I understood perfectly: it was the sound of my own voice screaming. But at the time I thought that it was somebody else's voice, high-pitched and hoarse, horrible and repellent, screaming:

'I'm telling you for the last time: I'd like you to take these sleeves off and add wide ones, of crêpe de Chine!'

And at that point a miracle happened. Madame d'Ivanova suddenly fell silent. She opened up my bundle calmly, with a business-like air. Then she began to wave a tape measure she had somehow acquired and said:

'I can buy the necessary materials for you. Don't worry. Come to see me at the end of the week.'

She saw me out very politely. In the hall, she even told me, 'Be careful. Watch the trunk there.'

I understood everything. She despised me. And as I went down the staircase, aglitter in my diamonds of vulgarity, she stood on the fourth floor landing and smiled her quiet, uncanny smile.

And now history will be our judge, into the bargain.

It's a hard life . . .

A Conversation

TEFFI

'Don't worry, my dear Ivan Petrovich. Everything will sort itself out in time. The main thing is not to lose your *bonne humeur*.[1] If life in Berlin has become impossible, it's quite clear that you will have to move to Paris.'

'Do you really think so?' Ivan Petrovich spoke slowly, his voice gloomy and full of misgiving.

'Now just you wait, we shall find you a *meublé*[2] somewhere . . .'

'And which *bezirks*[3] are the cheapest to live in?'

'I beg your pardon?'

'I asked, which *bezirks*?'

'Good Lord, Ivan, you've completely forgotten your Russian. Who ever heard of anyone saying "which *bezirks*"?'

'So how would you say it in Russian, then?'

'In Russian they're called *arrondissements*.'[4]

'Do you really think so?'

'Tssk. Do I really think so? I don't think so: I know so. By the way, please don't be angry with me if I seem a little *bilieux*.[5] I got out of bed the wrong side this morning.'

'Why?'

'I just did. Anyway, it's something that has always vexed me, hearing people making a mangle of the Russian language.'

'Excuse me, Nikolai Sergeich, but I don't think you can say that: "making a mangle of . . ." Please don't be angry, but I am fairly sure . . . Fine, fine, I won't say another word, I'm sorry I spoke . . .'

'So you're the expert, are you?'

'You know, you really have a marvellous little place here. Very *bijou*.'

'Yes, not at all bad. A little on the cold side. There's no heating, but the view is marvellous. Of course, this is just the back yard you can see here, but if you hang halfway out of the window (you have to hold on, of course) and turn round – like this, so you're almost on your back, see – then you can see the Eiffel Tower. It's very handy!'

'And don't you feel the cold?'

'Aren't you a rum one! If it's five degrees outside, then it's at least as warm as that inside. And of course, you don't get the wind inside either.'

'I see. It's *dazu*,[6] as they say.'

'I beg your pardon?'

'*Dazu kein Wind*. There's no wind, *dazu*.'

'I don't understand you. You know, you're a strange fellow.'

'Never mind, no hard feelings. It's an ill wind that comes straight from the horse's mouth.'

'Pardon?'

'Just a saying.'

'Well, as I say, we'll find you a *meublé*. I'll ask around. I won't be satisfied until I see you settled in a comfortable *meublé*. Vodovatin – do you remember him? the infantry general – he makes coloured hats out of raffia now. Very nice, they are. Very nice. And Krylov, the chemistry professor, has found work as a chauffeur. Baron Zelf has become a gypsy soloist. And Admiral Kelt does manicures. I had a letter from Constantinople the other day. Our crowd are beginning to find their feet there, too. Petya and Sonya have opened up a little drinking den. What are you looking for? Just drop your ash straight on the floor. They don't go in for these *cendrier*-thingummies[7] here. I wanted to ask you, by the way. I need a fresh ear. Which is better: "Leave me *in* peace" or "Leave me *at* peace"?'

'Maybe you should say "peacefully"; after all, it's an adverb you want. For instance, you can say: "He went peacefully out of his mind with rage."'

'I think it would be "He went *quietly* out of his mind with rage." And I think you can use "at peace" as an adverb. You do hear that. "At perfect peace." "At perfect peace, he flung himself downstairs."'

'Flang.'

'I beg your pardon?'

'*Flang*. Sing, sang. Fling, flang.'

'Flim-flam?'

'The past tense of *fling* should be *flang*, not *flung*.'

'Or is it *flong*?'

'Wait! I think we need a fresh ear. I'm such a pedantic when it comes to Russian. It's all we have left after all. It's our national treasure.'

'To tell you the truth, I find it hard these days to tell what's an *echt*[8] Russian phrase and what isn't.'

'What are you talking about?'

'What is not *echt russisch*. *Echt* Russian.'

'Etruscan?'

'Sorry?'

'What nonsense in this? Why drag Etruscans into it?'

'I still don't quite understand what you're saying. But you know, it's a pity about all the old Russian words that are dying out. *Dever, merin . . .*'

'Yes, wait, the *dever* is the wife's brother, isn't it? And the husband's brother, that's the *svoiak*, and then there's the *shurin*.'

'So what's the *shurin* in relation to all of them, then?'

'Well, I think the *shurin* is the wife's brother. And the *dever*, now, that's the brother of your — what do you call it now? — your wife once removed.'

'But there's no such thing . . .'

'Hang on, don't interrupt. Then there's the *svekrov* and the *snokha*, the wife of the *snokhach*. And then there's the *zolovka* and the *nevesta*, the *zolovka*'s sister, I think. And the brother of the *snokhach*, which is the *zolovka*'s *dever . . .*'

'Then what's the *merin*[9] in relation to all of them, then?'

'I can't remember a thing! I'll have to look it up in Larousse. Awful! Do you know, the other day a young soldier came to see me, one of our Russian soldiers, asking for some addresses. So I sent him to the Frickes'. I explained how to get there, and he said, "Right then, I'll go as far as the cathedral and *therefrom* no more than a stone's throw." And he used the word "therefrom" – *ottenteleva*. Can you imagine? *ottenteleva*? How about that! There is a man living in Paris who says *ottenteleva*. I can tell you, when I heard that I could almost smell the birch trees. I saw it all in my mind: a fence, and a shirt hanging out to dry, a red calico shirt with white patches under the arms . . . a wagon, its wheel thick with tar, wisps of straw stuck in the tar . . . a horse with a rope bridle – the kind you won't see anywhere else in the world. Up climbs the wagoner, straightens out the harness, *gee-up* and *clip-clop, clip-clop* through the wide wood, up to some place called Mashkin's Bend and then "therefrom", *ottenteleva*, it's just a stone's throw, no more than forty versts if you go by the wild country. That's exactly what they'll say . . .'

'You're not crying, are you?'

'What, me? Of course not. Well, at any rate, not because of that. And you? What's the matter with you?'

'Nothing. I'm fine too. It's not that. It's just that my nerves are on edge. *Ich bin nervös . . .*'

Moscow in Shame

IVAN SHMELYOV

When the sun sinks in the ocean, when its last glimmer is extinguished – suddenly, there, in the opalescent distance, comes a smoky scintillation, flashes within the twilit clouds. A living pulse behind them. Are these the crosses of heavenly belfries, is this the flicker of their tolling? . . . Look – the horizon has grown dark; the ocean undulates, heedless, turning a deep blue in the night.

Anyone who has lived by the ocean knows this valediction of the sun – the marvellous play of light. It saddens me to see it. It calls to mind smoky sunsets, the lustre – smoky gold and the tolling of bells. Their tolling plays in that lustre: it has been engraved in my soul ever since childhood, it has become the light itself.

Once there was a tolling of bells; the living soul could hear it. Holy Kitezh . . . It spurned shame and found shelter in the abyss. Its cathedrals and their tolling live on incorruptibly to this very day in deep Lake Svetloyar.[1] Kitezh has hidden itself, submerged, pure, till the Gladsome Morn.

Moscow has gone nowhere; she lies there submissively, smouldering.

There was no miracle of Svetloyar. Why did she not burn in the fires, instead of offering herself up, like a slave, to mockery?! . . .

I remember Moscow in disarray – the smoke and fire of explosions above the cupolas, the glint of the Kremlin eagles shining out of the black night, the flashing of crosses and towers. The crosses called out like beacons. The serene cathedrals had taken fright.

I remember my old Zamoskvorechye district – the darkness of autumn nights, the desolateness of the streets, the solitude of blind alleys and passageways. Shadows hid around corners. There were no human faces to be seen – only shadows. And so on throughout Russia.

I recall the autumnal dark of the disarray, the troubled patter, whispers – husks and wind.

'There was a sailor here. They've outstripped us already – now we're under *them*! . . .'

'If only they'd stick to one side. What did he have to say?'

'Said we're not to be afraid. "Your side has been secured . . . Carry on," he says, "and we'll instil order." '

'Or-der . . . They're shooting at the Kremlin!'

'What's more valuable: people or brickwork?'

'There'll be no miracle here! . . .'

'There could be one yet . . .'

'There'll be disgrace. If they're tearing churches down . . .'

'There was an almighty bang! So loud . . . The dome?'

'The things they're letting them get away with! . . .'

'Who's going to stop them? They've toppled the leader.'

'Sounds as though they're shooting over us.'

'It's coming from Vorobyovka. They've got all Moscow in their sight! . . .'

'Incomi-ing! They're taking out all the belfries now . . .'

'And the people aren't doing a thing! In the old days, they would have raised the alarm.'

'People were tougher in the old days. Minin, Pozharsky . . .[2] Look!'

'There's no one to rally around. If there were someone to rally around . . .'

'I wish they'd get a move on . . .'

'They're setting up. The Army Staff's at Teremok, by the Serpukhov Gates. They're laying telephone lines . . .'

'In a tavern! So why are they shooting at the Kremlin?'

'What's the use of hiding behind saints? Over there, beside Pushkin, him, the one with the goatee, he's just come from the government . . . says they categorically must cordon off the church.'

'The one in the hat? . . .'

'Wait, don't startle him . . .'

'Really, that's how they ought to do it: go out on to the Kho-dynka[3] and have it out. But here, in the city, among the people . . .'

'There's no one to rally around. If there were someone to rally around . . .'

'Not one of them knows his history! Until some illustrious figure shows up . . .'

'One did.'

'Him again, in the floppy hat! Let's hear what he's got to say . . .'

'Why is he . . . what's his name . . . forever going about. He's always going off and showing up somewhere! Authority should rule from a single point. But the minute they start going off . . .'

'Wait, he's coming closer . . . No, he's making for the gates! . . .'

'Why does every great power have to have an eagle? What d'you think it means? . . .'

'If you're a power, you need to be power*ful* and stand fast. It's as Kostomarov says . . . Minin, Pozharsky . . . To think he was anointed.'[4]

'What a waste of oil.'

'Look, look! They're in the Butikov factory![5] They'll have a fine view from the loft.'

'It's a disgrace! . . .'

'Over there! He's hiding behind that corner . . . Ran right through the gates! . . .'

'Well, now . . . they'll answer with their heads for this one.'

'No doubt. Otherwise it's all talk, and they won't see the point.'

This was all a long time ago. The wind was blowing husks.

I remember Moscow in disarray, given over to capture through a lack of zeal, the impotence of power; lone heroes fighting with their bare hands; and the 'respectable world' – the final mockery.

I remember Moscow in shame: a rowdy clamour beneath red rags draped in tinsel, in that farcical gold leaf you find in taverns. 'On-ward! . . . On-ward! . . .' – their licentious, lewd cry, sodden skirts billowing in the wind, over naked legs, ankle-boots splashing through puddles, open jackets, errant kerchiefs about their necks, heads bare to the elements, voices hoarse from shrieking. Dissolutely, drunkenly they plodded beneath the rain, through the filth. Herds wandering through Moscow, lowing for feed!

I remember the severe faces, too – depressed, alarmed.

The drunken Moskva River, full of bacchic boats, bare-chested sailors, accordions, whores ... And the Church, golden, mirror-like, tossed about on the drunken river.

Parks trodden down to a glossy finish, the boulevards' crushed flower beds, and packs of wenches, plump-cheeked, bare-legged, on round stump-legs, cows in calf, draped around a soldiery reduced to shreds, red ribbons on their stockings, decked out in looted wears. Suitors at their heels, with ribbons, topknots, puttees, sniffing them, rubbing up against them.

The herds ran riot – the stench of dung was overpowering.

I remember their keepers, too. They would tear past, roaring, gazing with their proprietorial eye, luring them with fodder.

I can see the stricken Kremlin, the cathedrals' punctured cupolas, calling out from behind the walls with their shimmer. I can see the battered tower, Spasskaya's now silent clock. The Nikolsky Gate, the icon of Saint Mikola, the miracle: a red rag smouldering, falling in tatters upon the people – Mikola watching the people.[6]

The saint, painted over, boarded up.

The herds resting beneath the walls, eyeing Minin, in mockery, beneath a red flag.

I remember the Great Entrance – the last, Holy one.

Moscow was crying out, standing by the Kremlin walls, begging for a miracle. I remember a Holy Flood: thousands upon thousands of people. Black around the Kremlin. Every street clogged with black ...

'Let God arise, let His enemies be scattered . . .'

Moscow prayed. She stood wall-like by the walls themselves.

No miracle was worked.

I can hear it even now, in the far-off distance, the cry of an Orthodox nation.

Gazing at the cathedrals behind the walls, the belfries silent.
No miracle was worked.

The smoky gold of sunsets, the anguished glimmer of belfries, the sultry summer nights, luminous and muffled, in
dread . . . Volleys of executions at night . . .

Russie

IVAN SHMELYOV

For Ivan Alexeyevich Bunin

Today I heard talk of Russia. And in what a spot!

A remote corner – a wooded, primeval place. Through a narrow creek the ocean enters a thicket, lapping at the roots of the pine trees. Crabs are playing in the sand, venturing into the heather, getting lost and staying there as the tide goes out. There are jellyfish melting in the brilliance, starfish drying out. The pines are shedding their cones, which float out to sea. There's a point of exchange where the ocean meets the forest. People seldom turn off from the highway here: there's nothing to look at – just sand and pine trees. The road isn't far off; automobiles tear along it, hallooing to the thicket. And long after they've gone clouds of off-white dust hang in the air.

Here the locals have their own ways.

Among the trees, the resin-tappers wander about mutely, knocking with their long scrapers, like woodpeckers, flaying the tree down to its flesh, revealing its veins – milking its 'sugar' into pots . . .

'These are our forest cows,' they say of the pines here.

Everywhere is steeped in resin, amber, viscous – becoming sugary, sticky. Splinters crackle in the heat; as though glazed, the wood chippings sparkle; the sugary resin runs down the pines' ridges, the little pots overflowing with sugar – the sweet smell of resin is suffocating. It's an odd and painful sight to see the pine trees like this, their open wounds. Wherever you look, they're weeping, bleeding, begging passers-by for alms – each one with its own little bowl.

Such are the local customs.

How wonderful it is here in the July midday; the heat makes everything around crackle, torments you with languor, turns thoughts to resin.

When the tide is out, the little children go about collecting cockles and mussels to sell. The boys are just like ours: britches about their necks or rolled up to the waist, and their voices are similar, too – only they aren't as quick-tempered, they don't fight. Their faces, however, are quite different; they're swarthy, somehow beetle-like, and their eyes and noses are different, too, as are their ways. There's something lacking. Spry curiosity, a roguish, brazen grin? Something's missing. You will recall how there was talk of 'a downtrodden people'! No, ours don't look downtrodden. They're younger, more brazen – that's a fact. They're more boisterous, too.

A little donkey stands harnessed to a cart, ears drooping, nibbling at the heather now and then, dozing. There's a keen smell of cockles and the sea coming from the crate on wheels. A fisherwoman, her wet trousers rolled up to her hips, with a red basque and a little hat with a wide brim, is groping avidly in the sand for cockles, barking at the children.

'Look lively, you slacker! . . .'

Her legs are pillars, her hands red and raw, but her accent is pleasant and her *r*s roll off her tongue. You close your eyes – a high-class lady at an institute. It sounds as if she's rinsing laundry. You look – she's slapping a young boy about the cheeks. The boy stands there obediently, just turning his head.

Here they have their own ways.

It was in this foreign corner that I unexpectedly heard talk of Russia:

'*Russie!* . . .'

It was a strange sensation, as if someone were calling you in the desert – fear and joy.

But I must recount how it happened.

I was lying under a pine tree, soaking up the sun and the resin, not thinking about a thing. Perhaps I was in a reverie . . . The tide had gone out, and the little pools it left behind were sparkling like mirrors. I could hardly keep my eyes open. The little donkey suddenly began to bray, languorously, mournfully, and tailed off, sobbing. The fisherwoman tipped the mussels into a crate, swigged from a bottle, rested her hands on her hips awhile, sighed heavily, and said '*Bon!*' to something, before going off again to pick cockles. There was a smell of warm red wine in the air, and I too thought, *Bon!* It was torpid, sultry. Bees were buzzing and crawling among the heather, cones were crackling in the pine trees, and the resin-tappers were hacking away. As I lay there squinting, listening to their knocking, I thought of our Russian summer, our peaceful sky. And it came back to me so vividly – with all its smells and sounds.

. . . I'm sitting on the edge of a birch forest. I hear a cool rustle, see the green little hearts fluttering. There's a smell of birchwood, the bitterness of its sweet, dry stumps, the fresh meadow hay with its warmth. Among the tall grass, among the sparse panicles already shedding their blossom, the tracks in the road are visible, even from the spring fork, where we would take a detour to the grove a little higher up. You can even spot a nest in it, made of flax and grass – belonging to some trusting little birdy. No one has come this way since spring. Beyond the road, beyond the sparse shrubbery, are meadows on a broad, even incline, stretching as far as the dark willows of a stream, which sparkles in pools here and there in the clayey banks, in the little holes of sand martins' nests, with the murmurous pebbles of its shallows. The meadows are aflutter with activity. The harvest: colour everywhere, white kerchiefs and shirts, russet shelters made of hay, carts, with skirts hitched up on the shafts and withered birch branches to provide shade. Throughout the bright yellow meadow, dark crests of mowing, glittering new rakes, hay pitched in light stacks. On a dark cart a peasant, completely crimson in the sun, dancing about, treading it down. It's being tossed to him on pitchforks. Harnessed to the cart is a tiny horse, although you can see it as far as the shaft bow, tossing its head, kicking the horse-flies under its belly. Beyond the stream, fields of grain – taller, yellower – beyond them, threshing barns; a long country road, lined by willows: someone's prosperous estate – a high green island, the arrow-like sails of a windmill, a belfry with a green cap, and in the distance, under the heavens,

by the dark ridge of a pine forest, white spheres billowing up
like spinning wheels: a freight train crawling along. What an
unembraceable expanse! I can even hear the lads calling to one
another in the woods, the hollow echo unrolling in the desolate depths behind me. And somewhere quite nearby, a pure
and tender maiden's voice wistfully sings a song . . .

It's all so vivid, so unforgettably vivid.

The roar of a motor car came from the road; it halted. Voices
drew nearer, and a trio appeared. One man, guiding with his
hand, admiring the scene. The others, taking to binoculars to
inspect it. These arrivals appeared to be tourists, English by the
looks of it: travelling caps and Kodaks. The first man, plump
and of modest stature, was evidently from these parts, sporting
the customary crumpled shirt and rigid straw hat of a local
businessman. He said something, rapidly, enthusiastically – his
gold teeth glittering. The tourists looked around, consulted a
little book, marking things with their nails. They quickly got
out the camera apparatus and photographed the hillock, on the
side of the bay where the local man was pointing out the picturesque fisherwoman in trousers bent over in the mud, the dozing
little donkey and, of course, me. I heard a torrent of words. The
fat man was repeating in delight:

'*Très joli! Très joli!* . . .'[1]

The English mumbled in agreement.

'Am I not right, gentlemen? Just like a little Switzerland . . .
How pretty! . . .'

'*Très joli!*' the answer rained down, like dried peas.

'Such a rarity! A terrific height for dunes, sixty-three metres!
Practically mountains! The whole ocean from here . . . *très
joli*. For a hotel, or maybe a stylish villa . . . Bear in
mind . . . only, please, keep this between us . . . a commercial
enterprise, a company is being put together, with a vast amount
of capital . . . Fifty million! Then . . . ! We'll apportion land
for golf.'

'There will be golf?'

'Why ever not?! People will come and ask, "Is there golf?"
We'll set aside a hundred acres.'

'Hmm . . . !'

'There's enormous potential. A magnificent casino, right on the *mer sauvage*![2] The bright lights of culture! . . .'

They drew closer and sat down. The fat man unrolled a sheet of paper, and then again there was that rattle of dried peas:

'*Très joli! Très joli!* . . .'

The hacking in the forest fell silent, and a resin-tapper came out from behind the pines with his inevitable pouch and a long scraper over his shoulder, wearing a soiled jacket and a cap covered in resin. He gave a sullen '*Bonjour*', spread out a newspaper, extracted a bottle of wine, some bread and a little knife – and set about his lunch. He fastidiously sliced off thick wedges of bread, chewing unhurriedly, glancing at the pine trees, at the visitors, and taking measured sips from the bottle. By the alertness of his face, I could see that he was listening to what the three of them were saying. Judging by the way he was looking at the visitors and the manner in which he was slicing the bread with the knife, I could tell that these people interested and worried him. He began fussing about and grunting. His face stretched out sharply, his thin lips drawn into a sarcastic grin. He shook his head and muttered angrily under his breath:

'Foreigners, hotels, villas . . . Those agents certainly know how to cut a deal. But where does that leave *us*? . . . *Non, portez ailleurs vos coquilles, là-bas!*'[3]

He waited for the fat man to lift his head from the plans and shouted amiably:

'*Bonjour*, Monsieur Lafont. Business going well?'

'*Bonjour*, François,' said the fat man. 'Not too badly. And you?'

'Me? . . . *Donnons bœuf – avons œuf*.'[4]

'We-e-ell,' drawled the fat man. 'Resin's on the up, like rubber.'

'What do we care for rubber? You aren't planning to bleed all our forests dry all the way to Arcachon, are you? – along with the lot of us?'

'*Your* . . . forests!? Which are *yours*? What are you trying to say? . . .'

'What is there to say? . . . It's no good having roads in forests, if you ask me . . . for rubber!'

'And why is that?' The agent's shoulders flinched.

'It just isn't. There's no room. You mightn't even be able to drive past an oncoming driver. And it would be sticky too . . .'

The tourists were listening intently but seemed not to catch the meaning of anything: the resin-tapper's talk was impure, forest-fashion.

'I simply cannot understand you,' the fat man said in astonishment, looking at the pine trees.

The resin-tapper measured on the bottle with his nail and drew out as much as he required.

'You understand me all right. While we were sodden in the trenches, you were trading in waterproof sacks, for dugouts. Now you're trading in sodden land? . . .'

'I am. What of it?'

'Well . . . the buyers had better tot up their losses beforehand.'

'*Ne faites pas la bête!*'[5] shouted the agent angrily, tearing off his hat and smacking it on his knee as he would a carton of cigarettes. 'What are you trying to say? . . .'

'What am I trying to say? I wouldn't waste my money on the official paper, if I were you. The wind changes! Our woods, your woods . . . Have you forgotten what it was like five years ago, what people were saying back then? . . .'

'And what were they saying? . . .'

By now the resin-tapper had finished his lunch; he packed up his bag and scraper and, without answering, walked off into the pine forest. Soon the tapping of a woodpecker could be heard once again.

The tourists interrogated the agent, who explained to them at length, tapping his hat against the little bones in his fingers and nodding towards the wood; now I heard distinctly, instead of the sweet '*très joli*', an entirely different word, which made me wince.

'*Russie!*'

Then I heard it again. And again.

Now all three of them were talking. The agent was enumerating something with his fingers, pointing somewhere, high over the forest, and amid his impassioned, disjointed speech the quivering word leaped up:

'*Russie! . . . Russie! . . .*'

And the other two – who were English, of course – repeated in their own tongue, with a sort of hissing through their teeth:

'*Russsssia . . . Russsssia . . .*'

They were talking about my homeland.

Lost, I could but listen. They were talking malignly, mockingly, haughtily:

'Plague, pestilence. Asiatics. Never had any laws or culture. Slaves, heathens, cannibals. The Tsar and the whip. Drunkards, savage peasants, Cossacks. All of them executed by the Tsar; they always loved the lash. Filthy animals! No sense of honour, they betrayed us. Now these savages want to destroy culture! They're spreading their disease! They ought to be taught some culture, they ought to be reined in. A fine future ahead. They ought to be colonized, they ought to be crushed in embryo . . .'

The agent was shouting loudest of all. He even spat and trod it into the ground. And everything went in circles:

'*Russie . . . Russie . . . Russsssia . . .*'

Finally they quietened down, took to examining the plans once more, and the phrase '*très joli*' rang out again.

I didn't utter a word. What could a savage, a slave who had felt the lash of the whip, who himself had fled from *there*, have to say to these people? They knew all about it; they knew it through and through. They had been told everything. For decades people had called them 'the finest, the most cultured', cast out by tsar-executioners for speaking the truth. They know: *Russie!* It means the Tsar and the whip. A country of oppressed slaves and hangmen. The crack of the lash can be heard the whole country over. The Tsar poisons the people with drink, extirpates them with famine, takes the last shirt off their backs. Constables, Cossacks, factory owners, industrialists, landowners . . . squeezing your last copeck out of you, thrashing you. They've all read dozens of books – they know this *Russie*, this country of eternal winter and darkness, where people go about in animal hides, where they eat human flesh. A great desert, utterly devoid of culture.

They are Europeans – and know everything. What could a savage, who knows neither law nor morals, have to say to them? They would crush my words beneath their sturdy hob-nailed boots – the inarticulate prattle of the inscrutable *âme slave*,[6] feigning depth and meekness.

I would say . . . But what do I have to say – *now* ? . . .

The car sets off. Ringing in my ears are the words:

'*Russie . . . Russie . . . Russie . . .*'

Who made her famous for this, brought her to her knees? 'Tsar-executioners' and 'the whip' – as if that was all there was to her! Who slandered her so, who robbed her so?

A thought that had been lulled to sleep stirred and drew me far away and deep inside.

'. . . Russia in chains. Imperial executioners, oprichniks. Hangmen, constables, gendarmes. The gendarme's jackboot. A downtrodden, backward people, in the clutches of kulaks, landowners, priests, taverners and gendarmes. Tsar-taverners. The country bleeding to death. The Crown Fatherland. Ortho-doxy, autocracy, nation . . . The infamous three tenets. The imperial eagles of prey. The Christ-loving host! Little brutes in uniform! . . .' – a savage shout and a cry.

I thought of all the little books, full of slander and malice, in which everything had been preened: the heart of life had been snatched out, all the colours stamped out, the proud pages torn out. Reams of talentless sheets, full of grandiloquent libel; arti-cles in daily rags – in every language, and nothing but distortion everywhere. Not a word of kindness, not even one spot of light. Not a single word of pride in Russia or her actions!

And so – she is rotten, dead, malign. Her temporary pass-port has already become a reality. Her slandered image has been justified. She has become a scarecrow, a parable. What words can you say?!

Russie . . . Russie . . .

The tide flowed out. Its dark-blue waters were now barely visible. Dirty sand and rotting seaweed was all that remained, and the young lads were rooting about in it. The wrathful fish-erwoman again slapped one of them – a backhand to his face – and roared:

'*Merde!*'

The little donkey's braying was heart-rending; it was pleading to go home. The fisherwoman dropped the mussels with a crash, hit the donkey with her basket, threw me a sharp glance and made ready to leave. Picturesque from afar, she had turned out to be rude, whiskered and sallow-faced, with heavy, severe eyes. Her trousers proved not to be trousers at all, but rather a skirt skilfully twisted up around her hips. She jumped up angrily into the cart and rode off through the sands, the young lads running alongside.

It was already past noon. The glaring sun was heavy with heat and the smell of resin. I could hear the snapping of pine-cones splitting, the crackling of wood chips and shavings, the hard tapping at the pines, the scraping on the bark, the crackle, the flaying. And amid all this rustling and noise, ringing in my ears, swimming before my eyes, was this tremulous word, crepitating in a foreign language – *Russie*.

Having managed to extract myself from the resin, I could no longer hear the crackling and breathed more freely – and then an enormous sky-blue motor truck, with twoscore or more flickering dots, drowned me in its roar and heat, dousing me in waves of dust.

Shadows of Days

IVAN SHMELYOV

Into the quiet arena of visions and dreams
Bursts the spume of the bellowing swell.[1]
Fyodor Tyutchev

I

It's as if I'm on the Place de l'Étoile, among a crowd. Whether
it's evening or night – I can't tell. The sky, as black as soot,
looms threateningly, oppressively. Not a single star to be seen.
Beneath the sombre Arc, by the tomb of the Unknown Soldier,
there comes a gust of wind: it tears at the eternal flame. The
pale lights of taxi-cabs retreat uneasily, their red eyes glancing
around. The tramcars are in a rush to depart. Everyone is waiting for something, waiting in trepidation. Their faces are
hidden – just heads and hats; everyone is heading *there*. But the
flame is already ablaze, hurling itself under the vaults of the
Arc. Billowing smoke, thick, black, as from oil. The advertisements' bright lights grow dim – glowing crimson, dirty, amid
the smoke. Someone's saying that the oil storage tanks have
caught fire . . .

I'm waiting for someone. I watch the flame – a desolate fire.
I know – the storage tanks are here somewhere, in Presnya.[2]
Over yonder there's a cemetery, and the oil from there, from the
ground beneath it, is viscous. The blaze is coming from there.
I'm terrified, I want to leave, but – it's difficult. I look on in
anguish: to the right, downhill, the Champs-Élysées, vast,
deserted, ablaze; the light is pallid and plaintive, in milk-clouded
globes, like in Moscow, during the frost. I must go there, but
why? I don't know. Peace awaits there.

Someone shouts:

'Make wa-a-ay!'

The voice is heart rending, strained.

I know it: it's picking its way towards me. I wait in trepidation.

It's an old man. His face is familiar – but who he is, I can't quite recall. He's short, frail, wearing a priest's hat, his eyes are watering, and he has a straggly beard – like a beadsman. He's carrying a little red bundle under his arm, as if he were on his way to the bath-house; only the truss isn't towels, but apples or Communion bread. I'm so happy to see him, a kinsman, from my own country. I want to ask him something important. But he winks:

'Come on, come on! . . .'

He knows something. People make way for us. He whispers:

'From Place de la Concorde . . . via Berlin, then right. The last train . . .'

My heart soars. Tickets, visas . . . ? We'll never make it.

He runs, clutching his tails. I see that it's our cabby, 'a good sort', only he's very old. He's been sent to fetch me . . . But how odd: his thick peasant's coat is fluttering about, like a sarafan, unfastened, and is sweeping the floor; silver baubles line the cuff; a beaver hat, with a little padding and cornering, and a fox-fur lining at the neck – the sort worn by coachmen.

I run in trepidation: we'll never make it, the last train. We'd better take a cab – via Berlin, then right, it isn't far. It's doable even without the visa.

We sprint along the glossy asphalt. It's slippery. Not a soul is headed in our direction. Behind us, peals, explosions. I look back – the flames have grown taller, the Arc glints through fiery, black clouds of smoke. A fire? . . . Still running, I check my pocket: *carte d'identité*. What about money? . . . How shall we escape? . . .

The old man runs, trailing along his little bundle. He seems to know *everything*. Visas are being sold on Place de la Concorde, in some sort of booth. Who is he? So familiar . . . Alexei, our coachman? But he was taller, and had a black beard . . .

and he died while I was a student. He died, and yet he lives – it isn't strange.

The Champs-Élysées recedes endlessly, downhill, illuminated by the cold light of the dull, milk-clouded globes. The lights are strange, different. The old ones were greenish and resembled little pails. But these whitish globes – where have I seen them before? In childhood, in the foyer of the theatre, by the doors? The lights of bygone days.

In the distance everything has frozen, like a black river. The dirty ice flows and glitters dreamily, like smooth asphalt. The pallid lights are drawing nearer: the taxis, uneasily flitting off towards the Étoile, are all empty. In the neighbouring streets, all the lights have been extinguished; there is only blackness. I recall an avenue of lights, shop windows, automobiles and hotels – where was all this? Dark, blind buildings. They've all gone. Now there's just one road – straight, amid the deathly, cold lights. Soon they, too, shall be extinguished.

I run in trepidation. The Champs-Élysées, my final road.

I can hear everything being deserted behind me, the high-pitched shattering of glass. Have the globes been extinguished? Still running, I look back. A crimson glow behind the dull glass, which fades to nothing. I hear the globes emptying. Here's a streetlamp. I run up to it – it dims, a red coal, and extinguishes. But farther on they're still flickering. I cry out and point to the lamp – it dims.

'They're going out! . . . Why are they going out?!'

Because of smoke, from the Étoile . . . ?

The little old man – I think he's a priest – shouts incoherently:

'The Elysian Fields! . . . The end! . . .'

There's a tapping on the asphalt behind us, a hopping like a grasshopper. I see – a dark figure on crutches catching up with us. I hear how laboured his breathing is, I want to take a good look at him, but his face is hidden. His service cap is pulled down to his nose, his head is bowed, his old greatcoat billows as he runs, lashing at his sticks. I know he's one of us, the poor devil. I feel so sorry for him; I want to call out to him . . .

Out of the darkness – an enormous, shadowy haycart. It bears down on us, swaying, sputtering . . . It has blocked the road – and all of a sudden it's dark all around. From beneath the earth comes the voice of a peasant:

'Steady-y-y! . . .'

Toppling down like a mountain, it buries us. I claw my way through, scattering clumps of hay all around . . . the road, quiet, empty, lit. Behind us – crutches.

'Look, look! . . .'

Is the peasant under the hay?! . . .

The avenue is chock full of these clumps – a hayloft. The clumps tremble and move: the peasant stirs beneath the hay. Beyond the hayloft, the sky blazes – a fire is raging. The Arc flickers against the sky. A black pillar of smoke; above it a storm cloud, orange underneath, glides off to the right. It's the oil that's burning. I see sparks tumbling down on to the hay. It'll catch! . . . It was a fool's business bringing it here . . . it will be lost!

The peasant hops about on the hay, flailing his arms.

We run. From the black streets – voices, uproar. *Has it begun?* . . . The lights have gone out; the blaze gives us light.

A shadowy, empty square. Buildings without windows. In the murk little boys whistle and whoop; they run – they trample. Black trees. Crooked, tangled branches against the red sky, like twisting crows' nests. Behind the murky mountain that is the Grand Palais, the sky is ablaze. Les Invalides? . . .

To the right, a bridge is on fire. Beyond it, beyond the winged steeds, against a background of flames, is a cast-iron cupola. Above it – glittering. Across the incandescent sky – whirlwinds, smoke. I see – Les Invalides has caught fire.

Behind me – crutches. With one, he points to the cupola.

'The cast iron . . . it's turning black! . . .'

I hear someone calling:

'Hurry-y-y!'

A familiar voice. I can scarcely see him, on account of the fire – he's waving. I know: he'll take me *away*. It's both joyous and terrible. *There* I'll meet . . . The past reaches back. *There* – is peace.

But I must leave.

Place de la Concorde, the last train. Is there something there . . . ? I see – like a crimson blotch, something's aflame. Bonfires? The noise reaches me.

I rush off, afraid to stay. *He* knows this. He looks at me so sweetly:

'It's all right . . . don't be afraid, young sir.'

He winks. I want to remember – who on earth is he?

'Here, take this . . .'

And out of his kerchief he extracts a little ball of Communion bread.

I recognize it, the cheap Communion bread of my childhood – the bread of the poor. The little ball looks like a church. There's a little cross outlined in red on its cupola. Joyously I accept it, and within it is that distant, bright, holy childhood of mine. I peer into his bundle. Grushovka apples, little trifles! I look into his eyes. Familiar, they twinkle with kindness. Wrinkles, a haggard face, a wedge-shaped beard . . . My God! I've remembered . . . It's the old psalm-reader, from the parish almshouse. Nikolai Arsentich, the psalm-reader from back home. He's come for me.

He whispers:

'Hurry! The last one . . . from the Place de la Concorde . . .'

Both joy and the agony of loss come to me in a flash.

I sense how much I need him. I love him, just as I did when I was a child – for his wrinkles, for his caressing hand, for the tapered candles he places before the icons, for the strange words – I don't understand them, but they caress me – for looking like the icon.

He has come for me!

It comes to me in a flash.

He would stroke my head, give me Communion bread, little churches like this, lead me to the altar, show me the book dripped with wax – it smelled of God – and wink at me sweetly. Before the Saviour he would lay out little apples streaked with crimson, tickling them with the holy brush . . .

My whole being soars up, sweetly, as in a dream.

I recall the lovely icons, *my* icons. They exist only in one's childhood: each child has *his own* one – alive to him alone. He nods his head and reads ... The candle dozes, then awakes and quivers and drips wax on his fingers, on to the old book. From an icon another little old man looks down, blinking sweetly. I recall his rattling voice, I hear the unfathomable sacred words: ' ... Therefore is my spirit overwhelmed within me ... I go mourning all the day long ...'[3] It flows with a mysterious sorrow. Whereas my soul is so lucid, so tranquil.

Through the windows – snowdrifts, stars. He's already reading, 'Thou who at every season and every hour ...' – somnolent, nocturnal words. The candles are snuffed. The night street shows blue. The snowdrifts are swept in mounds – you could drown in them. It has been snowing heavily all day. Great bales in snow-capped rows. It's so quiet on our little street, so desolate – everything blocked up with snow. How the spades crunch; how they shovel, how the clumps thud ... The cart steals along, as if on down; there's a spade standing like a post in the snow. A cabby sails past noiselessly; at the corner, a little horse snorts – full pleased – and kicking up the ash-like snow beneath its legs. Atop the posts, atop the fences – little mounds of snow. Soft, powdery. Lanterns covered in snow shine drowsily; dogs dig up the snow with their snouts. Beyond the fence, among the birches, a crow croaks hoarsely, foretelling more snow – without waking. The windows cast a radiance over the snow, themselves rose-tinted from the icon lamps. You go inside – it's warm, cosy, the stove bench is being warmed for the night. On top of it, under a lamp with a green shade – a precious new *Around the World*,[4] and a heel of black bread. You read awhile, the cocks crow. Through the frozen windows – the twinkling of stars, a silver-framed Saint Nicholas in the corner, the icon lamp casting little moustaches on him ...

The wrinkles of that dear face conjure up everything. Joy, loss – all in a flash.

He's been sent for me ...

But didn't he die? . . . How is it that he's . . . in Paris? with us? . . .

He died, and yet he lives. It isn't strange.

He drags along his bundle as he goes. I follow – behind him.

The glow is masked by a shadow – a palace of some sort, dark. Where the fire is, the sky is lightly tinged with rose. The roofs are turning black.

A forest, black trees. Beyond the thicket, in the distance, the horizon glows a smoky crimson. A country house? The trees give off a greenish light. It's strange. The lights have gone out all around, but . . . ?

The trees retreat, I descry the fiery letters – *Restaurant*.

A mirrored wall. Glittering chandeliers, crystal garlands, stars. The glitter of silver, the ring and sparkle of crystal, the shimmer of frosted glass. Potted tropical flowers.

A restaurant? . . . Don't they know that the lights have gone out? . . .

I see amid the lustre a rosy mass – shoulders, breasts, starched snow-white shirt fronts, bald patches, the entwining of naked arms, the shimmer of tail-coats. I sense the warm, intoxicating aroma of wine and powder, flesh and flowers. I watch how they cling, how they drift languorously among the lights, heads cast back. They recline in armchairs, glasses in hand, sniffing cigars. Waiters advance, then freeze decorously along the walls. But I hear no music. It's strange. They seem *alien* to me, as if from another world – not even alive. Something like . . . Americans?

A strange restaurant.

Among the trees – a reddish glow. I see charred stumps, the bloody reflection of the glass in the lanterns. The Great Obelisk[5] is flickering.

The Place de la Concorde, the last train . . .

There's a rumbling. Carts, wheels, horses, mountains of luggage – a rag-tag band? . . .

The sky is ablaze, the cupola of Les Invalides. Two turrets, like two nuns in peaked habits, stand against the background

of sky, one facing the other, uneasily. Trees behind the Concorde, chambers, the Obelisk – bathed in a bloody light.

How on earth shall we get through? . . .

On the plinths – rearing steeds. Their manes streaming like
fire, their bared teeth red. There's a ditch behind them . . . I
dash over and see: feet in buckles, stockings, camisoles, swollen faces, wigs . . . There's shouting:

'Some people have been crushed . . . !'

Khodynka,[6] Presnya? . . . Crushed people in pits . . . *Here?!*

I'm alone. I'm afraid.

Bonfires smouldering. Gypsies beating basins, playing cards.
Cauldrons smoking, horses jerking their heads about. There
comes a thundering noise, something like a tambourine . . .
buffoons? Some people, in jumpers with polo necks – thieves? –
lugging fur coats. Teetering, in wide pleated velveteen trousers,
with a drawn face, like a hare wearing a cap, a man – a swindler – follows me. I feel fear and loathing. With scarves at their
necks, the scoundrels – they're doing indecent things to a young
lady. She's wearing a sky-blue plush cloak, thrashing her arms
about, putting up a struggle; her cape flies open, leaving her
swollen stomach vulnerable; a little watch dangles on a gold
fob. They drag her into a corner and thrust themselves upon
her . . .

There's shouting: 'Make way!' They're carrying someone
upright. Men on horseback are making threats. Haven't I seen
this somewhere before . . . ? In the bloody light, *something* –
with posts . . . Executions? . . . By some new show-booths, in
the distance, there's a black wall of people. Youths are clinging
on to the trees, waiting.

The Great Obelisk towers over everyone. Red stone. Its millennia have awakened, blinking at the fire, streaming. The
sombre chambers, the windows, the pillars, the lanterns under
the arches – everything flickers. From the balconies showmen
cry out over the throng.

I peer in all directions: where on earth is the train? It must
be towards the gardens. I shan't be able to get there directly.
I see suitcases, and people scuffling over them. People with

wolfish eyes, in torn scarves; apaches in leggings, with hidden
knives; stout women with moustaches; whores; the rabble . . .
snatching, lugging fur coats . . .

I force my way through. Snow-white shirt fronts, tail-coats . . .
The restaurant? . . . Side-by-side with the tail-coats – ladies with
bared shoulders crowding together. They're surrounded, being
robbed. They're tearing off their tail-coats, pearls, bracelets.
Whores in rags crowd around; ladies put up a fight. His mouth
agape, a cross-eyed man paws at them . . . The teetering one,
with the hare's mug, plays with a fat one, tickling her under the
arms. A fat man with a cigar looks on blearily, sweating. The
one with the mug grabs him by his tails, like a sack, and shakes
him out of the coat. They're giving the tall American a beating:
no dice!

I'm – *outside*. I must catch the last train.

They're waving from the balconies. Tiers of faces, as at the
theatre. They're shouting:

'Vi-i-i-ctory!'

The one at the front is short, a gnome. His dark little head
is shaped like a wedge. He's wearing a fur coat – like the one
belonging to the woman who bakes the Communion bread,
with its sheen. A fox-fur collar down to his elbows. The little
eyes bore into you. His mouth is rat-like, he squeaks; yet the
squeaking, like an awl, pierces the skin.

Another one – thick-set. Hat like a tower, raccoon-skin
coat, like a mountain – elephant ears. The coat of an arch-
deacon, while his moustaches . . . are those of a Romanian
cymbalist: like screws.

Yet another – beetle-like. Drooping moustaches, nose like a
nail, sour mouth: as though he were sniffing something. And –
a stolen fur, of polecat. Behind him – a man with no forehead,
but quite a mouth; his moustache, 'for piquancy', shaped like
an arrow; a greatcoat with beaver trim on one shoulder and a
red lining; a shirt smeared with grease.

Behind them, a flock – peaked otter caps, dog-hair hats,
wolfskin overalls, polecats, camelskins, cloaks, short sheepskin jackets, plaids, peaked hoods . . . They jab their fists in
the direction of the Obelisk, calling for it to be hauled off

somewhere far away. I sense that this stone is *theirs*, the rabble's thousand-year-old aspergillum, the nomads' god. They've hauled it across the earth since time immemorial.

Down below, they're shuffling about in confusion: carrying little books, poorly dressed, with nervous faces. They argue, whisper, quarrel. Their movements are indecisive, impotent. Some agree; others protest silently. There's a rustle of paper, the glint of spectacles . . .

I know: they'll be carted off any minute now. Behind them, behind bars – there's a clanging; snouts in animal hides are waiting; there, they're being released . . .

There's blood everywhere: the Obelisk, the sky. It glows inside the glass of the lanterns, streaks across the stonework, streams on to the trees.

I can't get past. I cut through towards the Obelisk. A peasant with a sack gawps at me. A pot-bellied little horse, and a sleigh; hay under the horde's feet: they're feeding. I ask where the train is. He isn't listening, just looks out ahead, in the direction of the balconies; they're tossing clothes and fur coats to the crowd. I see: he's come for the loot.

By the stone, behind bars – little old men in robes and turbans of many hues – Magi, as it were. Their faces are hidden; all of them on their knees, heads crowded together: they're inspecting something on the ground. I look in dread: a yellow lick of flame. The eternal flame? . . . Is the oil here too?! . . . They're practising sorcery, fanning it . . . Magi? Is it fires they're fanning . . . or – *light*? Silently, heads together.

The gypsies beat their basins. The horses neigh. Something like a tambourine thunders. Cauldrons smoke, and there's a smell of meat. Foul fumes, nauseating.

A subterranean staircase. The metro, a train standing at the platform. A little door, a chink of light. Visas? . . . A woman behind a counter, packs of something. It's a bistro, but it looks as if they might be visas. The woman throws down a pack of Marylands[7] – three francs' change, our gold ones. I run, the gas burner flickers: a corner, tables piled up to the ceiling, like a partition. In the corner – tortured young faces, mortal anguish

in their glances. Martyrs, our very own! I shout: 'It's the last
train, get a move on! . . .' They say nothing, as though in slumber. I cannot reach them. I throw down the gold and hear its
ring. I run – slip by them, from behind. A wall. I knock, as if on
a void. Where are the doors? Boards everywhere, new ones, the
smell of pine. Stairs, stairwells, holes. I crawl along the ties,
crosspieces, beams. I spy through the holes – deep down – only
lights, bonfires, smoke. I'm terrified: I'll fall into the breach.
The steps have collapsed, there's no handrail. And I hear:
crutches, behind me. I look around – it's *him*, on crutches. He's
walking on the beams.

I crawl out on to the landing. There's nowhere to go: it's the
last one, the size of a board. There's nothing to grab hold of, I'll
fall . . . The sky shows dark blue, the stars are out. In the terrible depths, spots of red – lights, bonfires. In the distance – the
blaze, and a cupola the size of a five-copeck coin. Two turrets,
like two nuns, in pointed habits – two staffs, in the terrible
distance.

I hear a familiar voice:

'Hurry-y-y!'

I run along the little planks, in the wind. It's crisp, frosty. The
locomotives are enveloped in white clouds of smoke. A platform, crates. It seems to be lightly snowing. The train is strange:
benches in the carriages, along the walls. I see: a little old man
waving to me. I'm so happy, I run towards the carriages, grab
on . . . My hat?! . . . Lost. Baggage? . . . I cannot recall. *Everything* I had was there . . . The train will be leaving in a moment;
it's too late. In the carriage, under me, there's an orchestra playing. Bismarck is travelling with us, en route to a congress.

A whistle. I see: far away, he's flapping like a bird, on crutches,
his old greatcoat billowing in the wind. He catches us up, makes
the jump! I'm so glad, I cry out from happiness. Who is he, a
relative of mine? I can't make out his face.

We're on the move. The crystal stars are so bright! Fir trees
lash at my legs. Snow, forests. While the music plays, tenderly.

'We've passed Berlin! . . .'

A peasant's voice: it sounds like 'Bur-r-rlin'.

*

Birch trees, among the stars. It looks like – Kuskovo.[8] A long barracks at the foot of a hillock. The grille windows are misted over; the dim light of a bath-house. A little old man runs thither through the snow. What shall I do? . . .

It's snowing heavily; there's a platform. I'm – alone. Now what? It's shameful to go about without a hat. I peer through the window – the lamplight shines yellow. I see . . . Am I – *here*?! . . . Is it *that* horror? . . . I stand there. Out from the darkness floats a lantern. Through the window I can see the waiting room, an empty counter. Someone by the door . . .

A voice from the darkness, hoarse:

'Come in, we're just locking up!'

Snow has drifted in by the door. I see a bell and a rough rope. On the bell, a strip of snow. I stand there, freezing. Still, I keep trying to peer inside. A counter, a man asleep. *Someone* is waiting behind the door . . .

I'll go in right away . . .

2

En route from Paris – I'm somewhere just outside Moscow.

Night, heavy snow. A remote, deserted station, not a carriage in sight. Even the tracks are hidden: everything's covered in snow. On the platform not even so much as a footprint, everything is smooth, pure – total isolation. The snow is somehow lifeless, it doesn't crunch – like cotton. While everything else is as one would expect: sheds, gardens, birch trees. Lights in the station windows.

I look around. How alone I am! . . . Where am I going, and why? – I don't know. I have no hat, no luggage. The snow sticks, like it does in March. Shining through it, there's a dim light coming from the lanterns. Behind the station a dog is barking, anxiously: it listens awhile, barks awhile, into the void. It listens again. It's dark there.

How can I escape this place? Through the station, without a hat? It would look awkward. Through the garden? There's a cabby somewhere ... There are railings everywhere, like prison bars. An acute pang of anguish. Why am I here? I try to recollect: something ... the bath-house? ... How many years I've gone without a bath-house! They're all in the bath-house – there's not a soul in sight. Tomorrow is a holiday.

The little terminus is squat, long, made of boards, and splashed with snow. I try to make out the writing above the entrance – 'Moscow', it looks like. The grille windows have steamed over; the light shines out meagrely. I look intently ... Dear God, am I *here* ... ? But how on earth did I get ... here?! ... I feel sick, I want to go back but my legs crumple. The snow sticks, the dog barks – despair.

I look in disgust: the dingy waiting room, the stove looming black, foot-bindings drying out ... a man in a shaggy hat is asleep ... the greenish smoke of his cheap tobacco, a skew burner in the lantern, a trickle of lampblack running down. There's *someone* behind the door ... It's so dreadful, I can't go in.

I hear – a person ... ? He hawks viscously, like an invalid. The lantern is dangling, its fireguard sullying the snow.

A slave, again ... To run around, lost, filling out those vile forms ... How awful it all is!

A voice from the shadows – hoarse, dull:

'Come in, we're just locking up.'

I think: I need a smoke ... Should I say I'm from these parts, just taking a walk? ... I grope for my cigarettes – Maryland, they'll see ... I'm out of matches.

I walk like a local. I try to whistle, but my lips have gone soft. The *carte d'identité* in my pocket! ... The snow is thick, there's a drift by the door; no one has come this way in a long time. I jerk the door handle, but I can't open it ... The lantern seems to be floating. I see a bell, a frozen rope with a little knot, on the bell a strip of snow. I stand there freezing, still trying to peer inside. A counter, a man ... asleep? There's *someone* behind the door. I feel an itching torpor in my legs – should I flee?

I'll go in right away ...

*

A tall barracks on stilts – a box stand of sorts. A dark, stained wall, an arch supported by beams. A little lantern glows yellow amid the emptiness. To walk here is disgusting – the floor is slimy, sticky. The sharp stench of a bull pen; the sweetish odour of rot is nauseating. I can't . . .

I look around; where on earth is the way out? *There* . . .

I see a barrier in the distance, a turnpike. Shadows flit about.

Revulsion, and the terrible desire – *to see*. They're hiding.

I know: they cannot be here, this is 'Europe', a special place – outside.

Empty tables between partitions, like boxes at the theatre. A peasant of some sort. He's lying on a bench, beneath the window. A blind window. A long, tight-fitting lambskin coat, a crimson sash, boots with studs, a cap, his fist in his pocket . . . Aquiline nose, swarthy face . . . A gypsy horse trader? I'm worried: if he wakes up, 'Europe' will be lost.

I inspect the counter. A frightful-looking dish of aspic and some yellowish lard. Behind the counter there's someone watching me – he seizes a ladle and shoves it into the aspic. I recognize him as the *garçon* from Motte-Picquet and wave him away in horror – no, I don't want any! He scoops some out and brings it over to the table. Pointing to it with his finger: 'Eat!'

There's a partition behind me – there are more people there. The loud clatter of crockery – like a restaurant. A waiter with a napkin is looking. Am I really to eat *such a thing*?! . . . I feel nauseous, but I want to placate him . . . He looks like an Italian, with a goatee; he's peeping out from behind the wall: am I there? I play the foreigner – this is 'Europe' – and I say to the *garçon* from Motte-Picquet, wishing to placate him:

'*Voilà, monsieur . . .*'

I hand him a five-franc note.

'Here, some foreign currency . . . I'm from Paris and about to return there . . .'

He looks at me impudently and says in Russian:

'All the same, you must give your *signature*. On the forms, all fourteen of them, sir! I'll be right back . . .'

He disappears somewhere. I'm alarmed. A head peeps out over the wall: am I still there? I understand, and skulk away, to where 'Europe' is. I walk like a foreigner. *There* – appears a waiter; he thrusts a piece of paper at me. I see a door, only a fraction ajar . . .

I recognize the station – Vindavsky.[9] The red broadcloth, the glasses, the chandeliers, the suitcases. The first- and second-class waiting room. *They* are there.

They're all wearing masks and fur coats. The Paris train leaves: first stop Riga. I see a short man, his head held erect, dressed in a woman's coat, the fox-fur collar down to his elbows. There are others with him, supporting him, leading him, all – with reverence. He jabs his finger towards the door, at me. I'm terrified, but I keep my grip on the door handle: this is 'Europe'. All the people here are foreigners, and everyone is heading to Europe. Everything on them – right down to their suitcases – is foreign. They're all of them foreigners, in Russian fur coats. By the exit – in felt caps with red stars – our ones look like fools. Cap in hand, their eyes bustle around, keeping watch.

I look – the fox-fur collar is coming towards me! . . . I slam the door and run . . .

The platform, a void. An enormous locomotive. I see a man:

'For Paris?'

He rummages in a bag of some description.

'Cancelled.'

Someone waves to me. The greaser – he smells of lubricant. He takes me somewhere. There's no longer a train, but a field. He whispers:

'Straight on, straight on . . .'

A familiar voice, but the face is hidden; it's dark. We walk along a deep corridor; the floorboards bow underfoot. The cracks between them glitter with gold: beneath us is a brightly lit hall, and a hubbub. I tread carefully, peering into the cracks: people are milling about, slamming doors, searching for something . . . I know: *that* man himself is there, among the furs.

'Here's the exit . . .'

It's a friend, a relative – perhaps my late father. I want to embrace him . . .

I'm alone. The door is bolted, the brickwork rumbles. I see pure snow, I gulp the air.

A long barracks, a bath-house. Wet windows, and shadows within. Water in a ditch; it smells of a bath-house. Log walls, the wood rotten: the bath-house is rotten through. The little window is slimy. I examine the scene – it's crowded: bodies standing, up against one another, tightly packed. Shoulder blades, ribs, necks – all bony. Steam fills the air, which fizzes with the noise of the bath-house, the drumming of water buckets. It's too crowded to enter. I look for the doors – there aren't any. I'm afraid: how they're packed in, how they rub up against one another! . . . The steam appears to be coming from them; it's cold there. I shout:

'Let me i-i-in! . . .'

The heads sway and crowd together – like the sea swell. I'm terrified: the bath-house will tear apart, the walls will burst . . .

Night. Snow. I'm in the alleyways. The snow is off-white – it must be the moon. Dead houses, closed gates. I'm lost, I don't know where *mine* is . . . Here's a crossing, but there's no one to ask. What town is this? Dead ends, oil lamps. Klin . . . Ryazan . . . ?

A cabby crosses my path, from one lane to another, shadow-like. I hear the muffled sound of his sleigh on the tracks. Black manure, kitchen gardens. Where am I? . . .

The Sukharev Tower, judging by the eye of the clock. Of course, it's Meshchanskaya. A quarter to . . . seven! But why can't I see anyone?

O Lord, where is this? . . .

Sadovaya?[10] It's empty, and there are no gardens. Fences. Everything is muddled. How can it be so . . . forgotten?! . . .

Another cabby clatters down a lane. Nearby, by the sounds of it. Zhitnaya? A dead end, a railing . . .

I see – a church. I think it's . . . ? No, it's not tall enough.

The one where I was baptized was tall, with a green dome. The doorway is the same. It's aged, of course . . . I recognize Saint Nicholas in the snow, and the fence. Here's the vestibule. Yes, it is the same church. It's locked.

I press my aching bosom to the door, kiss the railings. Snow has swept into the vestibule. The font used to stand here . . . a white font, it would always stand here. How often I would climb these steps and look through the railings! It would stand there, the white font, on a little pedestal. The old font, *my one*. I remember, into it . . . I press myself against the door and weep. There is no font. A *single* sharp sensation passes – through me and through the church. The white font . . . There's a connection between us. I cry out from pain through the railings, into the darkness. O Lord! . . .

Night. Spring. I'm in my patron's study. I'm wearing tails; I have to attend the District Court, for my defence.

I find the austere, calm, sedate study so agreeable. Dark portières. A deep leather divan, armchairs, a cabinet with green curtains, the bronze faces of sages. I see Cicero's smooth skull, the Tsar Liberator with his topknot,[11] the Laws. The Wise Statutes on a table. The table is long and stands by the window. A candle is burning. The window is open. A portière gently billows. From the garden wafts the smell of verdure and the night. The lilac is in blossom. I see its racemes. The candlelight falls on them, on their dark, lustreless leaflets. Silence. Light from the street lamp spills on to a poplar, bathing its whitish little leaves.

'Let us discuss this . . .' says my patron, lighting a cigar from the candle.

He is good-natured and calmly impressive. I'm pleased. I know – he is dead. But this means nothing: he is – *somewhere else*.

I say:

'But how are you *now*? You have that same study, all in order. And the Statutes? . . . They haven't touched you? . . .'

'They cannot . . .' he says with gravity. '*They* do not know. All this . . .' – he circles the study and points towards the garden – 'is *outside*! The Law . . .' – he seizes the Statutes and fans the pages – 'You know, even Justinian . . . "pending inheritance"?'

I recall something: yes, Justinian . . . ? A 'pending inheritance'? He continues, weightily:

'Well, let us discuss this. The "pending inheritance" . . . You mustn't confuse matters: this isn't escheat! . . .' – he threatens with his finger – 'No! I *know*. When the legal heir is unknown, or when his whereabouts are unknown . . .' – he points somewhere beyond the garden – 'but he . . . *exists*! The presumption . . . that, well, he exists *somewhere* . . . as it were, po-ten-ti-al-ly. Let us discuss this special case . . .' – he gesticulates beyond the garden. 'In such a case, the vast inheritance is pending, as it were, waiting for his appearance before the law – *id est, momentum juris*.[12] Is that clear? While here . . .' – he indicates the cabinet, his quiet study – 'here, sir, is guar-di-an-ship! Elusive, moral . . . Allow me to put it another way: spi-ri-tual guardianship, *tutela spirita*. That is why . . . they *cannot*! Do not let us talk of the right: to all intents and purposes they *cannot*! *Impotentes*. It is beyond the reach of corruption. *Ergo: victores sumus!*[13] It's obvious. Do you follow?'

I understand perfectly – we understand perfectly. I believe and am convinced that there is guardianship, that my patron knows everything. They *cannot*. That is why this study, this table, these Codes, this lilac through the window, the caretaker on the other side of the fence, the little cupola of the Church of the Assumption somewhere there – that is why everything is so fixed: the 'pending inheritance' and guardianship. Yes.

It suddenly occurs to me:

'The *carte d'identité* . . . Do I need . . . my identity?'

He catches my meaning from these few words. He looks at the clock – his clock is a curio, a chronometer – he smooths out his little fair beard, scratches his forehead.

'We'll arrange it. Let us go to Kamergersky[14] – they're putting on Chekhov today. Are the guardians not there . . . on the walls, in the auditorium?' He winks. 'You'll emerge from there with full rights. The law exists! . . .' He points to the many volumes.

I understand: there is such a law. My patron knows everything.

So pleasant is the feeling that I desire to see the little cupola of the Church of the Assumption. I look through the window: I can't see it – the poplars are obscuring the view, so big have they grown. The moon seems to have come out: a delicate light throughout the garden. While beyond the fence there are measured steps. The caretaker is here, and the solicitor's maid. Quiet laughter.

I hear a rustle behind the shrubbery.

'It's my dog Milord . . .'

I know: the maid had taken Milord out for a walk. I feel serene.

'Shall I spend the night . . . ?' I say.

'Naturally. Well, let us go. Bismarck will be there . . . And if Bismarck . . .'

I understand: if Bismarck . . . !

My patron leaves to get dressed. I doze off.

Is that Milord barking? . . . A lorry rumbles. Is that a knock at the gates? . . . I listen – voices, in the garden . . . ? It's *them*, they've come for me . . . I know it. I snuff out the candle. I dart across the study cloaked in darkness. It's easier to see the window in the moonlight. The trees and the wind are whispering. Footsteps below the windows. I listen – a scratching at the window sill, they're climbing up . . . I watch as their peaked caps draw into view, I can see their heads in the window . . . I grab something and I scream, I scream . . .

Milky stripes. Twilight. I don't understand the words but, bringing joy to my ears, I hear:

'*Marchand d'habits et peaux-o-o!*'[15]

Paris?! . . . I'm in Paris . . . In the little street there's a *marchand d'habits*, a rag-and-bone man with his animal hides. I recognize the milky stripes – light streaming in from the shutters. There's a clatter of buckets, lorries are taking away the rubbish . . . Morning. The shadows have disappeared.

I lie there for a long time as I recover my senses. It's agony for me. I'm in Paris, so far away . . .

All day long I'm not myself. I touch my head: so much *in there*! Everything. From the first ray of light until – death. A whole life, a great treasure of lives. But here, a *marchand d'habits* – my last treasure? My last joy? Filthy rags and animal hides ... His voice rends the air, covering – *everything*. Like the clarion at dawn, in the days of old.

It's strange.

Spindleshanks

SASHA CHORNY

Ivan Petrovich trailed the angular profile of his wife with his eyes as it flashed by in the mirror, glanced at her spindly legs and sighed.

The door in the anteroom slammed. She was gone . . .

Ivan Petrovich poured out some beer for an old acquaintance who had just come to Paris from his home town of Narva and affably took hold of his sleeve.

He had long needed a patient listener, an earnest, old-fashioned provincial, who could fully understand him and empathize with him.

Those damned Russian Parisians have got so thick-skinned that you could bare your soul to them all the way down to your liver, and they'd only tell you to go stuff yourself with moth-balls and put yourself in storage. They're barely scraping by, but they're still kowtowing before the latest fashions. Mutton-headed self-hypnosis, that's what it is . . .

– You remember what my Natasha looked like back in Narva. A meadow blossom! Glowing with health. She really turned heads on the street: all those curves – natural, no padding! Round shoulders, apple cheeks and so forth . . . A regular cello!

Made you want to put her into an advertisement for Dutch hot chocolate.

From the primeval Eve to, let's say, Pushkin's Olga, this tradition held firm: a man – whether he's Onegin, the Demon, or Pechorin[1] – had to have muscles all over, because he's born to command. But a woman, glory be to the Creator, is a gliding swan, a poufy soufflé, a ripe peach – no bones jutting out all over the place!

Take Rubens, for example, or our own Kustodiev, or some sensible ancient Greek sculptor – they're all on the same page. If it's Venus you're depicting, then make her look like Venus;[2] if it's a woman, she should look like one; no need to whittle her into a stave, to turn sweet sorbet into vinegar. The only exception was Diana, because she needed sinews for hunting, and not much else besides.

– Or, for instance, take old Russian folk songs: 'Face round and fair', 'my juicy little apple', 'honeybun'. Just look at how round the words were! The peasants had a wholesome taste: a woman reaps the harvest and she's also the one who gives birth. Skin and bones need not apply. And they danced back then just as well as they do nowadays.

She-bears – what she-bears? Some floated lighter than dandelion fluff on the dance floor – extra weight not a hindrance!

'When I dance before young boys, I don't show off all my toys, but when I dance before grown men, why, I show them all I can! . . .'

Even a Grand Marshal wouldn't be able to resist!

– Or, take, for example, your old-fashioned wholesome Turkish taste. I haven't visited any of the old-time harems myself, true, but I've seen enough postcards and read enough of Pierre Loti[3] to form an impression of what they were like. They brought in lovelies from all over the world. Turks aren't allowed to have wine, so they go crazy for suppleness. Their cupolas are round, their crescent moon is round, and, correspondingly, so are their women. They didn't even allow women to walk around needlessly, so that they wouldn't lose any of their curvatures. Made them take Turkish delights internally, and rose oil externally . . . Now that's beauty!

I can just see them now, lounging around some fountain: wave rising upon wave . . . The on-duty eunuch is sniffing smelling salts, he's so worked up . . . Praise Allah! . . . Ah, to hell with it . . .

Similarly, King Solomon, a man of refined taste, in his 'Song of Songs', indicates pretty clearly: 'The curves of your thighs are like jewels, the work of the hands of a skilful craftsman.' This shows that he too waged no war against suppleness, yet he was as wise as they come . . .

But now . . . Have you seen what my Natasha did to herself, following everyone else's lead? Started out as a beautiful Houri and finished off looking like one of the Furies.

'Why did you plane yourself away like this?' I ask her. 'Just looking at you makes me feel all uncomfortable. Not much left to you except for tragic eyes and a spine – think you'll impress the world looking like that . . . ?'

'So don't look, you caveman,' says she. 'Head up to Lapland and marry a seal cow . . .'

Oh, good heavens! Isn't there a pleasing middle ground between seal cows on the one end and spindleshanks on the other? Why go to extremes?

She doesn't even deign to respond. Just looks down her nose at me, as if I weren't her husband but an old, peeling spittoon, and that's the end of it.

I sidled up to her once, on one of our good days: 'Tell me, Nata, little darling, just who are you doing this for – sharpening yourself into a toothpick like this? Not for me, I hope. You've known my tastes since we were young. And if you're doing it for others, God forbid, then where will you find those perverted he-goats who would enjoy looking at your flatlands?'

She didn't say word, just narrowed her eyes, like a panther ready to pounce. I spent the next two hours begging forgiveness in front of her closed door. I had to donate a hundred francs for a Chaliapin[4] benefit concert before she forgave me.

– And what suffering she puts herself through . . . Saint Sebastian himself never suffered so much.

She has the same old Narva-style appetite. But what does she do? . . . In the morning she sucks on a piece of toasted bread crust; for lunch, she juices two lemons; in the evening, she rinses out her mouth with Bulgarian acidophilus.

I sometimes wake up at night, switch on the light, and see

her lying there beside me, staring up at the ceiling, lips trembling, eyes dry and hungry ... Like a vampire.

I even find myself edging away from her – wouldn't want her to sink her teeth into me.

And what's the reasoning behind this? Why, bread makes you fat, potatoes make you chubby, meat makes you bloat, milk makes you chunky ...

They've got an intake schedule for every food product.

On top of that, she does a full fast day once a week, to promote lightness of gait. Of course, it goes without saying that on each of those fast days she eats me alive – she's so cranky.

And afterwards she either feels her solar plexus fall into the pit of her abdomen, or her sympathetic nerve gets all twisty, or else her stomach does not digest properly.

And why would the stomach be fool enough to digest properly, I ask you, if it gets no pleasure out of life other than lemon juice and massage? Then there's the anaemia. All her red corpuscles are so hungry that they're devouring her white ones, so there is nothing left in her veins but some watery whey.

She also gets vertigo. In other words, she's got the whole catalogue of ills. She says that she feels the floorboards rock under her. Well, that's only logical: if a woman has been turning herself into King Tut's mummy for the third year in a row, never mind the floorboards, the pavement itself will start rocking under her!

– I've begged my wife's doctor: 'Be an angel, do something! She's melting away like a candle for no reason at all! Before you know it, there'll be nothing left of her except for the wick!'

He just shrugs. Some friend he is.

Why would he do something about it, when his savings account benefits directly from all the indigestion and vertigo ...

His own wife, mind you, is German and so plump that it makes me upset just to look at her. Probably fattens her up with fish oil, the lousy crook!

– Even my daughter, a thirteen-year-old sprat, is crazy about it. Slimming down her silhouette ... She hardly has any flesh on her bones, what silhouette?!

'Listen, you ninny,' I tell her, 'you're growing – you need to feed yourself! When I was your age, I used to steal raw dumplings from the kitchen, that's how greedy I was for food.'

She just snorts in response, says something in *lycée* French that you can't find in any dictionary, and turns away.

'Who do you think you're snorting at, you little spindleshanks? At your father?'

Her mother stands up for her: 'Kindly don't interfere. I'm not raising my daughter to become a wet-nurse.' Then she calls me an apathetic pot of borscht, takes up her manicure set and sits herself regally by the window. Her nose and collarbone – that's her entire silhouette.

– Even my aunt, a respectable, flabby-looking woman who lives across the street from us and hawks ladies' lacy underthings, is also trying to follow their lead.

Now, if a woman is genetically inclined to it and is entering her twilight years, then, naturally, her sides begin to bulge out. She can't deposit them in some safe. That's just the order of things.

Since my aunt doesn't have any extra francs to spend on a masseuse, she lashes herself with rubber hoses and squeezes herself into elastic girdles all the way up to her chin. Some femme fatale . . .

Instead of normal food, she eats raw carrot peelings and some kind of crackers she buys at a store for sufferers of gout: they don't contain any flour or yeast – barely anything there at all, in fact.

All you hear is, 'I dropped three centimetres last week, thank God . . .' That's three centimetres that she worked hard to put on, that's her sweat and blood, so to speak . . .

Now that the stuffing's gone, all she has left is empty skin folds. They flap beneath her jaws. She looks just like an ox on Ukrainian fields. It's hard to take . . . Who is she trying so hard for, anyway? A hundred-year-old invalid would turn away in disgust.

– And they're all obsessed about weighing themselves.

As soon as the entire gang pushes their way into the metro,

my aunt rushes to the automatic scales, throws a coin into the slot and plunks herself on, to take stock of her inventory, so to speak. Then it's my wife's turn, then my daughter's . . .

One notch less on the scale, and they're beside themselves with joy . . . Lost some living flesh, how fabulous . . . Was it worth crossing the border for this?!

In a year, I bet, they'll have to weigh themselves on the food scale at the *épicerie* – there will be about a kilo and a half left to each of them, not more than that.

– But the big question is: what am I suffering for? I've got myself a bit of an income – I buy up various Louis XX antiques at the Salle Drouot[5] and then resell them. I run around non-stop, like some trained monkey at a fair. Haven't I earned my daily borscht?

I come home, sniff the air – once it used to smell of food, now it just smells of face powder.

So, because of their egoism, I too must turn myself into some kind of starving dervish. Borscht is supposedly bad for me. At my age, I should just drink milk of magnesia. What am I, an oyster? And what have they got against my age?! At forty-eight, a person just develops his real appetite, achieves a real taste for things . . . Look at the way the ancient Romans ate when they were my age . . .

I even dream of dumplings now; platters with geese and buckwheat pilaf drift before my nose in my dreams. But as soon as I grab one of them by the drumstick, I wake up . . . So I walk barefoot to see what's in the sideboard, but there's nothing there except for gramophone records and cans of milk of magnesia, may it rot in hell! . . .

Of course, I understand their starving female psyche: if I should eat a bit of salami in this cramped flat, they'd wake right up – the smell alone would overwhelm their souls.

I'm not a tyrant to torture my nearest and dearest.

So, during the day, I grab a couple of cold *pirozhki* on the go at some Russian store and eat them sitting on a wet bench, like some misbegotten child. It makes me bitter just to think about it . . .

I've started going to restaurants. The portions are all sparrow-sized, while the prices are ostrich-sized. Instead of the comforts of home, you're surrounded by strangers' jaws chomping, rushing, chewing last-year's fat ... All unpleasant types too – can't even find anyone to clink glasses with.

And then for the rest of the day your tongue is coated with fat, as if you've been licking some Laplander across her bare back.

– Yes, sir ... Fashion ... Who declares what's in and out, and when they do it, is simply beyond me. All right, let it drag on for a season or two, I'd understand that, but why keep it going for ever? That's what fashion is for, after all – to be driven out by counter-fashion ... Long skirts are in again, so why not switch to full figures?

No, they don't want to hear anything about it. Never shall we return, they say, to draught-horse sizes. It's only now, they say, that women have really sprouted wings ... We'll never exchange our fast-paced grace for Rubenesque fish bellies. But personally I think that if some pranksters were to publish a proclamation tomorrow that it is now the fashion to wear a curling iron as a nose ring, women would rush out in droves to pierce their noses. Mine would be the first in line, no doubt ...

– And another thing: why can't those idiot tailors just call it off? They could go in cahoots with the manufacturers, publish a fashion manifesto – and that would be that!

Clearly, a full-figured woman would need a ton more material, and you could charge her more for the work. Doesn't it cost more to upholster a sofa than a chair? Farmers and store-owners also stand to benefit if half the population – the entire female half of it – finally starts gobbling up natural food products after all this self-induced hunger!

You know, I'm even thinking that maybe this entire global economic crisis we're having is due to women starving themselves ... It stands to reason, doesn't it?

– I've been considering something ... Should I, perhaps, move my tribe back to Narva? I could open up a Parisian salami shop there, or else start exporting Estonian arts and crafts to Paris. Maybe people still live normally in that little backwater, like they did in the old days, without tying themselves up in knots. Ladies are ladies – a centimetre here or there makes no difference.

You're smirking? So it's reached Narva, has it? I see . . .

I bet you that even the Samoyed women up by the North Pole can now crawl in and out of the eye of a needle. Fashion. Oh, well . . .

Why aren't you drinking your beer? To your health! Leave the grave to the dead, but the living must be fed, as they say . . . I'm getting all worked up talking about it – shouldn't have even started . . .

Pompeii

VLADISLAV KHODASEVICH

To live two hours from Pompeii for six months and leave without seeing it is indecent, unthinkable. But still, I'd been putting it off for some reason, as if I felt some sort of foreboding. Finally, I settled on it. But it was 13 April, and a Monday at that – a day that was doubly onerous.[1]

By tram to Castellammare, by train to Torre Annunziata, then by cab. The day is cloudy, with only occasional sunshine, though the atmosphere is leaden. The road is white, dusty, covered in weeds. On both sides: vegetable gardens, water channels, gullies. The occasional house built of porous limestone, flat roofs with no eaves, windows without glass – those Italian houses that from the very day of their creation look like ruins. Everything is bare, flat, dusty, stony, scorched by the sun and eroded by the winds: the valley of Pompeii. The ennui of antiquity hangs above the road. The ash of Vesuvius seems to have eaten into everything here.

Vesuvius rises up on the left, rust-brown, its summit obscured by smoke. Almost black at the crater, it lightens and disperses into a whitish cloud, stretching out south-eastward.

At the entrance to Pompeii there is a little square, jammed with motor cars and open carriages. It is enclosed at one end by a modest hotel, the Hôtel Suisse. This lively establishment by the gates of the dead city immediately recalls those stalls selling crosses, wreaths and memorials that like to live near cemeteries.

A little curved road, strewn neatly with sand and bordered with lush verdure, leads from the entrance towards the excavations. Here, after the bustle of the square, the noise

immediately fades away, leaving only the crunch of sand underfoot. And the little road looks like a path in a graveyard.

There are calico sedan chairs dotted around on both sides –
for those who are too ill or too rich to go on foot. Now and
then they bear people – 'That way!' – farther down the path. It
looks like a cemetery.

Presently we enter through the gate: Porta della Marina. To
the right, beneath an archway, there is a door to a little museum.
Oh, what horror! In a cemetery office you're told only who
lies where – while here you're shown inside the grave, what
transpires within. On display is a collection of household
implements uncovered during the excavations: dishes, bowls,
tools, pots of rouge, padlocks, door locks, statuettes. And here
we have the inhabitants themselves: casts of people buried by
the ash. One, a writhing skeleton in rags, its mouth agape, full
of teeth; another covering its head with a toga – a last gesture
of desperation; a third, naked, lies on its back, bow-legged, in
a glass grave. A dog in a broad collar, reduced to convulsions,
curled up, like a caterpillar. Here, the 'secrets of the grave' are
revealed. Here, the virtue of the grave is outraged, its only right –
the right to secrecy.

We leave and enter the 'city'. There is something quite marvellous about its deathly silence and order. What with the
number of streets, squares and walls still intact, it's impossible
to think of it as a heap of ruins. Indeed it is a city, but a city from
whose face everything temporary, accidental, transient, has
been erased: Pompeii has been wiped clean, tidied up, 'decked
out', like a corpse.

The windowless backs of the houses, giving on to the streets,
are almost identical. Evidently the building work here was uniform even when the city was alive. Denuded by time, deprived
of their rendering, they are now no different from tombstones
in a cemetery.

Narrow but straight regular streets reveal the simplest of
vistas, intersecting at right angles. They are far straighter than
the streets of any modern Italian city. Uniform plaques with
numbered areas and districts are nailed to the corner buildings. Each building has its own number, too; at the crossroads,

by the pavements, plaques that are a little bigger – with street names – have been affixed with iron nails: a useful fabrication, necessary even for the tourists' orientation. Glancing at the numbers and names, however, one is constantly reminded that resurrected Pompeians would now find themselves resultantly lost in their own city: they are all approximate, arbitrary designations, bestowed in our time at the tyranny of scholars – just as it is in a cemetery, where the living, for their own convenience, name avenues after the dead.

Tourists here go about like visitors to a cemetery, never blending into the scenery. Like flocks of birds, small groups of young, gaily dressed English girls flit about. Occasionally, from behind a low wall, as if from behind a mausoleum, the ginger-moustached head of a German peeps out. Everyone moves in an erratic way. Only the keepers and guides walk and talk here with any certainty. For them alone, as for sextons and grave-diggers, is the dead existence of Pompeii a routine, a way of life.

Yet still, for all Pompeii's many similarities to a graveyard, there is always a sense of some important, essential difference, too. And suddenly it begins to dawn on you.

A cemetery is idyllic. Peace reigns there. Those who have trodden their path on earth we bear to a cemetery, to a city of *peace and those at peace* ... What is the grave to us? *Parva domus, magna quies.*[2] But in these little houses there is no great peace at all. There is reconciliation in a graveyard; here there is just horror. Everybody died, yet none was reconciled with anything. Here the people were buried, taken by death not only in the midst of their earthly journey, but also, one might say, with one foot poised to take its next step. Everyone here died in terror, in frenzy, in passion, in rage. It was a thousand times worse than on the field of battle. Violent deaths befall those, too, but every man is in part prepared for it; he sees in it even the littlest bit of sense: on the field of battle one man may be moved by patriotism, another by the thrill of glory and heroic poses, a third by a sense of duty. A fourth – at worst – goes because he has been given the order. No one here saw any sense in what happened. They perished in nonsensical terror and, according to Pliny's testimony, offended the gods – doubtless because they were sitting drinking, eating, measuring, weighing, fighting, embracing. And now, all of a sudden, you die, without the time to finish your drinking, eating, measuring, weighing, fighting, embracing . . .

> . . . And when, sans strength, the lovers came to rest,
> And sleep invincible subdued them, masses
> Of cinerous dust then fell upon the city,
> And the city was buried under ash.
>
> The centuries passed – and, as from avid jaws,
> We tore the past out from the earth, and found
> Two bodies there, symbolic of immortal passion,
> So incorruptible in their embrace.
>
> O, raise on high this sacred monument,
> This living sculpture of eternal forms,
> So that the universe shall ne'er forget
> That passion which transcended every bound.[3]

Lord, what soulless decadence! 'O, raise on high . . .'! No, for the love of God, hide it away, show it to no one, bury it again!

Death passed through here, touching everyone, delivering none from his earthly mask, purging none of his meagre, wretched horror. When a man dies of illness, of his body's exhaustion, his earthly cares leave him by degrees; the accidental and temporal fade away – anxieties, troubles, all the marks of his profession. The mask falls – and a face is revealed. It isn't a cobbler, a doctor, an actor who dies – but a man, a servant of God. It's the same when the death is sudden, if the sense of it is in some way deliberate: through heroism, sacrifice, perhaps even suicide, the desire to 'return the ticket'. There is a moment of purification, of catharsis in each of these deaths. At Pompeii there was none of that. They died just as they were: not men, but bakers, cobblers, prostitutes, actors. Thus it was that they 'crossed the great divide' – in their filthy, earthly guises, covered in the sweat of fear, of greed, of passion. At Pompeii, every step reveals a terror – of a death 'without repentance', of a transfiguration into an 'otherworldly' baker, an 'otherworldly' owner of a tavern or lupanar.

That is why Pompeii resembles not only a cemetery, but also something far worse than that: a house where the robbers have rushed in and slaughtered the residents in one fell swoop. They were boiling, frying, eating, breathing in the reek of onions – and right there, they were slain. We see the scattered remains of food, shreds of garments, broken crockery, traces of a brief, desperate scramble. The sight is terrible, and yet it inspires no awe, as is always the case in places of senseless catastrophe.

At Pompeii terror envelops you not on account of the number of victims. Here a modern man may startle a good few thousand Plinys with his tales. Here, it is not the quantity, but the quality of death.

Since the buildings and the houses here are turned with their backs to the street, each time you go inside one, you feel some thievish notion, as if you are not simply entering, but creeping, stealing into it. You go in, and it's as if at any moment, from this little room or that one, from some pit, the master of the house will crawl out into the light of day, disturbed by your presence. Perhaps he's that same bow-legged man lying in the glass grave. You go in, and it takes your breath away – not the fires of hell, but the onion, the eighteen-and-a-half-centuries-old onion. The pungent smells of Roman cookery seem to have spread over Pompeii. The city was small, artisanal, practical; here they knew the value of money and every kind of 'productivity', the emblems of which are strewn everywhere, in the form of various bulls, goats, swine, boars – and far more suggestive images, too. There were once many brothels and public houses here; the population had a robust love of eating, drinking and sleeping their fill. Pompeii was destroyed at supper time.

Here, a dreadfully uncouth, greasy, sticky life passed into an equally uncouth and ignominious death. And one knows not what would be more distressing: that the city were better preserved, or that it had been more violently ruined. The former bears traces of a suffocating life; the latter of a suffocating death. Here people lived and died in dingy, cramped quarters, with no windows and only a single door.

I imagine it would feel strange and unsettling to walk here in bare feet. And to touch something with your hand – no, not for all the world. There was once a terrible incident in my youth. On returning home from school one day, I found on the window sill a little round parcel. The newspaper on it was crumpled and full of holes. I stuck a finger into a hole – and recoiled in terror and disgust: coarse hairs and dry skin. Lying on my window sill was . . . a human head. Yes, yes, a real severed human head: a mummy brought as a gift. Pompeii reminded me of this incident at my every step.

The little rooms in the brothel are the most suffocating of all, the most cramped. They haven't been properly cleaned: the black remnants of ash have eaten into everything, probably along with the remains of ancient filth and human sweat. There is a black, ever so slightly greasy film covering everything: the wide stone beds, each occupying half the darkened box room; the thin partition walls; the posts of the doorways, from which the curtains have disappeared (or perhaps they were never really there to begin with?); in the cracks of the chipped paintings depicting the *what* and the *how*, the sight of which immediately brings on nausea and shortness of breath; and, finally, forgive me, in the round-holed board of the latrine (right there between the little rooms), which, not without a certain pride, our guide indicates to us: indeed, perhaps this is the only surviving example from antiquity. And when you manage to get out into the street – the exclamations of Petronius' characters seem to fly after you: true, the base, tedious, eternally vulgar, impenetrable (like the Pompeian night) events of the *Satyricon* unfolded a little later – though it was in these very parts.[4]

And so, a tour around the different buildings, the different rooms, contemplating the tasteless Pompeian artwork, with its insipid drawings and discordant colours on oil-cloth – each time you pray to God that the room be smaller, so as to pay homage to culture and snobbery all the more quickly. Even those that are somewhat better (for example, the little nauma- chia on one of the walls, completely out of keeping with the local style) bring no joy. How pleasant it is to examine this naumachia; yet it would be pleasanter still to run away from here.

Just for an instant, somewhere in the distance, beyond the railings, an image of Orpheus flits past – the only hint of a ghost in this city of people buried alive. Yet it passes – and again there is nothing to breathe amid the ancient twilight.

In schoolbooks, it is written that Christianity brought the Gothic spire into the world – an ascent upwards. Here you can witness this simple truth for yourself. The leaden, inert, squat cube of the Pompeian home – what inescapability, what flat- ness, what tedium! And these million-*pood*[5] weights, falling like deceptively light ash from the rationalistic heavens of the Latin world – oh, what inescapability! Now you can believe and you can see how great, probably, was the yearning for the Saviour in some of these souls – from the suffocating heat, from the flesh, from the ash.

It's hot. There are still a couple of buildings to inspect. The street's vista ends in the great mass of Vesuvius, as though cutting into it. I raise my eyes, and I see: playing in the black puffs of smoke, there are flickers of lilac, the colour of wine. This isn't fire; this is only its reflection in the clouds of steam. But all the same! There, high above Pompeii, the mouth of the dragon is breathing. I recall 'the wicked flame of earthly fire'.[6] And the ground seems to grow hotter beneath my feet. Away from here!

O dear, spirited, jovial cabby, riding to Castellammare! O dear, spirited, unfossilized little galloping horse, bearing me swiftly along – with every second farther and farther hence!

The cabby, it so happens, spotted me in Sorrento. He turns around, engages me in all manner of conversation about my nationality, my domestic situation. At any other time, I would perhaps have demurred, pretending to be an Englishman. But now, I muster all my knowledge of Italian and reply to each of his questions, so that he should feel well disposed towards me and crack the whip all the more often. And how cheery, how beautiful: somewhere off to the left, in the distance, is a tall, white belfry.

Atlantis

VLADISLAV KHODASEVICH

Usually Urenius is the first to arrive – when half the cellar is still in darkness and a single bulb is all that illuminates the firm leather divans, the wax-polished tables and the clean tiled floor. At two o'clock in the morning, when they will ask us to leave (though we shall argue and be outraged, shouting that the clock has been purposefully set ten minutes fast), the floor will be strewn with cigarette ends, and cards will be strewn across the tables covered in grimy mats, and the chairs will freeze in various expressive, at times fantastical, patterns, alone and in groups, like the characters in the final scene of *The Government Inspector*.[1]

Urenius takes off his coat, extracts a newspaper from his frayed pocket and sits under the light bulb. Around twenty minutes pass before Arkhangelsky arrives carrying a suitcase and an umbrella. Inside the suitcase are stockings, cigarette holders, glass beads, mosaic brooches and rings with large imitation rubies and sapphires – all these will be inspected and tried on by the ladies between play, while he tells them how the night before a certain wealthy Englishwoman bought rings or beads just like these.

Having deposited the suitcase in the corner, he carefully hangs up his coat, hat, chequered scarf, goes up to Urenius, touches him on the shoulder and shouts in his ear:

'I'm afraid that I'll forget my umbrella again. I forgot it here the other day.'

Urenius lifts his dishevelled head, curves his gentle, broad mouth into a smile and says:

'Yes, yes, with pleasure, just as soon as the others arrive.'

On swollen legs Madame Zwick slowly descends the staircase.

'Oh, this dreadful darkness again!' she says. 'Mr Arkhangelsky, tell André to give us some light at once.'

'Hold your horses, there's no one here yet.'

'But I don't want to sit in the dark. Thank you. I shall be able to see quite enough of it in the grave.'

Two more people appear presently. An experienced cinematographer would not reveal their faces just yet. He would show the staircase, and on it, behind the cast-iron spindles, a close-up of two pairs of legs, right in front of the audience's nose. One pair is in galoshes, with the frayed hems of some old mud-spattered trousers flapping over them. The other is in boots, not that they are at all chic, but durable, with thick, sturdy soles, and well polished. As they descend, the first legs reveal a senile tremor above a pair of trousers that are stretched and shiny at the knee. It is clear from all this that they belong to a poor man who, if not having been shy since birth, was made so at some point once and for all. The second pair of legs, too, are no longer youthful, but their step is assured, even menacing; they are clad in dark-brown trousers of good material, with a respectable crease down the front.

Light is cast on the stairs from only one angle, from the hall upstairs, and, as they come down, the newcomers are plunged stepwise into the penumbra. There their vague features greet Madame Zwick and Arkhangelsky. All four of them move off into the depths of the cellar. They make up a nightly group there. Urenius continues reading the newspaper under the bulb.

Meanwhile, Yasha Litinsky and Chernolesov arrive, our *jeunesse dorée*,[2] true Parisians – it has already been two years since Yasha became a Frenchman. He burrs, he talks with a disparaging mien – essentially, he has dropped in just to see what is going on; perhaps he won't even stay, and will instead pay a visit to the cinema, or to a girl – it isn't yet certain. Chernolesov looks like a sportsman: no hat in summer or winter, tall, tanned, bare-necked, a pencil moustache. It's best to avoid playing with him; yet Madame Simplonskaya, whose husband has left her, thinks that, for all her portliness, she is a fine, healthy woman, with her own womanly needs. It is for this reason that she plays with Chernolesov every evening.

For the sake of such guests as Yasha and Chernolesov, the lights must be turned on. The owner, without leaving his post at the cashier's counter, extends his hand towards the marble switch plate – and the cellar lights up. Now colourful paintings can be seen, hung on dark-crimson wallpaper with splashes of gilding. The paintings depict scenes at the races. Horses with flared nostrils galloping in a frantic rush forwards, their necks outstretched, flying through the air; they're being whipped by hunched-over jockeys in billowing harlequin silks; in the distance loom the grandstands with a blurred scattering of spectators. The other pictures show horses galloping and falling in the indistinct depths, while in the foreground there is a green lawn, blue and pink dresses, military uniforms of the last century; narrow redingotes, grey top-hats and lace parasols. There are five pictures in all. A sixth was smashed to pieces by a drunken Negro the year before last. To cover a hole in the wallpaper, the proprietor has hung a print of a painting by Brueghel, which, for a franc, he purchased along with the glass; the human heads, deprived of their bodies, look like misshapen potatoes trying to devour each other; the most emaciated face with its large nose plunges its only tooth into the fattest one, like a blunt knife in a pillow.

One after another, the parties assemble: six or seven tables, and on the eves of holidays even more. André rushes from one table to the next, handing out decks of cards, clattering about with saucers and glasses and taking orders. Play begins. The first ribbons of tobacco smoke hang in the air; the routine exclamations come from all corners.

Having migrated to Europe and traded ponderous whist and sedate préférence for the more neurotic bridge, already we no longer say, as our fathers and forefathers did, 'piquentia', 'David and Alexander' or 'I'll take your queen by the whiskers', and so on, but 'triphylandopoulo', 'pique-pique-pique' and 'frustrate their knavish tricks'.[3] Every now and then, one hears the threatening 'contre!', the poisonous, hissing 'sur-contre' and then the gloating 'I'll teach you to be contrary.'

Mostly our play is neurotic – the Chekhovian era, so to speak, with its gentle rustle of cards and the poetry of a winter's evening, has receded into the past. In our cellar there is uproar. Sometimes the owner, leaning over the banister, will instil quiet with a threatening clap of his hands. Then we shall warily quieten down, as Madame Simplonskaya gazes into Chernolesov's eyes, squeezes the round joint of his knee or, having tipped some coffee into her saucer, treats her restless mutt, which has worms in its mouth.

The Astrologist

MARK ALDANOV

In the autumn of last year, the author visited a number of French and German astrologists in Europe. Their communications and séances have served in part as material for the current story.

I

Madam,

I have received your letter, and I thank you for your confidence in me. I have immediately set about the complex computations that compiling a horoscope requires. This work is yet far from complete; however, already I can be certain that your fate appears to be most auspicious.

Further to this, I am already able to draw numerous conclusions with respect to your personality. Your character is exceedingly attractive. You are very intelligent, although your detractors deny this. You are woven from contradictions. You are strong and brave at times, but occasionally you yield easily to the not always salutary influence of others and lose your mettle and courage. You passionately thirst for life; however, at times you feel great spiritual exhaustion. There are several contradictions in your complex nature that you do not yet know yourself. Not everybody sees your rare and exceptional qualities.

Are you happy? I do not believe so. Yet opportunities for great happiness lie in your fate. You have already let slip several of them, which you, most likely, have not even suspected. An experienced guide could make you the happiest of women. I offer you my well-proven skill in this capacity.

You mention you are interested, more than in your fate, in the attitude to you of the man whom you love. But is one not linked in the most intimate way with the other? It is my belief that you were made for this man, and that you are able to bring him happiness. Regrettably, the details you provide regarding him are quite insufficient. For a certain answer to the questions troubling you, I shall have to compile a horoscope for this man, too. I must therefore know his date of birth. Additionally, there is a great deal that can be discerned by means other than astrology. You will be aware that I am not merely an astrologist. Please do not judge me to be immodest when I say that I owe my world renown in equal measure to my knowledge of chiromancy, oneiromancy, ophiomancy, rhabdomancy and economancy – the great and ancient sciences to whose study both I and my forebears have dedicated our long lives.

All this will require a private meeting and consultation. You ask about my terms. As you will naturally be aware, I am by no means mercenary and should gladly work in the interests of people entirely free of charge, if only there were not in this an element that my clients found beneath their dignity. Your personality is so alluring and your fate so interests me that I am prepared to offer you preferential terms, which I do not offer even to the most famous writers, doctors or advocates who have long honoured me with their confidence. I offer you the following:

1) For the contents of this letter I shall take nothing from you.

2) Your full horoscope will cost you two hundred (200) marks. From ordinary clients I would usually take twice this. Before the war I had occasion to compile horoscopes for representatives of the Anglo-American plutocracy, such as Franklin Roosevelt, Rockefeller, Vanderbilt, the Dukes of Westminster and Norfolk and Sir Walter Scott. They paid me thousands of dollars, which I donated almost entirely to charitable causes.

3) If you wish also to have the horoscope of the man mentioned in your letter, I shall charge you for both horoscopes a total of three hundred and fifty (350) marks.

4) If you would do me the honour of visiting me on Wednesday, at 10.00 a.m., the consultation, with card reading, will cost you only fifty (50) marks.

In anticipation of your prompt reply, please accept the assurances of my utmost devotion.

Heil Hitler!

After the signature came the date: '13 April 1945, 10.30 sidereal time'. The letterhead was engraved with the name and address of the Professor, his telephone number and the words: 'Please enclose a stamp for reply.' His name was long and strange. Before, he passed himself off as a Hindu, but since the outbreak of war he had said he was Indonesian.

The Professor reread his copy of the letter and sighed. He did not like to deceive people; but then, one had to live. *Lord, how much in life is built upon human credulity, and what a misfortune it would be if people were not so gullible!* he thought again. Perhaps it would have been best not to mention the Anglo-American plutocracy in the letter, especially now, given that affairs in Germany were not going so well. But the Gestapo often read his correspondence. However, on the day that he wrote the letter, the situation had improved: the Russians were no longer advancing, the radio commentators were saying that a rift had now opened between the Bolsheviks and the democracies. President Roosevelt had died, and the commentators were interpreting this as a great coup for the National Socialists. Perhaps it would have been better not to mention Walter Scott either: however, from long experience the Professor knew that the vast majority of his clients were uneducated people. *The letter is well written. No woman doesn't think herself intelligent, with rare, exceptional qualities and a complex, contradictory nature, that she was made for the man of her affections and that her detractors fail to appreciate her.*

There was nothing of interest in the letter he had received

from this woman. The majority of his clients declined to give their names in the first instance and asked him to reply via poste restante. Later, many of them, particularly the women, would not only give their names, but reveal everything about themselves, right down to the most intimate of details. The Professor would draw his initial conclusions from the style of the letter, the paper and the handwriting. Before a consultation he would always read over the request and a copy of his reply. The years were telling on him: his memory had grown feeble, and recently he had begun to prattle on and repeat himself more often than people do.

On this day, since morning, he had felt a familiar unpleasant sensation in the pit of his stomach, which usually, although not always, presaged a fit. He had slept poorly and awoken very early; the first thing he did was to open the window, fasten his dressing gown, so as not to catch cold, and listen. People in Berlin had been saying that at night one could hear the distant thunder of cannon. *No, I can't hear a thing . . . There weren't any attacks overnight. Oh, it's time to get out of here . . .*

He was a diminutive old man with yellow hair around a yellow bald patch, with cunning little yellow eyes, a yellow beard and a weary yellow face. The Professor suffered from a liver complaint, but he hid this as best he could, lest his trade suffer: though his clients could not demand that an astrologist be immortal, still he was not supposed to fall ill. He was a pure-blooded German, but with the years there had appeared in his countenance something oriental – which was not without its dangers: he could be taken for a Jew. He spoke with an indeterminate foreign accent, rightly calculating that no one in Berlin would know how a German-speaking Indonesian would sound. Of course, the police knew exactly who he was. However, astrology was not *verboten* in Germany. The Führer himself had been known to use astrologists in his time. The first of them, Hanussen, had been assassinated some while ago – which could be attributed to his Jewish lineage. Hitler's new astrologist, Dieterle, was rumoured to be constantly by his side, in the Reich Chancellery, at the front, at the Eagle's Nest, and even now in the underground bunker on Wilhelmstrasse. Recently the astrologist Wulff had begun to visit Himmler. The Professor was acquainted with Hanussen, with Dieterle and with Wulff; he spoke of them always with politeness and restraint, much as a good doctor might speak of other doctors, while inwardly he was unable to bear them and took them for charlatans.

He went through to the bathroom – there had long since been no hot water – and for around forty minutes set about his ablutions. Cleanliness was an obsession of the Professor's; he would say to his lady friends that any civilized man could have but one ideal in public life: to live to a time when bathing every day was just as imperative as eating every day. Having perfumed himself with strong *oriental* scent, brushed his beard with a golden comb and clipped the yellow hairs protruding from his nose, he put on a black suit made by the best tailor, with two inside pockets and turn-ups on the trousers – admittedly it had been made some time ago, when fine English cloth was still being imported to Berlin from Holland and Belgium. The Professor was not rich. His savings, amassed from years of toil, had dwindled away during the era of inflation. Sceptics he knew, to his great annoyance, would scoff: 'How is it that the stars didn't inform you that the mark would go to the devil?' True, his earnings had increased under Hitler. Everything that had taken place in Germany was so strange and fantastical that, evidently, people had begun to believe again in sorcery. Clients appeared even from among the new masters. The Professor feared them, but they too feared astrologists; however, they paid poorly, haggled, and at times would allude to their connections. He would give the dignified reply that he had some connections of his own, but in this instance he would concede to a discount. On account of his innate goodness and *joie de vivre*, the Professor was not overly fond of National Socialism and even before 1933 had been given to calling Hitler 'the Dauber'. The Professor had held no great love for the Weimar Republic either – due in most part to inflation – and had dubbed Ebert 'the Saddler'. Real life was what came before the first war. The Professor hated war and felt dejected when maps began appearing in the newspapers.

His modest apartment was furnished part in the Gothic

style, part in the oriental: something between Indian and Turkish. The Professor had been married twice. Both wives left him: the first had declared that he was too stupid for her; the second that he was too smart. Neither had any interest in astrology, and so they found his company tedious. *Usually people divorce because they have nothing to talk about with one another*, he lamented. But then, he had not been much grieved by this and found there to be certain advantages to bachelordom: for example, it was most pleasant to sleep alone – one could turn on the lamp whenever one so desired, turn it off whenever one fancied, take as much of the duvet as one wanted. His lady friends would complain that he was forever telling the same stories, for the most part having to do with astrology. This puzzled him: was all this really so boring? Yet there were times when he himself was astonished to find that he had nothing to talk about: so little had happened to him in those seventy years, during the most tumultuous period in history. Every now and again he would invite a former lady friend to dinner, always at some fine restaurant, and order expensive wines. He was never mean with money, although he would frequently recall with mild distress the hundreds of marks he had simply thrown away. He was exceedingly courteous to each of his acquaintances, men and women, and would say only nice things to their face, knowing how little these people were indulged and how much they appreciated it. When travelling to a spa by train, in the carriage, wearing a smoking cap and slippers, he would offer his fellow passengers confectionery and praise the amenities of the railway. The Professor would even make an effort to speak flatteringly of the weather, as though granting that even it required compliments. He tried not to speak of politics at all, particularly since the July of the previous year: the plot had shaken him even more than the war – wars would always come about, but if German field marshals were being hanged, then absolutely anything in the world was possible.

Breakfast was served in the dining room. The Professor did not keep a maid or a cook. He always felt a vague sense of unease whenever there was an outsider in the house. Breakfast had been prepared by the charwoman Minna, a morose, taciturn woman, who came for only two hours each day. She was entirely indifferent to the identity and occupation of her employer, but would give the apartment a good cleaning. Before, Minna would cook fried eggs with speck, porridge and stewed fruit. Now all these were difficult to obtain. Liver stones prohibited the fried eggs. In the morning the Professor would drink only two cups of coffee with toast. However, breakfast remained one of the greatest pleasures in his life. The coffee was tolerable, although he recalled real coffee, the sort that was served during the reign of Kaiser Wilhelm, the sort he would drink at Kranzler's, Bauer's and the Café Victoria.

At breakfast the Professor unfolded the newspaper, and his face altered. The Russians had begun an offensive across a 200-mile-long front. Ten Soviet armies were attacking simultaneously. The Führer's order to the soldiers on the Eastern Front was published on the front page. 'Our supreme enemy, the Judaeo-Bolsheviks, have launched their Asiatic hordes against our Fatherland; their aim: to put an end to German civilization. We anticipated this attack and since 11 January have established a reinforced front,' read the Professor, cursing. *I know just how the Dauber anticipated this. He should go back to painting fences!* he thought. ' . . . This time the fate of all Asiatic marauders awaits the Bolsheviks. They shall perish outside the walls of our capital . . .' *So that's it. They've already reached 'the walls of our capital'*, thought the Professor gravely. 'The moment Fate wiped the earth clean of the world's greatest military criminal of all time, the outcome of the war was sealed . . .' The Professor failed to grasp immediately that the greatest military criminal of all time was President Roosevelt. *The Dauber seems to have completely lost his mind* . . . The situation on the Western Front was no better than on the Eastern one. General Patton's Third Army had crossed the Czech border. The First Army under General Hodges, too, was sweeping forward. *Would that they got here first, and not the Russians!* thought the Professor. *Of course I must flee, but how? I ought to have gone to Switzerland long ago* . . .

He sighed and went through to his study. On a wall in this large luxurious room hung an enormous painting depicting a

procession of fakirs on the Ganges, and on another the signs of
the Zodiac. On the shelves stood marvellously bound ephemeri-
des. On a small narrow table covered by a yellow velvet cloth
with embroidered oriental characters lay a crystal ball and an
antique card case. At each end of the table stood two tall Gothic
chairs. Everything was in perfect order. The room smelled pleasant and strange. The Professor opened a Gothic cabinet and
donned a yellow cloak and a white turban. Despite this habit of
many years, he still felt some shame in putting on this garb.

There were still ten minutes until his client's appointment.
He carefully locked the door and switched on the radio. An
underground German radio station usually broadcast at this
time. The Professor had his suspicions: he very much doubted
the existence of secret radio stations in Germany. Moreover,
three-quarters of its broadcasts seemed like flim-flam to him.
An angry voice suddenly, in the middle of saying something,
began shrieking that things for Hitler were now at an end. He
could no longer even hope for a conflict between the Bolsheviks
and the democracies: President Truman had taken the firm
decision not to include in his cabinet Byrnes, who would have
opposed granting any concessions to Russia, while the appointment of Molotov as the head of the Soviet delegation in San
Francisco testified to the true spirit of friendship that Stalin felt
towards the new president of the United States.

From the hallway came a very short, somewhat timid and
plaintive ringing at the door. The Professor hurriedly switched
off the radio and turned the dial to another, faraway frequency.
Then he increased the flame under a copper cup filled with
eastern aromas and went into the hallway. He opened the door,
placed his right hand to his turban and admitted the lady to his
study.

2

'Pray be seated,' he said with an Indonesian accent, offering the
lady a Gothic chair and scrutinizing her closely. Personal observations of clients formed the principal source of his predictions.

He was observant, was a shrewd judge of people (less now than formerly) and understood his clients very well indeed. 'A cross between Freud and a swindler,' said a foreign writer who had visited him out of curiosity.

The lady wore a heavy veil. This was in no way out of the ordinary: many of the Professor's female clients chose to conceal their appearance at first, although he could never have known them, and they would lift their veil only after ten minutes or so. *Well-heeled, young and, I'd imagine, beautiful,* thought the Professor. Women now flustered him less than before, but still they did fluster him (just last year he had completely gone to pieces when, for the first time in his life, a woman had offered him her seat on the bus). *Very nervous . . . There's no need to demand the money up front: this one will pay . . .* Clients occasionally cheated him: they would refuse to pay for their horoscope and even abuse him. This usually happened in those rare instances when the horoscope turned out to be inauspicious. The Professor knew perfectly well that inauspicious horoscopes were disadvantageous, and so he steered clear of them in so far as he was able. However, whenever a client demanded too great a slice of happiness, when some grim-visaged woman longed for a fiery romance, when an old man who had spent half a century on the stock market wanted his shares in Allgemeine Elektricitäts-Gesellschaft to double, then the Professor would refuse: one should never spoil one's reputation with the uniformity of auspicious predictions. If the client were to raise his voice or start to cause a scene, the Professor would curtly remark that he bore no responsibility for the display of celestial luminaries and that he made no demands on payment. In such instances he would not place his hand to his turban, but he never threatened to summon the police. He had no affection for the police even in the days of Kaiser Wilhelm.

'You have come at an early hour: the hour of Saturn,' he said slowly, in a rich, deep voice. He usually said exactly the same thing: mainly to give his client time to calm her nerves. He liked hearing himself speak, too. 'The earlier we commune with Fate, the better. I always rise before dawn, and every morning I feast my eyes upon the great miracle of the world. Dark night flees the rising Sun. Spectacular and majestic is the appearance of the greatest of the celestial luminaries. The first streaks of magenta appear in the east, while the horizon in the west is still dark. The Sun rises. The Sun is risen. Every earthly creature greets it. Birds sing. Everything rejoices in the new day. Only the weak and mad do not rejoice in this daily miracle. And why?'

'I . . . I don't know,' the lady whispered. The Professor, however, did not expect an answer: he knew that even a person of quick wit would find it difficult to answer his question. He continued to study the lady. She did not look at anything: not at his cape, not at the signs of the Zodiac, not at the painting. A woman of easy virtue? No, of course not. An actress? Not that either . . .

'The Sun,' the Professor continued, 'is suffused with reason. Kepler, the greatest among all the world's astronomers and astrologists, knew this. Do you recall his treatise on Mars? Therein he wisely declares: "The planets must possess reason: otherwise they should not be able to follow their elliptical paths with such regularity, in full accordance with the laws of motion."'

The lady clearly did not recall Kepler's treatise on Mars. She sat there in silence, gazing fixedly in front of her.

'Your coming here, madam,' said the Professor, 'indicates that you have accepted my offer and my terms. Before we move on to the cards, I must ask you several questions. You are passionately in love with one man. Fate is usually sympathetic to our passions, so long as they are pure, not ruinous to our being, and do not harm others. You wrote that you have cause to doubt this man's love for you. He is unmarried, has promised to marry you, but has not made good on that promise. Is that so, madam?' asked the Professor. He addressed his female clients differently: some as 'my sister', some as 'my mistress', some as 'my soul's joy', and some simply as 'madam'.

The lady nodded silently.

'There should be no secrets from an astrologist, indeed there cannot be: the stars will tell me what you would hide from me . . . Are you in an illicit relationship with this man?'

'No . . . Yes,' she whispered, hesitating somewhat.

'Do you suspect he loves another?'

'No.'

'Perhaps he is in need of money, which you haven't in your possession? . . . I ask this not to cast aspersions on him. Some of the most upright men do not marry because they cannot support a family . . .'

'Money has no place in this,' the woman cut in.

'How then do you explain his refusal to do his duty?'

'That . . . That's precisely what I wanted you to tell me.'

'And so I shall,' said the Professor, placing the crystal ball in front of the lady. 'This sphere contains the water of the Ganges. Place your left hand on it. But first, naturally, please take off your glove. And, if you don't mind, I'd ask you to lift your veil. Of what use is it here? Why conceal your face, when I am entering into communion with your soul?' The lady lifted her veil. She was indeed very pretty. *There's something common about her. She looks as strong as an ox, but she has the eyes of a maniac, a most strange combination* . . . As was his custom, he wanted to establish whether this woman projected a good or a bad principle of life, but he found himself at a loss. *No, her face doesn't express any goodness. Passion, yes. Unrequited passion.*

'The left. I said the left,' he corrected her. When the lady had placed her hand on the globe containing water, the Professor remained silent for a few moments and poured the liquid into the copper cup. The pleasant, slightly intoxicating smell intensified.

'*Susabo! Mizram! Tabtibik!*' the Professor intoned in a hollow voice, placing his hand on that of the lady. Her hand was cold. Her entire face grew pale. *Very nervous*, he thought without taking his eyes off her. Then he closed his eyes. He himself felt somewhat uneasy. *What a pity that I mentioned Walter Scott in the letter . . . She isn't stupid . . . Poor woman . . . She'll meet a bad end*, he thought, preparing his answer.

'I can't . . . I can't go on with this!' whispered the lady. The Professor opened his eyes and said severely:

'You must remain silent. Your words have broken the chain

of the spirits. Now I'll have to re-establish it.' He stood up, wet-
ted his hand with liquid from a little crystal bottle, wiped it
with a snow-white handkerchief, placed it again upon the lady's
hand and closed his eyes. His face also began to grow pale. A
moment later he lifted his hand and placed it to his turban.

'You will be happy. You will live to an old age: another
forty-nine years, seven months and sixteen days.'

'What about him?' asked the lady, gazing at him lifelessly.
Evidently his words had made no impression on her. This
wounded the Professor a little.

'Let us move on to the cards,' he said, as if not hearing her
question, and took the card case from the table. 'As you will
know, the cards in the deck correspond to various human char-
acteristics. You are the Queen of Clubs. The Queen of Clubs
denotes goodness, nobility and intelligence, with a certain
instability of character.' He began to deal. 'The card to the
right indicates the nature of a person. The one to the left tells of
what awaits him. You see, I was not mistaken: the Queen of
Clubs lies to the right.'

He set aside the cards and raised his hand.

'*Susabo! Mizram! Tabtibik!*' he repeated even more solemnly than the first time, and, as before, without drawing his
eyes from the lady, picked up the deck again. 'The nine of diamonds . . . Madam, you are on the eve of important decisions.
Very, very important ones. The nine of diamonds fell to the
Argonauts when they decided to board the *Argo*. The six of
hearts . . . A noble, selfless deed,' said the Professor, shaking
his head, as if in doubt. 'The eight of hearts . . . What you have
hoped for so long and passionately will come true . . . I think
you will be happy.'

'So you aren't certain.'

The Professor paused for a moment.

'Madam, in life there are two principles: good and bad. No
man is given to know which of these is the stronger. On first
appearances, hatred is mightier than love. Yet in life only the
good principle is lasting. The eternal principle of love is the
only thing that brings happiness in life. Hatred brings success,
but it does not bring happiness,' he said and lapsed into thought,

watching the woman with distress. The Professor seemed suddenly to recollect something. 'That's all I can say to you for
now. But, as you know, your horoscope has not yet been fully
drawn up. Readings of the celestial luminaries do not usually
differ from card readings. However, there are always exceptions. The great Wallenstein was one such exception ... But
then, was he really so great? With great people of this type, it is
essentially just their energy that is special. All of their ideas
were worthless. Perhaps even as people they were worthless
too ... Not all of them, of course,' interjected the Professor,
thinking better of it. 'This, of course, doesn't pertain to such an
exceptional man as the Führer ... You ask whether the man
whom you love will marry you. I must refer you to what I said
in my letter. In order to be absolutely certain, I must compile his
horoscope as well. If you are hard up, I can give you a discount.
The second horoscope will cost you a total of one hundred
marks. Money is of no interest to me at all.'

'Money isn't the issue! But ... I cannot tell you his name ...
It would be indiscreet of me.'

'I do not require his surname. Indeed I haven't even asked
yours. For the sake of convenience, however, may I be permit-
ted to know your given name? ... But then, that too is
unnecessary. The progenitrix of womankind was Eve,' with a
smile the Professor said what he said to all his female clients
who did not wish to give their name. 'Thus shall we call you in
the horoscope. I require his date and year of birth or the date
and year of his conception. Nothing more.'

'What? ... How do you? ... How is one to know the date
of someone's conception?'

'Of course, in the vast majority of cases one can only know
the date of conception approximately. However, the celestial
luminaries do not alter their position in the Houses of the
Zodiac in the blink of an eye. A few days' error is of no great
consequence. Indeed, in antiquity dates of birth were not
known with complete accuracy, and yet their horoscopes were
drawn up and proven with time ... Surely you know the birthday of the man you love?'

'No ... Yes, I do ... He was born on 22 April 1889.'

He's none too young, her chap! thought the Professor with a certain astonishment. He took his fountain pen, filled it with red ink and wrote down on his notepad in red, legible handwriting with a few flourishes: 'Born 22 April 1889.'

'Both horoscopes will be ready in a week. Drop by on Wednesday, again at the sidereal hour of Saturn ... At ten o'clock in the morning,' the Professor clarified and recalled that in a week he might be gone already. 'Or, if you would like, pay me now and I'll send you the horoscope by post ... poste restante, of course.'

'For the love of God ... for the love of God, tell me sooner!'

'Very well, on Tuesday.'

'Earlier still, I beg of you. Can I not have the horoscope tomorrow? Or even the day after?'

'In that case I should have to work throughout the night. For you I should be willing to do even this, but I require the assistance of a young Siamese whom I have initiated into the most basic mysteries of our science. He helps me to make the calculations. You will understand, of course, that I cannot take advantage of his industry. This will cost you an additional fifty marks.'

'I'll willingly pay whatever's necessary. Can it not be tomorrow?'

'No, tomorrow is impossible,' sternly said the Professor. He argued only for appearance's sake: it made no difference to him when he drew up the horoscope. 'I know with what trepidation people await my predictions. Believe me, you have nothing to worry about: already it is becoming clear to me that your horoscope will be an auspicious one. He will marry you.'

'Do you think so? Are you certain?'

'I am almost certain. Almost,' said the Professor solemnly.

3

Four hundred marks was no trifling sum. Yet the Professor's mood improved only for a few minutes. The unpleasant feeling in the pit of his stomach would not shift. *There is one true happiness in the world: never to feel the existence of a single part of one's body. This is a happiness that we begin to value only as it disappears*, thought the Professor. He had a penchant for philosophy, and in his youth he had conquered half of *The Critique of Pure Reason*; only upon reaching page 300 did he decide that there was no reason to torture himself. *I am neither a Privatdozent nor a fakir.* All in all, he had read a great many books.

The Professor hid the money in a secret compartment of his bureau. Minna would steal only in kind: pilfering sugar, coffee, more rarely bed linen, but she would never take money. It was better, however, not to lead people into temptation. In the compartment lay 5,000 marks, 350 Swiss francs, ten gold coins from the days of the Kaiser, a gold cigarette case and two rings. That was all the Professor had. He had no insurance policy, since he had no faith in currency; he did not keep his money in a bank, since he had no faith in banks. At the sight of a soldier with luxurious moustaches, his head proudly cast back, the Professor, with a sigh, mused that in those golden years a man without faith in banks might be taken for a psychopath, while no one had even heard of falling currency. *Yes, it's awful. Everything's so loathsome now. Perhaps it's still possible to fly away.*

One client, a dignitary or a high official who was well disposed towards him and much more amenable than the others, had contrived to find him a place on an aeroplane. The Professor had a Swiss visa at the ready: he had long sensed that *their* whole business was folding up – so much had he grown into the role of the oriental magician that now it was as though he viewed the Germans as an outsider, and in his thoughts even spoke of *them. Everywhere in the world, a lot hangs on luck, but for* them *absolutely everything depends on it. They're cynics and nihilists without even realizing it themselves*, thought the Professor. Nevertheless, leaving was difficult. He loved Germany, Berlin – so pleasant in former times – his apartment, his furniture and possessions. *Minna will ransack the whole place . . . And what's to become of me? Do I mean to leave for ever? Where politics is concerned, nothing is 'for ever'. But when a man is approaching seventy, this 'for ever' doesn't mean all that much* ... Some while ago, he had begun reading medical articles in the newspapers ... *Then again, the horoscope yielded such marvellous results* ...

The Professor did not believe in chiromancy, nor in ophiomancy or in rhabdomancy. He did not believe in dreams at all: they were usually too silly even for the silliest of clients. However, he did believe firmly in astrology – real astrology. He recalled how Theagenes had foretold his fate to Octavius, how Scribonius had compiled an astonishing horoscope for Tiberius, how Nostradamus had predicted world events four centuries before they came to pass. For his own clients, he went to no great lengths: one could not spend a month on each person. On his own horoscope, however, he worked long and assiduously, and only recently had he finished it. He extracted a notebook in a handsome leather binding.

The notebook contained wonderfully drawn charts, pages of calculations, texts that laid out the conclusions. Everything was written in inks of different colours, in an old-fashioned script. On the day of the Professor's birth, the Sun and Saturn had aligned in the Ninth and Tenth Houses of the Zodiac. Thus had it been on the day of Louis XIV's birth, and this king had lived for seventy-seven years. Mars ruled Saturn. This usually betokened nothing auspicious. The influence of Mars told on the fate of Sadi Carnot, who, although he did become the President of the French Republic, was stabbed to death by an anarchist. *True, under certain circumstances the influence of Mars can be paralysed by Venus, and that is precisely how things are in my case. A first-class horoscope ... But still, it's necessary to leave. There's enough money for two or three years of modest living, even in Switzerland. Then again, the prospect of modest living is singularly unattractive.* Such were his erratic thoughts of several things all at once.

Suddenly there came a ringing from the hallway, entirely unlike the first: authoritative, long, unbroken. This was how people from the Gestapo often rang. The Professor sprang to his feet and made for the door. *What on earth is this? Is he out of his mind?* ... The visitor did not release his finger from the button. A tall, very broad-shouldered man in a black civilian overcoat did not walk but rather burst into the hallway. *A burglar!*

'What's the meaning of this? . . . What do you want? . . .'

'I've come to you . . . On an important matter,' said the strange man in an unpleasantly hoarse voice. Obviously he was no burglar; a burglar would not have rung like that. Nevertheless, the Professor continued to look at him in perplexity. The strange man's face had been slashed from his ear to his mouth, leaving a terrible scar. *Where have I seen him before? . . . Who is he? What is he after?* The strange man, without taking off his overcoat, walked into the study, threw a quick glance either side of him, fixed his grave eyes on the proprietor and, without waiting for an invitation, sat in a high Gothic chair, which creaked slightly under his weight.

'I humbly pray you be seated,' said the Professor, forgetting his Indonesian accent. His heart was pounding. Even he could not understand the reasons for his agitation. This man could harbour no malign intent whatsoever. *Who is he? What a savage mug! . . . The scar isn't from a duel, and most likely it's recent . . . He has a military bearing, but then which of them doesn't? He's poorly dressed, although everything is brand new and expensive. He doesn't know how to wear them; he's unused to it . . .*

'Are you this . . . magician?' asked the man with the scar.

Perhaps he's drunk, thought the Professor. *If he'd been sent by the Gestapo, he would have been polite and courteous.*

'I'm not a magician but an astrologist,' he intoned quietly. 'I tell people their fortunes, mainly based on the science of astrology. On occasion, I also employ chiromancy, oneiromancy, ophiomancy, rhabdomancy and economancy,' he added. The Professor would always begin with exactly the same things; however, he did not tell this visitor about the rising of the Sun, about the birds, or about Kepler. The man with the scar immediately interrupted him.

'I don't know anything about these *mancies* of yours! I was told that you tell fortunes using cards, palms and the stars.'

'Dare I ask who might have referred you to me?'

'That is of no consequence.'

'Truly it is of no consequence to me. My science, which embodies nothing unlawful, is open to all. Apart from racketeers. Every now and then people do come to me, wanting to know when the war will end. Doubtless they'd like to know for stock-market manipulations. However, the celestial luminaries take no interest in monetary affairs, and the alignment of the planets in the heavens cannot be used for profit that would be at variance with the will of the Führer,' said the Professor with a look of utmost innocence. He had heard that the Gestapo had recently been sending agents provocateurs to fortune-tellers, inquiring after future levels of military borrowing. *We'll soon see whether he asks who has been to see me on such matters.* The Professor had a ready answer: that he never asked the surname of his clients. However, the man with the scar posed no such question.

'So what do these "celestial luminaries" reveal? . . .' he asked.

No, he's no agent, thought the Professor. *Maybe he's a client from the Gestapo – there are many of them. Or maybe he's not from the Gestapo at all.* He knew perfectly well that many Gestapo agents had a very peaceable and genial look about them.

'Our science,' he said, already more calmly and with an Indonesian accent, 'is based on one fact alone, verified by centuries-old wisdom. This fact consists in the following. In the life of every man there are two moments when his fate is written in the heavens and fixed for the rest of his life. These are the day of his birth and the day of his conception. Although, the wise men of antiquity would determine the alignment of celestial luminaries also on a third date: the day of the man's death.'

'Why on the day of his death?'

'In order to determine an auspicious day for his burial: to ensure a hospitable welcome for him in the hereafter,' said the Professor, who saw that a hospitable welcome in the hereafter was of no interest to this client. *Naturally, he's a grubby materialist, just like the rest of them,* he thought scornfully: he could not bear materialists. *A Nazi, to all appearances . . . This, too, we shall soon find out.* 'It is advisable,' he continued, 'to supplement the revelations of the celestial luminaries with magic cards. There are different systems of fortune-telling by cards. I, for instance, never use the Ancient Egyptian system of tarock, because everything there is based on the comparison of a man's fate with letters of the Hebrew alphabet. This would be incommensurate with the precepts of the Führer. Every letter of the Hebrew alphabet, as I know from censorious literature, carries a certain meaning. Thus, the letter *shin* denotes the approach of madness, while the letter *lamed* points to the gallows.'

'*Lamed*?' repeated the stranger, starting.

'Yes. As an Aryan, I do not care to use this system, although it was precisely by this that Aristotle foretold Alexander the Great's future.'

'*Lamed*! To hell with *lamed*!' said the stranger angrily. *Just as I thought: a Nazi. Hardly likely to be an officer. More likely from the Gestapo, or an informer*, thought the Professor.

'Indeed. There are, however, purely Aryan systems. Do you wish to limit yourself to cards?'

'How much will all this cost?'

'For you, I would charge twenty marks for a card reading and the same again for a palm reading. A horoscope would be more expensive: fifty marks,' said the Professor. He named a paltry fee, if only so as not to cause an argument and all the quicker to rid himself of this man.

'I'll give you fifty marks all in. That's more than enough.'

'The money is of absolutely no interest to me. Agreed,' said the Professor. 'Be so kind as to show me your hand.' *What a hand! He could be an executioner!* The hand belonging to the man with the scar was fat and enormous, with hairy, stubby fingers. *The fingers are shorter than the palm: bestiality. His life line is regrettably on the long side. Though here on the head line there's an island: perhaps he'll go mad. That is, if he isn't already half mad. I haven't seen such an abhorrent specimen in a long time!*

'Your life line is very long. This almost guarantees you a long life. True, it is red and broad.'

'And what does that mean?' quickly put in the man with the scar.

'It attests to strong passions. Forgive me, you have a difficult nature,' said the Professor. Strictly, he was no longer looking at his client's palm, but rather, while hiding his disgust, at his face. 'You have a network of enemies. Dangerous enemies, but you too are a dangerous enemy of theirs.'

'What will become of them?' asked the stranger, listening very attentively.

'From your hand, I can foretell only *your* fate. If you desire to know the fate of your enemies, you should turn to cards and to a horoscope ... I shall go on. In the world there are two principles: that of love and that of hatred. You do not show the principle of love. Your head line—'

'What does the head line reveal?' the man with the scar broke in.

'It reveals a man's intellectual and moral traits ...'

'That doesn't interest me,' said the stranger, drawing back his hand so sharply that the Professor started. 'Let's move on to cards. But since you didn't finish the palm reading, I'll pay you less for it. How many lines are there in all?'

'Five,' drily answered the Professor, although there were nine lines.

'You wanted twenty marks for the palm reading, so I'll deduct sixteen.'

'Very well ... Do you want to know your fate or that of your enemy? Your principal one? Splendid,' he said, and took the deck in his hand. According to convention, he was required to say here: '*Susabo! Mizrakh! Tabtibik!*' but the Professor had a vague sense that he should now dispense with this. *What sort of man might his enemy be?* He began to deal.

'The king of hearts,' he noted with uncertainty. 'But I cannot tell you about your enemy on the basis of this card. The king of hearts denotes a peaceful nature, wholly devoted to religion, charitable and philanthropic deeds.'

The man with the scar laughed coarsely.

'Yes, this card has nothing to say about him.'

'Indeed, I said to you that his card would be the first on the left ... The six of spades. Just as I thought.'

'What does the six of spades mean?'

'The six of spades betokens terrible deceit, uncovered too

late. The six of spades fell to the Trojans when they allowed the Greek horse to enter their city walls.' *It seems to have worked*, thought the Professor. *He isn't laughing any longer.* 'The three of spades: worse still. The *danse macabre*, the Parcae's dance . . . I shouldn't like to be in your enemy's shoes. Perhaps you won't require me to compile his horoscope?'

'When could it be ready?'

'It usually takes three days . . .'

'I must have it tomorrow.'

Strange, strange, thought the Professor. His unaccountable agitation grew. To this client he did not mention the young Siamese, nor did he demand an additional fee.

'Very well, I'll send it to you tomorrow. Be so good as to tell me the date of birth or the date of conception of your . . . acquaintance,' he said, once again extracting the fountain pen from his pocket.

'How am I supposed to know the date of a man's conception, damn it?!'

'An error of a few days is of very little significance. The celestial luminaries do not alter their position in the Houses of the Zodiac in the twinkling of an eye. You need only subtract 270 days from his date of birth.'

'The date of his conception is the seventeenth of July, 1888,' said the man with the scar after thinking.

'The seventeenth of July, 1888,' repeated the Professor, jotting down on the same leaf of his notebook: 'Conc. 17 July 1888.' The unpleasant sensation in the pit of his stomach suddenly grew stronger. 'That's everything. Tomorrow I shall send the horoscope wherever you specify.'

'I'll come to collect it myself, at eleven o'clock tomorrow morning,' said the stranger. The Professor had wanted to say that he would not be at home tomorrow, but instead of this he put in hurriedly:

'I can send it poste restante. Of course, it's entirely up to you.'

'Listen here,' said the stranger suddenly, in an irresolute, almost imploring tone. 'I can see that you're a good sort . . . Do you only predict events? What I mean to say is, perhaps you're able to . . . Perhaps you're able to influence them as well?'

So that's it, thought the Professor.

'No, I cannot influence them,' he replied coldly. His self-confidence had increased just as that of his client diminished. 'I can tell you what will happen to a man, but his fate does not depend on me. Probably, having seen his cards, you wish to help him? No, here there is nothing I can do. The cards have shown a terrible fate looming before him. If it is what the horoscope confirms, no power can save your acquaintance.'

'You guessed correctly that I wanted to help him,' said the man with the wound, standing up.

Having seen him out, the Professor returned in the most dismal state of mind. He was experiencing a feeling as though after this client's departure he needed to open the window in his study and sprinkle the Gothic chair with carbolic acid. *Naturally, he means to do someone a nasty turn. But then, that would imply he isn't from the Gestapo. Gestapo agents can do that easily enough without the help of astrologists . . .* The Professor had wanted to get back to his horoscope, but he felt that he was no longer in any condition to concentrate. *Shall I have a drink?* he wondered. The Professor went into the dining room and, although it was strictly forbidden by his doctor, he gulped down three glasses of cognac. He began to feel better. Returning to his study, he sat down and absentmindedly gazed at the notebook – then he grew pale.

On the page, one beneath the other, were written two dates: 22 April 1889 and 17 July 1888. The Professor mentally added 270 days. The blood drained from his heart. *What is this? . . . Lord, what on earth is this? . . . It can't be . . . Yes, of course, it's him! . . . After all, I did tell them that an error of two or three days made no difference. They've both altered the dates, each after their own fashion. But who are they? What do they want? What did I tell them? . . . O Lord! . . .* It was now clear – crystal clear – to him that the woman and the man with the wound were inconspicuously covering their tracks, talking about one and the same man: Hitler.

But if that is so, then I must run! Run now, this very instant, the Professor said to himself. He realized that he had become mixed up in something terrible. *Admittedly, I didn't say anything to her. Just that she would marry him ... He might not like it very much ... But* him! *I slandered* him! Deceit, the Trojan horse, the *danse macabre*, the terrible fate, the absence of power to influence anything – it all flashed through the Professor's mind. Who on earth was he? Plotter? Provocateur? Each was worse than the last. Dozens of innocent people died because of that plot. He clearly understood that for people mixed up in any way, however remotely, in a plot, there was only one salvation: to run, to run without looking back, to run without a moment's hesitation.

Breathing heavily, the Professor paced about his study and dining room and drank another large glass of cognac; he then opened the secret compartment and stuffed everything that was there into his pockets, taking with him the leather notebook. He always kept his passport on him. *Am I really forsaking this all for ever? ...* He lowered the blinds and then raised them again. *If he can't get me a place, I cannot return here in any case. Should I leave a note for Minna? No, that won't be necessary ... Of course now she'll ransack everything ... Perhaps I dreamed it all? ... Perhaps I've gone mad? ... After all, the horoscope was auspicious! ... What if it's auspicious precisely because I'm leaving here right now and shall fly to Switzerland this evening? No, no, I cannot stay here! ... Should I take anything with me? What if they're already watching me? It would be better to come back for things at dusk ... First of all, I need to know about the aeroplane ...* He donned his overcoat, locked the door behind him and stepped into the street, looking about.

4

In the deep, two-storey underground bunker there were telephones, radio sets, telegraph machines; typewriters clicked away, a continuous, almost imperceptible drone came from the engines below, while above the distant rumble of shelling grew daily. With much-too-sprightly resolute steps, field marshals and generals passed by the kitchen and through the canteen, trying not to look around them, as though feeling ashamed. Equally quickly, but now with a less resolute air about them, people who in recent years had been more important than field marshals descended the stairwell to the lower floor of the bunker, accompanied by policemen and bodyguards. Day and night, up and down the corridors, stairwells, the canteen, the little connecting room that had been dubbed the 'conference hall', ran secretaries, menials, drivers and messengers in confusion, bumping into high officials, astonished at seeing them while on the hoof.

All their faces were green with bloodshot eyes, exhausted from lack of sleep, from the eternal electric lighting, from the eternal hum, from hurrying, from fear, from the desire to appear calm, from the cramped quarters and, most of all, from the sweltering heat. Despite the artificial ventilation, there was not enough air fifty feet below ground. Order was still maintained somehow, but there could be none of the former discipline, respect or servility. Telephone operators or warders from the Begleitkommando[1] could sometimes be found in the canteen 'having a bite' (it was no longer permissible to say 'dining' or 'lunching') practically beside – although not quite beside – people whose names over the last twelve years had been mentioned constantly in newspapers around the world. And although these people feigned pleasure at a friendly acquaintance with their young colleagues and smiled at them amiably, little was now left of their prestige following the embarrassment of those first days. From the room on the left side of lower floor, which served as an office for the Führer himself, hysterical cries could be heard on occasion even on the top floor. Into this room secretaries now went on tiptoe, and high officials very nearly followed suit. At the doors were posted sentries with savage looks about them from the Reichssicherheitsdienst,[2] and detectives from the Kriminal Polizei[3] cast hasty glances over passers-by. But everyone understood: however one might twist it – if the enemy army was approaching Berlin, it meant that the Führer was not altogether the Führer. The pluckier ones, especially among the military, would shrug their shoulders, hearing from the office or the conference hall the wild, guttural cry that over the radio had only recently instilled fear in the world.

At a table in the canteen, some clerical personnel were expressing fervently what happiness it would be to die for the Führer. The high officials nodded their heads approvingly. Very few thought about this seriously: they knew they would be sought out and shown no mercy. Before long, they were recalling what they knew about Valhalla, about the Nibelungen, about the final scene of *Götterdämmerung* and Brünnhilde's leap into Siegfried's funeral pyre. Thinking about this more than anything, choked with desperation, hatred and rage – total victory had been in their grasp! – was the cleverest of those left in the bunker, a man more gifted than Hitler, who spoke better than he, who had failed to become leader chiefly because of his incompatible appearance.[4]

There were even people in this underground complex prepared to save their own head at the price of Hitler's. Now it was being voiced mentally: save Germany from the madman. One of the highest officials, practically the Führer's closest friend, a first-rate architect and engineer, passing through the vault with a polite smile, bowing amiably to his young comrades, exchanging firm – many without uttering a single word – handshakes with other high officials, poked his head into the ventilation unit and finally made a long-disputed decision: to introduce poisoned gas into the pipe, best of all Tabun or Sarin, which had been prepared in case of chemical warfare – that way they would die in a few minutes – an easy, painless death – and the Führer, too, and the highest-ranking personages. *Yes, it would be easy enough*, mused the official, contemplating the technical particulars. Leaving the bunker, he set about enacting his plan – afterwards, he was very aggrieved to learn that the bunker contained a bypass vent, thanks to which the Führer might have been able to survive.

However, this officer and the generals, who again now considered Hitler an untaught madman, along with those who had accompanied Hitler into the bunker to assist him in committing suicide, could not always cast off their doubts: what if he found a way out of this hopeless situation? What if he wriggled out of it this time, too? For a decade he had been attended by unprecedented good fortune. According to the rules of logic, according to the laws of probability, he ought to have found himself in the grave long ago: in a new Valhalla or in a pit for those who had been hanged. But not everything in the world adheres to the rules of logic or even to the laws of probability.

The vast majority of those people amassed in the bunker did not themselves know why they were being kept there, what their leaders were waiting for, what they were hoping for. They thought almost exclusively about how to save their hide from the 'Cossacks'. Simplest of all would have been to slip out of the underground complex. But this was strictly forbidden; the inertia of discipline somehow managed to retain some effect, and it was perilous to leave the bunker under ever-increasing artillery bombardment. People soberly hid everything from one another: their thoughts, their emotions, the contents of their wallets, cases, bags and money belts. But they all drank, even the women, a great deal more than usual, and sometimes their tongues loosened up. In a whisper people would say that the only option left was surrender: 'If we were talking about the Americans or the British, it would of course be a different matter. But Russians! Cossacks! . . .' – 'How would it be better if the Cossacks took us without a surrender?' – 'That's true, but . . .' – 'Who knows, maybe it'll be easiest to come to some arrangement with the Russians. Stalin's a very shrewd man, I've always said so.' – 'Yes, but will *he* agree to a surrender?!' – 'Whatever the case, we cannot die along with our wives and children just because *he* won't agree to it!'

It happened that a rumour spread through the bunker, that in another bunker, in utmost secrecy, an aerodrome had been built, that in it were dozens of the latest, best aeroplanes, waiting in reserve, that they would soon take them all away, along with their families and belongings. By and by, more accurate reports arrived: the aerodrome was located under the ruins of the Hotel Adlon, sixty-two aeroplanes would carry everyone off that evening, at the stroke of midnight. The women rushed to pack their cases, stuffing their jewels and currency into ever more secret places ('In all this confusion, one might so easily be robbed!') and pleading with their husbands: 'Isn't there any way we could get to Motzstrasse before take-off to pick up the silverware that's lying there – poor Frau Cohen, her things are sure to have disappeared – I just can't forgive myself for having left so many things at home when we came to this damned bunker – but you didn't say a word to me – we're talking about important things here – how could I have known? – well, is it really the woman's job? – God, who could have imagined it? . . .'

5

In one of the remaining chambers of the new Reich Chancellery, an elderly clerk with a bewildered, exhausted face was receiving those who arrived. *A good thing he's old*, thought the Professor, who knew from his twelve years of experience that in Germany now one could only deal successfully with elderly people. The clerk looked at him in astonishment and, with equal astonishment, glanced over his permit and instead of filling out the visitor forms suggested searching for the high official in the bunker. 'He isn't here. Everyone's in the bunkers now; ask there.' – 'In which bunker exactly, and will they let me in?' softly began the Professor. 'Look in all of them! Most likely he'll be with Goebbels,' said the clerk exasperatedly and, seizing a card on which was printed 'Führerbunker', wrote something on it. 'I'm sincerely grateful to you, but if . . .' – 'Try them all! For God's sake, go!' shrieked the clerk, grasping his head in his hands. 'Forgive me. The old formalities are gone now.' The Professor had taken no offence, but he was baffled, particularly by the fact that the clerk had referred to the Minister for Propaganda simply by his surname. *Yes, clearly things are going very badly for them*, he mused – not without pleasure, though nevertheless with alarm: unfortunately *their* affairs were tied to his.

It took him more than an hour to make his way about the bunkers on Wilhelmstrasse, but he still could not reach his goal. The high official was nowhere to be found. In one Dienststelle[5] they said that he had gone to the front and was expected any minute in the Führerbunker. 'So shall I wait for him there?' asked the Professor boldly, and, receiving no answer, he set off for the bunker. As soon as he found himself at the main underground complex, located beneath the old Chancellery, heavy shelling began. As the people ran below, they no longer asked to see passes.

The Professor paused for a moment to get his bearings: it was as though nothing so awful had happened. Only it was difficult to breathe. He walked along the corridor. A young woman was taking a break at her typewriter, fanning herself with a sheet of paper. She scrutinized the Professor closely, extracted a compact mirror from her bag and made up her eyebrows with a pencil. At the end of the corridor, by a short flight of stairs, stood a sentry. 'I suppose those are the Führer's rooms?' asked the Professor without his Indonesian accent. There was nothing so awful about the girl either, and he was less afraid of women. She laughed as she painted her lips. '*Her* rooms are first, Eva's,' she said. 'She has her own bathroom – not exactly how we live! Anyway, there's no hot water, and the pipes were put out of order this morning,' the girl added joyfully. 'His rooms are further up, to the left of the conference hall.' The Professor was taken aback. Who was this Eva, if they called Hitler *him*! . . .

Having taken a wander around the corridors, he sat down wearily on a stool in the corner of a room that served as a canteen. He was terribly hungry and thirsty but decided not to ask the grim-looking man behind counter, who was angrily dishing out beer and sandwiches. Passers-by occasionally glanced at him in astonishment, but no one questioned him. People were talking about the shelling; it was getting heavier by the minute. *I must act very, very diplomatically*, thought the Professor. Growing bolder, he approached one of the groups, walking up with an ambiguously ingratiating smile: each of them might think that he knew the others. Smiling sweetly, the Professor listened to the conversation. They were discussing dinner: there would be fried eggs and sausage. 'I'd give half my life for a smoke,' said one of them. 'Half your life? That might not be much now,' replied another. Everyone laughed gaily – exaggeratedly so. They don't seem to be very busy. Odd . . . Perhaps everything is done on the lower floor.

The high official had not returned by evening. People were saying the bombardment had been like no other. From agitation, or possibly from the cognac he had drunk, the Professor began to feel pain. He barely made it to the man in charge of facilities in the complex, explained to him what the matter was, having called the high official 'a close friend' of his, and asked permission to spend the night there. 'To go out, they're saying, means certain death.' The clerk muttered something angrily – evidently each new person here was considered an enemy – however, he ordered a camp bed to be allocated to him. They billeted the Professor in a very small box room with three unmade camp beds, situated next to the lavatory. The two youths who were already there did not so much as nod in reply to his courteous greeting and presently walked out into the corridor, cursing as they went.

The air in the room was frightful. In the first minute, the Professor doubted he would manage to last there for even a quarter of an hour. He hid his leather notebook under the mattress and collapsed on to the bed. He knew that when in pain it was best to sit with his back not leaning on anything. *Oh, if only he would come tomorrow, if only he could find space for me! . . . Lord, what can I do? . . .* He had not brought with him his pyjamas, soap or even a toothbrush. Of his medicines, he had only belladonna: he had purchased it at a pharmacy the previous evening and had forgotten to take it out of his coat pocket at home. Making an effort, without a sip of water, the Professor swallowed the pill.

Half an hour later he was feeling better. He took off his coat, folded it so that nothing would fall out of the pockets and lay down, placing it under his head. He mused that there were bound to be fleas, mice, even rats in the bunker. He thought he would never sleep a wink. However, his thoughts soon became muddled. *But the horoscope was auspicious, ever so auspicious*, he told himself. On occasion he would employ the Coué system, but it gave good results only when life's circumstances were getting better and better, every day in every way.[6]

The youths returned late and, by the looks of it, tight. He noticed that they were wearing white socks. *That means they belong to his youths, to those fanatics. They must serve in the kitchen or the canteen* . . . They, too, lay in their beds, without undressing. As he drifted off, he could vaguely hear their conversation. 'So, haven't you flown off yet?' the elder one asked sarcastically. 'Not yet,' replied the other, pausing to think, evidently not having understood the joke right away. 'Are those sixty-two aeroplanes still under the Adlon?' – 'Yes, they're still there.' – 'Where will they take us to? Moscow?' – 'Certainly not! Why would they? There are Russians in Moscow. They're taking us to Berchtesgaden.' – 'What are we going to do in Berchtesgaden?' – 'What do you mean, what are we going to do? Defend the Führer and Germany. They've built impregnable fortifications there.' – 'As impregnable as the Siegfried Line, or better still?' – 'Better still, they say.' – 'They also say that in the refrigerators there they've got forty million geese with apples ready, and just as many bottles of Rheinwein. You always were an idiot.' – 'That isn't true at all,' replied the second, pausing for thought.

At daybreak the Professor awoke and again heard the muffled, continuous rumble coming from above. He glanced at the clock and sighed: it had just gone eleven. The youths in the room were gone. He felt a terrible thirst. There was no shoehorn. He had to shove his index finger behind his heel, which felt awkward and painful. He grew tired immediately. His wallet was safe, the leather notebook lay under the mattress as before. *What if he still hasn't come?* thought the Professor, adjusting his collar, tie, then beard. *I wonder whether there's anywhere to wash around here* . . . He went out, his head in a muddle. Probably the belladonna . . .

Suddenly, the door behind him crashed open. The Professor looked around and was dumbstruck. Coming out of the lavatory was the Führer. By force of habit, the Professor stood to attention, raised his arm and in a broken voice shouted: '*Heil Hitler!*' However, he immediately felt that it would be better not to shout. The Führer cast a quick, suspicious glance at him – a look of horror flashed in his eyes. In the lamplight,

Hitler's face was of a sallow, jaundiced colour, haggard and ill-looking. He was hunched over, one of his hands drooped, and his fingers were trembling. *You'd simply never recognize him*, delightedly thought the Professor, who had seen him several times up close and from afar. Hitler straightened his back slightly, also raised his hand, probably wishing to impart a look of majesty to himself. *True, it's very difficult for a man to take on a majestic air when he's just coming out of the latrine . . . Could his own one have been damaged? . . . Or is this for associating with the masses: the Führer sharing a lavatory with ordinary people! . . . The hunted animal! Well, one can't go on hunting others for ever*, thought the Professor, watching in amazement as Hitler went. Ahead, people threw themselves against the wall, standing to attention and raising their arms, but nobody shouted any salute.

A queue had formed in front of the counter in the canteen. There was no coffee. A sandwich and a mug of beer were thrust into the Professor's hands. He retreated with them into a corner and propped himself up against the wall, so as not to fall over. *Cold beer is strictly forbidden when you have liver stones, it's much worse for you than cognac*, he thought. But he was desperately thirsty. With great relish, he drank the whole mug in a single draught, then bit off a little piece of bread. Suddenly, about twenty paces from him, he spotted the man with the scar! He was drinking something straight from the bottle, throwing back his head as he did. The Professor dropped his sandwich, shrieked and bolted down the corridor on tiptoes.

He collapsed onto the bed in the little room. His pain immediately magnified. Half an hour later, it was unbearable. He thought he might be passing a stone: the doctors had told him it could happen. Little by little, his groans turned into cries. He had never felt such pain before in his life. He wanted to reach for the belladonna, but even this was beyond him.

The elder of the youths stepped into the room, looked at him in perplexity and asked what the matter was. He asked the question brusquely, rather because he did not know how to speak any differently. 'A doctor . . . For the love of God, call a doctor!' whispered the Professor. The young man shrugged and went out. In the bunker were the Führer's doctors, who were constantly giving him special medicines, specifically concocted for him, and one doctor for ordinary people, who worked almost around the clock.

About twenty minutes later, the doctor for ordinary people arrived with the youth; he examined the Professor and gave him an injection. 'He'd fare better out of here, in somewhere like a hospital, wouldn't he? What good is it doing him lying around here? He'll only stop people who work all day from sleeping,' said the youth angrily. 'Perhaps you could send a car for him?' asked the doctor. In the bunker many people now spoke only in tones of sarcasm. 'Lie here. I'll drop by later,' he added.

The Professor's pain began to ease, then it disappeared completely. In a delirium, he warmly thanked the youth, saying fervently how much he loved the Führer, that President Roosevelt had been a wonderful person, that President Truman would probably be a fine fellow too, and that the Americans would be there soon. They would arrest that villain, clean that lavatory, purify the air and give a lot of money for the restoration of Germany, like they always did. He said he would receive an enormous indemnity from the Americans if Minna had ransacked his apartment, that he would presently leave for Switzerland, where they did not allow such terrible people to walk freely. He also said that he dearly wanted to take a bath and that any civilized man had only one aim: bathing ought to be just as necessary as ... The youths, by now quite drunk, were conducting their own conversation. 'You idiot, I'm telling you, he's going to marry Eva. She's said herself that she'll soon be Frau Hitler,' said the elder. 'I'm no idiot, and you're always lying,' replied the other. 'I've never told a lie in my life! Say what you will about me, but no one can call me a liar!' – 'Well, I can!' – 'She's called Eva Braun, and she's a witch,' continued the first youth. 'The Führer can't marry a witch,' objected the other. Faltering, the elder said something about the newly wedded couple, about a honeymoon, about Cupid and Venus. The Professor did not listen to their conversation, just as they did not listen to his ravings. Yet the word

'Venus' reached his consciousness. Tears welled in his eyes. On the day of his birth, the Sun and Saturn had aligned in the Ninth and Tenth Houses of the Zodiac. Mars could do nothing, for the good and powerful goddess Venus had bound him up by his hands and feet.

6

How long had he lain there in bed? Afterwards, the Professor could not tell: he had lost track of time. The doctor came in to see him every day, gave him something to drink and an injection. One day he asked him his name and noted it down. This augured nothing good, although the Professor now felt much better.

'Doctor, is my situation dangerous? Tell me the truth,' he whispered.

'It was. But I think the danger has passed,' replied the doctor. 'I should say: the danger from the *illness*. The Russians are two miles away,' he added with a smile while leaving.

Russians? What Russians? Two miles away? thought the Professor perplexedly. *Two miles – meaning they've reached Berlin? I must have misheard him ...* However, he felt no alarm at this. What did the Russians matter to him? *As if they could prevail over the will of Venus!* he thought, and again dozed off. When he awoke, it was strangely silent. The Professor pricked up his ears: could he hear the continuous rumble coming from above? *I think I can ... No, I can't ... Oh, how tired I am, how weak I am!* He put on his shoes, rested after this exertion, brushed down his coat as best he could and went out, slightly unsteady on his feet.

There was no one in the corridor. The bunker appeared to be deserted. Even the sentry posted by the short flight of stairs had vanished. In the conference hall, two soldiers and that same girl were there. On the table in front of them was a bottle. On the very first day, the Professor had spotted one of these soldiers, a middle-aged Obersturmbannführer. His face was gashed all over with scars from duelling. *But he didn't have a monocle before* . . . All three of them were smoking, which had been strictly prohibited before. They looked animated, almost merry, but rather bewildered at the same time. The girl smiled at the Professor, as at an old acquaintance.

'Where have you been? At the wedding?' she asked. She slightly faltered as she said this. The Obersturmbannführer removed the monocle from his eye and then replaced it. The second officer, an artillery captain, seemed displeased by the girl's remark.

'What a business, what a business!' he said. 'People are losing their heads! What's the point of it all? . . .'

'The point is clear enough,' replied the Obersturmbannführer, paying no heed to the stranger. 'The point is that Schicklgrubers[7] shouldn't be in command of the German army.' He again removed his monocle, which evidently gave him pleasure, and was about to pour himself some cognac but found the bottle empty. 'Regrettably, he was musical. Wagner killed him. And that foolish woman was also something out of the Nibelungen . . . *Walküre bist du gewesen!*'[8] he declaimed melodically. The artillery captain sighed. 'We'll see what Dönitz does . . . No, people are losing their minds, simply losing them. You'll see: a new Kant or Hegel will come along and explain it, and all will be clear, like a bolt of lightning!'

'The wedding was held in the map room. They served champagne. For Eva, naturally, they found some,' said the girl, painting her lips.

'Then he publicly announced his intention to kill himself,' noted the captain with another sigh. 'Or rather, he didn't announce it, but hinted at it. Had he announced it, then even *they* wouldn't have organized a ball.'

'It was such a scream. I danced with Bormann; he's a marvellous dancer,' said the girl.

'Why ever not with Goebbels? That dandy was made for dancing. They say he's going to kill himself today as well. A pity they didn't all do it earlier – especially Schicklgruber,' said the Obersturmbannführer. He pronounced the word 'Schicklgruber' in a particular way, affectionately sarcastic, drawing out the first letters as though it made all the difference.

'Goebbels wants to poison his children,' said the girl. 'He doesn't care since they aren't his. She was unfaithful to him every step of the way. He was drunk when he married her ... Who was that poor actor chap? ... I also saw your unfortunate field marshal,' she said, turning to the Obersturmbannführer, whose face twitched.

'How did it happen, anyway? Some are saying he shot himself in the mouth – others, through the heart.'

'Eva poisoned herself,' said the girl. 'Kempka told me so. He carried her out into the garden.'

'I heard they shot Göring there last night,' said the captain.

'Rubbish! Herr Reichsfeldmarschall slipped off to Carinhall long ago.'

'Most likely to deck Emmy out in diamonds again,' the girl put in. 'What did he see in her? Not only is she no beauty, but she isn't even pretty ... Although I heard he's gone to Bavaria to establish a new line of defence.'

The Obersturmbannführer broke into fits of laughter.

'A fine defence and a fine defender. "No bomb shall fall on German soil." Is he still burning?'

'He was an hour ago,' said the captain. 'I saw him from a distance. 'They'd been wrapped in white sheets, but his black trousers were still sticking out. The smell was terrific. I had to get away.'

'Sorry, who is burning? I don't understand,' the Professor boldly asked the lady. His head had stopped working entirely. The Obersturmbannführer turned to him, as if noticing him for the first time only now.

'S-S-Schicklgruber,' he said gleefully. 'S-S-Schicklgruber and his wife. *Monsieur et Madame Adolphe Schicklgruber.*'

'What a business, oh, what a business!' repeated the captain sadly. 'But you'll see: a new Kant will come, and all will be as clear as day.'

In the canteen, where there were many people, was the high official who patronized the Professor. He was greedily tucking into something. On seeing the Professor, he waved to him amiably, although there could be no thought of fleeing to Switzerland now. The high official shook his hand firmly – just like an equal – and did not even ask how he had come to be in the bunker. Nothing could astonish anyone now. He was like that Italian Fascist who would say the only thing that could astonish him was a pregnant man: 'Everything else, I've seen.'

'What a business, eh?' he said, and explained heatedly why he had been late and had not been able to say goodbye to Hitler. Then he immediately regretted his words, changed tack and informed the Professor that he would be leaving presently for the front again. 'It seems you were right about everything,' he said, laughing.

'How so?'

'Not you personally, but you astrologists. Just the other day, Hitler sent for his horoscope, and it turned out that the stars had predicted everything: his rise to power, the war in 1939, two years of dazzling victory and then a crushing defeat.'

'The celestial luminaries are never wrong. Our science is based in fact, verified by centuries-old wisdom,' said the Professor.

'Of course, the horoscope also said that in the April of 1945 Hitler would gain total victory,' continued the high official. 'Do me a favour, give me another glass of wine,' he said amicably, turning to a passing waiter. Evidently he was beginning a new chapter in his life, as a simple, average, very ordinary person. The waiter looked at him with contempt and walked on without acknowledging him. The high official's face twitched, but he immediately smiled condescendingly, with the look of Napoleon about him, enduring insult en route to St Helena.

'So the planes are still flying, then?' asked the Professor after a period of silence.

'What planes? . . . The front is now at the Anhalter Bahnhof. But the subway is still clear: we're using it for troop transports, supplies, and even artillery . . . You live in the western sector of the city, don't you? So do I. Shall we go together? We can catch a transport and go back to the Kurfürstendamm with the wounded. Tell me, you must know some Jews, mustn't you? You know I've never been an anti-Semite; I even said to Hitler that his anti-Semitic policies were damaging . . . Between you and me, he wasn't quite right in the head,' said the high official confidingly, lowering his voice by force of habit. 'If you only knew

the sorts of things he came out with in his final days! General
Steiner told me. His orders were full of utter nonsense, he threatened to execute anyone and everyone, although no one took any
notice of his orders or threats . . . We must have some friends in
common – Jews, or Social Democrats at least? They haven't all
died.'

'But how do we get to the subway?'

'I don't know. I can wait for you for ten minutes, no longer.'

Tripping as he went, the Professor ran down the corridor.
From the rooms along it, people were leaving hurriedly with
little suitcases, night bags and knapsacks. In his little room,
the Professor grabbed his leather notebook, picked up the
handkerchief he had dropped and ran out. The door to the
lavatory was wide open. Standing there with boots over his
bare feet was the elder of the two youths. He was throwing his
white socks into the washbasin.[9]

Auto-Suggestion

DON AMINADO

I think it's high time that we discussed auto-suggestion.

Everything that can be suggested to those around us has already been suggested – including the fact that we are not an emigration, but Russia abroad.

Suggestion, as everyone knows, can yield dazzling results . . .

Europe fusses over us like a child with a new toy and just doesn't know where to put us.

Thus, from an *international* perspective, we've landed on our feet.

But in our private lives – our common, day-to-day, humdrum lives – there's still some way to go before we'll see our bread buttered on both sides.

One cannot suppose that all two million of us can sing in gypsy choruses, dance the *kazachok* and munch on pressed caviar in the intervals.

There are those who don't eat at all.

I make no concessions: there are no inextricable situations, and an émigré who has absolutely nothing to eat could always, in a worst-case scenario, just die of hunger.

However, excepting auto-education, auto-inoculation and auto-intoxication, only one thing remains:

Auto-suggestion.

According to that Frenchman Coué,[1] one must say to oneself each and every morning:

'Every day, in every way, I'm getting better and better.'

Though it doesn't do to drag out the conversation.

Once said, you ought not to argue.

Otherwise, you'll end up with a split personality and twice the expenses: ten photographic identity cards, two Nansen passports,[2] four soles to mend ... To say nothing of tram fares, conjugal happiness or the cost of postage stamps.

Auto-suggestion should be performed in a very tactful, delicate manner.

One should never bawl at oneself.

'Oi, you! Damn it, you good-for-nothing b—st—d! Can't you see you're living in clover, and with each passing day it gets better and better?'

Such a technique bodes no good.

Man will begin to run from himself.

Why in fact poison the relationship with one's self, when there are so many extraneous selves with which to do similarly? ...

It is best to address oneself not in the second person singular, or even in the more polite second person plural, but in the first person singular.

'I feel fine. I am happy. I feel very fine. I am very happy. It is precisely because I am so happy that I feel so fine ...'

If a morning dosage has no effect and a person still does not feel fine, then auto-suggestion must be continued throughout the day, into the evening, and even until dawn.

Cases have been known of a friendly chat with oneself going on long past midnight.

Thus must one continue from day to day, until death itself – then the results will not be long in showing themselves.

Let us take, by way of example, the most prosaic émigré occurrence.

Monsieur X orders a suit on credit. The suit is ready.

A month passes, during the course of which Monsieur X goes about in his new suit, conscientiously devoting himself to auto-suggestion.

Meanwhile, the tailor devotes himself to making more suits, and to making up his accounts as well.

Monsieur X's subconscious suggests to him that it would be wise not to walk down the street in which the tailor lives.

While his conscious suggests to him: why ever not, since the suit is paid for?

The conflict between the conscious and subconscious is unpleasant, all the more so since the tailor is clearly on the side of the subconscious . . . and resolves to pay Monsieur X a visit.

The rest is obvious.

The tailor, being of a coarse nature, presses for his money and brings an action against X, while the latter, of a more inspired nature, believes in all good faith that the money has been paid long ago.

Need I state that the final victory nevertheless falls to Monsieur X, in spite of the fact that his new suit is being sold at a public auction? . . .

Left in only his underclothes, Monsieur X suggests to himself that these are not underclothes at all, but a magnificent tail-coat and trousers, just slim-fitting.

And when a man is able to suggest a thing like that to himself, it's nigh impossible to disabuse him of the idea.

'I feel fine . . . What wonderful tails I'm sporting! How cheap it is to live in France! . . . And tomorrow it will be cheaper still.'

A Scattering of Stars

IVAN LUKASH

I sleep above a precipice, by the sea.

You wrap yourself in a blanket, lie down on the warm earth, on quills of grey grass, and all night gentle bursts of wind from the sea roar in your ears and with a fresh shiver rush across your face. At dawn your shirt and blanket are damp from the dew, and the freshness of the sea clings to your face and hands.

Above the precipice soldiers and officers sleep side by side. At night, in the wooden huts, the sultriness is unbearable. They sleep, just as I do, on the ground, wrapped in blankets; only one or two of them have fashioned unsteady, creaking beds from the boards of tinned-food crates, lest a scolopendra or a scorpion suddenly attack their leg.

Along the precipice, in the brown clayey sand, they've built dugouts, which they clamber into on their haunches. Below us, at night, on a terrace farther down, more men stretch out on the ground, asleep. The thin, silvery, weary crescent moon keeps its timid watch over us by night, drenching and dragging across the dark sea its slender glittering chain.

The terrace below drops down towards the sea. There is a grey track, and grey dykes built with stones of considerable size. Still farther below gleams the white of the round-pedimented building where General Kutepov[1] lives. Rumbling beyond the building, misty teams of white horses.

'G'morning, g'morning, 'rexcellency!'

The clear early-morning air is rent, reverberating with a cheery salutation from the general's escort. General Kutepov rises with the sun.

Our men begin to stir on the precipice, too. Half-asleep,

huffing and puffing, they pull on their yellow soldier's breeches over their underdrawers. Crouching down, they wrap their feet in long grey-brown English puttees, a *sazhen*[2] in length.

Pale, bare-headed Greek women with bulbous noses and black manes of dishevelled hair bang shutters, standing in the rectangular window frames dressed only in their night-gowns, and shake out their rugs and bedclothes over the kitchen gardens.

They flap loudly in the morning hush.

The sun emerges from behind a little flock of dark-blue clouds that had been dozing until just moments before it rose. It had been a crimson twilit disc, but now it's like a great circular shield, cast from brilliant yellow gold. A golden kitten's little ball climbs a thread into the deep airy blue of the sky.

The grass – a brilliant yellow, like gold – is overlaid with a quivering of dark-blue shadows. Bright gold on the soldiers' faces, droplets of wet gold in their squinting, drowsy eyes. My neighbour, a tall, gaunt volunteer from a flying squadron, raises his face skywards. His nose is snub and one of his eyes is hazel, the other a pure sky blue. The vari-eyed volunteer is an incorrigibly jovial chap and a joker.

'Eee-ho-ho-ho,' he greets the morning with a joyful horse-laugh.

But the golden kitten has already bared his claws, and the backs of our necks are hot, and we must get up; we must shake out our trappings.

A dazzling gold tiger crosses the blue desert, launching millions of scorching claws at the earth.

In our grey building below there's a hullabaloo: they're brewing the morning tea. Beneath the collapsed stone awning of the hearth they've laid a fire, and on it, in turn, they place their cans and mess tins, which get covered in a fluffy down of soot and ash.

They gad about just in breeches, without shirts. Bronze backs and bronze faces dusted in soot. Their eyes all seem to be made up. They go about like devils in an inferno, casting spells over bubbling brews, squatting, soldiers and officers together.

Delicately they make way for one another. Delicately, lest it be obvious, they try to do one another thousands of the littlest services, thousands of the smallest acts of human kindness.

'Sir, I'll throw some more wood on the fire for you.'

'Very well, very well. Thank you . . . Please do.'

'Would you fix me some tea, Sapunov, or put it on to boil?'

'Right away, Captain, I'll just nip upstairs.'

'Why go up? Take a pinch of mine.'

Here everyone maintains an air of decorum, here every gesture betrays a delicate courtesy, a delicate agreeability.

The hearth smokes. The smoke stings and everyone rubs their eyes, squinting, snorting like little pup-devils by the scorching heat of the inferno.

The sharp-clawed sun has already warmed the dust hanging over the grey-brown terrace. Morning lessons have begun by the trucks.

They're learning about the engine. A little group of white shirts stands in the wasteland next to the trucks, while one of them explains in a mellow bass, with a velvety croak:

'If I incline the cylinder now, there'll be an explosion . . . Is that understood?'

'Yes, sir. If you incline the cylinder now . . .'

Teetering and swaying, some soldiers with makeshift yokes across their shoulders come marching single-file down the road running along the stony grey bank of the Turkish cemetery. The orderlies are drawing fresh water from the fountains.

Gaily the water tinkles in their tin buckets. It splashes about, and behind the orderlies, among the grey dust, stretches out a line of dark, damp blots of spilled water.

My volunteer neighbour, too, is carrying buckets. As he sees me, he squints first with the hazel, then with the blue eye, and smiles.

'Make way! . . . The water-carriers are on the move.'

On the other side of the bank, in the wastelands, where like Cyclopes rows of heavy flagstone benches have been set out, sit white flocks of white shirts. Glowering under the sun, they rustle with their workbooks, writing; and every now and then the enormous spectacles of a young officer-cum-professor flash heavenward in beams of dazzling light.

'Now let us follow the parabola towards point B . . .'

Sketched in chalk on a rusty iron board are line segments and sectors, falling arcs and a white web of algebraic formulae.

Nuzzled into the little chinks in the stone bank are a slip of a Turkish girl and a young Turk in a red fez, which blazes in the sun like a ruby. Both of them crane their slender golden faces and watch through their hazel eyes the beams of dazzling light from the effendi's terrifying spectacles. They watch and chirrup timorously.

The soldiers' wives are queuing up at the Zemgor[3] office – many of them carrying children in their arms. They're waiting in line for the dole-out of bread and semolina.

Bathers stretch out down towards the beach, caps pulled over their foreheads. Crunching evenly and firmly with his boots, a white guard clomps past. They all shoo him away in unison. Once he is shooed, they strike up a rousing chorus:

'Yo-ho, our sorrow's no woe . . .'

Meanwhile the sharp-clawed sun is already spreading its golden haze of sultriness. The closeness weighs heavily towards midday, like a millstone. At midday, across the burned wasteland, white dust roams drowsily.

Lustrous with sweat, the Sergievsky men[4] are half-asleep on duty, swaying gently, their black, spindly legs splayed like a pair of compasses. Here and there the shops close their shutters. Shaggy-haired dogs steal into the marble basins of fountains that have run dry, searching for cool and shade on the cold stone.

In the coffeehouses around midday they sip bitter coffee from little white cups, washing down each hot mouthful with cool, clear water from tinkling glasses misted with condensation. At shop counters Russian soldiers while away the hours trading, sans urgency, plump-cheeked tomatoes and sharing muskmelon amongst themselves, cutting it into succulent orange slivers. On the counter stand little mountains of green rind and a wet porridge of stringy melon seeds.

Dusty desolation.

Amidst the heat's golden haze, the sea falls silent; it dies away and is clouded over by a lilac mist.

But the heat and the dusty white desolation will persist until evening . . .

. . . Until evening, when the sun yellows and cools, and the flocks of dark storm clouds begin to seek light shelter around it. Until evening, when above the blue outlines of the mountains the sun's splendorous lances rise up and stop still, before cooling and being extinguished in the evening ocean. But then the crimson ocean will shimmer, rushing beyond the mountains without a sound.

And so a blue and tender evening rings out over Gallipoli.

Solitary, cooing, the song of a cornet-à-piston appears somewhere. Somewhere two women's voices strike up: sweet and harmonious. They're singing something from *The Queen of Spades*.

'Tis evening, the linings of the clouds have darkened . . .[5]

Probably they are pupils from the arts school rehearsing a duet for an evening concert.

Two soldiers climb into a truck – the same one at which that very morning someone had been teaching the little flock of white shirts about explosions in an inclined cylinder – and sit on the worn leather seats. They prop their feet on the round steering wheel, legs bent double to their chin. One of them has an open book resting on his knees. They both lean over the white pages, and I hear one of them repeat again and again:

'Der Garten ist grün, der Garten ist grün . . .'[6]

Meanwhile the other has turned away from his neighbour, repeating in the fashion of a tongue-twister:

'Ich bin, du bist, er, sie ist . . .'[7]

They are learning a foreign language. They take foreign-language courses here, at the public university, at schools, at the lyceum and at the library. They learn by copying out textbooks, each into his own exercise book. The learning is non-stop. Some young officers have already graduated; senior years take exams at the lyceum; thousands have graduated from the public university; hundreds, with desperate Russian vowels, though very assuredly and enthusiastically, now chatter away in the camps in French and English.

In Gallipoli there are as many as 6,000 Russian students. In

Gallipoli there are as many as 20,000 young peasant lads, yesterday's factory hands, lyceum students and clerks.

In Gallipoli Russia's youth is performing a monastic feat.
Where else would you find Russian youth like this, men radiant
in spirit, having condemned themselves to blood and heroic
deeds, men who have withdrawn to the white monastery of
Gallipoli to bear closed, pure witness? . . . Green is our garden,
precious our Russian hope, our Russian youth, our novice Alyosha, the third and youngest of the brothers, who will come to
replace us all, even the cold, mad Ivans, who are the devil's kin,
and the Don Quixote Mityas who squander their souls, and the
abominable Smerdyakovs. The third brother, our dear Alyosha,
behind whom, whitewashed in a deluge of blood and pus,
stands the third Russia.

The evening sky is already a deep blue. The white pages of
the open book are barely visible, and inside the truck they keep
reciting German words. That will do, gentlemen – do you hear
the sound of the evening, and how the stars, lofty and nebu-
lous, have come out in shy, flickering clusters? . . . That will do,
gentlemen!

Der Garten ist grün, der Garten ist grün . . . The phrase
haunts me.

In the evening I love to walk through the streets as they turn
a deep blue.

Glowing red dots as I meet cigarettes head on. Voices in a
fading murmur. Ruined walls gleaming silently – dark blue,
listening.

The blue evening listens in, and everyone hears its delicate,
deliberate breathing. The drifting dust listens, too, as do the
marble turbans among the tall grass, and the grey, creaking –
like decrepit old men – Greek buildings and people.

The music of the blue evening is shy and flits away from loud
chatter, from footsteps, from the trundling jolt of the cart.
The music of the evening is shy, and because of this the voices
speak so cautiously and so sensitively, and the people pass by
so quietly, without stamping about, and this is why the burning
cigarettes smoulder so gently.

On the stony steps of the grey buildings and along the

escarpments by the Turkish cemetery sit soldiers in dusky-white coveys. They are listening to the evening, and their evening talk is soft and quiet. Someone laughs, but even his laughter isn't loud. Laughter, like a gentle plashing in a dark creek, when the water radiates in silvery circles away from a glimmering silver roach.

Amid the blue air everything is ghostly and gentle. I listen to snatches of soft Russian patter, which combine to form a sort of nocturne. I walk on, hoping to find, to pick out the whole tremor of chords in this song, but I cannot, and it grieves me that I cannot.

'Tomorrow we're going on detail,' I hear from the blue murk.

'And she was so fair, and she would say *merci* in French, and everything was as it ought to be. I met her in Odessa. Ah, those were the days . . .'

'The Reds hacked him to pieces with their sabres. Budyonny's men charged.[8] Made mincemeat of us. It was horrible. He was left under the horses . . .'

'So I'm on patrol, and she comes right at me, like this, and turns through the field. Some old crone. I can see her in the moonlight. "My boy," she says, "don't shoot, give me something to drink." I do, then I tear into her: "How did you get here?" – "From the Dnieper, across the marshlands. I've come for my son. He served with you Whites." So I tell her: "Go to the division headquarters, old woman . . ."'

'We were just outside Kakhovka. The infantry had got into a scrape . . .'

'Let me tell you: they're saying that every nation will rally to Russia's side and sort things out . . .'

'You're talking oats. You may well have some decent oats, but we in Melitopol – you've seen for yourself – have excellent wheat . . .'

I listen to the soldiers' evening chatter, and it seems to me as if they have always talked like this, softly throughout the blue evening, of encampments, division headquarters and campaigns – Skobelev's men in the camps near Tashkent, the powdered guardsmen of Empress Elizabeth in field tents outside Berlin, and the moustachioed Carabineers of Alexander

I, crowded around campfires on the roadways of Paris's suburbs . . .[9]

I saunter towards the sea, towards the rocks. The rough stones are already cool. A little above me, along the escarpment, I spot the dusky white of four shirts. I cannot make out their faces in the deep-blue twilight. A lone cigarette smoulders. I listen.

'You were on the gun crew – how would you know anything about shaft horses? For four years I drove our shaft horse. I knew both of those horses. The one on the left, chestnut, young, named Leda, and the one on the right, chestnut too, but with a blaze and a large rump – she had a bowed pastern and would drop on to her hind legs . . . She was called Dreamer. Let me tell you about them. The team never knew a better horse than my chestnut Leda. She would haul a gun at full tilt, like the wind, with her chest, while Dreamer, of course, was a hard-working mare, but how could she ever hope to keep pace with Leda when she pulled from her hind and not from her chest . . . Do you remember how our battery took a beating just outside Novorossiysk? Dreamer took a hit in the stomach from a shell, and her guts spilled out. We were retreating, but she, my friend, still jerked her head and tried to stand up. And that she did. She walked with her guts trailing beneath her belly. She soon fell behind . . . Leda made it to Novorossiysk, though. That's where we left her when we embarked. There were horses wandering about on the ice by the pier, unwatered, unfed. In little teams they edged nearer and nearer to the water. They were drawn in by the moisture of the water – just wanted a drink, those horses did. A team of them trotted up to the pier, but we were already in the boats by then. I have a good eye for horses. I spot my Leda among them: craning her neck towards the water, whinnying, nostrils flaring. She's thirsty. "Oh, Leda," I think. And, my friend, I see her suddenly, with all four legs, leap into the water. She couldn't bear the thirst . . . She went crashing down, placed her lips to the sea salt and began jerking her head about. She jerked her head, Leda did, but she was soon swept away by the current. I couldn't watch, my friend. I walked away, but she drowned of course . . .'

Silence fell over the escarpment. And the misty scattering of stars listened to the human silence . . .

'Yes, here is Russia,' says General Kartsev, his turbid grey eyes fixed on me, in a café where I've come from the sea to drink a glass of wine.

General Kartsev is a judge in the court of honour. General Kartsev is an old military instructor, a strategist, an expert on the Imperial Russian army, a traveller and a warrior.

The military runs in General Kartsev's blood; his forefathers before him served in the Life Guards. There doesn't seem to be a single war, a single Russian campaign since the eighties in which General Kartsev has not had a hand. Just one little medal hangs on his threadbare tunic: a steel sword inset among a steel crown of thorns, on a St George's ribbon, a token from the Kornilov Ice March.[10] And from the silver engraving on a Cossack sabre trails a frayed scrap of ribbon belonging to the St George's Sword, which is awarded for bravery.

Bald and slow to his feet is General Kartsev. He's snub-nosed, his eyes stare, and a wispy grey beard sprouts from his neck. Looks like Socrates, does General Kartsev, this judge in the court of honour, this 'god of war', as the young officers in Gallipoli call him.

He has recently lost his last kinsman on earth. Now his staring eyes are always moist and, truth to tell, he'll never refuse another glass of rough red wine or cinnamon-perfumed amber cognac.

His talk is wise and magnificent. His senile staring eyes have seen much in their time. India, the steppes of Tibet, Paris, Japan, campaigns and quiet books, the torches of bivouacs and green library lamps. His valuable archives, the correspondence of his fathers and grandfathers with the tsars, his diaries – all lost.

I tell him of what I've seen in Gallipoli, of the soldiers, of Lieutenant Misha, of the ulcers from saltpetre, of the volunteer with one blue eye and the other hazel. I tell him how I've heard the live heart of Russia beating here, beneath furled banners.

'Russia breathes here,' says Kartsev. 'I don't know how it is for you over there, among the émigrés, but Russia lives here. Russia in all her splendour, pure and chivalrous. I'm off to

Constantinople shortly. You see, a Russian officer has chal-
lenged a Frenchman, a certain Lieutenant Boucher, to a duel.
Boucher had been rough with one of our women, the officer's
wife. A challenge was sent. Boucher replied with some vague
letter – not quite a refusal, not quite an apology – and a French
representative replied along the lines that if we're eating their
tins of food then what honour could we possibly have? We
replied that tinned food and a soldier's honour are two different things. We said we'd tell the neighbouring armies how a
French officer refused a challenge. And so now the commander
of the French corps has summoned me to Constantinople.'

The god of war smiles, staring at me with his dimly glinting
eyes.

'But Russia lives on here, that's for sure. Just listen to the
army and you'll hear she's alive, all right. You see, my boy,
you'd been thinking of the old army, as it is in Kuprin's *Duel* –
all these Romashovs, Captain Slivas and Shurochkas in their
silk stockings – but of our army, of Gallipoli, you knew nothing. You see, if your lot over there doesn't pay attention to
what's going on here – they'll make a grave error. These men
aren't relics from the Civil War, nor are they some black rabble,
nor even bandits or thieves. They are a new army, a fresh cadre
for Russia, which has undergone ordeals such as you cannot
imagine.'

The general sips his wine unhurriedly, wetting his whiskers,
droplets of wine hanging at the ends of them, like rubies.

'Here, we see things not as they're printed in the papers.
The Reds have an army, and a very strong one at that. They
have fine, competent commanders. There are many scoundrels
in the world, but we shall never sit at a table with scoundrels,
even if it means they lop off my head at the neck . . . We aren't
politicians, but we have our soldier's creed: Satan and God do
battle on Earth. Today Satan has won. But we shall be victorious, for God is with us. This is our credo. And this is why we
shall meet every ordeal and rise to every human sufferance.'

The old man let his head slump on to his hand. He lapsed
into thought at the table, like an old knight from a tale of long
ago, like a hulking grey-headed master of some chivalric order.

'You have to understand the army . . . All this braiding and piping – I dare say you'll have laughed like the rest of them at such folly. But did you know that the strongest armies are those where every regiment, every unit is distinct, has its own colours, takes pride in its own history, its own covenant of blood and glory. Take the German army, for instance. Its downfall was its standardization, its numbered regiments, its grey uniformity; when the colours fade, so too the thriving soul of the army withers. And you'll recall how the French numbered army, at Charleroi, fled under attack from Pomeranian grenadiers. Our army flourished under Elizabeth and Suvorov. Its decline began with Milyutin's standardization and Vannovsky's numbered regiments.[11] Bureaucrat-officers, numbers, bearded cannon fodder by the million, an unbroken stretch of grey pawns . . . Our army used to be in the hands of people, the likes of which you'd never seen. In the hands of hermit-officers, monk-officers, who knew nothing but their regiments and their men. We even had such officers, men for whom their regiment, their own company, their own platoon, was dearer to them than anything else on earth, dearer even than their sweethearts.'

I listen to the general's paradoxes, and a satirical snatch from 'The Crane' comes to me, and I begin to ponder its meaning differently . . .

> All the colours of a poster
> Make a true Kornilov man . . .[12]

Probably that's how it has to be: for him to be decked out head to toe in his regimental colours, for him to fly the flag and carry the tune. The newer regiments at Gallipoli jealously guard all their distinguishing marks newly won in the Civil War: stripes on their cuffs, skulls above crossed swords, black-and-red epaulettes for Kornilov's men, crimson velvet ones for Drozdovsky's,[13] while in the old guards they solemnly pass on, in order of seniority, the yellow shoulder braiding of aiguillettes, with the silver monogram of Catherine the Great.

Outside, night has fallen . . .

In a luminescent mist a scattering of stars flickers over Gallipoli. The beam from a lighthouse, with its golden shadow, cuts through the starry mist and lands on the dark sea with quivering golden wings. The lighthouse looms white in the distance – the Fener, as the Turks call it. Yesterday I was there with some friends . . . I hadn't expected to meet the actress Astrova there – the bright, airy comedy actress from our South. She has followed her husband, an artillery captain, to Gallipoli. There was also Plevitskaya, and the young Kovalenskaya from the Alexandrinsky's stage.[14]

As I stroll along the nocturnal street, I recall how radiantly and archly Astrova looked at me.

'So you're leaving us? A pity, a pity . . . I'm sorry for you – that you're leaving . . . In your Parises and Constantinoples you'll have no Russia anywhere. But here we have Russia. I'm sorry that you're leaving.'

I stroll beneath a twinkling of stars. Far away, the sighing of brass horns sings an old waltz. In the black water by the pier blue starlights ripple like bashful fireflies and the reflections of the café windows toss about. Their reflections are like long and tender eyelashes.

On a floating restaurant, at a narrow little table, I meet Lukoshkov, a commander in the Foot Guards. By the veranda's dark railings the water exhales a cool, night-time freshness. A tacit throng of bright, delicate, nearby stars hangs in the sky.

There is a light felucca sleeping, its slanting mast raised, but through the black web of rigging the scattering of stars barely glimmers. Perhaps the felucca isn't asleep, but dreaming and listening.

Slender and pale is Guardsman Lukoshkov. At his white shoulder there is a faint clinking from the ends of the yellow braiding of his aiguillette, which bears Catherine's monogram. Lukoshkov, dignified right down to his manicured nails (the nails of a Petersburg Guardsman), is soft-spoken, affable but ever so reserved. Now, though, the stars have drawn closer to us, and in his eyes I glimpse their tacit blue flicker. Perhaps this is why our flickering conversation is so strange.

'The world has lost its beauty,' says Lukoshkov, stroking his chin with his long fingers. 'Beauty has forsaken the world. Eve-ryone lives on flesh. The world's soul is being dragged through the mud. The world has no inspiration. The world of today has lost its wings, ever since the war.'

His signet ring clinking against the glass, he pours himself some wine. He turns to look at the scattering of stars and tells me a strange story, of strange chivalrous love . . . A friend of his had lost his Beloved. The friend was alone under the stars, and his Beloved was dead. And it was impossible to forget her, nor could she ever be forgotten. But his Beloved will come one day, for Love is everlasting, Love is immortal and will never shed its white light. His Beloved will come, like a star falling to earth, and his friend, who is perhaps still here, on earth, will meet her, or maybe there, where the starry mists glimmer.

I walk alone in a mist of stars. I walk to my precipice and think how we have already forgotten tales such as this. Such chivalrous tales of Immortal Love and the Beautiful Lady.

When I pass by the curtained window on the terrace below, where you live, my darling, you will already be asleep. Just like when you were a child, so long ago, in Petersburg, pressing your fiery little scarlet cheek to your bent white arm. And your chestnut plait will come loose and gently tickle your delicate eyelashes.

You will already be asleep, my darling. But if you weren't, I would crouch on the floor by your mattress and begin to tell you strange and wonderful tales of explosions in inclined cyl-inders, of trajectories and parabolas in a wasteland, of German vocabulary in a truck, of a chestnut mare called Leda, and of knights and their chivalrous love.

Do you remember how, long ago, when we were children, brother Zhenya would make us believe that at night, in the kitchen, he would sit on a stool, having taken a large teapot so he should have something to drink on the journey, and then fly off on the stool to travel the starry sky?

Do you remember, he would tell us how the stars greeted him up there, where the angels live. How there are mournful angels with wings as dark as sorrow, furled, and how mournfully they look down on the earth at night. How there are gladsome angels that sing in the evening, and how the earth resounds with their singing ... Do you remember, Brother Zhenya would insist that, just like you, the angels would practise their exercises on the piano, and that, just like our grandmother did, they had cages with kindly old grumbling parrots ...

Are you sleeping? I've come to tell you strange tales of stars scattered on earth, tales of men whose souls blaze like luminaries.

A Literary Studio

GEORGY ADAMOVICH

Two young writers, a youthful poet and a budding critic hatched a plan to write a novel together ... This is not an imitation of Krylov's 'Quartet',[1] nor is it a fable: it truly happened a few days ago in Paris. There are in Soviet Russia so-called 'literary studios' – what's to stop them springing up here, too? So, a couple of youths decided to write a novel together. Their purpose was twofold: on the one hand, they very much wanted to get rich; on the other, they lusted after fame and recognition.

'Right now, the public is craving a good novel,' said one of the writers. 'Publishers are dreaming of a good novel. But, you see, a good one, captivating in content, dazzling in form.'

'I would call it ... a "shock novel",' thoughtfully noted the critic.

'My dear, you've clearly been reading too many Soviet journals! Our public demands first and foremost that there be no trace of such jargon, and that the old spellings be observed.[2] That's the minimum curriculum. What's more, there should be no Komsomols or collective farms. We need something more tender, more romantic ... a moonlit night, she an innocent girl, he an enamoured youth. We need something original. We had better start with the moonlit night.'

They argued, wittering on until they finally agreed that what was needed was a moonlit night in spring. Several versions were prepared for the next meeting:

'For a long time that night I sat by an open window, and along with the intoxicating perfume of blossoming roses carried in from the now quiet, as though enchanted, garden was the trilling and chirping of a nightingale, singing, just as it had done a thousand years ago, that same eternal song of love. O Rapture, how my heart fluttered, filled with that same inexpressible, unoccasioned, gratifying bliss, in which this garden was enveloped—'

'Enough, enough,' they stopped the reader. 'It's Bunin all over.'

'And it's bad Bunin at that. Bunin writes incomparably better.'

'Yes, of course Bunin writes better. Strictly speaking, it's not Bunin, but ... Well, what does it matter who it is? The point is that everyone will think that we're aping Bunin. Bunin has a monopoly on nightingales.'

'Next version!'

'If at times, in those far-off, distant years when I was still a child, the moon and spring would always create upon me an impression that I, still lacking the refined sensitivity I would later acquire, was at that time unable to comprehend with any clarity, then now, having come to know and understand that sometimes she, as it seems to me, embodies that quality, which, precisely on such a moonlit night, appears somehow magically, doubly and yet at the same time relatively sharply reflected and able even imprint itself on the soul with a power, such that I would be (or was) only later truly in a position to understand, while the view of these low flowerbeds bathed in a sort of milky light still caused something to stir in me softly, although even then I marked that it was not the beauty of nature that ever since childhood I—'

'Excellent,' said the critic, blinking. 'Excellent! That's just what we need. It continues the Proustian tradition.'

However, the successor to Bunin protested.

'The Proustian tradition? For a start, hardly anybody has managed to wade through your Proust in the original. And this mix of French and Nizhny Novgorod[3] ... well, who needs it? They may well praise us in the newspapers. But no one will ever read it.'

'Gentlemen, people are now talking about a revival of Symbolism. We have such a version.'

'And so it was night. Someone clutched at a flat, white disc in the sky. And the anguish that engulfed the earth ascended to meet it. There was man, and there was the moon. Nothing else in the world existed, apart from man and the moon.

'Someone was sitting by a window, thinking: I govern the earth, for I am man. And the milky, crystalline, sonorous rays glided across the face of the sitting figure . . .'

'What do you think?'

'I think there are some things you'll never revive.'

Each version was rejected. So the author of the future novel decided to ask an intelligent man, an ordinary reader, who himself had never written so much as a single line, which description of a moonlit night in spring he would find most moving. The man paused and replied:

'"It was a moonlit night in spring." That's all you require.'

'You jest.'

'No, I'm quite serious.'

Ramón Ortiz

GEORGY ADAMOVICH

He was twenty-nine years old. His name was Ramón Ortiz
Menéndez. He was an Argentine.

If only a type of ray existed that would allow you to determine the composition of the air – not of oxygen or hydrogen,
but rather the kind that radiates from people's passions – those
ethereal, melancholy, homeless particles that suddenly affect
our mood, or suddenly force us into making a decision that
mere moments ago seemed like sheer madness – the kind that
cause all sorts of other 'suddenlys'. And if such rays existed, how
fascinating would it be to analyse the air of a gambling house.
Not a new one, of course, where nothing has as yet had time
to linger. But one such as this, with heavy, sumptuous, dusty
yellow-and-pink damask over the windows, with lustrous velvet
and carved oak chairs that for forty years have been drawn to
and from the table, to people, to catastrophe and sudden good
fortune, and to much, much else by a clean-shaven old man,
who no longer pays attention to anything other than the hour
hand on the clock that delivers him from his labours. With what
is the air suffused here? What has that yellow-and-pink silk
soaked up over the last half a century, and what envelops a person here?

Ramón Ortiz entered the hall cheerfully, joyfully even. He
had been living in the south of France for three weeks already,
and this good cheer never abandoned him here. Following the
humiliating and difficult settling of accounts that he had faced
over there, at home, and the doubts he felt about the future,
which he found difficult to imagine, Ramón Ortiz was gradually beginning to recover here. He mistook the professional

flattery and the perfunctory obsequiousness that surrounded him for respect, sensing his mistake but delighting in it anyway. On one occasion, he had bought himself two neckties, and when the shop assistant asked him whether he would like to take them with him or have them delivered, he, without knowing why, replied:

'Yes, have them delivered.'

And when he gave his address, he called himself a baron. The Such-and-Such Hotel, Baron So-and-So. Then, realizing that this might lead to a misunderstanding, he mumbled something and placed his purchases in his pocket. But the way in which the portly and ageing sales assistant looked him in the eyes as he handed over the shopping bag with the words: 'You're welcome, Monsieur le Baron,' and then silently and with hurried little steps ran to the door, so as to open it in time, as well as his bow in the doorway – all this delighted Ramón. He decided that from now on he might sometimes call himself a baron. Ramón Ortiz was a frivolous young man. But worst of all, he had little money. He had around 20,000 francs left, but how long would that last him? And in any case, the money wasn't his. He couldn't go home, nor was there any reason to do so. He was going to have to settle here.

The previous morning Ramón Ortiz had already decided that today was to be his last day of idleness. No – decided wasn't quite the right word. He had wandered along the sunlit promenade, whistling a little, looking around at passers-by and thinking that today, after breakfast, he must sit down at his desk, take up a pencil and make a plan of whom he was going to appeal to and how. The main thing was to think everything over properly, without rushing. There was no point in writing to his father; he wasn't going to answer, but his uncle might still recommend him to someone in Paris, if he asked him nicely. Ramón Ortiz could already see himself in his grey travelling coat, with a small suitcase in his hand. He would climb out of his car, smile politely and offer up a special new polish for cleaning leather belts, or something along those lines. How many would you like? Give me a trial sample of a hundred pots. A hundred pots – he pockets one franc a pot, that's a hundred francs. If one has several clients a day, that would settle every-thing. So boring – women – if only Anna were to come in her little white dress . . . Everything would be settled. But he had to begin today; he couldn't go on living like this.

Ramón Ortiz went to the casino almost every evening. He didn't play himself, but merely watched others, mentally placing bets, mentally chalking up his losses and wins. He desperately wanted to play, but it was a little daunting to begin, and it seemed to him that everyone would look at him if he asked for a card. On one occasion the table had been fifty francs short. The croupier looked at him probingly: 'Fifty francs?' Ramón Ortiz clutched at his wallet but, seeing that someone else's fifty-franc note had already landed on the table, he was thrown off and continued to hold his hand on his left side, under his jacket, pretending that he had chest pains and grimacing. Today, Ramón Ortiz had decided to play – and to win. Not much, 500 francs at most, and after that he would come here every day, as though he was going to work. He knew the faces of a few play-ers who won every day in just that way, little by little, but consistently and unerringly. It wasn't at all hard, all one needed was discipline. Yesterday's plans had come to nothing: after breakfast he had felt sleepy, so Ramón Ortiz did not write any letters, and at any rate there was no point embarking on such an important task on a day when your head ached and you wanted to sleep; it was far better to put it off till tomorrow. To wake up early with a clear head and get down to work, to really think everything over and make a decision. And so another day went by. In the evening Ramón Ortiz slightly trembled as he walked into the casino, he felt a kind of icy coolness within, as though he had lost weight. As he handed over his coat, he thought an odd number on the hanger would be a good sign. The girl smiled, handing over his ticket, and said: 'Nineteen.' She had never done this before. Ramón Ortiz was unable to keep silent: 'Your age, no doubt?' The girl seemed not to understand him. He wanted to sing and jump up and down from excitement. He smoothed back his hair and ran up the stairs.

As yet there was only a handful of players, and a free space presented itself at the main table. This wasn't a common occurrence, and Ramón Ortiz gladly noted it as another sign of fate's benevolence. He sat down at once, looked around with an affected look of boredom and, having waited for a few seconds, retrieved his wallet with a weak, trembling hand. The croupier looked at him attentively for a moment, sizing up the new player. Ramón Ortiz drummed his fingers on the table and looked away. His neighbour was a large, red-faced man who wore dirty clothes and had fleshy hands – 'a tradesman of some sort', thought Ramón. He sat muttering and mumbling something incessantly, addressed most of the other players as *tu* and cried out if anyone turned over a nine. He would pick up his cards in a secretive and conspiratorial manner, not looking at them straight away but lifting each one slowly away from the baize, as though he were having difficulty unpeeling them from the table. He would squint his eyes, cock his head and when he had seen what he had been dealt, he would once more press his cards to the table, or – if it was an eight or a nine – he would quickly turn it over and tap it with his dirty fingernail, as though he were inviting his opponent to deal him another card. He was not particularly lucky. But he played with caution and from time to time he would bury a thousand-franc note in his pocket, having first smoothed and folded it. Ramón Ortiz immediately felt a sense of trust towards him, and they exchanged two or three remarks.

The listless voice of the croupier announced: 'Thirty Louis, six hundred francs' – and when no one answered, he shrugged his shoulders. The tradesman stretched his hand towards the cards, when suddenly, as if struck by a felicitous thought, he turned to Ramón: 'Halves?' Ramón Ortiz, rigid with fear, nodded his head. The tradesman revealed a nine, promptly counted out 300 francs and stuffed them into Ramón's side pocket with an amiable wink. It was a promising start. Ramón Ortiz thought: 'Perhaps I should leave?' but stayed put, sensing that it would be rude to leave when he had only just sat down. To sit down, win and then to leave would be rude – thus he deceived himself for the second time and made a sign to the croupier, who was once again proffering cards. This gesture of his startled him, and he was overjoyed when it seemed as if the black-bearded gentleman in a tuxedo sitting to his left was reaching for his money and going to outbid him. But the gentleman pulled out a cigarette. The croupier placed the cards in front of Ramón. He grabbed at them, one after the other, trying to hide that his hand was shaking – and then he saw the nine. The tradesman mooed in approbation, while Ramón Ortiz, smiling casually, bent towards him and said: 'That's always how it goes, two nines in a row . . . always!' Within half an hour he had won several thousand. The stakes were not particularly high; it was still early. Ramón Ortiz felt pleased that he was the main player at this table. The croupier addressed him before he addressed the others, the clean-shaven old man inquired whether the draught from the open window was bothering him, and twice already a young lad with gold buttons had brushed down the baize in front of his seat, even though neither dust nor ash had gathered there. Ramón Ortiz gave the lad five francs, and called over another one, who had been standing by the door, and gave him five francs too. Ramón Ortiz was enjoying himself: he found the game entertaining, his chair was comfortable, the lighting was pleasant, and the people were kind and friendly. He smiled amicably at the young Englishman whom he had beaten, and when the latter got up to leave and began bashfully rummaging through his pockets without finding anything in them, Ramón gently shrugged his shoulders, as if to say: 'Truly, it's not my fault; today it's you, tomorrow it will be me.' The Englishman stared coldly at Ramón, without seeing him.

Only a few cards remained in the slender lacquered box. Ramón Ortiz promised himself he would leave as soon as this deck was finished – he had had enough for today, more than enough. It was his turn to deal. Without knowing what bet to place and firmly believing that it was impossible to lose now, he looked around the table and in response to the croupier's habitual and expectant silence, drily said: 'Who's betting what? I'm all in.' His voice, his eyes and the slouched way in which he sat, with a cigarette dangling from his extended hand – everything about him expressed indifference.

'All in, gentlemen,' the croupier repeated, suddenly reinvigorated.

A thin, tall and well-groomed old man with a monocle appeared at the door; beside him stood an old woman who looked like a schoolmistress. The old man held a liqueur glass in his hand; he had just finished dining. The young lad with the gold buttons ran up to him and asked whether to free a space for him right away or a little later. The old man nodded his head unintelligibly, but when the croupier repeated, 'All in,' as though it were a personal invitation, he pulled out several crumpled papers from his pocket, along with a handkerchief and a set of keys, and, selecting three large pale-purple notes, threw them on the table. It was too late to change his mind. Even if Ramón Ortiz had known in advance that he was going to lose, he would have dealt the cards anyway. All eyes were on him. It was impossible to go back on his word: better to lose than to do that. The old man slowly picked up his cards, chuckled, showed them to his wife and said: 'One more, please.' Ramón had six points. He pulled out an ace, tossed it to his opponent and, unable to contain himself, loudly shouted: 'Six!' – and even tapped on the table, 'like the tradesman', he thought immediately to himself. The old man chuckled again, showed his cards to his wife once more – and revealed a seven. He had bought an ace to his six, he had taken a punt and won. The table erupted with fawning exclamations. Ramón Ortiz jumped up as if he was about to run away. The croupier lifted his paddle, gently reminding him that he owed 3,000, as well as another several hundred francs for his smaller bets. Ramón Ortiz blushed, apologized and, no longer attempting to control his hands, began to count out the money.

Three thousand – it was almost all his winnings. Of course, if it hadn't been for this freak incident, everything would have been different. And wasn't it possible that he had had an eight or a nine? It was. And couldn't the next card have been a four, and not an ace – wouldn't that have been a good lesson for the old blockhead? And he would now be walking along the street calm and contented. He needed to win the money back, gradually, slowly, without getting carried away – that was the most important thing, not to get carried away. He still had some winnings left over; he ought to count his money. The croupier was shuffling the cards; Ramón Ortiz took out his wallet and began to sort through a wad of thousand-franc notes. The croupier glanced at him briefly, lowered his eyes and then glanced up at him again. There was no pity in his eyes, only a kind of tired, somewhat mocking, drily indifferent haughtiness – 'count away, count away' – which at some distance, having lost its way and worn itself out, might have bordered on pity . . . but didn't.

Ramón Ortiz had lost, of course. He had lost everything. There's no point going into detail or being magniloquent about it, especially since you've already guessed how this evening ends: the story is a banal one. At first he had simply wanted to win, but this didn't happen, after which he thought only of breaking even, and had indeed been close to his aim several times when, at the final moment, he would once again start to lose. He began to place money haphazardly, confusing the bets and no longer following the game – he was beginning to feel like he was rushing headlong into an abyss. To rush headlong into an abyss is terrifying, only a liar would say it was sweet. He had lost his resolve. Someone else was making decisions for him, refusing or accepting bets on his behalf. He had been dragged into someone else's cruel and inexplicable battle, one that he could only survive by a miracle – and he knew already that he couldn't, but no longer had the strength to liberate himself. Only once did the hope of salvation flicker, but Ramón Ortiz disregarded it. He counted over the money he had left, and the multi-coloured notes piled up in a heap alongside the white and red circular and square chips in front of him. Losing count, he threw back his head in frustration and helplessness. Right before him, holding on to an empty chair, stood a woman in a revealing pale blue dress; she had auburn hair and, although just perceptibly beginning to fade, she was still very attractive. She gazed at him attentively, and her nostrils flared, as though she were breathing in some kind of faint, fading smell. Ramón Ortiz's eyes met hers, his brow furrowed woefully, and for five or six seconds he could not tear himself away from this pale-blue spectre. His weakened mind struggled to grasp who she was, but a familiar excitement had already overcome his whole body,

and he felt a vague regret that this excitement was in vain, that
it was all slipping through his fingers when he could have been
elsewhere, could have been walking into a room with red and
bright-orange striped wallpaper and a huge bed, looking
around, turning to the *garçon* and busily asking: 'How much?'
The woman smiled demurely and shifted her gaze towards the
entrance door. The croupier's croaky voice could be heard saying: 'Twenty-five Louis.' Ramón Ortiz greedily snatched the
cards from his outstretched pallet. Warmth, happiness, tenderness, the room, life – it all disappeared as though he had flicked
a switch. The only thing that revealed his absentmindedness
was that he turned to his neighbour once more and suggested
they split the bet between them. The tradesman had long since
been watching him with alarm and curiosity. He recoiled,
silently refusing the offer. Ramón Ortiz drew two kings, bought
a jack and angrily hurled the cards across the entire table on to
the floor. The croupier betrayed his emotions for the first time:
with a hurt and bewildered expression of superiority he shook
his head disapprovingly.

After that there were no more stops. He descended farther
and farther downhill, with only a few inadvertent delays on the
way, but no more stops ... Twenty-three thousand, it was a
huge amount of money – everything he had. Where was he
going to get it? From whom? Surely all was not yet lost, no, all
was not lost; and, though it most certainly would be lost, it was
still too early to say that for sure. Perhaps his situation could
still change: he might draw a nine and win 23,000 rustling new
notes and then leave this place for ever. It wasn't possible to do
in one round. He had to put everything he had on a card and
then double his winnings. It was hopeless trying to win small,
he had to bet it all at once – that was the only sure way to do it.
What were they all smirking about? He would think about it all
tomorrow, what did it matter anyway – he would come up with
something. The main thing was that this was the only sure way
to do it. Trying to win small was a waste of money; he needed
to pick up the cards, win and then double it.

Ramón Ortiz looked pale, his chin had turned grey, and a
lock of hair had fallen on to his forehead. With a fitful and

decisive gesture he stopped the little box of cards that was being passed around the table. The bank was put up for auction. The croupier looked in astonishment at the player who was trying to obstruct him in this mandatory ritual, after which the bank would be offered up at any price. Emphatically, he declared: 'Five thousand two hundred francs,' and tried to move the little box forwards. But Ramón Ortiz had already drawn the first card and with his other hand was pushing all the money that lay in front of him towards the centre of the table, as if it no longer belonged to him. The tradesman grabbed him by the shoulder and whispered: 'Don't do it, luck's not with you!' Ramón Ortiz heard nothing. The tradesman hurriedly bet 500 francs, paused to think for a moment, then added another 300. The neighbouring table was on a break, the players were unoccupied, and so money poured in from all sides. '*Les jeux sont faits!*' declared the croupier authoritatively; narrowing his eyes, he turned over several of the notes with his pallet and repeated: 'No more bets.' Ramón Ortiz took out a cigarette, tapped it against the lid of his cigarette case, tilted his head from side to side as if his collar were too tight for him and, with a steady hand, lit a match. His eyes gleamed; he had regained his resolve. 'No more bets?' he asked again of the silent room, took another drag of his cigarette and, at last, rapidly dealt the cards: two into space, somewhere far off, God knows to whom, and two for himself . . . There was a pause. Another card there, another card for himself. And then an eternity, an eternity – the whole world had stopped.

Seven and five. At the far end of the table, over there, God knows who has seven. Ramón Ortiz has five. It's all over. The settling of accounts, the money, quick . . . He's sixty-five francs short. The croupier waits coldheartedly. Ramón Ortiz turns his wallet inside out, searches his waistcoat pocket. And then the gracious and handsome gentleman with the cards in his hands sympathetically assures everyone that it doesn't matter, that he knows Ramón Ortiz well and that he will gladly wait till tomorrow.

Ramón Ortiz rose up from his chair, tipping it over. The lad with the gold buttons, paying no attention to him, offered

up his place to another player. The woman in the light-blue
dress, who was standing to the side, gazed intently at the good-
looking gentleman who wasn't insisting on the sixty-five
francs. The clock showed twenty minutes past three.

He hurriedly went downstairs, threw his coat ticket on the
counter and grabbed his coat, as though he was afraid of being
late somewhere. Alas, there was nowhere for him to hurry to,
and his only remaining desire was to walk, and walk, and
walk, and it would be good if a harsh wind and rain were to
blow in his face. But there was no rain. Almost all the windows
were dark already, and all that was left was the matt moonlight of an occasional towering streetlamp. Faint music could
be heard in the distance. The sea lay to his left. Oh, the sea!
There's nothing more I can say. Oh, the misery! Like in some
hymn – and then silence. How could this happen? Everything
would eventually become clear if he just kept walking, if he
walked quickly and far; he had neither heart nor legs, he was
flying, not walking. Someone had to help him, had to save him.
Ramón Ortiz stopped. He thought: someone had to save him.
It couldn't be any other way. If he walked into the dark entrance
hall of some house right now, rang the doorbell of a stranger's
flat, woke up the first person that came out, took him by the
shoulders and shook him to wake him up properly, told him
everything, made him understand everything that had happened – then that man, in a dressing gown and a nightcap (just
like the ones in engravings), would sit down at a table and
write out a cheque for 23,000. And he'd even thank you for
waking him up. It couldn't be any other way. And if it were,
then there was no God – no matter that it was all because of
cards. Or, if he went to some kind of prefect or governor, then
he'd order for the bank doors to be opened up at night, he
would do all it took, he'd break the law, he'd steal, if only everything was explained to him. All he needed to do was explain
what had happened – it wasn't possible that man was so brut-
ish and malicious as not to understand. He couldn't be. Two
tipsy sailors walked by, and they too would understand . . .
only it would take a long time to explain. And Ramón Ortiz
had grown very tired. But he would still be saved. Everything

would be all right; and the sea lapped the shore gently, as though promising it. O, life! If only he could meet a woman – that would be best of all – and afterwards to fall asleep and tomorrow think about everything with a fresh head. You can't keep walking for ever. The one in the pale-blue dress, perhaps? But it was impossible to go back, it was hell there; those people were monsters and they certainly wouldn't understand a thing, not a thing. You can't keep walking for ever, Ramón Ortiz. He had reached the city limits; there were fields, allotments, little white houses. He stopped again. My God, my God – life! What about tomorrow? There was nothing left to think about tomorrow, and nothing to be done. It was absolutely clear: there was nothing to think about.

A woman in an off-the-shoulder black dress emerged from the bushes. She was carrying a basket of vegetables on her head – she was going to the city, to market, to sell them. Being alone was more than Ramón Ortiz could bear. He moved closer to her and spoke to her in his language: 'What should I do?' The peasant woman sidestepped him nervously and quickened her pace. Ramón Ortiz looked out towards the sea. Where now? Backwards, forwards. This one didn't understand me, and others won't understand either. You could go anywhere you want now, ring the bell and tell the story, clarify it and explain it and you would still be shoved out of that stranger's bedroom, and no one would care about any of this, each to his own, and tomorrow is a new day, and, most importantly, it will be light, it will be light soon, the sky is already turning pink, and everything is absolutely clear: there is no hope, and it's impossible to bear this any longer, for God's sake, I can't take it any more – the palms beneath the looming, threatening tropical clouds, Anna, angel, farewell, oh, what does it matter if it happens now or later, only get it over and done with, and no one will know, when, where, no one will remember, oh, what does it matter, only to do it before dawn.

Ramón Ortiz took out a revolver and shot himself.

Most likely this wasn't how it happened at all. I don't know. I made it up. I was reading a French newspaper just now, the kind that loves tragic stories, while simultaneously worrying that they might ruin their readers' nerves. The newspaper writes:

'Yesterday morning, near the St Geneviève bridge, the body of Ramón Ortiz Menéndez, an Argentine national aged twenty-nine, was found with a bullet wound to his temple. The reasons for the suicide are unknown. No money was found on the body. The investigation has revealed that the deceased spent his last evening in the gambling rooms of the municipal casino. Madame M., who resides in the village of F., recognized the body as belonging to an unidentified young gentleman whom she encountered at dawn at the aforementioned place. The Argentine was in a state of extreme agitation and attempted to engage her in conversation. The town doctor has issued his consent for the body to be buried.'

Alongside was a photograph: a man lying across the boards, vertical and calm. Only his head is visible, tilted back. His heavy lids are closed; it is all over.

I didn't know this dead man. I had never before heard his name. Most likely it all happened some other way. But I should like to talk to you, Ramón Ortiz. I don't know why I thought about you, you in particular; one reads about this sort of stuff a thousand times . . . But I should like to talk to you. I am an old man; I'm sixty-eight years old. Outside my window it is night and winter; my room smells of ether, some sort of blanket covers my legs, it's soft and warm – I'm not complaining. In fact, I don't complain about anything and – do you know what? – there are even some things I still hope for. 'And, perhaps, at my melancholy sunset, love will yet flash a parting smile.'[1] As you see, I'm joking, but I don't mean anything by it. It's only because I'm afraid to begin and I don't know where to start. Outside my window the snow is falling; the coal blackens in the hearth.

Enough. It's time. The eleventh hour strikes, and with it the head falls on to the executioner's block. It's time! I wish to speak with you, Ramón Ortiz. I'd like to tell you: you did the right thing. I am sixty-eight years old, a long life trails behind me, some successes even. How can I put this? I know what life

is. You see, even if a person hasn't experienced happiness himself, he can still feel how someone else might be happy – in love,
of course. The rest is nonsense, the rest is immaterial – but with
love there is no doubt – and to this day I want to light a candle
to her memory and beat my brow against a stone floor, remembering her. But this has all passed, where is she, the 'immortal'
one? Sorrow, bliss, her hands on my shoulders – where, where?
You see, even memory fades and physics triumphs. This is why
I am not blind now.

And I should like to tell you: what you did was good. Bravo!
For the anguish, the betrayals, the insults and the bitterness – I
say this calmly, having weighed it all up, and not because your
life was a failure (who knows how the rest of your life would
have turned out) – no, not because of that, but taken as a
whole, dear friend. I am bold enough to say this, instead of
saying, as they have: 'he tried his luck', 'he played at cards', 'a
good-for-nothing', 'should have got a job', 'nothing but froth',
'the dregs of society'. O, hypocrites! I don't mean playing
cards, of course, but rather that you understood that nobody
gives a damn . . . I, too, know this: no one gives a damn. And,
listen, the most frightening thing of all is that up there, on
high, it seems they're on their side and not on ours, they are for
them . . . or they're indifferent, which is the same thing. Bravo!
For the insults, for the anguish, for the cracks in life, for the
betrayals of everything and everyone and most of all, once
more – for the bitterness. My heart overflows with it, and I
cannot bear it any longer. Bravo, Don Ramón, you seeker of
universal justice! . . . I have told your story poorly, I have said
the wrong things, but now you understand me. In the end, I
take pity on you: the sea didn't overflow its banks, nobody
stopped you when you took out that revolver, you – a man, a
child, a living thing. There is nothing left to object to – I am
right. Where are you now? Can you hear me? Where are you?
I close my eyes, Ramón Ortiz, and stretch my hand out towards
you – out there, into the greyish greenness, into the haze, into
your icy refuge, which is shady and evanescent and which dissolves into that unfathomable, frightening pearl-and-ashen
dwelling place of yours, where I do not yet wish to go – I stretch

my hand out to you in friendship and in brotherhood. Can you hear me? If there is light and life somewhere – answer me, give me a sign. In the name of brotherhood, and as atonement for all the betrayals, honouring that lightning bolt which once flashed above the world only to disappear. In honour of our eternal acquiescence – give me a sign.

There you are. I thank you. It couldn't have been any other way; I knew I was not talking to you in vain. And even if . . . it was only the marble on my bedside table, I still know that I touched the cold hand you extended to me. I thank you.

An Experiment

YURY FELSEN

I

As I did almost every evening, I stopped off at a little café by
the Étoile and sat down next to the Polish journalist De K. (his
signature), a nightly patron, who was similarly at a loose end
and restless.

At a neighbouring table were two women who looked rather
fast. One was American: grey, with a fresh face and dazzling
teeth. The other was Hungarian: mutton that I had spotted
before on several occasions.

Listless conversation. The Hungarian, driving home some
point, suggested heading on and said outside:

'De K., you shall accompany my friend, and your acquaintance, me.'

There was no discussion, it was raining, we found ourselves
in an uncomfortable red cab.

I am not an adaptable person: with difficulty do I shift
from one psychological state to the next, especially when leaving behind my favourite – melancholy. But my old woman,
as I had treacherously christened my unexpected admirer, nes-
tled up to me, and so I was obliged – as one always is in such
circumstances – to affect blithe chumminess.

I scrutinize her. The coarse skin, flecked violet with age, of
an otherwise becoming face; rather coarse strong hands; grey,
powdered shoulders glimpsed under a flung-back cape. Her
entire being – as it had fleetingly appeared in the lead-up to the
taxi – was short, shapely, plump. Much flesh, energy, impatient

passion. Doubtless she had at one time been alluring. Her eyes –
intelligent, opaque, mocking – do not match her face.

I caution her: *fauché*.[1]

A deft, irreproachable word. She laughs.

'You're in for a surprise.'

We pull up at a fashionable Russian watering hole that I used
to frequent during my first wealthy years in Paris. Those same
officers disguised as doormen and waiters, a famous *tzigane*,
bored and shivering, that same rotund little fiddler with a face
like a caricature of the moon, those same Swedes, Americans,
fugitive Muscovites – my poverty did not tell on their stock lives.

It's nigh twelve, the tables are quickly freeing up, I shan't be
recognized. Our arrival is late and irrelevant. No one will see
our shameful pairing.

I have a curiosity for everything new, even for things most
untypical of me; even more do I love this posture of bold curiosity, and besides, it would be such a pointless bore to fear
some painted old woman who will foot the bill.

'Choose the champagne, otherwise they'll give you one
that's three hundred francs.'

A novice in an ambiguous role, I choose the cheapest one –
for a hundred.

She catches me, roars with laughter and orders another one,
a little more expensive.

I hasten to drink up the bottle myself. So as not to spoil the
game, I need to make myself insensible somehow. But the
champagne goes down like water or lemonade when you aren't
thirsty. Thus is a healthy body probably unaware of the poison
at first.

The fiddler is engaged to play for me. Instead of his violin,
he seizes an accordion – a mark of especial indulgence – inclines
his round, bald head, then lifts his eyes to the new ceiling frescoes, plies the instrument and gives it a few jolts in order to
squeeze out some exceptionally long, plaintive notes.

The Hungarian woman stops things angrily:

'He's Russian, he'll be scandalized by our songs.'

The fiddler has seen it all before; drowsy and devoid of any
national pride, he plays something Russian.

My *patronne* is an old Parisian: her chatter is more assured and plainer than that of any refugee adept. But it's a bore to chat and listen to rubbish. I try to move the conversation on at least to exhibitions and paintings – the easiest topic in Paris. *Échec.*[2] Prancing, often wild turns of phrase, always about the latest thing.

'*Pas une occasion, c'est une sensation.*'[3]

Our relationship is terribly unconvincing. It's impossible to develop any tone or tempo. No heartfelt drunken lyricism, no mutual trust, nothing that might cheer us or bring us closer together.

None too slyly she slips some money under my saucer, and we leave.

The few francs I had I gave to the driver who brought us here; I have no money for the cloakroom, but the Hungarian doesn't realize that we need some change, and she has avarice in her eyes.

2

The rain, the taxi, the love is over. We drive for some time to an all-night café. It's long and rather narrow. An aisle runs straight through the middle. Along each side crimson sofas and tables form individual booths, as it were. We sit in the farthest one. With us is our driver, a strapping forty-year-old Frenchman with pendulous moustaches, who is wearing gaiters and is dressed all in leather. He says nothing and evidently knows his place.

The Hungarian: '*Je veux . . .*'[4]

I conceal my amazement at her lack of decorum. I order a coffee and a Bénédictine. It's pleasant after a liqueur – in a single draught – to take a sip of coffee. The same taste: you cannot tell whether they are two scalding or two intoxicating beverages.

I grow drunk. The Hungarian has returned, rudely having changed her attitude towards me. Suddenly, the attention of our table is directed towards a petite woman, no longer in the

first flush of youth, holding herself erect. She has the look of a
cook about her, and curiously intent eyes that travel past you –
cold and indomitable. There's something in her that reminds
me of a holy fool.

The Hungarian dashes up to her, finds out her name (Marie)
and asks – or rather begs – her to join us. Marie seems almost
to have expected this and, as though playing on the stage, reluctantly, grandly acquiesces. The Frenchman and I are introduced.
Her hand doesn't bend in mine – good form, presumably.

We are being watched – a gentleman, serious-looking,
middle-aged, and two young things who make no attempt to
conceal their merry astonishment. I'm on sensationally good
form – either because of the drink or because of the certainty
that I shall never see these people again; nor will they ever
learn who is paying and why. There's no inherent shame whatever. After all, I'm conducting an experiment, internally and
externally; of my own free will have I embarked on this singular escapade.

Meanwhile, the Hungarian is raptly asking Marie all sorts
of questions. She is Breton – no more do I commit to memory,
for my curiosity has passed. At times polite participation is
required of me. I perform, as though on command. Then I
betray my table: I light a cigarette and smile, as if to say I've
got mixed up in this sordid business on purpose, for the sheer
hell of it. Before long, this too fails me – the gentleman and the
ladies leave.

I'm fast growing drunk. I am no smoker, and cigarettes
between alcohol always make me flag. I want the noise to
swell, to find some licence in it to reveal myself high-handedly.
Evidently, sober, I am much too convolute.

A new white liqueur is ordered. Unnoticed, I pour mine into
the Hungarian's cup. Amazement: '*Tiens, le café est arrosé.*'[5]

The fawning over Marie continues; I am forgotten. Both
women seem sordid and repulsive. The Frenchman makes
scarcely any conversation and clinks glasses only with me.
There is condemnation in his unassailable dignity.

I can sit no longer. Bored stiff, I walk along the aisle. The
customary loneliness among a crowd of people – no ready pose

or quick ripostes are necessary. Because of this, I gradually regain myself – I'm hindered by the noise, some memory loss and gross, drunken passivity.

A relatively young couple in one of the booths is exceedingly occupied with me. The lady smiles, points towards me; I remember her from somewhere. The man has blue eyes – bold to the point of impudence – and fine, becoming features. His gaze, impudent and at the same time sympathetic, immediately fascinates me. Assuredly, he motions me to come over. Russians, of course.

'I used to serve you at the Donon, you were such a gentleman, there was an American lady with you, you had such *bon-ton*. I recognized you at once, although I can't quite believe my eyes.'

She was correct, only the American had been a simple, dull Frenchwoman, and the restaurant was a much more modest affair than its name suggested.

'One does sometimes get into a fix. But you're no scoundrel, that much is obvious. Why don't you sit with us, with your own crowd?'

I'm touched by the faith of the man with blue eyes, thank him excessively and muddledly explain that I have no money on me.

'No matter. We drivers, cabbies – we have money enough.'

We ask each other a thousand questions. Russians have still not grown used to the fact that there are thousands of them in Paris, and they are congenial and curious about one another, like men in a barracks who hail from the same parts.

Our lady is called Zoya. She has a pale, delicate face, thick eyebrows and black almond eyes – all markings of a refined oriental type. Coiffured in the *grande beauté* style, her hair is smooth, knotted at the back with a parting in the middle. But her nails are dirty, and she is missing one front tooth.

My blue-eyed friend is handsome, self-assured and speaks for everyone. Doubtless in the past he was some pert student from the provinces, who saw a thing or two later on.

There seemed to be no romance between them – in any case, I was their sole occupation.

All this is extraordinarily agreeable: at last, after a precari-
ous, bleak evening, a veritable refuge. In order to reinforce it, I
ought to prove that I'm no 'scoundrel', nor a cadger. At home,
under lock and key, I have a few hundred-franc notes, which I
guard from myself. I concoct a plan and want to enact it at once.

'Chaps, why don't we go to mine? It's nearby. Would you
see me for the drinks?'

Impatiently, I hasten to leave. The man with blue eyes unexpectedly advises:

'All the same, do say goodbye to your Hungarian friend.'

In the end booth, a lavish feast is going on. I blow a kiss; no
one notices. Suddenly, the Frenchman with the pendulous
moustaches, whom I had entirely forgotten, hauls himself to
his feet.

'*Je vous emmène.*'[6]

He amiably comes to some agreement with the chap with
blue eyes – they are wearing identical caps. This strikes me as
especially touching, a high point in the evening's events, whose
impropriety and isolation I only vaguely comprehend.

The Frenchman purchases some Cointreau.

3

He drives ably, and soon enough everyone is at mine, in the
spotless, ordinarily quiet room.

I hang up the coats (one leather), which have been caught in
the rain. Zoya lies on the bed but now asks to be shown to the
bathroom. This is an inconvenience – one has to go through
the corridor. I explain and show her the way. The man with
blue eyes follows her out.

The Frenchman and I are left alone, and we drink the liqueur
from large glasses. I compose affected toasts: to the labours
that cast us together, to 'their' benevolence towards us, in general to the help the strong give the weak, and, inappropriately
(for it is private), to faith in love. For the first time in a long
while, I utter such shameful nonsense, which, I know, will
spoil my awakening.

The Frenchman remains silent, most likely in tacit approval, producing an even greater impression of quiet strength.

'Oh, yes, I owe you.'

'Forget it. What does it matter?'

But the whole point of the visit is the repayment of the debt. I open up my private little box containing notebooks that have been filled up long ago. One contains eight hundred-franc notes. I want to settle up and ask whether he has any change, but my guest is a gentleman.

The man with blue eyes calls for my assistance. Our lady has taken ill. She has difficulty breathing and is leaning her forehead against the window, crying. I place my arm around her naturally, pat her hair. A stiff, lithe, slight figure, which moves me at times.

We tend to her together, patiently, then we all three of us return to my room, where the taciturn Frenchman is sitting alone in front of the bottle.

We lay Zoya on the bed again. She continues to cry.

'To think, a husband at home, my girls . . . God, it's awful, what a life! I'm worthless.'

I somehow manage to calm her and find myself in a cloudlessly fine disposition. She falls asleep; we, the men, sip Cointreau – a nasty, saccharine drink. I am definitively drunk and, as always a second time round, blithely and gaily so.

The man with blue eyes baits me with an argument. I overreact because of a nagging suspicion that he doubts my sincerity.

It is light, seven o'clock. My drinking companions want to go; they deliberate whether or not to leave the woman with me. I have nothing against it but do not show my hand. Curiously enough, the Frenchman discourages the idea.

Having got ready with unusual speed, my guests say their thanks and farewells. I look out of the window; they go their own separate ways.

I fell into a deep sleep and awoke late with a squeamish feeling that other people had been here, and a memory of myself, of the others and of the baseness of it all.

There was a bottle on the table. In my pocket, the crumpled

hundred-franc note that the Frenchman had refused. The key in the little box.

I decided it must be the wrong notebook when I found no money in it. But there was none in the others either.

I told De K. about everything, except for the epilogue. He listened without smiling, if not ashamed for my sake, then harshly, like a grown-up, judging me.

The Recurrence of Things Past

YURY FELSEN

After everything I've described, wonder and joy sit uneasily
with me – our illogical ways make us opaque to ourselves, for
no sooner have we given death the slip than, fretting with anticipation, we take up the life we refused not long before, at its
more even passing. For me, today, everything that might have
come together has come together – spring, my first walk, elegant, cheerful women, playful, drunken, languid stares (and I
am gently warmed by them, in blind and bodily delight), our
old concierge sweetly squinting at the sun. It's strange to me
that, even now, Lyolya, even in your absence – alone, without
money or future, I am able to enjoy minutes of a happiness that
is, notwithstanding its naked brevity, almost total – and I can
truly enjoy it, not in the way of those without a ray of hope,
happy to get by, but in a way particular to those few who have
indeed been happy, with a reliable and benevolent memory –
and these flashes, though minute-long, are rekindled particles
of a past kept in me and impossible to efface. Perhaps every
illness – simple, external, known to medicine – is ultimately
bound up with our emotional state, and I am now not just physically well, but jubilant, sharply agitated by a stealthy victory of
the spirit. I have described to you many times the weighty matter of what I have taken to calling my inspiration – at present,
this stubborn need to carry each thought to its close, calling on
all the resources of my being, to track down the exact poetic
term, which has at times driven me to despair, appears to me in
a new light, or in another of its many shades: now it is a dim
stirring I might work into something greater, and its unruly,
palpable intrusion into the state of lethargy and indolence that

without fail precedes it is no longer that of a duty, bringing difficulty and hardship, but carries rather a splendour and a
charm.

This extraordinary state first arose at the café where I am
sitting, though sitting at any café is a source of nervous curiosity, with its host of strangers, acquaintances, adventures and
unexpected Russian meetings with friends thought forgotten
(everything that, alas, will never happen and suddenly does);
and I, without obstacle to my work, busy wholly and exclusively for myself, I am starkly and astoundingly alone, existing
apart. Without hurrying, I gather my extensive riches – the
wild, disjointed arabesques that bear your stamp – and slowly
fold myself into them. This is the root of the café's appeal, that
it allows me to bring together a host of pains and impressions
elsewhere scattered: I can focus in on you, on my ancient memories, on the diligent practice of my craft, and at the same time
take part in life, drink in its flavourful mixture of unattainable
coquettes, jealous, teasing stares and habitual poses, haughty,
bitter, wounded. Just as I noted this down, a radio, as though
clearing the sleep and phlegm from its throat, gave a boisterous, nasal snort. I gave up writing for a short while, listening
in to the music against my will, and suddenly forgot my task,
colouring the broken notes with a phrasing all my own: it was
the very beginning of that well-known opera by Wagner, with
its stately central theme, strident amidst competing voices, and
I caught, distinctly, once again, the difficult, contrapuntal
charm of my solitude in the café, the alternation of you and
not you, my present and past. I was reminded again of my
childhood, my first time reading this luxuriously slow, sombre
overture from the music over the piano, the stories of my
father, who loved it and never ceased to see in it a childhood
buried before, fabulously distant, careless and good; and in
this way everything came to me as one, the confluence of time,
family, St Petersburg, Russia, life abroad, everything that is
viscerally close and that usually comes to me when love will no
longer dislodge strange visitors with their alien attraction.
With love spent, such a chance melody is able to resuscitate
things past and join with a wind of sadness, though not sweet

boyish sadness, foretelling love and death, but one darkened, limp and spare after so many adult misfortunes. Now I, alone, am not saddened, even about you, and that at this minute, in these sunny, spring days, you, my love, are somewhere with someone else, as all the women at the café are with someone else (they have cocktail dates and, I think, long lines of lovers). In the same way, last night, at home, perhaps I was similarly lightened after having read a thrilling adventure story in which, to my amazement, the hero was not a captain, nor a brave patriot, but an admirably intelligent writer, little known, already forgotten, and one of those few justifications for our dull and dirtied modernity. For is it not amazing that now, in the dead black of war and revolution, amidst all the arrogant stupidity and baseness, an undaunted man of unceasing heroism of the spirit could appear, a man of total inner honesty and enormous, concealed kindness, not minded to promise anything, wholly true to his nobility, to his implacable candour? Suppose the assured victory of force, coarse and merciless (not just the silent crowd, as always guilty of nothing, but also its attendant, mercenary flatterers, the false prophets and traitors to poetry stirring its wrath, all those without the capacity to understand a wise heart's wisdom), suppose this force's victory – for me, the rectitude of the defeated would be all the greater and more true. For some reason, I thought of L., with his services for the advancement of Soviet society, of their expression in his bearing, in his eyes, and I felt outrage at those leading exemplary and respectable lives, placated whether by those revolutionaries and officials or this bourgeois life – all those willing to put their money on the victor after victory, risk-free, and whose seeming virtue cloaks the usual pliability. And indeed, in this motley, many-shaded though perhaps rather richly elegant café, to which I hauled myself only with difficulty, though Shura's apartment is close by, I find around me, peacefully reposed, light-hearted, loud and funny old men, with rosettes and ribbons on their breasts, and young, liberated dandies; and in my hopeless lowliness I find them somehow abiding, sturdy, but most of all 'at home', in a country that is theirs, dignified, righteous, composed. Of course my émigré poverty distorts all sense of proportion and often blinds me, but all the same an untold, understood division exists between them, their life and us, between the sure path that, save perhaps for difficult beginnings, they tread, and our perpetual stumbling, and there is something I jealously reprove in this hostile good fortune. Bending to some opaque force, I am driven to discover, to guess at my compatriots by smiles and gestures, to catch them speaking Russian, and at sweet leisure, to really talk my fill with them about our alien surroundings. I am, granted, making a slight mistake, and I ought not to indulge such a petty, ugly impatience in myself: but there, it is from this hostile quarter that the hero who conquered me appeared.

I am writing today with especial passion – evidently my new notebook has furtively inspired me with the possibility of great achievements to come: not with the naive curiosity we bring to what we excitedly await, slipping into a circle even less familiar, meeting youngish women, hurrying to a concert or ball, entering a half-darkened compartment of a train ready to depart – for then these happy, captivating possibilities open up for us what is later inescapable, ordinary and soon exhausted. But then, since childhood thick leaves of paper, gleaming with soft white, the light touch of a fine, silver pen, limpid indigo ink and my own measured hand have almost physically aroused me, compelling me to work diligently, as spring's first warmth brings us surely to love. I had only just written this when I thought how completely my possession at the hands of love permeates literally everything, even the chance comparison of such things – not that I don't know how unconvincing the joining of objects and ideas by outer appearance can be: as, for example, a chewed and blunted pencil appears sometimes like a dirty, ungroomed finger (a manicure corresponding with sharpening) – however winning these 'literary' means may at times be, I am convinced that every attempt to compare things and words fails to uncover their inner essence and simply leads nowhere, that in trying to remain cold and honest I avoid just so many obvious bluffs, so many cheap and dirty tricks; only the comparison with love remains irresistible for me. Just as a minute ago my pencil became blunt (and so the previous comparison) and it turned out that the sharpener that you, at my bidding, gave me had broken, so in my memory suddenly arose your nervous, determined departure, my limitless, pitiful emptiness, all the change that has taken place between us, suddenly illuminating the reason for my lightness today: I didn't plan to deceive by ascribing it to my convalescence, my first walk, spring, the mottled noise and the women and the café, the stately sound of Wagner or the story I had read, my new notebook and working habits, but had somehow forgotten the main point, your short dispatch, that you will soon return to Paris. I had truly at first registered something like fear at the thought of your arrival and of the ceaseless anxiety in store: do you remember how we often recited the disquieting old formula – 'though rest is dull, unrest is torture'? For months of illness and separation I rested, happily weaning myself off unguarded insult and bitterness, and in my spoilt and lazy state I came to fear them fretfully. Just now I suddenly felt how insistently, with what impatience I am waiting for you, carelessly as before, how little I care for peace or rest, how readily I shall accept whatever form of you: however you come – an indifferent, secretive adversary – you, Lyolya, will nonetheless be you, and you will certainly smile at me before we say hello and inquire amiably after my health, and with gratitude I shall trace that dear, unmatched silhouette of yours, I shall hear your enchanting voice, your infectious chesty laugh, and I shall be able to place my hope in something, even if, admittedly, without wishing to. Without especially wanting to, really out of kindness, you will invite me to approach, and we shall chat about something; and later, coming home, I shall try, with a light touch, to alter and embellish our conversations as my pale, deflated life, loveless, aimless, takes on once more a shade of risk, of struggle, of scope. Once more, our half-forgotten journey comes to me – your flat and Petrik, and Pavlik (no longer rival but husband), and our stormy, heated rows, with those softened pleas of mine, first born in illness, and this against the pleasant background of spring, troubles past, of propitiations to crafted sadness and the pull of wise and lucid kindness.

Leafing through the pages of my previous notebook, I find words only about death, about bitter longing, and I am amazed

at the changeability of my emotional state, almost as much as
that of my outer, bodily one: I recover and relapse with freak-
ish speed, almost as though able to grow more or less pretty,
like a woman with her *mauvais et beaux jours*.[1] I lose strength,
and can find it again – at the moment I am especially strong
(a reaction to long-standing weakness), and with you I shall be
inwardly free.

And so I have become used to you and to being in such a state
that I cannot imagine the monotony of a week without you,
without knowing that in the afternoon or evening I shall definitely see you; in which each of our meetings thrills me, for all
their apparent simplicity, as something momentous. The two
of us are alone together more than I had assumed or hoped,
and you can no longer conceal from me your disappointment
in Pavlik, nor that your admiration and respect for him are
finally spent: outwardly and in front of me you are constantly
sweet with him as before, you don't pick at trifling particulars,
you avoid sudden and painful rebukes (you didn't avoid them
with me); but all the same, at certain moments listening to him
simply bores you – after so much fruitless endeavour, I catch in
your eyes a subtle flash of irony, a fleeting, inadvertent gleam
of that shrewd desperation peculiar to you, and then you are
cordial and gentle with him, but speak to him with a wound-
ing condescension, as though mentioning some casual
acquaintance. All of this surely indicates my certain victory
(see how each of our victories springs from defeat) and in fact
I am increasingly assured – by many signs, clear and implied –
that by degrees you are moving from passion to seriousness
and civility, making a return from the journey that drove me
out: Pavlik is now driving himself out. I still bear the smart of
your not so distant decision, nor has all the preceding bitterness been effaced, but somehow these rest alongside my new
sense of triumph, of such firm and blithe delight that I begin to
think things could not be other than they now seem, that my
feverish joy on the eve of your return is a preview and presenti-
ment of this mighty triumph.

I am perhaps embarrassed that your attitude towards Pavlik

changed for such stupid, prosaic reasons: he suddenly found himself without work (there are cuts everywhere at the moment), lost his old assurance and, more flummoxed than he ought to be, he cannot, alas, assure that *sécurité*[2] so dear to you. *Pavlik's support stands as firm as stone* – your words, ringing with a note of acrid reproach directed at me. (Although the ability to procure precisely this everyday stability is a constituent element of every woman's attitude towards us.) I have, through no will of my own, become his equal: yes, he swore an oath, but he made a promise to you and broke it, and even my sneaking prudence now ranks over him. Pavlik is completely, literally without money and a stranger to no form of indignity – the rent for the flat, gas bills, fruit and cake for visitors, conversations over who will pay at cafés – all this is monstrously at odds with his old bachelor's independence (as often happens after marriage, with the inescapable increase in expenditure, even before the major catastrophes). You've had enough of this lowly life, of contrived lightness and cheer, of the jokey, student-like troubles: secretly, Pavlik irritates you. I know you well enough and I don't accuse you of worldliness, nor do I blame you for not turning out to be a heroic and devoted wife: you are patient and steadfast, but you cannot persist for two, and Pavlik is not a comrade to you and still less a commander. After his first few attempts to get it together he no longer puts his faith in any future effort; in misfortune he has done as all those cast down in misfortune do – he lies on the sofa, unkempt and unshaven, staring into the middle distance, with no need, of course, of your advice. I understand such indolence: like him I am assiduous and canny and have found myself on a safe path, however empty, difficult and demanding, though I never went looking for it. It seems to me that many of those who from time to time suffer misfortune find a curious buoyancy – that at the last, hopeless moment, they are saved by some chance event – and this buoyancy Pavlik evidently lacks; and so you will never have the support that you so dearly need. In his newest period of pitiful despair he has dropped himself with all his weight on Petrik, and will not count on anyone else; and every hundred or thousand francs shamefully extracted from Petrik is for you a deeply felt blow. Petrik has wangled a success without precedent, his pictures are selling at ever greater prices, which – given the general lull in business – is less an achievement than a miracle. He experienced what sometimes happens in Paris – sudden fashion, mesmeric fame, interviews, profiles and portraits in the papers, admirers, the envy of his associates; everywhere one catches the name unknown to none – Petrik Stebline. Ordinarily, people enjoying such success cannot understand the preoccupations of others, for success, no matter what the pursuit, seems to them within easy reach; and so each day, Petrik concocts new plans for Pavlik, only to later ascribe his failures to an absence of talent and will – all of which redoubles Pavlik's shame at Petrik's generosity; at the hundred-franc note extracted from Petrik's swollen wallet, proffered sweetly, discreetly, and added to a tally long without purpose; at the frenzied revelry at restaurants and at home; at everything that unwittingly underscores the basic imbalance between them. Now any unwarranted domestic expense or unnecessary purchase pains you, and recently I was astounded, to the point of acute yet impotent pity, by your meek, plaintive words:

'How marvellously simple it all is – so long as there's the least trickle of money coming in, we can put aright anything remiss; we have such a barbarous attitude to things, always replacing one thing with another. But if this trickle were to dry up . . .'

You must have had in mind laddered stockings, or something equally unremarkable, though for you something that was truly irremediable: I sympathize with you especially in this – our proletarian 'solidarity' somehow draws us closer, and you're innocently trusting of me. Do you remember how we climbed the stairs together on our way to the vernissage, to which Petrik had deigned to invite us, and how, smiling to one another, we exchanged glances; it was as if we shared a secret – two shy, unassuming people who had landed, by some error, at a glittering society event. Since that morning, Pavlik, in an attempt to make himself useful, had been hanging the pictures and drawings (for some reason the poor are always so fussily and selflessly accommodating), beaming as he met the guests – every puffed-up critic, every crone in pearls. The vernissage was set for the evening, according to that new recherché fashion; the electricity burned too brightly and (as in all suchlike accounts) one descried the shimmer of smoking jackets, diamonds and décolletés. 'All Paris' turned up at the exhibition, brash and snobbishly conceited: writers, stable-owners, bankers, deputies, marquises. Squinting with concentration, they examined the pictures for hours on end and expounded authoritatively to their bedaubed wives, who were charmed equally by the eloquence of their omniscient husbands, by Petrik's vivid imagination and even by the man himself, in his terribly narrow tail-coat: *'Ah, ses couleurs sont vraiment chauds, il est exquis, ce petit moscovite.'*[3] The success of it 'exceeded all expectation', and the steadily burgeoning throng scarcely blinked at the sight of a ballerina, in one of the pictures, with neither arms nor legs, covered in mysterious, sinister dark spots, and below which was flaunted, as everywhere else, that most proud-making of inscriptions: *'Vendu'*[4] – there had even been comparatively little of the usual necessary unscrupulousness. Having taken a brisk tour of the studiedly familiar paintings, you and I slipped off quietly to a corner to repose on a backless little velvet divan, jocosely sharing our observations, censuring the guests' vanity, which was at times so conspicuous from the sidelines, so trivial and so unfathomable compared to our own immediate cares, and this friendly chat seemed to bring me such comfort, as of old. 'Here comes our patron; Pavlik has given him the slip' – and you bowed ever so obligingly to that freakishly absurd man, who with shoulder and elbow had brushed past me. Hastily, almost teetering, he weaved his way through the crowd, forever in pursuit of some new squabbling clique, looking like a great puffed-up pygmy, with his broad, fat, balding, elongated head, bushy black eyebrows, grotesquely overgrown, one quite literally meeting the other – and, because of which, expressing unbroken, continuous wonderment – hairy, fleshy hands of rather dubious hygiene, a round, fatted stomach atop little spindly diminutive legs, stumpy and curiously mobile: there is a special breed of jolly, alacritous fat men who thrive in life and in business. He manifestly enjoyed posing, promoting himself, talking in a loud and clipped manner, thrusting out his chest and stomach, greeting guests in a

sweeping, familiar way, parading his close acquaintance with
every celebrity in the room – finally he came up to us in the manner of old Muscovy, merchant-like, moistly kissed your pallid
palm (in such cases they are wont to add: 'Well, how are we
getting on, my child?' or 'My respects, dear lady') and condescendingly proffered me his hand. We laughed royally back then
(if you believe Petrik and Pavlik) at his comical maladroitness
and endless social gaffes, even at his very name: Armand Grigorievich Davydov. Truly, though, that combination – the absurdly
French 'Armand', which was enough to make anyone laugh,
and, what was more, at the stock market, in Russian restaurants, amongst film actors and businessmen, he was usually
known, just a tad disparagingly, as 'little Annie Davydov'.
Quick-witted, unscrupulously capable people such as he surface
so readily these days, then they break away, vanish, flee from
debts, only to arise just as gaily and with the same commotion
once again, somewhere far off. Annie Davydov, that luminous
dreamer, had spent some considerable time in various cities and
had a knack for seeking out and seducing wealthy men – men
who were canny and wary of others, but who put blind faith in
him. He 'cultivates' them all differently, and, never demurring
from drunken surroundings, female assistance (one good turn
deserves another), or the deployment of his Kovnoan *'charme
slave'*,[5] he tries to bedazzle them with enticingly reasonable
profits – and so they forget risk, forget his woeful reputation,
and forget the fact that he spends, on the pretext of fictitious
bribes, such fabulous, vast sums on himself. With a strange and
stubborn naivety, even he himself believes in his proposals
(which is an undoubted strength of his) – and so the money in
his bulging pockets, which he carelessly extracts from there, the
toadying of the hangers-on and the contrived sycophancy of the
waiters and drivers are taken by him for genuine repute and only
fortify his conceit. When the war broke out, he found himself in
Moscow, where he had his first run of luck, and ever since then
that unduly familiar, gypsy-like, Muscovite merchant's style
retained for him the charm of magnanimity, sophistication and
wonder, and consequently he never exchanged this captivating
'magnanimity' of his for European commercial dryness. Annie

somehow flits instantaneously from one specialism to the next – half, needless to say, because he is bankrupted by each in turn – and is now a 'film magnate', intoxicated by the opportunities it affords him, by his career and fictive greatness, and so Petrik's plan is the most realizable one of all – to set up Pavlik in his former position: that is why he accepted on our behalf Armand Grigorievich's invitation 'to celebrate the happy occasion' and 'to get blind drunk, Moscow- style' – these words of Annie's contained both a ring of self-satisfaction, to the point of throwing down a challenge, and also something hauntingly sad.

And so we find ourselves in a drunken Russian bar, where our 'patron' is welcomed with a march, and where he democratically talks to a waiter with a title, to the musicians, to the fair-haired gypsy chorus girls and to the bellicose highlanders in tall astrakhan hats:

'My champagne, served just as I like it.'

Then begins the 'wild debauch', in which everything is uniformly sham – the gypsies, the menace of their daggers, Annie Davydov's wealth and his notorious magnanimity: he blatantly counts out the bottles, never rushes to open them, orders us coffee and liqueurs, partially expiating this with the phrase (borrowed from someone else): 'Champagne for the band!' For the sake of appearance, the musicians show their appreciation for this unnecessary act of generosity and artificially rouse themselves, a famous Romanian violinist in a frenzy of grease and sweat, Cossacks with swarthy faces and fine curled moustaches (like in old illustrations of Lermontov) dancing – never stopping, never wearying – in sharp-toed soft boots, drawing close to each other with inimical indifference, almost merging, stamping in time to the monotonous, viscid melody, and then coolly parting and with their merry, strong teeth tossing up daggers for them to plunge into the floor in the shape of a semicircle, as though they were spoils of war, so out of place amidst these surroundings. The gypsies, to the complaints of a guitar, steadily drum home their message – that 'love is gone' and that 'a blizzard's a-comin'' – and our French neighbours rapturously sing along ('*ces russes, ah, quelles voix chaudes*'[6] – clearly for them, everything Russian invariably falls under the category '*chaud*').[7] You and I are coolly sober and absorbed by more prosaic matters; I by yours more than my own, and I feel ashamed that it is beyond my power to help you. Armand Grigorievich is captivated by you – I recall (not without an inner chuckle) that caustic, wicked serenade: 'We four, four, four of us, we four, all four, we love you thus.' He can hardly expect to meet with success, but it seems the time has come to get used even to this impossible prospect: how often have I thought about the general public – how it is for them with their wretched simplicity, their plebeian, caricature-like appearance – yet here they are, fashionably dressed, they dance no worse than the rest, they spurn neither beach nor sport, and freely chat about any old thing, striving for intimacy, sympathy, or playing court in their coarse, cynical ways, thus seeing off rivals far more persistent and experienced than I (which has nothing to do with their financial advantage, despite the indirect assistance it affords them). It came so unexpectedly for me – Bobka, Shura, Pavlik, and the fact that you so callously preferred each one of them to me. But now you are on my side, and in my stead you deprecate Annie – not because he is more absurd than the rest, but because you have no time for coquetry, no time for vain women's games, and because I share this unremitting preoccupation of yours. You wince when he says, with the inflexions of an inveterate drinker, 'Ah, my thanks' to the musicians and the gypsies, or, congenially to me, 'Drink, professor!' – and the crumpled hundred-franc note, virtuosically snatched mid-air by the still-sweating violinist, only piques your vexation, although in your usual composed state you would be more patient and indulging. Trying to amuse you a little, while at the same time showing off in front of you, Armand Grigorievich began telling us about his latest business enterprises, the rapt approbation of his acquaintances, the repentance, the envy of his enemies, and their pathetic spats with him – he numbers among those 'naive egoists' who, upon meeting whomever, engage their bewildered companion with talk only of themselves, in the unbearable, puerile confidence that it hotly interests them, too. Such bores, besotted with themselves, occur in every milieu – amongst politicians, artists, actors – particularly when their intellect is not on a par with their achievements, and when they have no sense of reality, though the bravado of the rich, intoxicated by their money, is in fact a hallmark of unconscious modesty: any wealthy person will maintain that all his merit lies in his money, and that without this chance appurtenance he would be, in and of himself, nothing. Of course, he would fail to grasp my dissertation on modesty; then again, it's far from difficult to catch in the pretensions of many a millionaire something resembling a vague admonition, self-doubt or a complaint of 'unacknowledged genius'.

When we decided to leave (Petrik had been politely bored the whole time – he is against 'coarse, barbaric amusements' – while Pavlik was in a now permanently and resentfully listless mood), when you hinted at being tired, Armand Grigorievich called for the bill and, scrutinizing it, covered it with his hand, as if wanting deliberately to underscore that this honour, this customary delight, would not be ceded to any of us. He then folded in half the narrow ruled slip of paper covered in minutely written numbers, deftly slipping a crumpled thousand-franc note inside it, attempting to demonstrate through this his exceptional finesse. He had, a thing one rarely witnesses, a special ritual when dealing with money – from his gestures when paying for anything to the sentimental and edifying stories he told of those people who had helped him and whom he had been able to reward – a ritual peculiar also to those who enjoyed former wealth, the well-bred, respectable and haughty: since childhood I could recall examples of such things verging on religious rites – how people, with grand gestures, would in my presence extract from their pockets gold cigarette cases or watches with hinged cases, imparting (incongruous) significance to anything they did and prolonging their every action – all this has been lost, forgotten in our terrible, shifting days, and with a feeble sort of mimesis it surfaces among latter-day epigones like Annie.

Hospitable and obliging to a T, he took it upon himself to accompany us, and when we were alone together in the taxi, he suggested going to sit awhile longer in some 'quiet little spot'. I freely agreed to this – I found him curious in a way, and

even this slovenly nocturnal mode of life was irresistibly attractive to me: like all neurasthenics I come alive and am sociable
by night, while in the mornings I'm ill-tempered and reserved.
We found ourselves in a small bar, pricey, but relatively
comfortable, and Annie, having livened up a little from the
wine, became somehow more pleasant, more intimate, all the
while maintaining in the conversation, true enough, a hint
of condescending pretentiousness. He entertained me rather
importunately ('My dear, drink, eat, don't stand on ceremony!'), inquired after Petrik, after you, and confided in me a
series of sufficiently sober and vapid observations: 'Your Lyolya's a top-drawer gal, believe me, I know what I'm talking
about, though her choice of husband is idiotic, and she'll come
to realize it soon enough – you'd be a better match for her, but
then again, what she needs is a real man, one with capital and
character.' He was of course alluding to himself, although during his conversation with me I had failed to uncover any
character or depth – on the contrary, he was woefully limp, he
would harp on about his loneliness, about the ingratitude of the
many people who were infinitely indebted to him, their treachery towards him (notwithstanding the most recent tales about
those who had helped him): 'I'm well aware I buy each and
every one of them for a song, for champagne, for dinner. There's
no such thing as an altruistic friend.' Naturally, he failed to
mark that he stood to offend me with these words about champagne and dinner and so on, but I was ready for him well in
advance and took them in kind, replying as opportunely as I
could (so callously do we lose our sense of *amour propre* when
we decide to take no notice of someone). I stated that 'banking
on money' leads to inevitable failure, that we can buy only the
semblance of something, a phantom of a relationship, that
friendship is acquired through friendship, but he cut me off at
once, truly indifferent to this advice, unable even to hear me
out and, moreover, fearing a departure from his pathetic attitude. I'd had enough of consoling him and devised new topics
(friends, the past, Moscow), and he seemed to thaw at once: so
easily do we make friends with those people – hostilely disposed, hardened by life – when the mood takes us; indeed, each

of us has his own stock of shameful, secret, obscure memories, whether amatory or juvenile, and we must skilfully conjure them up in order to disarm someone in a flash. Thereupon I tried to exploit my patron's unusual excitement and began extolling Pavlik – perhaps too transparently, though at any rate, contracting, narrowing his eyes, he looked at me in astonishment and with enmity drily retorted:

'You simply do not know Olshevsky. He's a careerist and an utter nonentity.'

How strange, we apply this term so often to all sorts of people who are dissimilar to us, while elevating ourselves to a paragon: for me the nonentity was this 'Maecenas', with his intellectual blindness, yet for him it was Pavlik and I, with our naive obtuseness in matters of business. Though he attacked Pavlik for another, different, reason:

'Tell me: who was it that took him under his wing and for whom did he first work, and who would he be without me? A good-for-nothing, silly young lad. And how does he repay me? By being taken in by some worthless pittance and leaving me – and now he's out of pocket. So let him come running.'

I later discovered why Armand Grigorievich was contradicting himself, telling Pavlik to his face of the loyalty he had rewarded, and then complaining, after he had gone, of interminable treachery at every turn: in the first instance he was exacting revenge on Pavlik; in the second, he was venting his bitterness. I also realized that he would never forget nor forgive this 'betrayal', and that nothing would assuage him: to satisfy his pride, he has to see the most demonstrative results possible from his good offices, the grateful dependence of those whom he has made happy and 'taken under his wing'; he would never dream of helping someone without bragging or making a fuss, from afar, hiding behind the scenes, and is most of all indignant if strangers fail to mark his expenditures and oblatory services. Unconsciously I compare this to gracefully veiled help, anonymous good deeds, sweet, simple, heartfelt generosity, such as I ascribe to Petrik and probably Sergei N. too; therein lies the key to overcoming crudeness and selfish animal instinct, the key to 'humanization', flights of the soul, everything that holds a particular allure for me and that I value above all else, conscious of how much I am repeating myself, and even of how much in it is not at all new, preferring, as I do, truth to novelty. Truth such as this is hardly exact, however, and in their purest form our traits are neither malign nor lofty: quite probably even Annie Davydov is at times capable of some excitation on account of the joy he has occasioned; quite probably Sergei N. harbours dreams of reward, hopes for your gratitude, only right now he is embarrassed and will endeavour to quell those hopes within him; and this secondary impulse, this remorse, this effort, is immeasurably more important to me than that vague initial jolt, for such efforts change us, are even the making of us: they constitute our purpose, our future character, and doubtless the long trod path of man's struggle for nobility, for the agony of spiritual ascent, which is made up of 'secondary impulses', our dissatisfaction with past mistakes. And so, in contrasting these two extremes, Sergei N. and Annie Davydov, I am convinced of the vast disparity between the achievements of some and the failures of others, across thousands of centuries and generations, and thus a question arises, for which I do not have an answer: is humanity tending towards the better, or are these few instances of good forever hopelessly isolated?

My conversation with Armand Grigorievich ran dry, ending on an awkward note: eager to find a common language and to bait him without his noticing, I cited the figures of Sergei N.'s royalties over several years (breaking the confidence bestowed upon you), but in the blink of an eye he 'outstripped' me with such outrageous numbers, such vast quantities of money earned, spent, given away by him, that I (all too late) began to pity his lavish imprudence. Truly, one should never say sensational things in front of liars: they will always go one better and cheapen everything with their fabrications, while one has to hear them out patiently in order somehow to 'upstage' them and achieve a greater effect. All the same, these 'bluffers', devoid of any feeling of shame or fear for their ridiculous unmasking, often in life defeat the shrewd, calculating wise men, as though life bends to their fantasies: perhaps this triumph of flippancy, effrontery and stupidity (especially in financial affairs) is a sign of our times, of their alarming instability, the end of the bourgeois order – or is it always the case, in any age, that the more impoverished the heart and mind, the clearer and straighter the path? I did not enlighten Annie about my sceptical opinions of him; as usual I tried to ingratiate myself with him, and seemingly it worked.

Giselle

A Story of Bohemian Life

GEORGY IVANOV

The story begins from afar. But by a strange 'optical illusion' of plans hopelessly muddled (by war, revolution, fate) – it is precisely the beginning that I recall most clearly.

I remember that September morning in 1911 down to the last detail. The carouse started late – having been organized on the spur of the moment.

At half past eleven, Kokosha Kuznetsov – a jolly brawler, professional idler, thoroughly unknown artist and famed billiard player – suddenly remembered, or imagined, that it was his birthday, and that we just had to celebrate the occasion. The reason behind this decision, and behind the considerable delay in making it, came down to a long and, for Kokosha, felicitous contest in the Dominique billiard hall, a smoky and bespattered establishment that was, for some reason, held in especially high regard by the 'real players'. Kokosha waged battle for six straight hours against some fop who had, to his own misfortune, wandered into the Dominique. The 'fop' evidently hadn't a clue about the glory of Kokosha's cue, or about this billiard master's insidious manner of first feigning incompetence and only later, with passions rising and the stakes snowballing, suddenly demonstrating his fabulous skill, renowned throughout the billiard halls of St Petersburg.

The game ended at around eleven. Struck dumb by defeat and countless mugs of beer, the 'fop' left, having arranged a rematch for the following day. Then Kokosha, grinning blissfully, tossed the scorer a crumpled ten-rouble note and stepped out on to Nevsky Prospect – with the firm intention of celebrating his birthday in style.

And I recall the end of those festivities clearly, to the last detail. The horrific mess in Kokosha's flat – cigarette butts, scraps of food, empty bottles. Some of the guests had plodded off for home, barely dragging their feet, some were asleep, and some, who were either stronger or more judicious in their drinking, still sat upright, disgustedly chasing the last of their cognac with gulps of black coffee. The windows, which had not yet been sealed with extra putty against the coming cold, were flung open on to the murky, grey, slowly brightening Fontanka[1] – and in the 'clear, merciless light of day'[2] the picture before me seemed particularly unappealing. Yes, cigarette butts, bottles, puffy, heavy-eyed faces and eggs frying on a spirit-lamp . . . In short, a scene we've all witnessed dozens of times and can easily dredge up from personal experience. Of course, I would not only have failed to notice any of these details, but would have likely failed to preserve any memory of this 'birthday party' altogether, had it not been for one chance occurrence, which set this party apart from countless others of its kind . . .

Here is what happened. When the drunks were snoring in the corners, the coffee stains were spreading across the tablecloth, and the fried eggs' fumes were floating up into the grey cloudy sky – there was a ring in the hall. Yawning, the master of the house trudged off to open the door. A loud voice sounded in the anteroom (as I recall it now, a loud, young, and – especially striking to my ear at that moment – sober voice), accompanied by the jangle of spurs and the rattling of a sabre.

Kokosha came back into the room with a young, tall, rosy-cheeked, blue-eyed officer in a Guards uniform, with a cornet's epaulettes. I knew this fellow a little – a day-tripper in our Bohemia by the name of A. He adored the theatre, music, poetry. I'd first met him not too long before, in one of Petersburg's 'artistic' salons, and was immediately struck by his extraordinary beauty. There was something angelic about it. For men, beauty is, so to speak, a double-edged quality – in most cases, too handsome a male face looks foolish, just plain silly. But there was really something 'heavenly' in A.'s face, something one could go on admiring for a long time, like a painting, or a sunset over the sea . . .

And so I 'admired' A. for a while, having met him some-where, and then, of course, forgot all about his existence. Could I have imagined back then that, seventeen years later, I'd be writing about him in Paris? And could he have imagined that some kid-musician, to whom he had happened to be intro-duced somewhere entirely by chance, was destined to touch, many years later, the wisps of that strange cobweb in which he was to become entangled and perish? . . .

A. entered the room, beaming a rosy, sober smile (I remem-ber it clearly – he was smiling), deafening our ears, which were sensitized by drink and insomnia, with the loud, sober sound of his voice, the clanging of his sword and the silvery jangle of his spurs. He dutifully greeted each of us in turn, looking as if he noticed neither our own pathetic confusion nor that of our sur-roundings. He was offered a cognac. He drank a glass, refused a second. Having listened politely to someone's stupid joke, he rose to his feet, tossed a cigarette butt out the window and accompanied Kokosha into his office. Five minutes later, A. left. Kokosha explained that he had called (they were, it turns out, raised on neighbouring estates and had been friends since childhood) to pay a gambling debt. Roguish voices: 'He lost and swore he'd bring the money at the end of the month – and sure enough, at the crack of dawn. Splendid fellow, that A. – and what an Adonis! Bringing round the money like that – a good sport. That being the case, gentlemen, here are my instruc-tions – today, sleep it off, and tomorrow, get right back over here and finish the booze. Whosoever fails to appear is no friend of the retired Cavalry Captain Nikolai Kuznetsov.'

That happened in the morning. And in the evening a visiting friend informed me of something that was no longer news to anyone but me, who had been dreaming sweetly all day. Here is what he told me: A. had been found somewhere along the Chernaya River with a bullet through his head. He died in hospital without regaining consciousness. The only word he had uttered as he lay dying was 'Giselle'.

There was much talk about A.'s strange demise for a time. Everyone speculated as to what might have led such a hand-some, and, to all appearances, happy young man to commit suicide in so unexpected, so frightening a fashion. Some took these speculations even further – despite the fact that the inquest had established suicide as the cause of death, they debated about the revolver, the trajectory of the bullet, and conjectured about what the dying man's last word could have meant. Then, as usual, their interest in the case began to wane. A. lay in his grave, the chatter about him gradually died away, and soon he was forgotten by all.

A year passed, then another ... The war raged. The flower of the Russian Guards was lost in the famous Battle of Tannenberg. I remember, around that time, one officer made a melancholy remark in my presence: 'Our poor A. rushed it – had he waited a bit longer, he would have died a hero – a better end ...' Upon hearing these words, I momentarily conjured up A. as he had been in life – that smile, those rosy cheeks, those bright-blue eyes – and, for the duration of that moment, pitied him with that selfish pity of the bystander, which is, essentially, just a variety of human indifference – a polite variety of it ...

The second part of the story (if one can call this a story) – is rather foggy, troubled, vague. Of course, the period in which it occurred is itself vague, foggy, troubled.

This was August or September of 1917. The Provisional Government was still in power, St Petersburg was still the capital, and Russia was still at war. The Bolsheviks were still underground. But with each passing day, that 'still' grew more and more ironic. Still? For how much longer? Oh, perhaps a couple of months. And then ...

> ... Green star – brother of water, of the heavens –
> Petropolis, your brother, breathes his last! – [3]

as the most ravishing of Russian poets wrote about those days. In that dying Petropolis, against the terrifying background of Russia sinking to the bottom, there was, by the way, much reckless fun – and the nearer the end came, the more reckless the fun grew. There appeared – God knows from where, as if they really had sprung from underground – a horde of new people throwing around uncountable sums of money: women, Swedish industrialists, Cuban consuls. And every evening – God knows why, God knows for whom – they'd put on absolutely smashing parties.

I somehow ended up at one of these receptions. To this day I haven't the slightest idea of who owned that magnificent flat on Aptekarsky Prospect. I still see before me, as in a dream, the enormous gilded rooms, the mountains of expensive food, even greater amounts of wine and the crowd of unfamiliar guests – an elegant and insolent crowd emitting the complex odour of those days, which was a subtle mélange of Egyptian tobacco, the spirited scent of counterintelligence, L'Origan, Guerlain[4] and blood ... And ghostlier, foggier yet – as if it were a dream within a dream – looms the pale, slender and rather unattractive face of a woman. Her grey eyes stare sadly, with a touch of malice, and her painted mouth wears a cold smile. The face is both charming and repellent – one doesn't wish to remember it, but one cannot forget it.

Then even this shadow of reality disappears. There is a gap in my memory, a void. And that's no great mystery – it's simply that six months had passed since I'd last had a drop of wine. And here were Martell, and champagne, and liqueurs, as well as the awkward boredom of a man who's wound up among strangers, and who knows that, come what may, he'll have to stay there till morning: in the autumn of 1918, a journey through the whole of St Petersburg, from Aptekarsky Prospect to Znamenskaya Street, was no laughing matter. The empty, black, frightful Field of Mars, through which I'd have to pass on my way home, was enough to dissuade me all by itself ... Hence the gap in my memory – thanks to champagne, liqueurs and boredom. And when things begin to take shape again in my consciousness – they are no longer the gilded walls of the flat in which I'd drunk myself into a stupor, in which we'd met. It's something else – consisting of darkness, warmth, the scent of hair, the scent of warm skin, and a strange, sibilant, charming and repulsive female voice.

At first I don't quite understand what this voice is saying: 'We'll be so happy. But of course – we're already happy – so warm, so soft, so sleepy. We'll go abroad, big hotels, a rich, glamorous life.' What is she talking about? It all must be out of some novel. But her voice sounds so oddly insistent, so intensely dry. And why is she repeating the same things over and over again? I've already heard about us being happy, about us going abroad. And why does she keep insisting that I must remember this, must never forget it? The Ministry of War. Cabinet D. File N. What is all this – the novel's sequel? Now I'm fully awake (or so it seems). And in the half-light of an unfamiliar room I see a woman hovering over me in bed, making passes over my face like a hypnotist and repeating: 'You won't forget. You'll remember. Cabinet D. File N . . . We'll be happy. You'll remember . . .'

'What do you want from me?' I get out, barely able to turn my tongue. 'What do you . . . What ministry, what cabinet? I'm not in any ministry . . . I play the bass,' I manage to finish with a desperate effort – although I'm really a violinist, plan to overshadow Paderewski and, naturally, despise the bass. But at that moment I cannot recall the violin, any other kind of string instrument or any other musical concept at all, and so I settle for the bass.

Then she lies down beside me – quickly, softly, like a cat. 'Sleep, sleep, sleep,' she says in a rapid, tender, sibilant whisper. 'That was all nonsense. Don't give it another thought. Don't think about anything – sleep, sleep, sleep.'

She presses a glass to my mouth, lifts my head. 'Drink, drink,' I hear the tender, sibilant, insistent whisper and swallow something sweet and stupefying. 'Drink, drink. Sleep, sleep.' I drink and fall asleep. And through the veil of sleep I hear: 'It's all nonsense. Forget about everything. I love you – I am Giselle . . .'

All these details swam up in my memory only later, little by little, after a week, a month, a year . . . At first I could only recall the ambivalent sense of tenderness and revulsion with which I awoke (at my own home, having been brought there in a cab by some soldier early in the morning), as well as that strange, sibilant, insistent whisper: 'Sleep, sleep, sleep . . . I am Giselle.'

I had neither her surname nor her address – nor even the

186 GEORGY IVANOV

certainty that any of this had actually transpired, that it hadn't all been a dream. And, in truth, I didn't really wish to know what my nocturnal 'Giselle' went by in her passport, to know that she wasn't a ghost. Back then, the last thing I was in the mood for was continuing that strange dream – revulsion had clearly overpowered tenderness in my recollection of that night. While the thought that A. had died with that very same name – Giselle – on his lips didn't even cross my mind in those days . . .

And now for the epilogue to my 'story'. The epilogue takes place in emigration.

In the winter of 1923 my violin and I found ourselves in Germany. After Soviet Russia, from which I had just escaped – hungry, dirty, embittered – the Berlin of those days was to me nothing short of paradise on earth. The hunger that Germans complained about was a joke to me, and, after Moscow, I perceived the dereliction of their capital as a miracle of European luxury. I'd endured 'all manner of things' in the blessed USSR, had almost been killed, and now I could rest, body and soul. My violin fed me – I played mawkish tunes in cafés and nightspots, neither thinking of the past nor glancing into the future . . .

But that's not the important part. The important part is that during that winter of 1923, in a small, snow-bound town up in the mountains – a ski resort – I ran across her: Giselle.

The very same. Yes, the very same woman . . . who had brought about poor A.'s death.

I'll skip all the preliminaries: how I'd ended up in Schorne, as this town in the Harz was called, the description of my journey, of the natural landscape (though I find it hard to resist the chaos, so beautiful were those pines, that ice, the sunshine, with the colossal white Brocken in the background – a true snowy Eden). I'm skipping all of it – and starting directly: on the very first day, returning for breakfast after a long, tiring stroll in the cool, crisp mountain air, I nearly bumped into the woman at the door of my sanatorium.

She wore a white sweater and a short white skirt. Some sort of children's hat was perched, cute and sweet, atop her head, and, like a child, she was pulling a sledge. But the face was the same, completely unchanged, pale and thin, rather unattractive – at once charming and repellent . . .

I recognized her instantly. I don't know whether I'd have made up my mind to speak to her. But the force of chance that had brought us together was still at work: she happened to be staying at the same sanatorium, and, at breakfast, we were seated next to each other at the table d'hôte. I confess, I was quite grateful to chance. And – I also confess – in the foggy blend of the repellent and charming that swept over me at that moment, I felt that the charming had prevailed . . .

Now I skip over everything – those few days, that recurring dream within a dream. When I say a few days, I'm simply guessing – I don't remember how many there were: one, two, ten.

> I do not know if I dreamed long,
> But the awakening was strange . . .[5]

The awakening really was strange . . . By the way, dear reader, do you happen to know what a volta in a sonnet is?

Don't think me crazy – my question is relevant. Yes, the volta in a sonnet. At some point I made attempts at verse, and a poet friend of mine had instructed me in the intricacies of the craft. The volta is a sonnet's last line. It must 'turn over' the sense of the poem's preceding lines, throwing new light on the whole. It's all a matter of exactness, concision, dryness. And although I'm not writing a sonnet, but only a disjointed account of real events – in conclusion, I'd like to say a few words about what's most important.

. . . Berlin. A hotel room. Dawn. The window is flung open on to the murky, grey, slowly brightening Spree, and in the 'clear, merciless light of day' the picture before me is surprisingly reminiscent of another: a September morning in 1911, St Petersburg, Fontanka, Kokosha's flat, A.'s 'angelic' face . . . Now this face gazes up at me from a photograph that chanced to fall out of a suitcase, and that I chanced to pick up from the floor . . . And beside this face is another one – pale, rather unattractive. Its grey eyes stare sadly, with a touch of malice, and its painted mouth wears a cold smile. A sibilant voice declares indifferently:

'Yes, that's me . . .'

Recently I came across an issue of an American illustrated magazine. It featured a captioned portrait – a Soviet spy, expelled from America. The surname was different, but the face was familiar – charming and repellent. A face one doesn't wish to remember but cannot forget.

The Atom Explodes

GEORGY IVANOV

Lower thyself. Or I could say –
Soar high. It is one and the same.
Faust, Part II

I breathe. Perhaps this air is poisoned. But it is all the air I am
given to breathe. I have first a vague, then a painfully acute
sense of various things. Perhaps it is useless to talk of them.
But is life necessary or is it not? Does the whispering of trees,
the onset of evening, a fall of rain make sense or otherwise? I
feel both superiority and weakness before the world around
me: in my mind the laws of life are intermingled with the laws
of dreams. Thanks to this, no doubt, my perspective on the
world is seriously distorted. But it is the one thing I value, the
one thing that sets me apart from the overwhelming hideousness of the world.

 I am alive. I walk along a street. I go into a café. This is today,
it is my unique life. I order a glass of beer and enjoy drinking
it. At the next table sits an elderly gentleman wearing some
kind of insignia. In my opinion this sort of well-to-do old fellow ought to be eliminated. You're old. You're sensible. You
are the head of a family. You have lived a bit. Well, take that,
dog! He cuts an impressive figure, this gentleman. Which is
something to be valued. But what rot: 'impressive', indeed. If it
were handsome, pitiful, frightful, anything at all. But no, it has
to be impressive. They say that in England there is even a special profession – false witnesses who cut an impressive figure
which will inspire confidence in a courtroom. And not only
does it inspire confidence, it is itself an inexhaustible source of

self-confidence. One of the qualities of the hideousness of the world is precisely its impressiveness.

I am, fundamentally, a happy person. That is, a person disposed to be happy. Which is something relatively rare. I desire the simplest, most ordinary things. I desire order. It is not my fault if order has collapsed. My soul longs for peace. But my soul is like a churned-up waste-bucket – a herring tail, a dead rat, spat-out bits of food, cigarette ends, diving into the murky depths, then appearing on the surface, chasing each other. I desire fresh air. The sweet smell of decay – the breath of the world's hideousness – pursues me like fear.

I walk along the street. I think about the most varied things. A salad, gloves ... Among the people sitting in the café on the corner one will die first, one last, each at their allotted precise moment, determined to the last second. It is dusty and warm. This woman is beautiful, of course, but does not appeal to me. She wears a smart dress and smiles as she walks, but I imagine her naked on the floor, her skull split open by an axe. I think about sexual pleasure and disgust, about sadistic murders, about how I have lost you for ever, or how it is finished between us. 'Finished' is a pathetic word. Is it not as if, when one listens carefully for their meaning, all words are equally pathetic and terrible? The weak antidote of sense which with amazing rapidity ceases to be effective, and beyond this the mute emptiness of solitude. But what could they have understood of things that are pathetic and terrible – those who believed in words and sense, dreamers, children, the undeserving favourites of fortune!

I think about various things and, along with them, think incessantly of God. Sometimes it seems to me that God, amid a thousand unrelated things, is just as incessantly thinking of me. Light waves, orbits, tremors, forces of attraction, and amid all these, like a ray of light, incessantly thinking of me. Sometimes it even seems to me that my pain is a part of God's being. So that the stronger my pain grows ... A moment of weakness, when I want to say aloud, 'I believe, O Lord ...' Then a coming to my senses, which instantly asserts itself after this moment of weakness.

I think of the cross which I have worn since my childhood, as one carries a revolver in one's pocket – to defend, to protect one in a moment of danger. Of the fateful, inevitable misfire. Of the shining light of false miracles which one after another have enchanted and then disenchanted the world. And of the sole genuine miracle, that incurable yearning for a miracle which dwells within people in spite of all. Of the immense meaning of this. Its reflection in any consciousness, but especially a Russian one.

O, this wavering, uncertain, musical, masturbatory Russian consciousness. Eternally circling about the impossible, like gnats around a candle. The laws of life which have become one with the laws of dreams. Terrifying metaphysical freedom and physical obstacles at every step. Inexhaustible source of superiority, weakness, magnificent failures. Ah, the strange variants we produce, even now roaming like restless shades about the world: Anglomaniacs, Tolstoyans, Russian snobs – the most repulsive snobs in the world – and all sorts of Russian boys, the sticky little buds,[1] and then the eternal Russian type, knight of the splendid order of the intelligentsia, a scoundrel with a morbidly over-developed sense of responsibility. Always on guard, like a bloodhound always sniffing out injustice, no ordinary person can keep up with him! Ah, our past and our future, and our present accursed state of misery. 'And how alive the little child was . . .' Ah, this gulf of nostalgia, along which only the wind roams, bringing back from there the terrible Internationale and from here – plangent, astral, like a burial service for Russia, 'Lord, bring back the Tsar' . . .

I walk along the street, think about God, look into women's faces. There is one who is pretty, whom I find attractive. I imagine her washing herself. With her legs apart, her knees a little bent. Her stockings down below her knees, somewhere in the very depths of her eyes a velvety darkness appearing, her innocent, bird-like expression. I think of how as a rule the average Frenchwoman washes herself there carefully, yet rarely washes her feet. Why? But then they always keep their stockings on, sometimes even their shoes. I think about France generally. About the nineteenth century, which still goes on here. About bunches of violets at the Madeleine, sodden hunks of bread in *pissoirs*, boys on their way to their first Communion, chestnut trees, the spread of gonorrhoea, the silvery shiver of the Ave Maria. About Armistice Day in 1918. Paris went mad. Women would sleep with anybody. Soldiers climbed up the street-lamps, crowing like cocks. Everybody was dancing, everybody was drunk. Nobody heard the voice of the new century, saying, 'Woe to the victors.'[2]

I think about war. About how like a film it is life speeded up, its concentrated extract. That amongst the misfortunes which have befallen the world the war by itself was of little consequence. A jolt which hastened the inevitable, no more. Just as for a dangerously ill person everything is dangerous, so the old order collapsed at the first touch. A sick man ate a cucumber and died. The world war was that cucumber. I think of the banality of such deliberations and at the same time feel, like light or warmth, banality's reassuring caress. I think of the epoch which is disintegrating before my eyes. Of the two fundamental types of women: prostitutes, and the ones who are proud that they have refrained from becoming prostitutes. Of the inhuman charm of creation and the inspired hideousness of the world. Of nature, of the stupidity with which it is described in the literary classics. Of all the vile deeds people perpetrate upon one another. About pity. About the child who asked Santa Claus for new eyes for his blind sister. About Gogol's death: how he was shaved, terrorized by the Final Judgement, bled with leeches, forced to take baths. I remember an old lullaby: 'The cat Vorkota's stepmother was bad'. I return once more to the thought that I am a person disposed to be happy. I desired the most ordinary of things – love.

From my male point of view . . . However, a point of view can only be male. A female point of view does not exist. Woman does not exist, not for herself. She is a body and reflected light. And you absorbed my light and departed. And all my light went out from me.

For the moment we skate over the surface of life. About its

periphery. Over the blue waves of the ocean.[3] An appearance of harmony and order. Grime, tenderness, grief. Presently we will go under. Give me your hand, unknown friend.

Your heart ceases beating. Your lungs refuse to draw breath. Torment, close to elation. All is unreal apart from the unreal, all is meaningless apart from the meaningless. Man is simultaneously blinded and begins to see. Such orderliness and such chaos. A part, grown greater than the whole – the part is all, the whole is nothing. You guess that the clarity and finality of the world are but a reflection of the chaos in the brain of a gentle lunatic. You suppose that books and art are no more than descriptions of great deeds and voyages intended for those who will never travel anywhere and will never accomplish any deed. You imagine that within the atom, within a person who is outwardly in no way remarkable, but is nonetheless chosen, unique, never to be repeated, an immense spiritual life grows up and is then consumed. You suspect that the first person you come across in the street could be this unique, elect, never-to-be-repeated being. Innumerable contradictory suppositions, which seem to confirm, in a new key, some eternal elusive truth. One's secret dreams. Tell me your secret dreams, and I will tell you who you are. Very well, I shall attempt to tell, but will you hear me? All is smoothly walled in, not a single bubble can penetrate life's surface. An atom, a single point, a deaf-mute genius and beneath his feet the deep layer of subsoil, life's essence, the coal formed of rotted epochs. The world record for loneliness. So answer, tell, what do you dream of in there, in the very depths of your loneliness?

The history of my soul and the history of the world. They are bound together like life and dream. They have grown up together and merged into one another. Behind them, like the painted backdrop to a tragic drama, stands contemporary life. Embracing, interweaving and flowing together, they are borne away into nothingness with the terrifying speed of darkness, which light pursues lazily, not even attempting to catch up.

Fanfares. Morning. A magnificent theatre curtain. Of course, there is no curtain. But the desire for firmness, for solidity is so powerful that I can feel its heavy woven silk. From dawn to dusk blue-eyed craftswomen have woven it. One was to be married . . . It was not woven anywhere. Pass on. Pass on.

A dead rat lies in the waste bucket, amid cigarette ends tipped out of an ashtray, alongside the cotton wool with which a fiancée washed herself for the last time. The rat was wrapped up in a scrap of newspaper, but in the bucket the newspaper has unfurled and risen to the surface – you can still read scraps of the day-before-yesterday's news. Two days ago these were still news, the cigarette end still smoked in someone's mouth, the rat was alive, the virgin's hymen still intact. Now all of this, mixed up together, colours fading, vanishing, obliterated, flies off into nothingness, is borne away with the terrifying speed of darkness, after which light moves with the slowness of a tortoise, not even attempting to catch up.

The blade from a safety razor, attaching itself to a swollen cigarette end, reflects through the detritus a rainbow ray of sunlight, directs it on to the rat's face. It is grinning, there is pus on the sharp points of its teeth. How did it happen that an old, experienced, careful, God-fearing rat dropped its guard and ate the poison? How could a minister, a signatory of the Treaty of Versailles, be discovered embezzling in his old age because of a slut? Cutting an impressive appearance, with his hard starched collar, his Commandeur's cross,[4] 'Germany must pay' – and in affirmation of this axiom his firm signature on the historic parchment, signed with the historic gold fountain pen. And then the girl, stockings, pretty knees, her warm tender breath, her warm pink vagina – and then no more Treaty of Versailles, no more Commandeur's cross – a disgraced old man lies dying on a prison bunk. The ugly, respectable widow, wrapped in her mourning garb, departing for ever for the provinces, his children embarrassed by their father's name, his fellow senators shaking their bald heads in sad disapproval. Yet the instigator of all this ridiculous mess has already left it all behind, left it behind long ago, already at the moment when the bedroom door closed behind him, the key turned, and the past disappeared, and there remained only the girl on the wide bed, the

false promissory note, ecstasy, ignominy, death. Now, his fate
left behind him, he floats in frozen space, while the eternal
darkness ruffles the folds of his fussy, outdated frock coat.
Before him hurtle cigarette ends and historic treaties, combed-
out hairs and lacklustre great ideas, and behind him more hairs,
treaties, cigarette ends, ideas, gobs of spit. If the darkness
finally transports him to the foot of His throne, he will not say
to God, 'Germany must pay.' 'O thou, last love . . .'[5] – he will
mumble, in his confusion.

Intercourse with a dead girl. The body quite soft, only coolish,
as after a swim. A feeling of tension, of particular pleasure.
She lay as if sleeping. I did not harm her. On the contrary, for
these few trembling minutes life carried on around her, if not
for her. A star was fading in the window, the last jasmine flow-
ered. The semen dribbled out again, I wiped it away with my
handkerchief. I lit a cigarette from a big wax candle. Pass on.
Pass on.

You bore away my light, leaving me in darkness. All the
loveliness in the world was concentrated in you alone, completely and utterly. And I felt an unbearable pity at the thought
of you becoming old, ill, ugly, of you sadly dying, and I would
not be there with you, would not lie to you that you would get
better, would not hold your hand. I ought to have been
glad that at least I would not have to endure this torture. At
the same time it was here that the main thing, perhaps the
sole thing that constituted love was to be found. The feeling
of horror at this thought alone was the star which guided
my life. You are now long gone, yet the star still shines in my
window.

I am in a forest. The terrible, fairytale, snow-bound landscape of a disturbed, doomed soul who understands nothing.
Jars holding cancerous growths: intestines, a liver, throat,
womb, breast. Pallid foetuses in greenish spirit. In Petersburg
in 1920 this liquid was sold as a drink – it was known as 'baby
vodka'. Vomit, phlegm, malodorous slime slithering down
guts. Carrion. Human carrion. The striking similarity between
the smell of cheese and the smell of sweaty feet.

Christmas at the North Pole. Radiance and snow. The pure shroud of winter, spread over life.

Evening. July. People walking along the street. People of the thirties of the twentieth century. The sky begins to darken, soon the stars will be out. Stars of the thirties of the twentieth century. One could describe this evening, Paris, the street, the play of light and shade in the feathery sky, the play of terror and hope in a lonely human heart. One could do this with intelligence, talent, imagination, verisimilitude. But to create a miracle is no longer possible – one cannot pass off art's lies as truth. Not long ago this could still be done. But then . . .

What could be done yesterday has become impossible, unrealizable today. One can no longer believe in the appearance of a new Werther,[6] under whose influence the crack of the pistol shots of ecstatic suicides would ring out across the whole of Europe. One cannot imagine a slim book of verses causing contemporary man, upon reading it, to wipe away his involuntary tears and look out at the sky, an evening sky such as today's, his heart aching with hope. It is not possible. It is so far from being possible that it is hard to believe that it ever was possible. The new iron laws which have stretched the world taut like a piece of raw leather are impervious to the consolations of art. Moreover, these laws – still obscure, already irreversible – these soullessly just laws, which are either born out of this new world or themselves give birth to it, apply retrospectively: not only is the creation by some genius of a new form of consolation out of the question, it is already well-nigh impossible to find consolation in the old. There are people even now capable of shedding tears over the fate of Anna Karenina. They still stand with their feet upon the same disappearing ground which held the foundations of the theatre where Anna, resting her elbows on the velvet of her box, radiant with beauty and pain, suffered her disgrace.[7] This radiance barely reaches us. It does so in ever so slightly dimmed, slanting rays – perhaps the last reflection of what has been lost, perhaps confirmation that the loss is irrevocable. Soon everything will have faded completely. There will still be the play of wit, of talent, reading as entertainment, which does not oblige us to believe in it and has no power to inspire credence. Something like *The Three Musketeers*. That which Tolstoy himself was the first to discern, that inevitable line, beyond which there is no more consolation through imagined beauty, not a single tear shed over an imaginary fate.

I desire the simplest, most ordinary things. I wish to cry, to be consoled. I wish to look out at the sky, my heart aching with hope. I long to write you a lengthy farewell letter, insulting, heavenly, foul, the tenderest letter in the world. I want to call you an angel and a wretch, to wish you happiness and to bless you, and to say that, wherever you may be, wherever you may vanish to, the myriad particles of my blood which have never forgiven and will never forgive you will be forever bound to you. I want to forget, to rest, get on a train and leave for Russia, drink beer and eat crab on a warm evening in a floating restaurant on the Neva. I long to overcome this nauseating sense of numbness, where people have no faces, words have no sound, nothing has any meaning. I want to shatter it, no matter how. I want simply to draw breath, to gulp down air. But there is no air.

The bright lights and bustle of a café afford a momentary illusion of freedom: by dodging, jumping out of the way, you have evaded catastrophe. For a mere twenty francs you can go off with the pretty, pale-faced girl who slowly walks up and down the pavement and stops, meeting a man's gaze. If you nod to her now the illusion will solidify, grow firmer, will take on the pink complexion of life, like a ghoul after supping on blood, and will be extended for ten, twelve, twenty minutes.

Woman. Flesh. The instrument out of which man elicits the sole note from the divine scale which it is given to him to hear. A light bulb glows under the ceiling. Her face is thrown back on the pillow. I can think that she is my fiancée. Or that I have made a girl drunk and I am raping her, furtively, hurriedly. Or think nothing, trembling, listening, hearing astonishing things, awaiting the arrival of the moment when grief and happiness, good and evil, life and death will intersect in their orbits as during an eclipse, ready to join together as one, when the terrible greenish light of life-and-death, happiness-and-suffering will surge up, from the dead past, from your extinguished eyes.

The history of my soul and the history of the world. They have grown into one another, entangled with one another. Behind them, like the painted backdrop to a tragic drama, is contemporary life. The semen, with nothing to fertilize, ran out again, I wiped it away with my handkerchief. All the same, until it was finished, life still trembled there.

The history of my soul. I want to give flesh to it, but am able only to disembody. I envy the writer polishing his turn of phrase, the artist mixing his palette, the musician immersed in sounds, all these people of that sensitive yet heartless, far- and short-sighted, universally celebrated and utterly needless race, who have yet to become extinct on this earth, and who continue to believe that a plastic reflection of life is a triumph over it. If I only had the talent, that special creative spark in my mind, in my fingers, in my ear, I would need only a bit of invention, a bit of reality, a bit of sadness, a bit of grime, and then smooth it all out, as a child smooths out sand, decorate it with flourishes of style and imagination, as a cake is decorated with icing, and then it is done, and all is saved – the absurdity of life, the pointlessness of suffering, loneliness, torment, nauseating sticky terror, all are transformed by the harmoniousness of art.

I know the worth of this and still I envy them, for blessed are they. Blessed are the sleeping, blessed are the dead. Blessed is the connoisseur before a Rembrandt, with his pious conviction that the play of shadow and light on an old woman's face is an immense triumph, before which the woman herself is a nonentity, a speck, a zero. Blessed are the aesthetes. Blessed are the ballet-lovers. Blessed are those who listen to Stravinsky, and Stravinsky himself. Blessed are the shades of a world in the process of vanishing, slumbering through its final false, saccharine dreams, which for so long have lulled humanity. Leaving, already gone from life, they take away with them an enormous imagined wealth. What will we be left with?

The conviction that the old woman is infinitely more

significant than Rembrandt. Uncertainty as to what we are to do with this old woman. A painful urge to save and comfort her. The clear awareness that it is impossible to save or comfort anyone. The feeling that it is only by making one's way through a chaos of contradictions that one may arrive at the truth. That only through distortion can one draw near. That reality itself is unreliable: a photograph lies, and any document is deliberately falsified. That anything measured, classical, comfortable is impossible, unthinkable. That like an eel a sense of proportion slips from the hands of him who tries to seize it, and that this elusiveness is the last creative quality left to him. That when he finally does catch it, he discovers that what he is holding in his hands is vulgarity. 'In his arms the child lay dead.'[8] That every-one around him holds a dead child in their arms. That for him who would make his way through the chaos of contradictions to reach eternal truth, or perhaps only its pale reflection, there remains only one route: like an acrobat on a tightrope, to pass above life, across an ugly, tattered, contradictory shorthand account of life.

Photographs lie. Human documents are falsified. After losing my way in the Polizei-Präsidium building in Berlin, I happened upon that corridor. Its walls were hung with photographs, sev-eral dozen of them, all depicting the same thing: suicides and murder victims, as the police had found them. A young German hanging from his braces, the shoes he has taken off tidily set down beside the overturned chair. An old woman with a large blot on her breast in the shape of a cockerel – the clotted blood from her slit throat. A fat, naked prostitute with her stomach ripped open. An artist who had shot himself out of hunger or unhappy love, or from both at once. Below the shattered skull an extravagant artist's cravat, next to him on an easel various branches and clouds, the unfinished daubings of holy art. Star-ing eyes, bitten tongues, repellent poses, repulsive wounds – taken all together they become monotonous, academic, not shocking in the least. Not one bit of intestine slithering from ripped-open guts, not one grimace, not a single bruise has escaped the camera lens, but the most essential thing has escaped, is gone. I look at them and see nothing which might move me, which might provoke a tremor in my soul. I make an effort, but nothing happens. And then suddenly the thought that *you* are living and breathing here on this earth, and like a living thing the memory of your lovely, pitiless face.

And then suddenly I see and hear everything, all the misery, all the torment, all the fruitless prayers, all the final words. The hoarse cries of the old woman with her throat cut, the prostitute, her guts spilling out, fighting off her sadistic killer, and – as if it were myself – the talentless, starving artist dying. A lamp glowing. The dawn breaking. The tick of an alarm clock. The hands approaching five. Uncertain, then making up his mind, moistening his lips. Gripping the revolver awkwardly in his sweaty palm. The icy touch of the barrel against his feverish brow. The hate he feels for those who go on living, and the envy.

I would like to step out on to the seashore, to lie down on the sand, to close my eyes and feel the breath of God upon my face. I would like to begin from afar, with the blue dress, with our argument, the foggy winter's day. 'Over Georgia's hills nocturnal darkness lay'[9] – with words more or less like these I would like to begin to talk to life.

Life no longer understands this language. The soul has not yet learned another. Thus harmony painfully dies away inside the soul. Perhaps, when it is quite dead, and is cast off like a dried-up scab, the soul will once again feel primordially free. But the transition is slow and painful. The soul is in terror. It feels that one after another all those things which sustained life in it are withering away. That it is itself withering away. It cannot keep silent and yet it has lost the ability to speak. It mutters spasmodically like a deaf-mute, grimacing hideously. 'Over Georgia's hills nocturnal darkness lay' – it wants to pronounce, resoundingly, triumphantly, glorifying the Creator and itself. And yet, with a feeling of disgust bordering on enjoyment, it mouths some obscene filth scrawled on the metaphysical fence, some *'dyr bu shchyl ubeshchur'*.[10]

The blue dress, the argument, the foggy winter's day. A thousand other dresses, arguments, days. A thousand sensations running uncontrollably through the soul of every person. A small number that have become common currency and have found their way into literature, into public use, into conversation. And the innumerable remainder, which have yet to find literary expression, which belong still with the inchoate foetal world of the nucleus. But this does not make them any less crass, these thousands of unembodied banalities, patiently awaiting their Tolstoy. The suspicion that art, creation, as it is generally understood, is nothing other than the pursuit of one new banality after another. The suspicion that the harmony for which it strives is nothing other than some kind of superior banality. The suspicion that the soul's true path lies somewhere to the side, twisting corkscrew-like through the all-encompassing hideousness of the world.

I want to speak of my soul in strong, simple words. I know that there are no such words. I want to tell of my love for you, of my dying, of my death, of how a cross was placed over my grave and how time and the worms turned this cross to dust. I want to pick up a handful of this dust, look up at the sky for the last time and with a feeling of release blow upon my palm. I want many things, all equally unrealizable – to breathe in once again the scent of the hair at the nape of your neck and once again elicit from rhythmical chaos that unique rhythm which, like the detonation that brings down a rock face, will cause the all-encompassing hideousness of the world to collapse. I wish to talk about a man, lying on an unmade bed, and thinking, thinking, thinking, how to save himself, how to put things right, and unable to think of a way. About how he dozed off, and then awoke, and suddenly recalled how he had said aloud, as if talking about something unrelated, 'He was no Caesar. All he had was this love. But it held everything within it – power, the crown, immortality. And now it has collapsed, he is stripped of his honour, of his rank.' I want to explain in strong, simple words a multitude of unique, miraculous things – the blue dress, the argument, the foggy winter's day. And I want to warn the world against a terrible enemy – pity. I want to cry out so that all should hear me: people, brothers, take yourselves firmly in hand and swear that you will be pitiless towards one another. Otherwise pity, the greatest enemy of order, will attack and tear everything apart.

For the last time I want to summon out of the emptiness your face, your body, your tenderness, your cruelty, to gather up what is left of you and me, intermingled and decayed to dust, to hold it like a handful of ashes in my palm, and with a feeling of release to blow on it. But pity once more confuses everything, once more prevents me. Once again I recall the fog of a strange city. A beggar turns the handle of a barrel-organ, a monkey, trembling from the cold, goes around those idly watching with a saucer. They, from beneath umbrellas, morose, unwillingly toss him a few coppers. Will they have enough for the night, to find shelter, holding one another till morning . . .

I imagined this in the middle of a noisy ball – to the accompaniment of champagne, music, laughter, the rustle of silk, the smell of perfume. It was one of your happiest days. You were radiant with youth, loveliness, cruelty. You were joyful, you exulted over life. I looked at you, smiling, surrounded by people. And I saw the monkey, the fog, umbrellas, loneliness, poverty. And, overcome by a burning sense of pity, as by unbearable brightness, I lowered my eyes.

A shudder, evoking pity. A shudder which turns unavoidably into desire for revenge. For a deaf child, for senseless existence, for humiliations, for the holes in the soles of one's shoes. To take revenge on the comfortable world, the pretext is irrelevant. 'Anyone who has a heart' knows this. This almost mechanical transition from a confused feeling of pity to 'just you wait!', itself another form of impotence. Even the little creatures were disturbed, whispered among themselves, composed a lengthy 'protest pamphlet', 'You, Tormentors of Cats'. Asked whether they could not print it in the papers, so that everybody might read it.

The little creatures were inseparable from us. They ate from our plates and slept in our bed. The most notable of them were the two Swingeroos.

Green Eyes Swingeroo was good-natured, affectionate, never

harmed anyone. Grey Eyes, when he had grown up, turned out to have a strong character. He might even bite on occasion. We found them under a bench on the metro, in an empty date box. There was a note pinned on to the box: 'Swingeroos, otherwise Swingers, otherwise Swinglets. Australian origin. Need to be loved, fed and taken for walks in the Bois de Boulogne.'

There were other little creatures: Sweety, Toughy, Frowler, Chinesey, silly Tsutik, who would always make the same reply to any question, 'Yes indeed, Tsutik.' There was old Ruffiette, with her little duck's tail, uncouth in appearance, but with a heart of gold. Somewhere out of the way, shunned by the general company, inspiring hostility and fear, lurked gloomy von Klopp.

The little creatures had their own way of life, their own habits, philosophy, code of honour and outlook on life. They had their own animal country, whose borders, as by the ocean, were washed by dream. It was a substantial country and still not fully explored. It was known that in the south there dwelled camels, a white horse would go to them on Fridays to wash them and cut their hair. In the far north it was forever Christmas, there was always a candle-lit Christmas tree.

The little creatures spoke in a mixed-up language. They had some of their own Australian words, ordinary words that had been altered somewhat. In letters they would address one another as 'Your Wartship' and would write on the envelope 'To His Legcellency'. They loved dances, ice cream, walks, silk ribbons, holidays, birthdays. That is how they looked on life: What is a year? Three hundred and sixty-five birthdays. And a month? Thirty birthdays.

They were fine little creatures. They tried, to the best of their abilities, to make our life beautiful. They never asked for ice creams when they knew we had no money. Even when they were feeling very sad, they would dance and celebrate birthdays. They would turn away and try not to listen whenever they heard anything bad. 'Little creatures, little creatures,' the terrible von Klopp would whisper to them from his hole in the evenings, 'life is nearly over, winter is coming. You will be covered in snow, you will freeze, you will die, little

creatures – you, who love life so.' But they would huddle up
closer to one another, cover their ears, and calmly, gravely,
answer, 'That doesn't matter a bite to us.'

A man wanders about the streets, thinking different things,
looking into other people's windows. His imagination oper-
ates in spite of him. He doesn't notice its operation. He sits in
a café, drinks beer and reads the paper. Proceedings from the
Chambre des députés. Car purchase by instalments. He dozes
off, visited by absurd dreams. Ink spilled on the tablecloth. A
fish swimming past – the ink has vanished. He needs to lock a
door, but the key does not fit. English public opinion. A
cyclone. The fish turns out to be the key, that is why it didn't
fit. He wakes suddenly. There is no fish, no public opinion.
    Sitting in a café, drifting about the streets, looking into
other people's windows is nonetheless a better form of consolation than Anna Karenina or some Madame Bovary. To
follow a pair of lovers who huddle together over undrunk coffee, then wander about the streets, then eventually, with a
wary look around them, go into a cheap hotel, this is the equal
of, if not even superior to, the most perfect love poetry. 'There
steps a tiny foot, and golden tresses swirl.'[11] There it is, the tiny
foot, trotting along the asphalt of a Montmartre pavement,
and there a glimpse of the golden tresses, vanishing behind the
glass door of the hotel. This is today, this is a trembling, fleeting moment in my inimitable life – naturally, there is no
possible comparison – this is superior to all the poetry ever
written. The tripping of the foot has fallen silent, the tresses
have vanished behind the door. Let us wait and stay awhile. A
light comes on in a ground-floor window, there is a tug at the
curtain.
    The footman gets a one-franc tip and leaves them alone. A
light bulb beneath the ceiling, garish wallpaper, a white enamel
bidet. Perhaps this is their first time. Perhaps this is the most
blissful love the world has known. Perhaps this is what Napoleon fought for and what the *Titanic* sank for, so that on this
evening these two might lie beside one another on the bed. On
top of the blanket, on top of the stiff, marble sheet, the hasty,

awkward, immortal embrace. Her knees in their fallen-down stockings spread wide apart; hair dishevelled on the pillow, her face delightfully contorted. Oh, don't stop, don't stop. Faster, faster.

Wait. Do you know what this is? It is our inimitable life. Some day, a hundred years from now, someone will write a poem about us, though there will be nothing in it but sonorous rhymes and lies. The truth is here. The truth is this day, this hour, this fleeting moment. No one has ever parted your knees, and now in the bright light, on the white ironed sheet, I unceremoniously push them apart. You feel shame and pain. Each drop of your pain and shame enters fully into my swooning triumph.

Who are they, these two? Does it really matter? They do not exist. There is only a radiance, trembling on the outside, until it is over. Only tension, circling, burning-up, the blissful regeneration of the hidden meaning of life. The icy summit of earthly delight, illuminated by a flicker of light. Spermatic cords, testicles, the torn hymen, cherry blossom, knees pushed apart, swooning, stars, saliva, the sheet, trembling veins, shattering, shattering, uh . . . uh . . . uh . . . The sole note attainable by man, its terrifying sound. Oh, don't stop, don't stop, faster, faster. The last shudders. Warm semen, flowing towards the contracting, pulsating womb. Desire has described a full circle along a spiral thrust deep into eternity and returned, to emptiness. 'It was so marvellous that it surely cannot end with death,'[12] wrote the young Tolstoy after his wedding night.

In a café sits a man. An ordinary little man. One of those about whom after an accident people write: ten killed, twenty-six injured. Not a company director, not an inventor, not Lindberg, not Chaplin, not Montherlant.[13] He has read the paper and now knows the prevailing mood of English public opinion. He has finished his coffee and calls the waiter to settle his bill. Distractedly he thinks about what to do next – whether to go to the cinema or to save the money for a lottery ticket. He is calm, peacefully disposed, he sleeps, dreams absurd nonsense. And suddenly before him he sees the black hole of his loneliness. His heart ceases to beat, his lungs refuse to breathe. Torment, close to exaltation.

The atom is motionless. It sleeps. All is smoothly walled in, not a single bubble can penetrate life's surface. But if we were to dig into it, to stir its dormant heart. Catch hold of it, shake it, split it apart. Send a million volts through the soul, then plunge it into ice. To love someone more than oneself, and then to see the black hole of one's solitude, the icy black hole.

A man, a little man, a nonentity distractedly looks in front of him. He sees black emptiness, and in it, like a brief lightning flash, the impenetrable essence of life. A thousand nameless, unanswered questions, illuminated for an instant by a flash of light and immediately engulfed in darkness.

Trembling, exhausted, the consciousness seeks an answer. There is no answer to anything. Life poses questions and fails to answer them. Love poses . . . God posed a question to man – through man – but gave no answer. And man, doomed only to ask, unable to answer any question. An answer – the eternal synonym for failure. How many glorious questions have been asked throughout the history of mankind, and have any of them been answered? . . .

The earth's two billion inhabitants. Each of them formed of his own painful, unique, gratuitous, tedious complexity. Each, like the atom in its nucleus, enclosed in the impenetrable armour of his loneliness. Two billion inhabitants on earth – two billion exceptions to the rule. But the rule all the same. All repellent. All unhappy. No one capable of changing, of comprehending anything. My brother Goethe, my brother concierge, neither of you knows what you create and what life creates out of you.

A point, an atom, through which millions of volts pass. Very soon they will split it apart. Very soon inert immobility will turn into a terrifying explosive force. Soon, very soon. The earth has already shuddered. The foundations of the Eiffel Tower have already begun to creak. The turbid currents of the simoom are already swirling in the desert. Ships sink on the ocean. Trains plunge down embankments. Everything is ripped apart, falling, melting, crumbling into dust – Paris, this street, time, your image, my love.

A man, a little man, a nonentity sits with a fixed gaze. The waiter approaches him, hands him his change. The man takes a breath, stands up. He lights a cigarette, walks along the street. His heart has not yet exploded – as before it beats beneath his breast. Universal hideousness has not collapsed – like a cliff face, it holds up the world as before.

The blue dress, the argument, the foggy winter's day. The desire to speak, an urge to sing – of your love, of your soul. To let go, to pour out your heart, in strong, simple words, words which do not exist . . .

How did our love begin? Banally, of course. Like all that is beautiful, it had a banal beginning. There is probably no sense in protesting about this. Probably there was and is only one way for everyone – like an acrobat across a tightrope, to travel above life, passing through an obscure awareness of life. That obscure awareness that emerges in ultimate physical intimacy, ultimate inaccessibility, heart-rending tenderness, in the loss of all this for ever, for always. The light of dawn in the window. Desire has described a full circle and returned to earth. A child is conceived. What need is there for a child? There is no immortality. There cannot not be immortality. What need have I of immortality, if I am so alone?

The light of dawn in the window. Upon the crumpled sheet, in my arms, all the innocent delight of the world and the troubled question of what we have done to it. It is divine, inhuman. What can man do with its heartless radiance? Man is wrinkles, bags beneath the eyes, lime in the soul, in the blood, man is, first and foremost, doubt in his divine right to commit evil. 'Man begins with sorrow,'[14] as a certain poet said. Who would argue? Man begins with sorrow. Life begins tomorrow.[15] The Volga flows into the Caspian Sea. *Dyr bu shchyl ubeshchur.*

This day, this hour, this passing minute. Thousands of such days and minutes, identical, unique. This feathery Parisian sunset, fading as I watch. Thousands of such sunsets, over the present, over the future, over centuries past. Thousands of eyes, gazing with the same hope at the same dazzling emptiness. The everlasting sigh of earthly delight: I am waning, I am fading, I am no more. 'Over Georgia's hills nocturnal darkness lay.' Just as it lies here over the hill of Montmartre. Over the rooftops, over the crossroads, over a café sign, over the semicircle of a *pissoir*, where, with the same fearsome din as in the river Aragva, the water roars.[16]

Opposite the *pissoir* is a bench. Upon the bench sits an old man in rags. He smokes a cigarette end picked up from the pavement. His look is indifferent, dreamy. But this is a pretence. Alert, his gaze follows anybody who enters that section of the *pissoir* where a hunk of bread, swollen with urine, lies on a piece of newspaper. Here a worker with a fat neck unbuttons his fly as he walks. His legs wide apart, he urinates over the bread. A blissful tremor in the soul of the louse-ridden old wreck. Soon, with a glance over his shoulder, hastily folding over the wet newspaper, on which scraps of yesterday's news are still legible, he will take the bread home. Soon, soon, chomping, swallowing it down with red wine, picturing to the last detail the worker with the fat neck, a boy in yellow shoes, everybody, everybody who soaked this half-kilo of *gros pain* with their acrid, warm urine. Soon, soon. Torment, close to exaltation, the blissful tremor. As he departs he mutters something to himself. Perhaps his deaf-mute soul is struggling to mouth its own version of 'Over Georgia's hills . . .'

Sunsets, thousands of sunsets. Over Russia, over America, over the future, over centuries past. The wounded Pushkin rests on his elbow in the snow and on to his face streams the red sunset. Sunset in the morgue, in the operating theatre, over the ocean, over the Alps, in the prison-camp latrine made of wooden boards: every tinge of yellow and brown spattered on the walls, the rich stench on top of the fresh breeze coming through cracks between the boards. A new inmate, a rosy-cheeked boy, holding the door closed with one hand, hurriedly masturbates with the other. Panting, stifling a cry, he comes. Half a glassful, covering his fingers with sticky warmth, scattering the flies, spills into the brown sludge. The boy's face turns grey. He slowly pulls up his trousers. He still did not manage to conjure up the face of the fiancée left behind in his village. No doubt he will die in the war, perhaps this very year.

Sunset over the Temple.[17] Sunset over the Lubyanka.[18] Sunset on the day war was declared and on Armistice Day, when everybody danced, everybody was drunk, and no one heard the voice saying, 'Woe to the victors.' Sunset in the room where once we lived together, where your blue dress once lay on this chair.

The early Petersburg sunset has long since faded. Akaky Akakievich makes his way from his work to the Obukhov Bridge. Has his overcoat already been stolen? Or is he still only dreaming of a new overcoat?[19] A lost Russian stands in an unfamiliar street, before someone else's window, and his masturbatory consciousness imagines every sigh, every shudder, every crease of the sheet, every pulsating vein. Has the woman already deceived him, already disappeared in the feathery evening sky? Does it matter?

The sunset has long since faded. Work has long since finished. In a garret beside the Obukhov Bridge warm beer gurgles, tobacco smoke swirls. 'He was a titular counsellor, she was a general's daughter,'[20] sigh the insinuating, tender, velvety notes of a guitar. Here is nurtured the myth of the clerk in his garret, a myth that serves as self-defence and as a counterweight to the myth of Pushkinian lucidity. This myth is sulphuric acid, the secret dream that will disfigure, will corrode, will corrupt such lucidity.

Akaky Akakievich draws his salary, copies out documents, saves up money for his overcoat, dines and drinks tea. But this is mere surface, dream, debris, infinitely remote from the essence of things. This dot, this soul is immobile and so minute that it is invisible even to the most powerful microscope. But within it, beneath the impenetrable nucleus of isolation, is a limitless monstrous complexity, a terrible explosive force, secret dreams which are as corrosive as sulphuric acid. The atom is immobile. It is soundly sleeping. It dreams of work and the Obukhov Bridge. But if we were to stir it, grasp it, split it apart ...

The general's daughter, Psyche, the little angel, all dressed in muslin, runs into His Excellency's office, and the ink-rat, the little man, the nonentity, the fawning shadow in a second-hand frock coat executes a low bow before her. Nothing more. Psyche murmurs, '*Bonjour, Papa,*' kisses the general's ruddy cheek, flashes a smile; her muslin rustles and she flits out. And nobody knows, nobody guesses what kind of reality this is, or dream, or vanity ...

With his head befogged by the boredom of life and by beer, accompanied by the guitar's insinuating clamour, Akaky Akakievich leaves behind earthly vanity and superficiality and plunges down to the essence of things. His secret yearnings envelop the image of Psyche, and little by little his avid thought transforms into her longed-for flesh. The barriers which are so insurmountable by day fall away of their own accord. Silently he slips through the sleeping city, enters unnoticed into His Excellency's dark chambers, like a noiseless shadow, between the mirrors and statues, over the parquet and rugs, he makes his way towards the little angel's own bedchamber. He opens the door, stands on the threshold and sees 'paradise, such as is not found even in Heaven'.[21] Sees her petticoats strewn over the armchair, sees her sleeping face upon the pillow, sees the little bench upon which she rests her foot in the mornings, while she puts on her snow-white stocking. He was a titular counsellor, she was a general's daughter. And now ... Nothing, nothing, silence.

To the guitar's clamorous accompaniment, befogged by his secret yearnings, through his insistent, inflamed imagination, which for long hours, over long years has been constantly directed at the same point, he brings Psyche to life, has her come herself to his garret, lie down on his bed. And she arrives, lies down, lifts up her muslin skirts, opens her satin-smooth legs. He was a titular counsellor, and she a general's daughter. On meeting her he bowed to her fawningly, not daring to raise his eyes from his patched boots. And now, her legs wide apart, smiling her little angel's innocent smile, she waits submissively, for him to enjoy her to his heart's content, shattering, shattering.

'Stand firm, city of Peter, and resplendent,'[22] fervently exclaims Pushkin, in spite of his forebodings, and just about every society beauty appears in his 'Don Juan list'.[23] 'Nothing, nothing, silence,' murmurs Gogol, rolling his eyes in the darkness as he masturbates beneath the cold sheet.

'Stand firm, resplendent.' On the surface of life, in the clear, albeit setting, rays of the sun, so it would seem. Here is Paris still standing even now. On this fine summer evening it is indeed splendid. The chestnut trees, automobiles, *midinettes* in short summer dresses. The magic of headlamps flashing by around the most grotesque statues in the world. The scatter of flowers on stalls. Sacré-Cœur against the darkening sky. In spite of a sense of foreboding, the soul is hungry for life. There it is, among the light feathery clouds. 'I am waning, I am fading, I am no more.' And like the river Aragva, triumphantly, sadly, muted, the water in the *pissoir* roars.

But the sunset quickly fades, and nocturnal darkness yet more swiftly overwhelms man. It carries him away to such depths that, returning to the surface, he no longer recognizes it. But he will not return. In the black contentment into which his soul, corkscrew-like, twists itself ever deeper, what need has it for that already shaken steadfastness and disfigured beauty? Peter will be disembowelled from his grave and stood with a cigarette end in his mouth against the wall of the Peter and Paul Cathedral while the Red guards laugh at him, and nothing will happen, the cathedral will not fall down. D'Anthès will murder Pushkin, and Ivan Sergeyevich Turgenev will most politely shake his hand and nothing will happen, his hand will not drop off.[24] And of what concern is all that to us, here, down at the very bottom of our souls? Our deaf-mute souls, all indistinguishable, all different, have sensed a common goal and, corkscrew-like, through superficial, visible reality, are twisting, twisting down towards it. Our revolting, wretched, lonely souls have fused together into one and, corkscrew-like, twisting through the overwhelming hideousness of the world, struggle on towards God.

On meeting a man's gaze, the pretty, pale-faced girl walks more slowly. If you explain to her that you don't like to do it in stockings, she will gladly wash her feet in the expectation of a bit more money. Swollen slightly from the hot water, the toe-nails cut short, naive, unused to being looked at, kissed, having someone's forehead pressed against them – the feet of a street whore will turn into the pretty little feet of Psyche.

Your heart ceases to beat. Your lungs refuse to draw breath. A snow-white stocking is removed from the leg of Psyche. As slowly, slowly her knee, ankle, delicate childlike heel are exposed, years pass. As her toes are revealed an eternity has gone by. And now everything is complete. Nothing more to wait for, nothing to dream of, nothing to live for. Nothing more exists. Nothing but the naked feet of your little angel pressed against your deadened lips, and God, your only witness. He was a titular counsellor, she was a general's daughter. And now, and now . . .

The sheet is as cold as ice. Dimly night gleams in the window. His sharp, bird-like profile is thrown back among the pillows. Oh, don't stop, don't stop, faster, faster. Everything he longed for is his, but his soul is still not fully sated and trembles while it has not yet had its fill. While there is still time, while the night is not yet over, until the cock has crowed and while the atom, trembling, has yet to shatter into myriads of particles, what could he yet do? How to penetrate still deeper into this triumph, into the essence of things, how to dig it open, grasp it, split it apart? Wait, Psyche, stay, my sweet. Do you think that is all? The apogee, the end, the limit? No, you cannot deceive us.

Silence and night. Her naked child's heels pressed against deadened lips. They smell of innocence, tenderness, rose water. But no, no – you cannot deceive us. Corkscrew-like, twisting, through superficial, visible reality, insatiable passion moves, through the angelic flesh of its dream, in delirious pursuit of its own bloody, shameful essence. Tell me, beneath the innocence and rose water, what do your white feet smell of, Psyche? In the very essence of things what do they smell of, tell me? They smell the same as mine, my angel, the same as mine, my sweet. You cannot deceive me, no!

And Psyche knows it is impossible to deceive him. Her feet tremble in his tenacious, hungry palms, and, as they tremble, they release the uttermost thing that is in her – the most secret, the most treasured, since it is the most shameful: the slightest, most ephemeral smell, but which nonetheless no charms, no innocence, no social inequality can destroy. The same as mine, my sweet, the same as my plebeian feet, my angel, little schoolgirl, aristocrat. So, between us there is no difference of any kind and you have no reason to recoil from me; I kissed your ladylike feet, I gave up my soul for them, so now you bend down, you kiss my festering socks. 'He was a titular counsellor, she was a general's daughter . . .' And what shall I do with you now, Psyche? Kill you? What's the difference – even dead you will come to me now.

Across an unfamiliar city a lost man makes his way. Emptiness, like the incoming tide, gradually overwhelms him. He does not resist it. As he walks away, he mutters to himself: Pushkin's Russia, why have you deceived us? Pushkin's Russia, why have you betrayed us?

Silence and night. Total silence, absolute night. The thought that all is coming to an end, once and for all, fills the man with quiet triumph. He foresees, he doubtless knows, that this is not the case. But while this second continues, he does not wish to resist. No longer the property of life, not yet in the clutches of emptiness, he allows himself to be lulled, as by music or by inrushing waves, by this obscure, melodious lie.

No longer the property of life, not yet in the clutches of emptiness . . . At the very limit. Swinging on a spider's thread. The entire weight of the world hangs on him, but he knows that, while this second lasts, the thread will not break, it will hold it all. He gazes at a single point, an infinitely minute point, but while this second lasts, life's entire essence is concentrated there. A single point, an atom, millions of volts flowing through

him and shattering, shattering, melting down the nucleus of
solitude.

. . . The spiral was thrust deep into eternity. Through it everything flew by: cigarette ends, sunsets, immortal verses, nail
clippings, dirt from under those nails. Universal ideas, blood
spilt for them, the blood of murder and copulation, haemorrhoi-
dal blood, blood from putrid sores. Cherry trees, stars,
innocence, sewage pipes, cancerous growths, promises of bliss,
irony, alpine snow. The minister who signed the Treaty of Versailles flying by, singing 'Germany must pay', pus solidified on
his sharp teeth, rat poison showing in his stomach. In pursuit of
his overcoat, Akaky Akakievich flying by, with his bird-like profile, wearing canvas underpants stained with an onanist's semen.
All hopes, all spasms, all pity, all pitilessness, all bodily fluids,
all malodorous flesh, every mute triumph . . . And a thousand
other things. Tennis in white shirts and bathing in the Crimea,
the dream of the prisoner in a Siberian camp eaten
alive by lice. The different types of lice: clothes lice, head lice,
the special type of lice that burrow under the skin and can be
removed only by Politan. Politan, slimming pills, contraceptive
pills, ice floes on the Neva, sunset on the Lido and all
the descriptions of sunsets and ice floes in the useless books of
the classics of literature. In the ceaseless kaleidoscopic stream
glimpses of the blue dress, the argument, the foggy winter's day.
The spiral thrust deep into eternity. Shattered, fragmented, in
meltdown, universal hideousness, contracting, pulsating, racing
through it. At the very edge, at the end-point, all again merged
into one. Through the whirling, tremor and brilliance, slowly
clarifying, features now visible. The meaning of life? God? No,
as before, treasured, heartless, for ever lost – your face.

If the little creatures only knew what an important official
letter I am using their Australian language for, they would be
so proud. Even long after my death, they would still be celebrating, dancing, and clapping their hands.

'Your Legcellency Mr Commissar. Of my own free will, not
entirely sober of mind, yet with my memory fully intact, my
birthday celebrations are about to end. Myself a constituent
part of universal hideousness, I see no sense in apportioning

any blame to it. I would like to add the following, paraphrasing the words of the newly wedded Tolstoy: "It was so absurd that it surely cannot end with death." It is with astonishing, irresistible lucidity that I now understand this. But of course – switching once again to Australian – that does not matter a bite to your Wartship.'[25]

Klasson and His Soul

BORIS BUTKEVICH

In the spring of twenty-four, the Norwegian steamer *Munken Vendt*[1] called in at Beirut.

Serving aboard this cargo ship was a certain Klasson, a former officer of the Russian Imperial navy; on the Norwegian ship, as on the British one before that, he was considered the only experienced able seaman. He was an old stager. Bars the world over, from, say, Ienosu in Nagasaki to Antwerp's Schippersstraat, were well known to him. But of his officer's service, and of the fact that he was married, none of his fellow sailors ever learned from him.

On 18 May, in the afternoon, Klasson went ashore. He didn't announce this publicly, as others would, just as he didn't ask for leave; he left without a word, of his own volition.

As though half-asleep, he sat for a while smoking in the boatswain's deck chair, having kicked off his shoes and stretched out lazily, barefooted. He then went for a smoke on the upper deck and spat into the water. After this he was spotted at the deck ledge, wearing blue trousers and an old jacket over his striped vest, as he calmly descended the ship's ladder and, in a skiff belonging to an Arab boatman, headed ashore.

The skiff moored, as it was charged, at the customhouse. Climbing up the stone steps, Klasson passed through the customs building, and on this clear Levantine spring day lost himself among the crowded, narrow little streets of old Beirut . . .

He walked down canopied side streets, past cobblers, hatters, past jewellers and barbers; he passed stalls selling confections and the lavatories near the mosques. He felt surprisingly serene and not in the least bothered by the cries of the Eastern streets and the braying of donkeys.

Thus instinctively did he approach a maze of blind alleys housing brothels. In one spot, pipe in mouth, he paused to observe: the doors of a yellow two-storey villa open to the street, and the street, which curved round towards a dead end, entirely deserted at this hot hour. Through the open doors, by the entrance, he could see two women sitting on a rug, throwing dice and moving figures around a chessboard. The woman sitting on the left was fully in the sun: the sunlight adorned her inclined face with affecting, feminine shadows. She leaned over pensively, resting on her outstretched arm, her bracelets dangling about her short wrist. Her full, powerful legs, covered by grey silk stockings, were bared a quarter above the knee; necklaces, coins jangled on her breast. An alarming pleasure stirred in Klasson's chest: some blessed fear, a premonition – but, after spitting, he walked on.

From several doors they called to him. Sometimes he espied the interiors of cool, shaded rooms, carpeted divans or a broad French bed, the whiteness of a quilt as a half-naked woman nodded to him. However, he walked on.

Finally, he halted: the shutters of a window had just been flung open, and from inside the room, almost gloomy in comparison with the street, a young Arab woman beckoned him in. She was wearing blue silk undergarments, was not at all swarthy-looking, and a blue tattoo was just visible on her chin. Again she nodded, and Klasson answered her – he walked along the low railings towards the doors.

He liked this Arab woman. The insouciance of high noon extended also to her. Klasson was in no rush to go. And he, with his hard, clean-shaven face, his gold teeth, the coloured tattoo on his wiry but powerful arms, was to her liking; even his pipe, long and thin, lovingly polished after the previous day's cleaning, piqued her interest.

Klasson gave her money for wine. He lay there smoking in the room while she disappeared. Just lay there smoking. For so rarely is a man truly free, truly happy; then will he cease to ponder happiness . . .

Probably he drank more than she did – but he did not get drunk. On the contrary. She grew merrier, and her Arab reserve vanished; having stripped naked, she danced before him, singing gutturally as much to herself as to him. While he, looking on, sipped from his glass.

By the time he left, it had already grown dark; the stars were twinkling in the mild Levantine evening. Through the street lights, Klasson made his way towards the sea. He came out into the street running along the embankment, crossed over to the cement barrier and got up on to the embankment itself; the moon lit up the pavement, the sea and the wet pebbles on the shore.

Just then, two women walked past, laughing and talking like European women. Having sated himself with the moonlit sea, Klasson strolled on. The two women had paused on the busy evening footpath.

'Algy,' said the taller one, 'you might have donned a cunning disguise, but we've found you out! Good evening, you raffish waif . . .'

'Good evening, Algy,' repeated the other.

Klasson removes the pipe from his mouth: he has absolutely no idea who they are, has never seen them before in his life, and although he speaks English – who the devil is Algy?

'I see! Pretending that you don't know us, that you're someone else. Come off it! We're taking you prisoner. There'll be no limit to Uncle Austin's surprise – have you any idea, you poor wretch, how often he thinks about you! . . .'

Hereupon they take him by the arms. Concealing his pipe, Klasson tries to fall in step and listens to the incessant chatter of his escorts. Madgie and Glass: now he knows their names, and he also learns that his dog is with some Danny, that this year's champion at the Baker family's tennis tournament was Captain Glanger from Calcutta, that May has married, that . . . In short, Klasson learned almost everything that a certain Algy Davies would have done from these two loquacious lady friends of his.

They walked for rather a long time, but the talk never let up. And if one were to take into consideration everything that

Klasson had drunk at the Arab dancing girl's, it would come as no shock that his head had begun to spin most queerly and unusually.

The sea and the moon revealed themselves to him along this empty path, already beyond the city limits, and it was then (so Klasson would say) that he began to appreciate his escorts *in a different way*; in an entirely different way the sea basked in the moon's glow, in a different way the sky ascended into the unfathomable astral blue and . . . As though finding himself in a familiar spot, Klasson walked up a short gangway from the shore on to a lone white yacht.

The trio then proceeded down into a rather cramped cabin with soft divans lining the walls, and a long table, at the end of which sat a grey but stalwart-looking gentleman, smiling intently with his youthful, clean-shaven face. In front of him – patience, small Swiss satin playing cards, the backs of which were *already* familiar to Klasson: pink and gold . . .

'We began chatting blithely and drinking tea at this late hour' – thus Klasson would tell the story two years later to two Russians at a bar on Marseilles's Belgian Embankment – 'I ate *my* favourite cucumber sandwiches, although I must admit, *I* never did like them. We talked, and now the two girls were joined by the old man with his recollections of friends and family. And just imagine, in those moments I could picture clearly the countryside of the English Midlands, Tudor houses, lawns, riding to hounds, golf, tea in dingy drawing rooms, tobacco and the savour of aromatic spirits in the deep armchairs of smoking rooms, billiard parties with one of the ladies, Madgie, and so on, and so on, which I do not recall, nor shall I ever, most likely – but which in those small hours were mine.

'I then went up alone on deck. It was beginning to get light; there was a mist over the sea. The high embankment looked bare somehow, cold . . . I went ashore across the narrow gangway.

'I remember feeling cold, so I walked faster. I walked faster, teeth chattering, by now cursing aloud. Then I stopped. In my head – a dreadful hangover, a total loss of memory. How and

where had I passed the time? I dragged myself to the first bar
and began to mend myself. Thence to the ship . . .

'Only after an incident this winter, when one evening a
Negro from the *Atlantic* hit me over the head and I was laid up
in hospital for some time, did I recall this terrible night in
detail. And, upon my word of honour, I do not know where the
real truth lies here . . .'

The Life of Madame Duclos

IRINA ODOEVTSEVA

> ... And before my eyes, still,
> Are your uniform's colours
> And your bright, clear gaze.[1]
>
> Ivan Bunin

In the very first winter following her graduation from the institute, Manechka Litvinova got married to Monsieur Duclos. Manechka was an orphan, and her education and upkeep were paid for by her aunt. The aunt would bring her sweets on visiting days, and Manechka would always curtsey gracefully.

'You're an angel, *ma tante*! *Merci!*'[2]

After the institute, life was quite wonderful, rosy and empty. The aunt was an angel, and Pavlovsk was a paradise.

So, on that morning, when the aunt walked into her room – a white room, covered in pictures of her girlfriends from the institute – pinched her cheek and said: 'Now listen up my dear, I've found you a husband. A Frenchman. A rich one. You'll have your own house in Paris. How about that?' Manechka curtseyed just as gracefully.

'You're an angel, *ma tante*! *Merci!*'

They were married a month later. Monsieur Duclos was fifty, Manechka was seventeen. Monsieur Duclos would come to Russia on business, staying for no more than six weeks at a time. He had seen Manechka at the ballet and had fallen in love.

Manechka was proud. All her girlfriends were jealous. To marry a Frenchman and live in Paris! . . .

Her 'own house' turned out to be an enormous, grey, dark building.

Duclos wasn't a bad man. After lunch, he would blow cigar

smoke in her face. Manechka would cough and turn her pretty little head away, but she would try to smile nonetheless. Her husband was just being playful, after all.

'Ooh, my little savage!' he would say, kissing the back of her head.

Manechka learned very quickly the proper way to behave. The rules were quite different from Petersburg, but she soon earned the respect of the tenants, the concierge and even the baker on the corner.

On Sundays she would go for a stroll in the Bois de Boulogne with her husband. On Thursdays they received guests. The guests were always the same – Raffe, the industrialist, with his wife, and the tall, lanky lawyer Lanet, who was also a wealthy wine merchant. Duclos held the latter in particularly high regard.

The men played cards. The women discussed housekeeping, servants and fashions. Madame Raffe criticized eccentric trends and expensive tastes.

'Take a leaf out of my book,' she would advise Manechka. 'A carefully selected wardrobe will serve you well . . .'

Very occasionally, Duclos would take his wife to the theatre, to the Comédie-Française.

'No, but really,' he would say some six months later, 'I'm not sure I would have behaved like Rodrigo, had I been in his shoes.'

So that was Manechka's life – no disappointments, no excitements, comfortable, calm. The years followed on from one another, all of them empty and easy, all of them much the same. She felt like they were stacking up on top of each other, as neatly and effortlessly as the linen in her mirrored wardrobe.

So that was Manechka's life, although by then she wasn't Manechka any more, she was Madame Gaston Duclos. She never went back to Russia and she even started thinking in French.

She never left Paris. Let alone Paris, she never left Quartier de l'Europe, where their huge house was situated. Her 'own house'.

Then came the Russian Revolution. Monsieur Duclos was indignant.

THE LIFE OF MADAME DUCLOS

'It's a betrayal,' he would say, helping himself to some more gigot. 'Betrayal, pure and simple. They're our allies and they must keep fighting to the end.'

'And what about,' Monsieur Lanet would join in, giving Madame Duclos an angry look, 'what about your Russian shares? Will they pay out?'

Madame Duclos would try to reassure him with an embarrassed smile.

'They'll pay. Of course they'll pay . . .'

This is how it happened.

One morning in February, they awoke side by side in their large copper bed, just like they always did. It was a Sunday. And, as on every Sunday, they were in no rush to get up. They yawned and stretched sleepily, and discussed the pleasures the day ahead would bring.

'We're having duck with chestnuts for lunch, with pineapple cream.'

'And then we'll go to the Bois de Boulogne, and to the cinema in the evening.'

Monsieur Duclos put his arm around his wife's shoulders.

'Are you happy, my little savage?'

'I just hope it doesn't rain.'

She got up, pulled back the silk curtains and opened the shutters. The sky outside was a bright blue.

She smiled and went through to the bathroom.

'Tell them to clean my new suit!' he called after her.

She took a long and thorough bath and then went to the kitchen, where she placed a crystal bowl full of biscuits and two large, steaming mugs of cocoa on to a silver tray. They had three servants, but on Sundays she always served her husband breakfast herself.

She pushed open the bedroom door.

'You know, Gaston, today we—' But she didn't finish.

Monsieur Duclos lay across the bed. His face was blue and contorted. One of his fists was clutching at the covers. His thin, hairy legs were dangling off the bed.

Madame Duclos dropped the tray. 'Chocolate doesn't wash

out' ran through her head. But she didn't even glance at their plush, pink carpet; she just opened her mouth and screamed: 'Gaston!'

Her scream was so loud that it could be heard on the floor below, in the doctor's apartments. So, by the time that the frightened chambermaid had run out on to the landing to call for help, the doctor was already walking up the stairs to check whether everything was all right with the landlord.

Madame Duclos was an exemplary wife and landlady. And after the death of Monsieur Duclos, she became an exemplary widow too. Everyone in the Quartier agreed.

She never took off her mourning veil and wore only black dresses. She hardly ever went out. Everything in the apartment was left exactly the same as it had been when Duclos was still alive. She looked after his bureau herself. In the bedroom, his striped dressing gown still hung on the back of the door, and his bright-yellow morning slippers still stood by the bed. And his portraits still hung everywhere, draped in black mourning crêpe.

Madame Duclos even seemed quite proud of her widowhood. Her movements became sluggish, her face always melancholy, she hardly ever smiled.

But she soon realized that, at the core of it, her life had not really changed at all. If anything, it had just become that little bit duller.

And so the years ran on, one after another. Each as empty as the other. They stacked up quickly and effortlessly, like the linen in her mirrored wardrobe . . .

It was June. Madame Duclos was sitting at the small bureau in the drawing room, checking the accounts. The doorbell rang. It must be the property manager. But the maid announced:

'Monsieur Lanet.'

Monsieur Lanet called on her occasionally and together they reminisced about 'the good old days'.

She stacked the accounts into a neat pile, secured them under a heavy bronze poodle, fixed the tall hair arrangement on her head and went through to the reception room.

Monsieur Lanet was still standing when she walked in. He kissed her hand ceremoniously. He had never done that before. He was smartly attired, in a visiting suit. He was even wearing white gloves.

They sat down on the gold divan.

'How kind of you, my dear friend, to pay me a visit.'

Her voice trembled slightly. She no longer had an easy manner about her – she received visitors so rarely these days.

'How are you? How is business?'

'My health gives me no complaints, thank heavens.' He started, with confidence. 'My business affairs are healthy too. In addition to my existing shops on rue Notre Dame, rue Blanche and rue . . .'

Madame Duclos had, by then, quite composed herself. She nodded every now and again, without listening, and gave him the occasional polite and encouraging smile.

Poor man, how fat he had become!

'Two hundred barrels more than last year!' He finished. 'And how about you, my dear Madame Duclos?'

'My business affairs are also fine, thank you.'

Monsieur Lanet placed his hands on his knees and stuck out his elbows.

'Very fine indeed! If it's true that you have an income of one hundred thousand from the house and the shares alone, that is . . .'

'How did you know?'

He smiled, evidently quite pleased with himself.

'Oh, you can find out anything in Paris. I made some inquiries!'

'But why? . . .'

'You see, Madame Duclos,' he cleared his throat, 'I will have to start from the beginning. I have always admired you. Even when Monsieur Duclos was still alive, I felt the greatest respect for you. And now that four years have passed since that tragic day . . . and given that the late Duclos and I were the closest of friends . . .'

She listened, quite confused. He must be about to propose a partnership for some new business venture. She was by nature cautious and conservative and was preparing a polite refusal when he suddenly sat up and stretched out his short neck.

'I have the honour to ask for your hand in marriage.'

His voice was so loud that she was startled.

'What? What are you saying?'

'I hope that you will agree to make me the happiest of men.'

She stared at him in surprise.

'What? What are you saying?' she said again.

'I am asking you to be my wife.'

'Your wife? Monsieur Lanet ... Can you ... can you be serious?'

'I am absolutely serious! I am not one to joke about these things.'

He was agitated. His bottom lip was drooping, and his bald forehead glistened with sweat.

She was still staring at him in surprise.

'How could you? How dare you! You were his friend!' All of a sudden she blushed bright red and frowned. 'I want you to leave immediately and never visit me again.'

He grew red too.

'But allow me, Madame Duclos, I do believe that ...'

She jumped off the divan and stamped her foot.

'Leave! Do you hear me? Leave!' And she called out: 'Amélie, show the monsieur out.'

He spread his arms in indignation.

'This is outrageous! You should be honoured that I'd take you as my wife.'

Then he shrugged and walked out with as much dignity as he could muster.

She went through to her bedroom, drank a glass of water and unbuttoned the high collar of her dress. She needed to calm her nerves.

She sat down on her favourite armchair by the window and picked up her embroidery. How dare he! ... And he was a friend of Monsieur Duclos ... Her hands were shaking. The sharp needle pricked her finger. A bright scarlet drop formed on her pale white skin. She caught sight of it, quietly gasped, laid her head on the table and wept. Her scissors fell to the floor with a clatter.

She wept deeply for hours, until the tears drained all her strength. A warm breeze caressed her hair and her face. She lifted her head and looked out of the open window at the sky. The sunset had tinged it pink. Why had she been so offended? Thousands of widows remarry ...

Suddenly she heard herself laugh. It wasn't her usual laugh, which was dry, like a cough, but a deep, happy and bright laugh – just like Manechka Litvinova's, all those years ago.

The tears had left a peculiar lightness in her chest. Oh, to spread her arms and soar high above the houses, into the pink sky! Then she wouldn't have to be Madame Duclos – the woman whom Lanet the wine merchant was trying to woo.

To fly away ... but she couldn't muster the strength to spread her arms. Her hands lay on her lap, clasped lovingly, like sisters – white, thin and helpless. Her body was growing weak from the lightness. She looked at the scissors that were glittering on the floor, at the wet handkerchief, at the street-lights. The breeze ruffled her hair. Her collar was still open, and a coolness ran across her neck and down her back.

Madame Duclos wasn't thinking of anything. She felt oddly blissful. She listened to the faint beating of her heart.

She sat like this for a long time, until a servant came to call her to dinner.

'I will not be having dinner. That's all for today, you may go.'

Her voice was very quiet, which alarmed the servant.

'Madame is unwell? Should we call for a doctor?'

But Madame Duclos frowned impatiently.

'I told you, you may go now.'

The chambermaid closed the door softly and then ran all the way to the kitchen to spread the remarkable news: 'Madame will not be having dinner.'

The cook and the scullery maid oohed and aahed and shook their heads, then tiptoed to the bedroom door and took turns to spy through the keyhole, trying to see what was going on inside.

But there was nothing in particular going on in the bedroom.

The pink evening light generously lit up the room while Madame Duclos continued to sit in her armchair by the window. Her hands remained clasped in the same way. On her lips the same smile was playing.

The sky grew darker. It was almost night. A huge greenish moon slowly rolled out from behind a black house and hung motionless above a black chimney. White feathery clouds descended over it, like a flock of swans, covering it up completely for a minute, before flying on.

Madame Duclos sighed, slowly got to her feet and shook her head.

'Oh, how tired I am . . .'

She undressed without switching on the light. Her black dress fell mournfully on to the carpet. Her black stockings lay down next to it dutifully. She threw back the cover, laid her head on the pillow and closed her eyes. The cool sheets rustled around her. Her long hair fell about her shoulders and draped itself around her neck.

Leave it . . . it doesn't matter. She couldn't face getting up to brush it. The window was still open. A thin strip of moonlight ran across the carpet and lit up Madame Duclos's shoes. The copper bed shimmered dimly.

Madame Duclos opened her eyes and looked out of the window. She saw the moon as a round, green forest lake, and the moonlight felt moist. She suddenly felt desperately thirsty.

'Oh, how unhappy I am,' she sighed. 'There has never been such a strange moon. There has never been such a sad night . . .'

. . . She awoke. The window was wide open. Her dress lay in a heap on the floor. And even her hair hadn't been plaited. What had happened to her last night? But her recollections of the previous day were muddled by sleepiness and she couldn't quite remember or make sense of anything. The sun lit up the red silk covers, and only one thing was loud and clear in her mind – to live, live, live!

She jumped out of bed and walked over to the dresser barefoot. The mirror showed her a pale face with grey eyes, a straight nose and a small red mouth. Dark messy hair fell across her forehead and shoulders. This was her face – so young, so passionate. Yes, passionate. Pale and passionate, like the faces of George Sand's heroines.

She didn't look thirty-four. Only around her mouth were there some wrinkles – very thin lines, barely noticeable.

She smiled. To live, live, live! It wasn't too late. She could still do it.

Why had she even waited this long? She was free! Free and rich.

She sat down on the bed, putting on her stockings. She had such lovely legs, but her stockings were black and made of cotton. And her shoes were black and heavy. Who was forcing her to buy them?

She buttoned up the high collar of her dress and walked over to the mirror again.

In her clumsy black dress and with her tall, exuberant hairstyle she looked provincial. And her face no longer looked passionate and extraordinary. It was just a washed-out widow's face.

Who was forcing her to make herself so ugly? It was as if she had been doing it on purpose. 'A carefully selected wardrobe will serve you well . . .' she remembered. Yes, she had taken Madame Raffe at her word.

She laughed. Then she hurriedly put on her mourning hat and picked up her black gloves. Her heart was pounding. She was free, she was rich, she was in Paris. It was as if she had just arrived and was going to see the city for the first time today.

She left the house feeling happy and free, that same long-forgotten feeling with which she had walked out the doors of the institute for the last time.

Out on the street, she paused and took a deep breath of the gay Paris air.

To live, live, live!

In the milliner's on rue Royale, the shop assistant shrugged her shoulders.

'Unfortunately, we don't have anything for madame.'

'But why?'

'Oh, I can see what madame is after. Madame does not follow fashions.'

'Please show me your most fashionable hats.'

The shop assistant raised an eyebrow disdainfully, which meant: 'You wouldn't buy one even if I did.'

'Of course . . . But with madame's hairstyle . . .'

Madame Duclos impatiently let out her hair. Pins fell to the floor.

'I'm getting it cut short later today. But I'll try them on now anyway.'

The assistant looked at her with distrust.

'I'll take this one and this one too. And let me see that grey one over there.'

By now, the assistant was smiling sweetly.

'Grey doesn't suit everyone, but with madame's skin tone . . .'

Madame Duclos walked down the street, laughing. She was happy, happy, happy! How had she never realized that shopping was so much fun?

Elegant ladies passed her on either side. That was exactly what she was going to be like. She laughed again. It was like the fairytale about Cinderella. Right now, she was unsightly, but she was going to turn into a princess . . .

Madame Duclos ran into the vestibule. A short dress swished pleasantly around her legs, and a small hat sat snugly on her head. She carried a new handbag under one arm and a large bouquet of red roses under the other. Before, she would only have bought flowers to take to Monsieur Duclos's grave.

Her high heels clattered on the stairs. And their dry beat echoed the beating of her heart.

Oh she was so happy, happy, happy!

A door slammed on one of the floors above. Somebody was coming down the stairs. A young man in a grey hat walked down towards her.

She lifted her face, still smiling, to take a look at him. He stopped by the window to let her pass and tipped his hat. A slanting ray of sunshine fell on his fair hair. He looked at her intently, surprised. His eyes were large and greenish in colour. They were so bright that they seemed to her to be moist.

For some reason, his gaze reminded her of the previous night's moonlight, and for a second she felt desperately thirsty again, just as she had done then.

She walked past him, clutching the roses to her chest.

He muttered an awkward apology, threw back his shoulder nervously and ran down the stairs.

Who was he? A visitor or a new tenant? She'd have to ask the manager.

She opened her front door. The dark hallway was full of boxes, stacked one on top of another.

'There's been so many deliveries, I didn't even know if I was supposed to accept them! And the bedroom's full too—' The maid switched on the lights with a click. 'Oh! Madame!' She cried out in fright. A deep red flush of embarrassment spread over her cheeks. 'What has madame done to herself? Madame is unrecognizable.'

Madame Duclos threw the roses into her arms.

'Put these in water and bring all the parcels upstairs to my room.'

Cardboard lids hit the carpet with a dull thud. Scraps of silk wrapping paper floated helplessly in the air.

Dresses, pink slips, stockings, lace, artificial flowers all piled up in a merry heap on the bed.

Madame Duclos was excited and happy. She tried on shoes, dresses, hats. She looked at her small, round head, at her elongated, painted eyes, and at her lips – a bright red for the very first time.

Was this really her?

The servants stood silently and judgementally in the doorway. They had served in the house for the last fifteen years.

'I always knew this would happen,' the fat cook said when she returned to her kitchen. 'Madame has always had something debauched about her.' She squinted her left eye. 'She'll come to a bad end, just you wait.'

The chambermaid, whose face resembled a horse's, nodded:

'She'll come to a bad end.'

And the scullery maid was all too keen to agree.

'That's right. She'll come to a bad end . . .'

Electric bulbs shone brightly around a large mirror. The smell of perfume filled the air. A box of powder had spilled on to the carpet.

Madame Duclos looked pale and tired. She stood in just her slip, smiling, amid all the dresses, flowers and lace.

That was it – her first day in Paris. That was it – the first day of her life. And there were many more days like this ahead, each just as fun as the other . . .

She got into bed and switched off the lights.

The shutters were closed and the curtains were tightly drawn. There was no way that the moon could get through to her. It was better without the moon – calmer. She ran her hand across the back of her head. It was smooth – her hair was no longer in the way. How nice it felt, how light! Everything was light and nice now.

It grew deadly quiet. A face slowly appeared out of the darkness – a young face with large, moist, greenish eyes.

'Who does he remind me of? Oh, of course – Lidochka Petrovskaya. She used to throw her shoulder back just like that.'

The greenish eyes looked at her intently. Again, she felt a tickling thirst at the back of her throat.

'Water, please,' she whispered in her sleep.

In the morning, she found a letter next to her coffee. It was from cousin Jacques – Monsieur Duclos's brother: 'I hope, dear cousin, that you will finally agree to visit us. It's simply wonderful here this time of year. The roses are blooming. Our little Jeanne, you must remember her, is now engaged. Her fiancé . . .'

Madame Duclos thought of cousin Jacques – a large, loud man – and of his wife Thérèse – a kind woman, with a head of crimped curls, like a poodle's. They had come to stay with them in Paris while Monsieur Duclos was still alive and didn't seem to be able to spend any time at home – they wanted strolls along the boulevards, restaurants, theatres.

And now Jeanne was engaged. Little crybaby Jeanne! 'You must visit us. Let us know when to expect you.'

The 'must' was underlined.

The roses are blooming, and Jeanne is engaged. Madame Duclos smiled to herself, put the letter to one side and poured herself some coffee.

The roses are blooming. White, red and yellow, and butter-flies are dancing around them.

It had been so long since she had been in a country garden! The last time was when she was still at the institute, when she visited her aunt's estate.

. . . Weeping willows bent over the pond. Large carp with bulging eyes swam in the water. Silver birches rose up to the sky, like white candles. In the mornings, the grass was cold and wet with dew. It was such fun to run through it barefoot . . .

She stirred sugar into her cup. It will get hot in Paris soon. Why not visit them in Normandy? They were good people at heart.

Agreeing to visit would mean that she would have to run around the shops and buy, buy, buy. Linen dresses, straw hats, suitcases, a trunk.

It was the thought of a lacquered black wardrobe trunk that settled it. It was exceptionally spacious, with hangers and little compartments for shoes.

She couldn't buy it unless she went.

She got out of bed and wrote a reply. At this time on Satur-day, she would be in Normandy.

Only five days to go. She had to hurry! She rang.

'A bath, quickly, and then help me dress.'

That evening, when she got back, she ran into the young man in the grey hat again on the stairs. She got a good look at him this time.

He was tall and dressed in a shabby blue suit. He was very young.

She passed very close to him, although the stairs were quite wide enough. The tail of her silver fox brushed his shoulder. His pale eyelashes trembled. She thought he might have blushed. His greenish eyes looked at her just as intently.

She walked up to her door, still conscious of his gaze, and glanced over her shoulder discreetly.

What does he want? Why is he staring at her so? He was still standing on the same step, his head thrown back as he looked up at her from below. She couldn't read anything in the look on his face or in his gaze. But her heart started beating anxiously. She quickly unlocked the door and slammed it shut behind her.

The hallway was empty and cool. She sat down in an armchair and took off her hat.

'I'm tired,' she whispered. 'Those shops are so exhausting.'

But her heart was beating anxiously and excitedly, in the sweet anticipation of overwhelming joy.

So, that was the last of the shopping done. Yes, pretty much. And she had her ticket.

Madame Duclos walked into a patisserie on rue de Rivoli and sat down at a free table, trying to appear calm and confident.

There were so many dressed-up women. But she was no worse – she was probably even better – than most of them. It was silly to feel intimidated.

She fixed the white flower that was pinned to her shoulder.

People were looking at her. Let them. She found it quite flattering.

A girl in a lace apron brought her tea.

Most of the other women were with companions – gentlemen, as cheerful and dressed-up as they were.

Well, since she had no companion, she would have to imagine him. She took off her gloves, bowed her head slightly and poured herself some tea.

'Two sugars,' she says quietly to her imaginary companion. 'A spot more water. No, no cream.' She smiles at him as she stirs her tea. 'I'm going to Normandy tomorrow morning.'

And he – her imaginary companion – says:

'Do you enjoy travel?'

'Very much. Even though I haven't left Paris for the last seventeen years. Oh, don't laugh, I beg you. I really do love to travel. Let me tell you about Petersburg . . .'

She took a taxi home. Familiar streets, familiar streetlights. She felt a little sad. She was leaving tomorrow. She would be back in a month, but still . . .

Slowly she walked into the building in which she had spent so many years. Gently she placed a hand on the banister.

The oak staircase gleamed dimly with wax polish. A red carpet ceremoniously covered the stairs. Electric lamps, in the shape of decadent lilies, were already on, although the sun was still shining through the large stained-glass windows.

A door slammed on one of the floors above. Her knees instantly grew weak, but she carried on climbing the stairs. Only her heart beat faster, as if it was frightened. It was him. He was descending as slowly as she was ascending. She stopped on the landing, and he stopped there too. In the artificial, bluish light, his face looked pale and sad.

'What am I doing here?' she thought vaguely. 'I need to open the door.'

He was looking straight at her. His lips were moving, as if he were about to say something.

She started rummaging in her handbag, but her hands were shaking too much to grab hold of the keys. So she stretched out her arm and pressed the doorbell as if her life depended on it. The door swung open immediately. She went through, keeping her head down, not daring to turn around. The maid whose face resembled a horse's took her coat.

'Madame, the trunk has been delivered.'

'The trunk?' Madame Duclos ran a hand across her forehead.

Why was he staring at her like that? What was he going to say?

'The trunk? Oh yes, of course. Come, help me pack, Amélie.'

Cousin Jacques and his wife came to meet her at the station.

The ladies kissed. Cousin Jacques kept shaking her hands.

'I can't believe my eyes! Is it really you? You look completely different.'

Thérèse sighed.

'You look so young. This is what not having children is like! You know . . . I'm only three years older than you.'

'Oh, my dear Thérèse. You look wonderful!'

In the car, they kissed again.

'I'm so happy, Marie. We've been waiting for you to visit for years.'

Thérèse looked round and flushed. Her weedy hair was licked right back.

'You look so fashionable, Marie. But I can't. Not with a daughter that's old enough to be engaged! It's so much stricter here in the provinces . . .'

Madame Duclos looked out on to the yellowing fields, the green trees, the straw roofs.

'It's so nice here, Thérèse,' she sighed. 'So nice.'

And again, just like that time on the landing, she felt an anxiety stir in her heart – a sense of joyous anticipation . . .

'So, Jeanne is getting married?'

'Yes, a very good match. He's the son of . . .'

She wasn't listening. Her heart beat excitedly but ever so lightly. Soon . . . Very soon . . . But what? What? What? . . .

Jeanne and her fiancé were waiting by the garden gate.

Jeanne was sixteen. Her white dress was pinched at the waist and went all the way down to her ankles. Her hair was crimped in the same poodle style as Thérèse's all those years ago.

That meant that in twenty years' time, she would look just like her mother.

'Tante Marie!' she cried, draping herself around Madame Duclos's neck. 'And this is Pierre, my fiancé.'

The fiancé bowed awkwardly. He looked sweet and, most importantly, healthy.

Thérèse was right; he would make a good husband . . .

They ate dinner on the terrace. White moths circled around the night lamp and dropped on to the tablecloth. Cousin Jacques helped himself to some goose with apples.

'Poor Gaston loved this dish. If only he could have some now!'

Thérèse lowered her gaze sadly.

'Your poor husband . . .'

For a moment, everyone was silent. Madame Duclos looked out into the garden. A mist was rising from the pale flowerbeds.

Stars shone through the rips in the clouds, like silvery fish caught in fishermen's nets.

Cousin Jacques touched her elbow.

'Forgive me . . . I have upset you by bringing back memories . . .' He gestured towards Jeanne and her fiancé, who were sitting across the table. 'We shouldn't think of death when we have life in front of us.'

Madame Duclos turned to him, smiling.

'Indeed. A happy life,' she said slowly . . .

The walls were painted with a white oil paint. The bed was covered with a coarse piqué throw and a small 'Napoleon at Waterloo' themed painting hung above it. The floor had been cleanly swept and adorned with a small, colourful rug. There was an earthen vase with roses.

Everything was so simple, so cheap. How nice it was to be here!

Madame Duclos pulled her dress off over her head and filled the washbasin from the large water jug. The door opened, and in ran Jeanne, without even knocking.

'I thought you were still downstairs. I wanted to surprise you. You liked the jam, so I've brought you some more. It's such a treat just before bedtime!'

She placed a small bowl full of jam on the nightstand.

'Oh, how beautiful your underwear is! It's silk! Can I feel it? Will I lend me some – to take to my seamstress? All I get is long cotton shirts. Please can you tell Mama that nobody wears those any more.'

Then, without warning, she hoisted up her dress.

'Look at this! It's a secret, but I can show you because you're nice.' Just above her bony knees, Madame Duclos saw bright red garters, complete with enormous bows and ceramic cats' heads. 'Pierre got these for me on the quiet. If only Mama knew . . . ! Why don't you have some like these?'

'I've never seen such beautiful ones before. Now I will definitely go out and get some.'

Jeanne laughed in delight. Madame Duclos got into bed. Jeanne tucked her in and straightened the pillow.

'Is this all right?'

Crimped hair, dark, playful eyes and freckles danced in front of Madame Duclos's face. For a moment, she thought that she was back at the institute, with her friend Liza Galkina. With a rustling of starched skirts, Jeanne sat down on the bed.

'What scent do you use, Jeanne?'

'Mint oil. Mama won't let me buy perfume.'

She clasped her skinny hands to her chest.

'Tante Marie, I wanted to ask you . . . I can't ask Mama because she'll get angry and anyway – she's old, she's probably forgotten everything by now. But you're so young, so fashionable! Tell me, is it . . . Is it very scary? Does it feel very nice?'

Madame Duclos shook her head.

'My dear Jeanne, I'm afraid I can't help you. Ask your Mama. She's bound to know more than me.'

Jeanne was put out.

'You don't want to tell me. You think I'm still a child. But don't you know that I'm engaged already!'

'Don't be upset with me. I honestly don't know.'

But Jeanne was already laughing and playing with the pink lace around her neck.

'All my girlfriends are so jealous! Pierre is the best match in all of Rouen. I'm madly in love. The wedding's not till November. Of course, I don't mind waiting. It's quite fun, actually. But still . . .' Her face grew quite serious, and she sighed loudly. 'The sooner the better . . .'

At this Madame Duclos sighed too, taking Jeanne quite by surprise.

'Yes, the sooner the better . . .'

Jeanne was feeding chickens in the hen house.

'That's that.'

She threw the last handful of barley and took Madame Duclos's arm.

'Now, let's go on the boat. Oh, but wait . . .' Her eyes narrowed mischievously. 'Let me show you something.'

She opened the door to the barn. Some pigs stood around the sty, snorting lazily every now and again.

'See that fat one with the black spot?'

'Yes, what about it?'

'She'll be slaughtered tonight.'

Madame Duclos was startled.

'Slaughtered? Why?'

'What do you mean, why? What about the hams?'

A young farm hand bared his white teeth and laughed loudly.

'Why slaughter a pig? I can tell madame is from Paris!'

It was so hot that the windows were left open for the night. The stifling wind rustled in the trees. The white curtains flew out like two large, white wings, reaching into the middle of the room and then dropping to hang lifelessly again in front of the window.

Madame Duclos slept with her hands behind her head. She dreamed amusing, nonsensical dreams. In her dream she could tell that she was asleep and she smiled.

'How nice it is to sleep. And tomorrow will be another fun day. So nice!'

But suddenly the rustling of the trees and the amusing dream were cut through by a blood-curdling squeal. She sat up, throwing off the cover.

'What's going on? What is that?!'

The squealing was getting louder and louder. And only one thing was clear – that death would follow.

She leaped out of the bed.

'Murder! Help!'

And then she remembered – the pig. The pig was being slaughtered . . . She clasped her hands over her ears and buried her head in the pillow. But the squealing continued.

And then, just as suddenly, it was very quiet. Too quiet . . .

She switched on the light, cast a glance at the white curtains billowing in the window, reached for the glass. Her hands wouldn't obey her. Her teeth were chattering.

'Killed . . .'

She drank the water, spilling most of it on the little rug. She stood up and placed her warm feet on the painted floorboards.

'I need to calm down.'

A chill ran up her legs, rising higher and higher, all the way to her heart. For a moment, she thought that her heart had stopped beating.

'Death,' she whispered. 'Death!' She made her way back to the bed with difficulty and lay down again. 'I'm dying . . .'

But her heart was beating loudly and steadily in her left ear. She lay still, listening to the beat.

'That's my heartbeat. I'm still alive.'

She switched off the light.

'How dreary . . . Oh, how dreary! How frightening it is to die. How frightening it is to live. And why am I here, with these strangers?'

'I want to go home. Home!'

She looked very pale in the morning.

'Didn't you sleep well?' Cousin Jacques was worried. 'Did that damn pig wake you up too? How many times do I have to tell those idiots to stuff the pig's mouth with rags before they slaughter it.'

'Oh, it was horrible.' Thérèse pressed a podgy hand to her forehead. 'I have a migraine.'

A large mug of coffee was going cold in front of Madame Duclos.

'I'm very sorry,' she said. 'But I'm going to have to return home for three days. There are renovations going on . . .'

'What a shame! But what about your manager?'

'I'm used to dealing with everything myself. It's a shame, but it's only for three days. I'll take the one o'clock train.'

'Tante Marie! Can't you stay until tomorrow at least?' Jeanne was close to tears.

'Or at least – till lunch. We're having blood sausage.' Cousin Jacques rubbed his hands together with pleasure. 'From that very pig, the fat little squealer . . .'

Nobody met her in Paris. Of course – there was nobody to meet her.

She ran up the empty staircase and opened the door. The maid rushed to meet her.

'Madame? We weren't expecting madame. Madame wrote that she would be two weeks . . .'

Madame Duclos laughed.

'Are you annoyed that I'm back?'

'Oh, no, madame! But we haven't had time to clean the apartment . . .'

In the reception room, the shutters were all closed. The chairs wore striped jackets, like convicts. They looked like they were crouching, ready to pounce with a knife to your throat as soon as your back was turned.

She went through to her bedroom and closed the door to the reception room, shutting out the convicts.

This was her room.

She sat down in the armchair and stroked its back.

'Hello. How have you been? Was it very dull without me?'

But the armchair stiffened hostilely under her.

'All right, all right, don't be annoyed. I won't leave you again.'

She sat there and listened. It was very silent – the type of silence you find only in apartments that have stood empty for years. And all her things seemed alien and hostile.

'You're angry? You don't love me . . . Fine, don't, then. And to think that I rushed to be back with you! . . .'

She got dressed and went out. She wandered the streets for a while, went into a shop, bought a box of face powder.

She had a growing sense of unease. What was the matter with her? She was in Paris after all, she was home. What else did she need?

She was walking up the stairs again. Slowly, as if she were expecting something. A door slammed shut on one of the floors above. Her heart stopped and dropped into her stomach. She grabbed hold of the rail.

A little girl in a red coat skipped down the stairs. When she got to Madame Duclos, she stopped and curtseyed.

'Good day, madame landlady. Welcome back.'

Usually, Madame Duclos would pat her on the head and have a little chat with her, but today she just drily said, 'Hello,' and leaned against the wall . . .

The convicts' jackets were strewn across the floor. The servants were unrolling carpets and moving furniture around. Madame Duclos retired to the office.

'Amélie, please call the manager.'

The manager arrived fifteen minutes later.

'Forgive me for calling you so late, but I have just returned and want to know whether everything is . . .'

The manager's eyes were as honest as can be. They stared at her angrily.

'Everything, absolutely everything, is fine. You have nothing to worry about, Madame Duclos.'

'None of the tenants have served their notice? Nobody has moved out?'

'I would have written to you, Madame Duclos.'

'And their lodgers? . . .' She hesitated. 'The lodgers renting furnished rooms . . . Are there any new ones? And are all the old ones still here?'

Surprised by the question, he furrowed his brow.

'The lodgers? I confess, I'm not sure. I don't think there are any new ones, but the Levêques' lodger has moved out.'

'The Levêques?' Her voice trembled. 'A tall man . . . very young?'

'Yes, the Russian. He moved out yesterday. So, you see – everything is fine, as I have just had the pleasure of reporting to you. There is nothing for you to worry about. As for the accounts—'

Madame Duclos stood up.

'Thank you. We shall go through the accounts tomorrow.' Then she nodded. 'Good evening.'

The manager left. She remained standing by the desk.

He's gone . . . Gone! And he's Russian. She had to know. But it was too late now, she should ask tomorrow. No, no – now.

Madame Levêque opened the door herself. Her eyes darted this way and that in shock and surprise.

'Madame Duclos! What an honour. Please, do sit down. Over here, on the divan.'

Madame Duclos looked at her bird-like face, and at the lace doilies and gold picture frames cluttering the room.

'You had a Russian lodger. Can you tell me his name, please?'

'Nikolai Saveliev,' Madame Levêque pronounced with some difficulty. 'He left only yesterday evening. He didn't leave a forwarding address. Please can I offer you a cup of coffee?'

'No, thank you. Why did he leave?'

'Who knows with those Russians! He must have run out of money or lost his job.' Her face suddenly looked mischievous. 'You won't take offence, Madame Duclos?' She would never have dared to say this to the landlady before, but now that the landlady had cut her hair short and started wearing skirts up to her knees . . . 'Forgive me, madame, but he . . .' She giggled. 'He was in love with you, madame.'

'In love? With me? What nonsense is this . . .'

'Oh, quite in love! God forgive me!' Madame Levêque threw out her hands. 'He would spend the whole day standing around in the hallway, just to run out on to the stairs whenever you'd come home. Oh, how we laughed at him! He kept delaying his departure, waiting for you. He wouldn't stop asking when you'd return . . .'

'Perhaps, he just wanted to ask for help from a fellow countrywoman.'

'What do you mean – fellow countrywoman? Are you Russian, madame?'

'Of course. You didn't know?'

Madame Levêque shook her head in disappointment.

'I've lived in this house for ten years, and this is the first I've heard of it . . .'

But Madame Duclos was already on her way out.

'Your apartment is so cosy. Is this your little boy? And your cat? How lovely . . . Goodnight.'

Madame Levêque walked her to the stairs.

'Thank you for the honour! My husband will be disappointed to have missed you. Goodnight.'

Madame Duclos went straight to her bedroom. She stood in front of the open window, looking at the black roofs and the chimneys against the cloudy sky.

Then she sank to her knees and laid her head on the

armchair. The silk upholstery rustled gently. Madame Duclos was crying.

This was it. This was what she had been waiting for . . .

She quietly picked herself up, undressed and got into bed.

The cool sheets gently brushed her breasts and knees.

This was what she had been waiting for. Love . . .

Through the window, she saw the black sky suddenly light up. A large, green moon slowly rolled out from behind a dark cloud. It was as if this green moon was all she needed for total silence, total calm, total bliss.

Madame Duclos threw back her head and slowly stretched out under the cool sheets . . .

The shop clerk lifts a glass cloche. There is something red on the plate – it's moist and covered in flies.

'This is your liver, madame.'

The shop clerk giggles and reaches into the drawer, taking out two little disks that look like dried apples.

'And these are your ears, madame.'

Something is jumping all over the counter, hitting itself against the glass pane. It's wrinkled and ugly – it looks like a red pepper.

'And this is your heart, madame. You see – it's dancing. It's very happy, your heart.' The shop clerk laughs loudly.

Madame Duclos wakes herself up with a scream.

She needs to think things through. She needs to be practical. She's spent seventeen years in France, after all.

She finds an advert in a newspaper and goes to the address provided. She enters a grey building.

There is a plaque on the door: 'Private Detective'.

A young man with a sharp centre parting and piercing eyes greets her with exaggerated deference.

She sits down in a leather armchair.

'I need an address. Nikolai Saveliev. A Russian. I need it as quickly as possible.'

'You will have the address. I beg you to answer just one question . . . Can you describe him, please? How old is he?'

'The day before yesterday he was still living on rue Constantinople.'

'Can you describe him, please. How old is he?'

'I don't know. No older than twenty-three . . . He's very tall. Thin. His eyes are greenish . . .'

She blushes and fiddles with a glove.

'Forgive me, madame, but you must be completely open with me. As you would be at confession . . . Was it money or jewellery . . . These things happen so often . . .'

She sits up straight.

'How dare you! He's my friend's son. I'm Russian too.'

The centre parting gives a respectful little bow.

'Oh, madame, forgive me. I wasn't to know. These things happen so often. You shall have Monsieur Saveliev's address in three days. Payment is in advance.'

Madame Duclos doesn't go out. She sits by the window, waiting.

'I don't mind waiting. But still, the sooner the better.'

She can wait a little longer. Not too long, just a little . . . The letter she was promised arrived on the third day. Saveliev's address: Green Elephant Hotel, Marseilles.

'Amélie!' Madame Duclos was still holding the letter in her hand. 'Get me the train timetable. And pack my suitcase. I'm leaving right away.'

She couldn't get a sleeping berth, but what did it matter? The other passengers couldn't stop looking at the beautiful lady, who wouldn't stop smiling all night.

It's dark. The train stops. Lyons . . .

Madame Duclos fixes the hard little pillow behind her head. 'I've got you. Got you! And I won't let you go. You're asleep, you have no idea. But I'm on my way to you, to you, to you. And tomorrow . . .'

Outside she sees the sun, the round hills and the low trees of Provence.

And then she sees the sea – blue and sparkling. And then it's Marseilles.

She steps out of the carriage. She can hardly believe that she's walking, not flying.

This is it – Marseilles. City of light. City of happiness.

The high white staircase shimmers. She squints in the sun. The porter packs her suitcase into the taxi cab.

Straight to his? But how could she turn up there unwashed, wearing a creased dress, and with all her things! And what was the hurry now anyway? Their whole lives lay ahead of them. She had waited so long, she could manage another half hour of waiting.

At the hotel, the manager shows her a room.

'I can also offer you a bigger room, on the floor above. It has beautiful sea views.'

Sea views? What did she care about sea views.

'It doesn't matter. I'll take this room. Have my suitcase brought up.'

She rolls up her stockings. Her legs are still moist from the bath. She should dry them. She picks up her towel, looks at her knees and blushes violently. The towel falls to the floor.

It's so hot here. She can hardly breathe.

She didn't sleep at all. Her eyes must be puffy. It's a pity that he'll see her like this.

She walks over to the mirror.

No, her face is happy and excited. She just has rings under her eyes.

Her head is spinning from exhaustion, excitement and joy.

. . . She will knock softly, open the door and stand in the doorway. He will be reading by the window. He will turn his head and not even have time to get to his feet.

'Hello,' she will say, in Russian. She can see her lips moving in the mirror, struggling to remember the long-forgotten Russian word.

'Hello.'

She leans closer to the mirror.

'Kolya . . .'

And, so close now that she's touching the cool glass, she whispers:

'I love you. I love you!'

She must hurry. He might go . . . No, he isn't going

anywhere. He's waiting for her. And everything will be all right. It had to be.

The fat proprietor in braces says sleepily:
'Second floor. Number forty-two.'

Madame Duclos climbs up the narrow staircase. Only one thing could stop her now – her heart actually bursting from joy.

Number 42. She knocks. There's no answer. She waits and knocks a little louder. Again, no answer. She tries the handle, and the door swings open.

The room is shabby and almost completely empty. An unmade bed against a wall. A bottle and a piece of bread on the table. A pile of newspapers on the bare brick floor. And the bright, deep-blue southern sky outside the window.

'He's not in. He must have gone out.'

Well, in that case she'll wait here. A servant walks down the corridor, carrying an armful of dirty linen.

'Will Monsieur Saveliev be back soon?'

'Saveliev?' The man gives a low whistle 'There's no Saveliev here. He's gone.'

'Gone? Gone where?'

'To Russia. On a ship. Just now. If madame really hurries, she'll catch him at the port . . .'

Madame Duclos runs out on to the street.

'Taxi! Taxi! For God's sake,' she says, 'to the port, quickly! If we make it to the ship . . .'

Buildings rush past her. The taxi's green sign dances before her eyes. Her hat is skewed to one side. Her hair is all over her face. Madame Duclos sees nothing. She thinks of nothing. She just has to make it in time.

She doesn't take her eyes off the back of the cab driver's head. With every breath, every heartbeat, every drop of blood in her body, she wills the engine to run faster.

She just has to make it . . .

The taxi cab speeds down crowded streets, past shops, cafés and policemen, and swerves into the port.

. . . Slowly, grandly, a large, white steamer is sailing away from the pier, across the glistening blue waves. It's still so close.

'Farewell, farewell!' cry the people on the shore, waving their handkerchiefs in the air.

'Farewell, farewell!' can be heard from the ship.

The bright-blue sky, the bright-blue waves and the white ship – like a snowy mountain. A large French Tricolour flies in the wind. Black smoke rises into the sky.

She leaps out of the car and runs to the very edge of the pier.

'The ship . . . Is that the ship to Russia?'

Her happiness is sailing away. Her life is disappearing. Slowly, ever so slowly, into the bright-blue sea, in the stifling hot wind, under the bright-blue sky.

She can still see it, she can still breathe. The white funnels, the flag, the smoke . . .

And then there is nothing. No ship, no happiness, no life.

The Visit to the Museum

VLADIMIR NABOKOV

Several years ago a friend of mine in Paris—a person with oddities, to put it mildly—learning that I was going to spend two or three days at Montisert, asked me to drop in at the local museum where there hung, he was told, a portrait of his grandfather by Leroy. Smiling and spreading out his hands, he related a rather vague story to which I confess I paid little attention, partly because I do not like other people's obtrusive affairs, but chiefly because I had always had doubts about my friend's capacity to remain this side of fantasy. It went more or less as follows: after the grandfather died in their St. Petersburg house back at the time of the Russo-Japanese War, the contents of his apartment in Paris were sold at auction. The portrait, after some obscure peregrinations, was acquired by the museum of Leroy's native town. My friend wished to know if the portrait was really there; if there, if it could be ransomed; and if it could, for what price. When I asked why he did not get in touch with the museum, he replied that he had written several times, but had never received an answer.

I made an inward resolution not to carry out the request—I could always tell him I had fallen ill or changed my itinerary. The very notion of seeing sights, whether they be museums or ancient buildings, is loathsome to me; besides, the good freak's commission seemed absolute nonsense. It so happened, however, that, while wandering about Montisert's empty streets in search of a stationery store, and cursing the spire of a long-necked cathedral, always the same one, that kept popping up at the end of every street, I was caught in a violent downpour which immediately went about accelerating the fall of the maple leaves, for the fair weather of a southern October was holding on by a mere thread. I dashed for cover and found myself on the steps of the museum.

It was a building of modest proportions, constructed of many-colored stones, with columns, a gilt inscription over the frescoes of the pediment, and a lion-legged stone bench on either side of the bronze door. One of its leaves stood open, and the interior seemed dark against the shimmer of the shower. I stood for a while on the steps, but, despite the overhanging roof, they were gradually growing speckled. I saw that the rain had set in for good, and so, having nothing better to do, I decided to go inside. No sooner had I trod on the smooth, resonant flagstones of the vestibule than the clatter of a moved stool came from a distant corner, and the custodian—a banal pensioner with an empty sleeve—rose to meet me, laying aside his newspaper and peering at me over his spectacles. I paid my franc and, trying not to look at some statues at the entrance (which were as traditional and as insignificant as the first number in a circus program), I entered the main hall.

Everything was as it should be: gray tints, the sleep of substance, matter dematerialized. There was the usual case of old, worn coins resting in the inclined velvet of their compartments. There was, on top of the case, a pair of owls, Eagle Owl and Long-eared, with their French names reading "Grand Duke" and "Middle Duke"—if translated. Venerable minerals lay in their open graves of dusty papier-mâché; a photograph of an astonished gentleman with a pointed beard dominated an assortment of strange black lumps of various sizes. They bore a great resemblance to frozen frass, and I paused involuntarily over them, for I was quite at a loss to guess their nature, composition, and function. The custodian had been following me with felted steps, always keeping a respectful distance; now, however, he came up, with one hand behind his back and the ghost of the other in his pocket, and gulping, if one judged by his Adam's apple.

"What are they?" I asked.

"Science has not yet determined," he replied, undoubtedly having learned the phrase by rote. "They were found," he continued in the same phony tone, "in 1895, by Louis Pradier, Municipal Councillor and Knight of the Legion of Honor," and his trembling finger indicated the photograph.

"Well and good," I said, "but who decided, and why, that they merited a place in the museum?"

"And now I call your attention to this skull!" the old man cried energetically, obviously changing the subject.

"Still, I would be interested to know what they are made of," I interrupted.

"Science . . ." he began anew, but stopped short and looked crossly at his fingers, which were soiled with dust from the glass.

I proceeded to examine a Chinese vase, probably brought back by a naval officer; a group of porous fossils; a pale worm in clouded alcohol; a red-and-green map of Montisert in the seventeenth century; and a trio of rusted tools bound by a funereal ribbon—a spade, a mattock, and a pick. To dig in the past, I thought absentmindedly, but this time did not seek clarification from the custodian, who was following me noiselessly and meekly, weaving in and out among the display cases. Beyond the first hall there was another, apparently the last, and in its center a large sarcophagus stood like a dirty bathtub, while the walls were hung with paintings.

At once my eye was caught by the portrait of a man between two abominable landscapes (with cattle and "atmosphere"). I moved closer and, to my considerable amazement, found the very object whose existence had hitherto seemed to me but the figment of an unstable mind. The man, depicted in wretched oils, wore a frock coat, whiskers, and a large pince-nez on a cord; he bore a likeness to Offenbach, but, in spite of the work's vile conventionality, I had the feeling one could make out in his features the horizon of a resemblance, as it were, to my friend. In one corner, meticulously traced in carmine against a black background, was the signature *Leroy* in a hand as commonplace as the work itself.

I felt a vinegarish breath near my shoulder, and turned to meet the custodian's kindly gaze. "Tell me," I asked, "supposing someone wished to buy one of these paintings, whom should he see?"

"The treasures of the museum are the pride of the city," replied the old man, "and pride is not for sale."

Fearing his eloquence, I hastily concurred, but nevertheless asked for the name of the museum's director. He tried to distract me with the story of the sarcophagus, but I insisted. Finally he gave me the name of one M. Godard and explained where I could find him.

Frankly, I enjoyed the thought that the portrait existed. It is fun to be present at the coming true of a dream, even if it is not one's own. I decided to settle the matter without delay. When I get in the spirit, no one can hold me back. I left the museum with a brisk, resonant step, and found that the rain had stopped, blueness had spread across the sky, a woman in besplattered stockings was spinning along on a silver-shining bicycle, and only over the surrounding hills did clouds still hang. Once again the cathedral began playing hide-and-seek with me, but I outwitted it. Barely escaping the onrushing tires of a furious red bus packed with singing youths, I crossed the asphalt thoroughfare and a minute later was ringing at the garden gate of M. Godard. He turned out to be a thin, middle-aged gentleman in high collar and dickey, with a pearl in the knot of his tie, and a face very much resembling a Russian wolfhound; as if that were not enough, he was licking his chops in a most doglike manner, while sticking a stamp on an envelope, when I entered his small but lavishly furnished room with its malachite inkstand on the desk and a strangely familiar Chinese vase on the mantel. A pair of fencing foils hung crossed over the mirror, which reflected the narrow gray back of his head. Here and there photographs of a warship pleasantly broke up the blue flora of the wallpaper.

"What can I do for you?" he asked, throwing the letter he had just sealed into the wastebasket. This act seemed unusual to me; however, I did not see fit to interfere. I explained in brief my reason for coming, even naming the substantial sum with which my friend was willing to part, though he had asked me not to mention it, but wait instead for the museum's terms.

"All this is delightful," said M. Godard. "The only thing is, you are mistaken—there is no such picture in our museum."

"What do you mean there is no such picture? I have just seen it! *Portrait of a Russian Nobleman* by Gustave Leroy."

"We do have one Leroy," said M. Godard when he had leafed through an oilcloth notebook and his black fingernail had stopped at the entry in question. "However, it is not a portrait but a rural landscape: *The Return of the Herd*."

I repeated that I had seen the picture with my own eyes five minutes before and that no power on earth could make me doubt its existence.

"Agreed," said M. Godard, "but I am not crazy either. I have been curator of our museum for almost twenty years now and know this catalogue as well as I know the Lord's Prayer. It says here *Return of the Herd* and that means the herd is returning, and, unless perhaps your friend's grandfather is depicted as a shepherd, I cannot conceive of his portrait's existence in our museum."

"He is wearing a frock coat," I cried. "I swear he is wearing a frock coat!"

"And how did you like our museum in general?" M. Godard asked suspiciously. "Did you appreciate the sarcophagus?"

"Listen," I said (and I think there was already a tremor in my voice), "do me a favor—let's go there this minute, and let's make an agreement that if the portrait is there, you will sell it."

"And if not?" inquired M. Godard.

"I shall pay you the sum anyway."

"All right," he said. "Here, take this red-and-blue pencil and using the red—the red, please—put it in writing for me."

In my excitement I carried out his demand. Upon glancing at my signature, he deplored the difficult pronunciation of Russian names. Then he appended his own signature and, quickly folding the sheet, thrust it into his waistcoat pocket.

"Let's go," he said, freeing a cuff.

On the way he stepped into a shop and bought a bag of sticky-looking caramels which he began offering me insistently; when I flatly refused, he tried to shake out a couple of them into my hand. I pulled my hand away. Several caramels fell on the sidewalk; he stopped to pick them up and then overtook me at a trot. When we drew near the museum we saw the red tourist bus (now empty) parked outside.

"Aha," said M. Godard, pleased. "I see we have many visitors today."

He doffed his hat and, holding it in front of him, walked decorously up the steps.

All was not well at the museum. From within issued rowdy cries, lewd laughter, and even what seemed like the sound of a scuffle. We entered the first hall; there the elderly custodian was restraining two sacrilegists who wore some kind of festive emblems in their lapels and were altogether very purple-faced and full of pep as they tried to extract the municipal councillor's merds from beneath the glass. The rest of the youths, members of some rural athletic organization, were making noisy fun, some of the worm in alcohol, others of the skull. One joker was in rapture over the pipes of the steam radiator, which he pretended was an exhibit; another was taking aim at an owl with his fist and forefinger. There were about thirty of them in all, and their motion and voices created a condition of crush and thick noise.

M. Godard clapped his hands and pointed at a sign reading "VISITORS TO THE MUSEUM MUST BE DECENTLY ATTIRED." Then he pushed his way, with me following, into the second hall. The whole company immediately swarmed after us. I steered Godard to the portrait; he froze before it, chest inflated, and then stepped back a bit, as if admiring it, and his feminine heel trod on somebody's foot.

"Splendid picture," he exclaimed with genuine sincerity. "Well, let's not be petty about this. You were right, and there must be an error in the catalogue."

As he spoke, his fingers, moving as it were on their own, tore up our agreement into little bits which fell like snowflakes into a massive spittoon.

"Who's the old ape?" asked an individual in a striped jersey, and, as my friend's grandfather was depicted holding a glowing cigar, another funster took out a cigarette and prepared to borrow a light from the portrait.

"All right, let us settle on the price," I said, "and, in any case, let's get out of here."

THE VISIT TO THE MUSEUM

"Make way, please!" shouted M. Godard, pushing aside the curious.

There was an exit, which I had not noticed previously, at the end of the hall and we thrust our way through to it.

"I can make no decision," M. Godard was shouting above the din. "Decisiveness is a good thing only when supported by law. I must first discuss the matter with the mayor, who has just died and has not yet been elected. I doubt that you will be able to purchase the portrait but nonetheless I would like to show you still other treasures of ours."

We found ourselves in a hall of considerable dimensions. Brown books, with a half-baked look and coarse, foxed pages, lay open under glass on a long table. Along the walls stood dummy soldiers in jackboots with flared tops.

"Come, let's talk it over," I cried out in desperation, trying to direct M. Godard's evolutions to a plush-covered sofa in a corner. But in this I was prevented by the custodian. Flailing his one arm, he came running after us, pursued by a merry crowd of youths, one of whom had put on his head a copper helmet with a Rembrandtesque gleam.

"Take it off, take it off!" shouted M. Godard, and someone's shove made the helmet fly off the hooligan's head with a clatter.

"Let us move on," said M. Godard, tugging at my sleeve, and we passed into the section of Ancient Sculpture.

I lost my way for a moment among some enormous marble legs, and twice ran around a giant knee before I again caught sight of M. Godard, who was looking for me behind the white ankle of a neighboring giantess. Here a person in a bowler, who must have clambered up her, suddenly fell from a great height to the stone floor. One of his companions began helping him up, but they were both drunk, and, dismissing them with a wave of the hand, M. Godard rushed on to the next room, radiant with Oriental fabrics; there hounds raced across azure carpets, and a bow and quiver lay on a tiger skin.

Strangely, though, the expanse and motley only gave me a feeling of oppressiveness and imprecision, and, perhaps because new visitors kept dashing by or perhaps because I was

impatient to leave the unnecessarily spreading museum and
amid calm and freedom conclude my business negotiations
with M. Godard, I began to experience a vague sense of alarm.
Meanwhile we had transported ourselves into yet another hall,
which must have been really enormous, judging by the fact
that it housed the entire skeleton of a whale, resembling a frig-
ate's frame; beyond were visible still other halls, with the
oblique sheen of large paintings, full of storm clouds, among
which floated the delicate idols of religious art in blue and pink
vestments; and all this resolved itself in an abrupt turbulence
of misty draperies, and chandeliers came aglitter and fish with
translucent frills meandered through illuminated aquariums. Racing up a staircase, we saw, from the gallery above, a crowd of
gray-haired people with umbrellas examining a gigantic mock-up
of the universe.

At last, in a somber but magnificent room dedicated to the
history of steam machines, I managed to halt my carefree guide
for an instant.

"Enough!" I shouted. "I'm leaving. We'll talk tomorrow."

He had already vanished. I turned and saw, scarcely an inch
from me, the lofty wheels of a sweaty locomotive. For a long
time I tried to find the way back among models of railroad stations. How strangely glowed the violet signals in the gloom
beyond the fan of wet tracks, and what spasms shook my poor
heart! Suddenly everything changed again: in front of me
stretched an infinitely long passage, containing numerous office
cabinets and elusive, scurrying people. Taking a sharp turn, I
found myself amid a thousand musical instruments; the walls,
all mirror, reflected an enfilade of grand pianos, while in the
center there was a pool with a bronze Orpheus atop a green
rock. The aquatic theme did not end here as, racing back, I
ended up in the Section of Fountains and Brooks, and it was
difficult to walk along the winding, slimy edges of those waters.

Now and then, on one side or the other, stone stairs, with
puddles on the steps, which gave me a strange sensation of
fear, would descend into misty abysses, whence issued whistles, the rattle of dishes, the clatter of typewriters, the ring of
hammers, and many other sounds, as if, down there, were

exposition halls of some kind or other, already closing or not yet completed. Then I found myself in darkness and kept bumping into unknown furniture until I finally saw a red light and walked out onto a platform that clanged under me—and suddenly, beyond it, there was a bright parlor, tastefully furnished in Empire style, but not a living soul, not a living soul . . . By now I was indescribably terrified, but every time I turned and tried to retrace my steps along the passages, I found myself in hitherto unseen places—a greenhouse with hydrangeas and broken windowpanes with the darkness of artificial night showing through beyond; or a deserted laboratory with dusty alembics on its tables. Finally I ran into a room of some sort with coatracks monstrously loaded down with black coats and astrakhan furs; from beyond a door came a burst of applause, but when I flung the door open, there was no theater, but only a soft opacity and splendidly counterfeited fog with the perfectly convincing blotches of indistinct streetlights. More than convincing! I advanced, and immediately a joyous and unmistakable sensation of reality at last replaced all the unreal trash amid which I had just been dashing to and fro. The stone beneath my feet was real sidewalk, powdered with wonderfully fragrant, newly fallen snow, in which the infrequent pedestrians had already left fresh black tracks. At first the quiet and the snowy coolness of the night, somehow strikingly familiar, gave me a pleasant feeling after my feverish wanderings. Trustfully, I started to conjecture just where I had come out, and why the snow, and what were those lights exaggeratedly but indistinctly beaming here and there in the brown darkness. I examined and, stooping, even touched a round spur stone on the curb, then glanced at the palm of my hand, full of wet granular cold, as if hoping to read an explanation there. I felt how lightly, how naively I was clothed, but the distinct realization that I had escaped from the museum's maze was still so strong that, for the first two or three minutes, I experienced neither surprise nor fear. Continuing my leisurely examination, I looked up at the house beside which I was standing and was immediately struck by the sight of iron steps and railings that descended into the snow on their way to the cellar. There was a twinge in my heart, and it was with a new, alarmed curiosity that I glanced at the pavement, at its white cover along which stretched black lines, at the brown sky across which there kept sweeping a mysterious light, and at the massive parapet some distance away. I sensed that there was a drop beyond it; something was creaking and gurgling down there. Further on, beyond the murky cavity, stretched a chain of fuzzy lights. Scuffling along the snow in my soaked shoes, I walked a few paces, all the time glancing at the dark house on my right; only in a single window did a lamp glow softly under its green-glass shade. Here, a locked wooden gate ... There, what must be the shutters of a sleeping shop ... And by the light of a streetlamp whose shape had long been shouting to me its impossible message, I made out the ending of a sign—"... INKA SAPOG" ("... OE REPAIR")—but no, it was not the snow that had obliterated the "hard sign" at the end. "No, no, in a minute I shall wake up," I said aloud, and, trembling, my heart pounding, I turned, walked on, stopped again. From somewhere came the receding sound of hooves, the snow sat like a skullcap on a slightly leaning spur stone and indistinctly showed white on the woodpile on the other side of the fence, and already I knew, irrevocably, where I was. Alas, it was not the Russia I remembered, but the factual Russia of today, forbidden to me, hopelessly slavish, and hopelessly my own native land. A semiphantom in a light foreign suit, I stood on the impassive snow of an October night, somewhere on the Moyka or the Fontanka Canal, or perhaps on the Obvodny, and I had to do something, go somewhere, run; desperately protect my fragile, illegal life. Oh, how many times in my sleep I had experienced a similar sensation! Now, though, it was reality. Everything was real—the air that seemed to mingle with scattered snowflakes, the still unfrozen canal, the floating fish house, and that peculiar squareness of the darkened and the yellow windows. A man in a fur cap, with a briefcase under his arm, came toward me out of the fog, gave me a startled glance, and turned to look again when he had passed me. I waited for him to disappear and then, with a tremendous haste, began pulling out everything I had in my pockets, ripping up papers, throwing them into the snow and stamping them down. There were some documents, a letter from my sister in Paris, five hundred francs, a handkerchief, cigarettes; however, in order to shed all the integument of exile, I would have to tear off and destroy my clothes, my linen, my shoes, everything, and remain ideally naked; and, even though I was already shivering from my anguish and from the cold, I did what I could.

But enough. I shall not recount how I was arrested, nor tell of my subsequent ordeals. Suffice it to say that it cost me incredible patience and effort to get back abroad, and that, ever since, I have forsworn carrying out commissions entrusted one by the insanity of others.

The Assistant Producer

VLADIMIR NABOKOV

I

Meaning? Well, because sometimes life is merely that—an Assistant Producer. Tonight we shall go to the movies. Back to the thirties, and down the twenties, and round the corner to the old Europe Picture Palace. She was a celebrated singer. Not opera, not even *Cavalleria Rusticana*,[1] not anything like that. "La Slavska"—that is what the French called her. Style: one-tenth *tzigane*, one-seventh Russian peasant girl (she had been that herself originally), and five-ninths popular—and by popular I mean a hodgepodge of artificial folklore, military melodrama, and official patriotism. The fraction left unfilled seems sufficient to represent the physical splendor of her prodigious voice.

Coming from what was, geographically at least, the very heart of Russia, it eventually reached the big cities, Moscow, St. Petersburg, and the Tsar's milieu where that sort of style was greatly appreciated. In Feodor Chaliapin's dressing room there hung a photograph of her: Russian headgear with pearls, hand propping cheek, dazzling teeth between fleshy lips, and a great clumsy scrawl right across: "For you, Fedyusha." Stars of snow, each revealing, before the edges melted, its complex symmetry, would gently come to rest on the shoulders and sleeves and mustaches and caps—all waiting in a queue for the box office to open. Up to her very death she treasured above all—or pretended to do so—a fancy medal and a huge brooch that had been given her by the Tsarina. They came from the firm of jewelers which used to do such profitable business by presenting the imperial couple on every festive occasion with this or that emblem (each year increasing in worth) of massive Tsardom: some great lump of amethyst with a ruby-studded bronze troika stranded on top like Noah's Ark on Mount Ararat, or a sphere of crystal the size of a watermelon surmounted by a gold eagle with square diamond eyes very much like those of Rasputin (many years later some of the less symbolic ones were exhibited at a World's Fair by the Soviets as samples of their own thriving Art).

Had things gone on as they were seeming to go, she might have been still singing tonight in a central-heated Hall of Nobility or at Tsarskoye, and I should be turning off her broadcast voice in some remote corner of steppe-mother Siberia. But destiny took the wrong turning; and when the Revolution happened, followed by the War of the Reds and the Whites, her wily peasant soul chose the more practical party.

Ghostly multitudes of ghostly Cossacks on ghost-horseback are seen charging through the fading name of the assistant producer. Then dapper General Golubkov is disclosed idly scanning the battlefield through a pair of opera glasses. When movies and we were young, we used to be shown what the sights divulged neatly framed in two connected circles. Not now. What we do see next is General Golubkov, all indolence suddenly gone, leaping into the saddle, looming sky-high for an instant on his rearing steed, and then rocketing into a crazy attack.

But the unexpected is the infra-red in the spectrum of Art: instead of the conditional *ra-ta-ta* reflex of machine gunnery, a woman's voice is heard singing afar. Nearer, still nearer, and finally all-pervading. A gorgeous contralto voice expanding into whatever the musical director found in his files in the way of Russian lilt. Who is this leading the infra-Reds? A woman. The singing spirit of that particular, especially well-trained battalion. Marching in front, trampling the alfalfa, and pouring out her Volga-Volga song. Dapper and daring *djighit* Golubkov (now we know what he had descried), although wounded in several spots, manages to snatch her up on the gallop, and, lusciously struggling, she is borne away.

Strangely enough, that vile script was enacted in reality. I myself have known at least two reliable witnesses of the event; and the sentries of history have let it pass unchallenged. Very soon we find her maddening the officers' mess with her dark buxom beauty and wild, wild songs. She was a Belle Dame with a good deal of Merci, and there was a punch about her that Louise von Lenz or the Green Lady lacked. She it was who sweetened the general retreat of the Whites, which began shortly after her magic appearance at General Golubkov's camp. We get a gloomy glimpse of ravens, or crows, or whatever birds proved available, wheeling in the dusk and slowly descending upon a plain littered with bodies somewhere in Ventura County. A White soldier's dead hand is still clutching a medallion with his mother's face. A Red soldier nearby has on his shattered breast a letter from home with the same old woman blinking through the dissolving lines.

And then, in traditional contrast, pat comes a mighty burst of music and song with a rhythmic clapping of hands and stamping of booted feet and we see General Golubkov's staff in full revelry—a lithe Georgian dancing with a dagger, the self-conscious samovar reflecting distorted faces, the Slavska throwing her head back with a throaty laugh, and the fat man of the corps, horribly drunk, braided collar undone, greasy lips pursed for a bestial kiss, leaning across the table (close-up of an overturned glass) to hug—nothingness, for wiry and perfectly sober General Golubkov has deftly removed her and now, as they both stand facing the gang, says in a cold, clear voice: "Gentlemen, I want to present you my bride"—and in the stunned silence that follows, a stray bullet from outside chances to shatter the dawn-blue windowpane, after which a roar of applause greets the glamorous couple.

There is little doubt that her capture had not been wholly a fortuitous occurrence. Indeterminism is banned from the studio. It is even less doubtful that when the great exodus began and they, as many others, meandered via Sirkedji to Motzstrasse and rue Vaugirard, the General and his wife already formed one team, one song, one cipher. Quite naturally he became an efficient member of the W.W. (White Warriors

Union), traveling about, organizing military courses for Russian boys, arranging relief concerts, unearthing barracks for the destitute, settling local disputes, and doing all this in a most unobtrusive manner. I suppose it was useful in some ways, that W.W. Unfortunately for its spiritual welfare, it was quite incapable of cutting itself off from monarchist groups abroad and did not feel, as the émigré intelligentsia felt, the dreadful vulgarity, the Ur-Hitlerism of those ludicrous but vicious organizations. When well-meaning Americans ask me whether I know charming Colonel So-and-so or grand old Count de Kickoffsky, I have not the heart to tell them the dismal truth.

But there was also another type of person connected with the W.W. I am thinking of those adventurous souls who helped the cause by crossing the frontier through some snow-muffled fir forest, to potter about their native land in the various disguises worked out, oddly enough, by the social revolutionaries of yore, and quietly bring back to the little café in Paris called "Esh-Bubliki," or to the little *Kneipe* in Berlin that had no special name, the kind of useful trifles which spies are supposed to bring back to their employers. Some of those men had become abstrusely entangled with the spying departments of other nations and would give an amusing jump if you came from behind and tapped them on the shoulder. A few went a-scouting for the fun of the thing. One or two perhaps really believed that in some mystical way they were preparing the resurrection of a sacred, if somewhat musty, past.

2

We are now going to witness a most weirdly monotonous series of events. The first president of the W.W. to die was the leader of the whole White movement and by far the best man of the lot; and certain dark symptoms attending his sudden illness suggested a poisoner's shadow. The next president, a huge, strong fellow with a voice of thunder and a head like a cannonball, was kidnapped by persons unknown; and there are reasons to believe that he died from an overdose of chloroform.

The third president—but my reel is going too fast. Actually it took seven years to remove the first two—not because this sort of thing cannot be done more briskly, but because there were particular circumstances that necessitated some very precise timing, so as to coordinate one's steady ascent with the spacing of sudden vacancies. Let us explain.

Golubkov was not only a very versatile spy (a triple agent to be exact); he was also an exceedingly ambitious little fellow. Why the vision of presiding over an organization that was but a sunset behind a cemetery happened to be so dear to him is a conundrum only for those who have no hobbies or passions. He wanted it very badly—that is all. What is less intelligible is the faith he had in being able to safeguard his puny existence in the crush between the formidable parties whose dangerous money and dangerous help he received. I want all your attention now, for it would be a pity to miss the subtleties of the situation.

The Soviets could not be much disturbed by the highly improbable prospect of a phantom White Army ever being able to resume war operations against their consolidated bulk; but they could be very much irritated by the fact that scraps of information about forts and factories, gathered by elusive W.W. meddlers, were automatically falling into grateful German hands. The Germans were little interested in the recondite color variations of émigré politics, but what did annoy them was the blunt patriotism of a W.W. president every now and then obstructing on ethical grounds the smooth flow of friendly collaboration.

Thus, General Golubkov was a godsend. The Soviets firmly expected that under his rule all W.W. spies would be well known to them—and shrewdly supplied with false information for eager German consumption. The Germans were equally sure that through him they would be guaranteed a good cropping of their own absolutely trustworthy agents distributed among the usual W.W. ones. Neither side had any illusions concerning Golubkov's loyalty, but each assumed that it would turn to its own profit the fluctuations of double-crossing. The dreams of simple Russian folk, hardworking families in remote parts of the Russian diaspora, plying their humble but honest trades, as they would in Saratov or Tver, bearing fragile children, and naively believing that the W.W. was a kind of King Arthur's Round Table that stood for all that had been, and would be, sweet and decent and strong in fairy-tale Russia— these dreams may well strike the film pruners as an excrescence upon the main theme.

When the W.W. was founded, General Golubkov's candidacy (purely theoretical, of course, for nobody expected the leader to die) was very far down the list—not because his legendary gallantry was insufficiently appreciated by his fellow officers, but because he happened to be the youngest general in the army. Toward the time of the next president's election Golubkov had already disclosed such tremendous capacities as an organizer that he felt he could safely cross out quite a few intermediate names in the list, incidentally sparing the lives of their bearers. After the second general had been removed, many of the W.W. members were convinced that General Fedchenko, the next candidate, would surrender in favor of the younger and more efficient man the rights that his age, reputation, and academic distinction entitled him to enjoy. The old gentleman, however, though doubtful of the enjoyment, thought it cowardly to avoid a job that had cost two men their lives. So Golubkov set his teeth and started to dig again.

Physically he lacked attraction. There was nothing of your popular Russian general about him, nothing of that good, burly, popeyed, thick-necked sort. He was lean, frail, with sharp features, a clipped mustache, and the kind of haircut that is called by Russians "hedgehog": short, wiry, upright, and compact. There was a thin silver bracelet round his hairy wrist, and he offered you neat homemade Russian cigarettes or English prune-flavored "Kapstens," as he pronounced it, snugly arranged in an old roomy cigarette case of black leather that had accompanied him through the presumable smoke of numberless battles. He was extremely polite and extremely inconspicuous.

Whenever the Slavska "received," which she would do at the homes of her various Maecenases (a Baltic baron of sorts, a Dr. Bachrach whose first wife had been a famous Carmen, or a Russian merchant of the old school who, in inflation-mad Berlin, was having a wonderful time buying up blocks of houses for ten pounds sterling apiece), her silent husband would unobtrusively thread his way among the visitors, bringing you a sausage-and-cucumber sandwich or a tiny frosty-pale glass of vodka; and while the Slavska sang (on those informal occasions she used to sing seated with her fist at her cheek and her elbow cupped in the palm of her other hand) he would stand apart, leaning against something, or would tiptoe toward a distant ashtray which he would gently place on the fat arm of your chair.

I consider that, artistically, he overstressed his effacement, unwittingly introducing a hired-lackey note—which now seems singularly appropriate; but he of course was trying to base his existence upon the principle of contrast and would get a marvelous thrill from exactly knowing by certain sweet signs—a bent head, a rolling eye—that So-and-so at the far end of the room was drawing a newcomer's attention to the fascinating fact that such a dim, modest man was the hero of incredible exploits in a legendary war (taking towns single-handed and that sort of thing).

3

German film companies, which kept sprouting like poisonous mushrooms in those days (just before the child of light learned to talk), found cheap labor in hiring those among the Russian émigrés whose only hope and profession was their past—that is, a set of totally unreal people—to represent "real" audiences in pictures. The dovetailing of one phantasm into another produced upon a sensitive person the impression of living in a Hall of Mirrors, or rather a prison of mirrors, and not even knowing which was the glass and which was yourself.

Indeed, when I recall the halls where the Slavska sang, both in Berlin and in Paris, and the type of people one saw there, I feel as if I were Technicoloring and sonorizing some very ancient motion picture where life had been a gray vibration and funerals a scamper, and where only the sea had been tinted (a sickly blue), while some hand machine imitated offstage the hiss of the asynchronous surf. A certain shady character, the terror of relief organizations, a bald-headed man with mad eyes, slowly floats across my field of vision with his legs bent in a sitting position, like an elderly fetus, and then miraculously fits into a back-row seat. Our friend the Count is also here, complete with high collar and dingy spats. A venerable but worldly priest, with his cross gently heaving on his ample chest, sits in the front row and looks straight ahead.

The items of these right-wing festivals that the Slavska's name evokes in my mind were of the same unreal nature as was her audience. A variety artist with a fake Slav name, one of those guitar virtuosos that come as a cheap first in music hall programs, would be most welcome here; and the flashy ornaments on his glass-paneled instrument, and his sky-blue silk pants, would go well with the rest of the show. Then some bearded old rascal in a shabby cutaway coat, former member of the Holy Russ First, would take the chair and vividly describe what the Israel-sons and the Phreemasons (two secret Semitic tribes) were doing to the Russian people.

And now, ladies and gentlemen, we have the great pleasure and honor—There she would stand against a dreadful background of palms and national flags, and moisten her rich painted lips with her pale tongue, and leisurely clasp her kid-gloved hands on her corseted stomach, while her constant accompanist, marble-faced Joseph Levinsky, who had followed her, in the shadow of her song, to the Tsar's private concert hall and to Comrade Lunacharsky's salon, and to nondescript places in Constantinople, produced his brief introductory series of stepping-stone notes.

Sometimes, if the house was of the right sort, she would sing the national anthem before launching upon her limited but ever welcome repertoire. Inevitably there would be that lugubrious "Old Road to Kaluga" (with a thunderstruck pine tree at the forty-ninth verst), and the one that begins, in the German translation printed beneath the Russian text, *"Du bist im*

Schnee begraben, mein Russland," and the ancient folklore ballad (written by a private person in the eighties) about the robber chieftain and his lovely Persian princess, whom he threw into the Volga when his crew accused him of going soft.

Her artistic taste was nowhere, her technique haphazard, her general style atrocious; but the kind of people for whom music and sentiment are one, or who like songs to be mediums for the spirits of circumstances under which they had been first apprehended in an individual past, gratefully found in the tremendous sonorities of her voice both a nostalgic solace and a patriotic kick. She was considered especially effective when a strain of wild recklessness rang through her song. Had this abandon been less blatantly shammed it might still have saved her from utter vulgarity. The small, hard thing that was her soul stuck out of her song, and the most her temperament could attain was but an eddy, not a free torrent. When nowadays in some Russian household the gramophone is put on, and I hear her canned contralto, it is with something of a shudder that I recall the meretricious imitation she gave of reaching her vocal climax, the anatomy of her mouth fully displayed in a last passionate cry, her blue-black hair beautifully waved, her crossed hands pressed to the beribboned medal on her bosom as she acknowledged the orgy of applause, her broad dusky body rigid even when she bowed, crammed as it was into strong silver satin which made her look like a matron of snow or a mermaid of honor.

4

You will see her next (if the censor does not find what follows offensive to piety) kneeling in the honey-colored haze of a crowded Russian church, lustily sobbing side by side with the wife or widow (she knew exactly which) of the general whose kidnapping had been so nicely arranged by her husband and so deftly performed by those big, efficient, anonymous men that the boss had sent down to Paris.

You will see her also on another day, two or three years

later, while she is singing in a certain *appartement*, rue George
Sand, surrounded by admiring friends—and look, her eyes
narrow slightly, her singing smile fades, as her husband, who
had been detained by the final details of the business in hand,
now quietly slips in and with a soft gesture rebukes a grizzled
colonel's attempt to offer him his own seat; and through the
unconscious flow of a song delivered for the ten-thousandth
time she peers at him (she is slightly nearsighted like Anna
Karenin) trying to discern some definite sign, and then, as she
drowns and his painted boats sail away, and the last telltale
circular ripple on the Volga River, Samara County, dissolves
into dull eternity (for this is the very last song that she ever will
sing), her husband comes up to her and says in a voice that no
clapping of human hands can muffle: "Masha, the tree will be
felled tomorrow!"

That bit about the tree was the only dramatic treat that Golubkov allowed himself during his dove-gray career. We shall
condone the outburst if we remember that this was the ultimate
General blocking his way and that next day's event would automatically bring on his own election. There had been lately some
mild jesting among their friends (Russian humor being a wee
bird satisfied with a crumb) about the amusing little quarrel
that those two big children were having, she petulantly demanding the removal of the huge old poplar that darkened her studio
window at their suburban summer house, and he contending
that the sturdy old fellow was her greenest admirer (sidesplit-
ting, this) and so ought to be spared. Note too the good-natured
roguishness of the fat lady in the ermine cape as she taunts the
gallant General for giving in so soon, and the Slavska's radiant
smile and outstretched jelly-cold arms.

Next day, late in the afternoon, General Golubkov escorted
his wife to her dressmaker, sat there for a while reading the
Paris-Soir, and then was sent back to fetch one of the dresses
she wanted loosened and had forgotten to bring. At suitable
intervals she gave a passable imitation of telephoning home
and volubly directing his search. The dressmaker, an Arme-
nian lady, and a seamstress, little Princess Tumanov, were
much entertained in the adjacent room by the variety of her

rustic oaths (which helped her not to dry up in a part that her imagination alone could not improvise). This threadbare alibi was not intended for the patching up of past tenses in case anything went wrong—for nothing could go wrong; it was merely meant to provide a man whom none would ever dream of suspecting with a routine account of his movements when people would want to know who had seen General Fedchenko last. After enough imaginary wardrobes had been ransacked Golubkov was seen to return with the dress (which long ago, of course, had been placed in the car). He went on reading his paper while his wife kept trying things on.

5

The thirty-five minutes or so during which he was gone proved quite a comfortable margin. About the time she started fooling with that dead telephone, he had already picked up the General at an unfrequented corner and was driving him to an imaginary appointment the circumstances of which had been so framed in advance as to make its secrecy natural and its attendance a duty. A few minutes later he pulled up and they both got out. "This is not the right street," said General Fedchenko. "No," said General Golubkov, "but it is a convenient one to park my car on. I should not like to leave it right in front of the café. We shall take a shortcut through that lane. It is only two minutes' walk." "Good, let us walk," said the old man and cleared his throat.

In that particular quarter of Paris the streets are called after various philosophers, and the lane they were following had been named by some well-read city father rue Pierre Labime. It gently steered you past a dark church and some scaffolding into a vague region of shuttered private houses standing somewhat aloof within their own grounds behind iron railings on which moribund maple leaves would pause in their flight between bare branch and wet pavement. Along the left side of that lane there was a long wall with crossword puzzles of brick showing here and there through its rough grayness; and in that wall there was at one spot a little green door.

As they approached it, General Golubkov produced his battle-scarred cigarette case and presently stopped to light up. General Fedchenko, a courteous nonsmoker, stopped too. There was a gusty wind ruffling the dusk, and the first match went out. "I still think——" said General Fedchenko in reference to some petty business they had been discussing lately, "I still think," he said (to say something as he stood near that little green door), "that if Father Fedor insists on paying for all those lodgings out of his own funds, the least we can do is to supply the fuel." The second match went out too. The back of a passerby hazily receding in the distance at last disappeared. General Golubkov cursed the wind at the top of his voice, and as this was the all-clear signal the green door opened and three pairs of hands with incredible speed and skill whisked the old man out of sight. The door slammed. General Golubkov lighted his cigarette and briskly walked back the way he had come.

The old man was never seen again. The quiet foreigners who had rented a certain quiet house for one quiet month had been innocent Dutchmen or Danes. It was but an optical trick. There is no green door, but only a gray one, which no human strength can burst open. I have vainly searched through admirable encyclopedias: there is no philosopher called Pierre Labime.

But I have seen the toad in her eyes. We have a saying in Russian: *vsevo dvoe i est'; smert' da sovest'*—which may be rendered thus: "There are only two things that really exist—one's death and one's conscience." The lovely thing about humanity is that at times one may be unaware of doing right, but one is always aware of doing wrong. A very horrible criminal, whose wife had been even a worse one, once told me in the days when I was a priest that what had troubled him all through was the inner shame of being stopped by a still deeper shame from discussing with her the puzzle: whether perhaps in her heart of hearts she despised him or whether she secretly wondered if perhaps in his heart of hearts he despised her. And that is why I know perfectly well the kind of face General Golubkov and his wife had when the two were at last alone.

6

Not for very long, however. About ten p.m. General L., the
W.W. Secretary, was informed by General R. that Mrs. Fedchenko was extremely worried by her husband's unaccountable
absence. Only then did General L. remember that about lunch-
time the President had told him in a rather casual way (but that
was the old gentleman's manner) that he had some business in
town in the late afternoon and that if he was not back by eight
p.m. would General L. please read a note left in the middle
drawer of the President's desk. The two generals now rushed to
the office, stopped short, rushed back for the keys General L.
had forgotten, rushed again, and finally found the note. It read:
"*An odd feeling obsesses me of which later I may be ashamed.
I have an appointment at five-thirty p.m. in a café 45 rue
Descartes. I am to meet an informer from the other side. I suspect a trap. The whole thing has been arranged by General
Golubkov, who is taking me there in his car.*"

We shall skip what General L. said and what General R.
replied—but apparently they were slow thinkers and proceeded
to lose some more time in a muddled telephone talk with an
indignant café owner. It was almost midnight when the Slavska,
clad in a flowery dressing gown and trying to look very sleepy,
let them in. She was unwilling to disturb her husband, who, she
said, was already asleep. She wanted to know what it was all
about and had perhaps something happened to General Fedchenko. "He has vanished," said honest General L. The Slavska
said, "Akh!" and crashed in a dead swoon, almost wrecking
the parlor in the process. The stage had not lost quite so much
as most of her admirers thought.

Somehow or other the two generals managed not to impart
to General Golubkov anything about the little note, so that
when he accompanied them to the W.W. headquarters he was
under the impression that they really wanted to discuss with
him whether to ring up the police at once or first go for advice
to eighty-eight-year-old Admiral Gromoboyev, who for some
obscure reason was considered the Solomon of the W.W.

"What does this mean?" said General L., handing the fatal note to Golubkov. "Peruse it, please."

Golubkov perused—and knew at once that all was lost. We shall not bend over the abyss of his feelings. He handed the note back with a shrug of his thin shoulders.

"If this has been really written by the General," he said, "and I must admit it looks very similar to his hand, then all I can say is that somebody has been impersonating me. However, I have grounds to believe that Admiral Gromoboyev will be able to exonerate me. I suggest we go there at once."

"Yes," said General L., "we had better go now, although it is very late."

General Golubkov swished himself into his raincoat and went out first. General R. helped General L. to retrieve his muffler. It had half slipped down from one of those vestibule chairs which are doomed to accommodate things, not people. General L. sighed and put on his old felt hat, using both hands for this gentle action. He moved to the door. "One moment, General," said General R. in a low voice. "I want to ask you something. As one officer to another, are you absolutely sure that . . . well, that General Golubkov is speaking the truth?"

"That's what we shall find out," answered General L., who was one of those people who believe that so long as a sentence is a sentence it is bound to mean something.

They delicately touched each other's elbows in the doorway. Finally the slightly older man accepted the privilege and made a jaunty exit. Then they both paused on the landing, for the staircase struck them as being very still. "General!" cried General L. in a downward direction. Then they looked at each other. Then hurriedly, clumsily, they stomped down the ugly steps, and emerged, and stopped under a black drizzle, and looked this way and that, and then at each other again.

She was arrested early on the following morning. Never once during the inquest did she depart from her attitude of grief-stricken innocence. The French police displayed a queer listlessness in dealing with possible clues, as if they assumed that the disappearance of Russian generals was a kind of curious local custom, an Oriental phenomenon, a dissolving process which perhaps ought not to occur but which could not be prevented. One had, however, the impression that the *Sûreté* knew more about the workings of the vanishing trick than diplomatic wisdom found fit to discuss. Newspapers abroad treated the whole matter in a good-natured but bantering and slightly bored manner. On the whole, "L'affaire Slavska" did not make good headlines— Russian émigrés were decidedly out of focus. By an amusing coincidence both a German press agency and a Soviet one laconically stated that a pair of White Russian generals in Paris had absconded with the White Army funds.

7

The trial was strangely inconclusive and muddled, witnesses did not shine, and the final conviction of the Slavska on a charge of kidnapping was debatable on legal grounds. Irrelevant trifles kept obscuring the main issue. The wrong people remembered the right things and vice versa. There was a bill signed by a certain Gaston Coulot, farmer, "*pour un arbre abattu.*"[2] General L. and General R. had a dreadful time at the hands of a sadistic barrister. A Parisian *clochard*, one of those colorful ripe-nosed unshaven beings (an easy part, that) who keep all their earthly belongings in their voluminous pockets and wrap their feet in layers of bursting newspapers when the last sock is gone and are seen comfortably seated, with widespread legs and a bottle of wine against the crumbling wall of some building that has never been completed, gave a lurid account of having observed from a certain vantage point an old man being roughly handled. Two Russian women, one of whom had been treated some time before for acute hysteria, said they saw on the day of the crime General Golubkov and General Fedchenko driving in the former's car. A Russian violinist while sitting in the diner of a German train—but it is useless to retell all those lame rumors.

We get a few last glimpses of the Slavska in prison. Meekly knitting in a corner. Writing to Mrs. Fedchenko tear-stained letters in which she said that they were sisters now, because both their husbands had been captured by the Bolsheviks. Begging to be allowed the use of a lipstick. Sobbing and praying in the arms of a pale young Russian nun who had come to tell her of a vision she had had which disclosed the innocence of General Golubkov. Clamoring for the New Testament which the police were keeping—keeping mainly from the experts who had so nicely begun deciphering certain notes scribbled in the margin of St. John's Gospel. Some time after the outbreak of World War II, she developed an obscure internal trouble and when, one summer morning, three German officers arrived at the prison hospital and desired to see her, at once they were told she was dead—which possibly was the truth.

One wonders if in some way or other her husband managed to inform her of his whereabouts, or if he thought it safer to leave her in the lurch. Where did he go, poor *perdu*? The mirrors of possibility cannot replace the eyehole of knowledge. Perhaps he found a haven in Germany and was given there some small administrative job in the Baedecker Training School for Young Spies. Perhaps he returned to the land where he had taken towns single-handedly. Perhaps he did not. Perhaps he was summoned by whoever his arch-boss was and told with that slight foreign accent and special brand of blandness that we all know: "I am afraid, my friend, you are not needed any more"—and as X turns to go, Dr. Puppenmeister's delicate index presses a button at the edge of his impassive writing desk and a trap yawns under X, who plunges to his death (he who knows "too much"), or breaks his funny bone by crashing right through into the living room of the elderly couple below.

Anyhow, the show is over. You help your girl into her coat and join the slow exit-bound stream of your likes. Safety doors open into unexpected side portions of night, diverting proximal trickles. If, like me, you prefer for reasons of orientation to go out the way you came in, you will pass again by those posters that seemed so attractive a couple of hours ago. The Russian cavalryman in his half-Polish uniform bends from his polo-pony to scoop up red-booted romance, her black hair tumbling from under her astrakhan cap. The Arc de Triomphe rubs shoulders with a dim-domed Kremlin. The monocled agent of a Foreign Power is handed a bundle of secret papers by General Golubkov ... Quick, children, let us get out of here into the sober night, into the shuffling peace of familiar sidewalks, into the solid world of good freckled boys and the spirit of comradeship. Welcome reality! This tangible cigarette will be very refreshing after all that trashy excitement. See, the thin dapper man walking in front of us lights up too after tapping a "Lookee" against his old leathern cigarette case.

The Lady from Monte Carlo

DOVID KNUT

I was waiting for an acquaintance in the lobby of a respectable Paris hotel when I stumbled upon the following announcement:

'The renowned philanthropist Madame D— has passed away in Monte Carlo, where she had lived uninterruptedly for forty years. The deceased was only sixty-two years of age.'

Sixty-two years ... That meant that she would only have been fifty when I made her acquaintance some twelve years ago. She cut an elegant figure, had the youthful gait of an athlete, but her appearance was that of profound old age. And yet, framed as it was by fine fairytale-white hair, there was not a single wrinkle on her face. Old age had imparted to her a pair of fixed, sparkling, almost motionless eyes – as though she constantly saw the shadow of death behind every man, the shadow of ruin behind every object ...

Madame D— was no more. Madame D— had died. Now no one would learn her secret, and so I was saved from crippling nightmares, oppressive heat and madness.

Never again would I feel this terror, this relentless temptation – to dash to the station and into a carriage, to go to her, to knock on her door, and grasp her elegant, slender hand, to fall on my knees, to tell her of my situation, of my despair.

Thank God it was now too late, she was no more. Soon it would seem to me, as it had done at times already, that I had dreamed her, an apparition, a figment of my imagination.

Peace unto your ashes, unhappy, noble woman.

*

That memorable summer of my acquaintance with Madame D—, I had resolved to travel down to Nice and Monte Carlo.

I had little money, the hotel where I was staying in Nice stood on a dull street, which reminded me ad nauseam of certain quarters in Paris, and, having seen over the course of several days my fill of splendid hotels along the Promenade des Anglais, the fairground beauty of the seaside casino, and the fat, gorged gulls, those graceful scroungers of Nice's animal kingdom, I left for Monte Carlo.

The countryside at Monte Carlo enchanted me. But the town itself seemed much too clean, impracticably smart and tidy, the people always decked out in their Sunday best and wearing the latest fashions, even the villainously brought-up children, the type to say: *'Tenez, monsieur le mendiant, voilà un sou que mon excellente mère me donne chaque semaine pour les pauvres.'*[1] Even the palm trees there looked like stage props, while the policemen at the crossings seemed to have stepped out of an operetta, in their dazzling uniforms synthetically combining the attributes of an admiral, a general and a doorman.

Having toured the surrounding areas even by motorboat, and having gone to hear an open-air concert given by the symphony orchestra in a municipal park, I stopped by the casino before leaving. It seemed as comfortable as could be. Naturally, I threw several tokens left and right – my luck was in. I even noticed that some people, after exchanging glances mysteriously, began to follow my game.

I played cautiously: having thought of some number, I would frame it with a series of adjacent numbers (which diminished my winnings); however, noticing it was in fact the original number that often came out, I plucked up the courage to stake almost all I had won on number twenty-six. The croupier proclaimed: twenty-six.

I raked in a magical mountain of tokens and went to the cashier to exchange them. For an instant I imagined they wouldn't take them, that they would tell me, winking conspiratorially, and not without reproach: 'What's all this! You can't do that. Go and play a trifle longer. You understand, two or three hundred, *ça va*,[2] we'll gladly exchange that . . . but thirty thousand . . . It's just . . . I'm sorry.'

Or else: 'Well, have it your way, we'll cough up. One thousand is more than enough. Very well . . . Here's another two hundred francs. Put yourself in our shoes.'

However, the cashier amiably handed me a wad of banknotes, and, having left him some change, I made my way dizzily towards the exit.

All in all, after three days of gaming bliss, to which I had soon become accustomed, so much so that I began to feel a definite pride – the pride of a successful gambler (I was sure I was in some way worthier, more gifted, more intelligent than my neighbours at the table, whom I probably – I could now swear to this – regarded with disdain) – after my transferral to a first-class hotel opposite the casino, in a single evening I almost unwittingly lost everything.

I recall standing insensibly by a table for half an hour, despite an inexplicable feeling of shame before 'my' croupier.

I recall how a slow gentleman of aristocratic mien, having exchanged the occasional phrase in French with a wistful madonna who had come up to him, banged his fist on the table and with a distorted face unexpectedly bellowed a most indecent string of obscenities in Russian. I looked at the madonna. Her delightful childlike face expressed an infinitely wistful tenderness.

To put it briefly: my affairs were in a bad way. With ever greater effort, I obtained ever smaller sums, the hotel bill soared, like a malignant abscess, the day of my departure began to drift from one calendar leaf to the next, and in the hotel's office I was now met with an unpleasant fixed stare.

One warm evening, as I was walking to the casino, I stumbled upon an odd scene. On the restaurant terrace, sitting in an awkwardly extended chair, was an old woman, rubbing her emaciated leg in its black stocking. Some people were embarrassedly lingering around her, speaking to her with sympathetic alacrity in their faces, clearly hoping to help, while the old woman, with unconcealed vexation, was turning away her head. The haughty maître d'hôtel, dashing out from the restaurant, deferentially murmured:

'*J'ai tout vu, madame. Je suis témoin, madame.*'[3]

The old woman raised her head and screamed:

'*Allez-vous-en!*'[4]

'*Des chauffards de cette espèce méritent une punition!*'[5] said the maître d'hôtel, pressing on.

Two men were shouting at the driver, who guiltily shrugged his shoulders.

Unexpectedly for me, I walked up to the old woman decisively.

'*Où voulez-vous rentrez, madam, chez vous ou à l'hôpital?*'[6]

'*Chez moi,*'[7] she growled.

'*Vous pouvez nous conduire chez madame?*'[8] I asked the driver.

He slammed the car door. The old woman screeched the address. The vehicle moved off.

'*Rien de grave?*'[9] I asked the strange woman.

'*Non,*' she replied stoically.

Preoccupied by my wretched state of affairs, I asked no further questions. We drew up at an opulent villa. I helped the old lady out of the car. The driver handed her a small book.

'*Ma carte, madame. Pour le constat.*'[10]

'*Non,*' said the old lady and rang the bell.

She offered me her hand. '*Je vous remercie, monsieur.*'[11]

'*Vous pouvez venir me voir un de ces soirs,*'[12] she added drily, already walking into the house.

What an old witch! I fumed inwardly.

The invitation was insultingly off-hand, as if the old woman were bestowing upon me the greatest honour. Her whole behaviour recalled that of a patron with her petitioner. I shrugged and got into the car which had been waiting for me.

Several days passed. I sat at the casino's magical green table. A dispassionate man in black, on a low dais, was calling number after number, and every intonement of his reverberated in my heart like a judgement.

At the other end of the table, I spotted my new acquaintance. Even now, as on the restaurant terrace, she was surrounded by toadies to whom she paid no attention. The little pile of tokens in front of her grew and grew . . . I was about to go and watch her game, but in the eyes of the people around her there was so much sweet pus, thraldom, lust, masochism, that I turned away. The old woman did not notice me.

Within me was the chaos of ruin, smoke and dry tears filled my eyes, my hands and back were damp with anxiety, while my legs responded with trembling when I calmly stood up and, with an unwarranted, excruciating smile, made for the exit, sensing that no smile would ever fool any of these indifferent people, that my eyes might have betrayed me entirely, had the people not been eternally – tragically – lost and dissociated from one another, that there was no one to make an effort for, nor any reason, that the world stood in sin and wickedness, while man was but stone unto man.

At the exit I was caught up by an immaculate old man wearing a smart pair of waxed moustaches.

'Young man,' he said atitter, 'Madame D— requests your presence.'

'Whoever is Madame D—? You must be mistaken. I don't know any Madame D—,' I explained to the unrelenting old man, and suddenly espied a somewhat lame old woman with a stick, the very same, making her way across the hall towards me.

She greeted me. I bowed to her frostily. The old woman scrutinized me with her unmoving eyes.

'You are in bad humour, sir.'

Taken off guard, I was even at a loss to respond.

'You are invited to take tea with me,' she breathed grandly.

'Thank you, ma'am. I should be honoured.'

'Wait, wait. You haven't quite grasped my meaning. I am asking you,' she punctuated, like an order, 'to accompany me now.'

'Ma'am,' I replied, no longer able to contain my irritation, 'I am regrettably busy. I have a prior engagement today.'

Once again she fixed her gaze on me, hypnotizing me with her eyes.

'There is no need to be rude,' she edifyingly remarked. 'Give me your arm, sir. My motor car is downstairs, on the square.'

*

It was the strangest tea. We drank in silence from exquisite antique cups and then, also in silence, we each drank a glass of cognac. Dazed and devastated by the experience, by the hopelessness of my situation, by the cognac, the silence, the comfort of the armchair, I melted, unwittingly lost all conception of place, circumstance, time, unwittingly fell into a drowsy semiconscious state, and for a moment I comprehended nothing, hearing someone's half-familiar voice, calling from a distance, from the depths of a world left behind some while ago.

What was it? Who? Why?

A fraction of a second later, with a jolt, everything fell into place. The voice belonged to the hospitable hostess, that old lady with the injured leg.

'I said, what are we going to do now, eh? . . .' she said, repeating a question that had evidently been posed already.

Suddenly, I realized that she was talking about me, about my losses, and that she had seen and understood everything . . .

'Ma'am,' I said, flustered, but she would not let me continue.

'Listen here, monsieur, monsieur . . . Oh, how foolish of me. How am I to know your name? . . . But not another word. It's of no importance now, you can tell me later. Let us begin with what really matters: naturally, you must have some idea of who I am . . .'

I shook my head.

'I've only just arrived,' I mumbled.

'But you must have heard my name,' she said in astonishment. 'For it is I, Madame D—, you know, "The Lady from Monte Carlo".'

I felt embarrassed.

'Forgive me,' I admitted, 'but I know nothing of you.'

She burst into laughter. Her broad, infectious, ringing laugh surprised me.

'Now see here,' she said, frowning momentarily, 'you aren't . . . you aren't telling me an untruth, are you?'

She watched and shook her head resolutely. 'No, you aren't.'

Silence.

'Well, so much the better, and the worse. Worse because it will take that much longer to explain. So listen carefully . . .'

Hers was an essentially uncomplicated story, yet I listened intently to 'The Lady from Monte Carlo', never taking my eyes off her. At times it seemed fantastic to me – my meeting with her, the lady herself, the bizarre story. The thought loomed: might she be mad? But I immediately realized that all was well, that before me was a so-called normal person, and that there was evidently much in life that was more complicated and mysterious than I had previously imagined.

. . . She was twenty when she first arrived at Monte Carlo. Then she had been exceptionally beautiful. 'That girl on the piano is me. Yes, yes. Do not pretend that you don't recognize me, sir.' Intelligent and quite capable, she was the private secretary of an eminent politician. She had a fiancé – just starting out on his diplomatic career. He was predicted to have 'a future'.

She arrived at Monte Carlo on holiday. Out of boredom, she visited the casino. Having lost all her money, she decided never to do something so foolish again, and wrote to her sister. Having lost all the money she received from her sister, she vowed 'never to set foot in the casino again' and with a sigh wrote to her employer. Having lost the entire advance given to her by her employer, she roamed the town, struggling (could she not ask the cashier at the hotel, say that . . . But what could one say! . . .), took a pathetic oath (never again, on no account) and decided to write to her fiancé – asking for a loan. It was all terribly embarrassing. For several reasons. Having lost this money, too, she made her way to the park and sat down on a bench – to despair, to perish, to die.

Not for long did she sit alone. A gentleman of exceedingly advanced years with a carnation in his buttonhole came up to her and raised his hat.

'May I take a seat?'

The old man immediately struck up a conversation.

'Mademoiselle, I am an old man. Allow me, on the merit of

these grey hairs' – the grey hairs were few, so it was rather the merit of his bald head – 'to speak plainly . . .'

And so, he would sit beside her at the casino, he would watch, he would understand everything; oh, he would respect her feelings, all right, he would bow to her principles, but on the other hand she did not have the moral right to refuse him . . . Yes, mademoiselle, the *moral right*. Her life ahead of her, she was young, and beautiful, she quite probably had sweethearts . . . Most likely she also had . . . Oh, do not remonstrate, there is nothing shameful here . . .

'Anyhow, here is my address. Repay me whenever you like. Men may meet but mountains never, as they say . . . Show a lonely old man a little attention: how much do you need to settle at the hotel and leave? Lord, I, too, have been in this situation. Will five hundred be enough?'

In the end he won. She ran off, trembling, blushing, unfortunate, happy, with three hundred francs in her handbag.

The hotel manager was not to be found in his office. Could she not drop in at the casino for a minute – to bet ten, no more? Who knows what might happen! Wouldn't it be wonderful – to give the money back to the old man and return to Paris in style? Just ten, and not a sou more. Ten was nothing!

She returned home late. She collapsed on to the bed without bothering to undress. For a long time she sobbed. A concerned waiter knocked at midday. No, she would not be going downstairs. She would take lunch in her room. *Merci*. She stared inanely at the coffee, its surface vibrating, chewing vacantly on a croissant. Then she changed her dress and left. Having taken a few steps down the staircase, she stopped in her tracks, went back to her room, upturned the bed and sloshed the coffee in the wash-basin.

Like an automaton she reached that same bench in the park, where again she spotted the old man from yesterday. She froze – if only he wouldn't notice her! Thank God, the old man walked past without looking. She sat on the bench for a long time. It was the end. Everything, everything was lost, ruined, irreparable, hopeless. How bleak! What an awful fool I am. Poor Jacques. Poor mankind. This damned invention. The old man was walking slowly in the opposite direction. He was clearly engrossed in some thought, he went along without noticing her, he was already exiting the park, her last hope, her salvation, and, pale from the burning in her chest, from the sharp pain in her stomach, from the onset of hunger – to be saved, to live, to be! – she ran after him, caught up with him and stopped. The old man was gladdened by the meeting.

'You haven't yet left?'

'Tomorrow,' she whispered, licking her dry lips.

'Give an old man some pleasure. Let's lunch together.'

She nodded, afraid to utter a word.

After the restaurant they went to the theatre, from the theatre he saw her home in a cab. The imminent parting drew nearer, pressing on her, like death.

When the lights of her hotel lurched into view through the window, she could not endure it; she burst into laughter, began to wail, laughed again and began to thump the walls of the stuffy silk box. The old man ordered the cabby to make haste.

How she recalled that evening, the endless rolling of the carriage through the nocturnal streets, the gas lamps of the quay, the conversation with the old man, or, rather, his unhurried monologue.

The old man proved to be an Alsatian, a former tutor at an *école nationale*. Two years of pedagogical activity had stirred in him such disgust for a life of labour that he, upon quitting the school, at first made a modest card-sharp of himself and then, after several years of painstaking study, devised a system for playing roulette that guaranteed a respectable steady income. Since then he had lived and worked, as he termed it, in Monte Carlo.

He marked the young lady at once and wittingly put her to the test. It was not by chance – far from it – that he had been in the park yesterday and today. The young lady belonged among the gamblers, and she could no longer control her innate passion, which had erupted so unexpectedly.

He, on the other hand, was old, lonely; he needed a collaborator, an honest, loyal person. He immediately felt a compulsion towards her. In life, he knew, one ought not to practise trickery, and one should heed these foolish palpitations of the heart.

His conditions: he would reveal his method to her, she would work in the casino, which would incidentally localize, as it were, her passion and bring her into line. When one harnesses the destructive power of a stream, it makes no difference how it is made to turn the millwheel. The income was split between them.

He made no attempt to conceal it: the work would be the dullest imaginable, and exhausting – truly, it was impossible to step away from the table even for an iota.

You would need to switch off every little spark of life inside you, to transform yourself into an automaton. It required superhuman training, and he warned her that it was exceptionally difficult. True, at first he would prompt her, help her . . .

Let her sleep on it. He did not want any rash decisions. If she found his proposition unsuitable, he would with genuine delight lend her – this time without any ulterior motive – the necessary sum.

The following morning she gave the Alsatian her reply: No! A man was waiting for her in Paris; he worked in the Ministry of Foreign Affairs. Perhaps you catch my meaning. The old man smiled in a fatherly way, accompanied her to her hotel, where he paid for his 'niece', whisked her off to the station and already in the carriage passed her an envelope – 'Please, don't worry. We'll settle up some day.'

She languorously waved goodbye to him with a handkerchief. A week later, after seven sleepless nights, she came to him in Monte Carlo. There were tears in her mirthless eyes. Six months later the old man was dead.

Thirty years passed, like a single day raised to the nth degree, uniform and polished, like a ball between two mirrors infinitely reflecting one another, while the anonymous ball is repeated an unfathomable number of times – and then one day a heavy motor car, while reversing, runs over her foot, and she comes face to face with a foreigner, to whom it would doubtless seem a great stroke of luck to possess her secret, for which she had already been offered everything under the sun and because of which, until now, the most complex intrigues had been woven . . .

'Another cognac. I have excellent cognac,' she put in suddenly.

'Thank you.' I struggled to regain my senses.

'Tell me frankly,' I asked, almost trembling, 'why, why have you brought me here, why have you told me all this?'

'Why? . . . I myself do not know,' she said wistfully. 'Tell me about yourself. I am not asking out of curiosity. I shall tell you why afterwards.'

She sat there, unrecognizable, younger and more beautiful seeming, her morose aspect transfigured, her sharp features softened.

I told her what I could, as I could . . .

'And do you think my "method" could help you live?' she asked.

I shook my head.

'Don't you think that you would pay for it just as much as I have, as much as that poor Alsatian did? Don't you think that this is about some hidden, profound and just law of retribution, compensation, equilibrium? Sometimes I feel like testing it on someone else, to make certain that it . . . isn't so.

'Perhaps this may seem strange to you, but it would be a joy, a consolation to discover that I had made some mistake, that my decision had not doomed me *fatally*,' she pronounced clearly, 'to ruin, to desiccation, to this mummification.

'You see, I am being candid. Your success, for example, would console me – personally, egoistically console me. What's more, I like you. Say,' she continued, without looking at me, 'how would you set yourself up?

'When and for how long would you play, for how many hours each day, for how many years? You know,' she said, interrupting herself, 'it's a terrible thing. Say you had enough to buy everything you needed, but in the end you would give it all up, all of it, for *this*.

'I had a beloved, a sister, interesting work, hobbies, youth, beauty, life – and I gave it all up, do you hear? All of it. Do you know what that means? All, all, all of it for this money. I turned into a machine for accumulating money.

'I was loved – now I am despised. By everyone. I was surrounded by people; now I am alone, or surrounded by monsters.

'I was once beautiful – I became ugly.

'I was once alive – but I very nearly became a corpse.

'Do you not think I've paid over the odds for our little method?' She jumped up from her armchair. 'Do you not think that it reeks of swindling, crime, madness?' She was already shouting.

I seized her by the arm, but she tore it away, unexpectedly placing both hands on my shoulders and – her inhuman, unmoving eyes drawing nearer to me, eerily aflame and wide open on her pallid face – said to me in a hoarse, calm voice:

'For the love of God, my dear boy. Leave this place. Go. Trust me, you must leave at once.'

I kissed her childlike hand. She kissed my forehead.

The evening was cold, majestic and indifferent.

Kunak

GALINA KUZNETSOVA

A little after nine o'clock in the evening, the order was given to set out.

From the station, a string of carts surrounded by people trailed slowly through the suburbs. Almost nobody knew where exactly the embarkation would take place.

Beyond the suburbs, a narrow, stony road led through the darkness, among some bare, thorny bushes. To one side, above the town, a far-off blaze could be seen: somewhere was already burning. The broad white beams of the town's searchlights were fraughtly flitting across the sky. They walked in pained silence, broken only by the cries of the drivers. The twisting road led up into the hills and down again into a hollow. The wheels creaked despondently over the hardened earth. At first they were cold, but the arduous walk gradually warmed them. No one spoke. In the beginning it seemed to everyone that the sea shouldn't be far off, over the nearest knoll, and everyone stared fixedly into the dark. But the road looped round again and again, knoll gave way to knoll, little stones stung the feet, and the carts rocked helplessly in front of their eyes ... It was especially difficult for the women in their high winter galoshes and long coats. Yet they carried on more patiently than the men, trying not to lag behind their carts, struggling with the fatigue of many days, with the ardent desire to sit down and rest awhile.

At last, something flickered up ahead. Beyond a dark gate, curiously dominating an empty field, a bonfire was alight, its flame red. Soldiers were warming their hands by it. From the darkness blew a sharp, cold freshness.

'The bay! We're getting close!' cried someone cheerily.

But it proved not to be so. For a long time they walked along the bank, slowly climbing down the hill, when suddenly the carts in front ground to a halt, while those in the rear kept pressing on, and around half an hour passed in agonizing, ever-growing impatience. Finally there was movement, and, before long, far below something big showed black, covered in several rows of tiny lights casting their glimmering gold reflection on to the oily black water.

The column halted at the foot of the hill. Immediately, the regular file of people disintegrated, scattered, and, having snatched their belongings from the carts with astonishing speed, rushed towards the water, where, unusually close to the shore, separated from it only by wide gangplanks, an enormous ship loomed, shining with hundreds of lights. These gangplanks could scarcely be seen for the dense, assortedly rippling crowds that were jostling with one another in a frenzy, shouting, making violent threats.

A small group of women had been pushed back. The tall captain, whom they were watching, swore and shouted in a terrible, hoarse voice that this was the transport of such-and-such a corps, that there were women and children here, that they were 'obligated' to let them through . . . He was met with the same hoarse cries, that everyone here was equal, that it was every man for himself.

Suddenly a coarse, thundering voice, bellowing out from the gangway, overwhelmed all the others:

'Silence! You damned swine! These are our wives! You're to let them through immediately! What are you standing there goggle-eyed for?'

The enormous double-deck ship was so crowded with people that it seemed utterly impossible to fight one's way forwards. Yet the captain, forever looking about, gave signals to the women, forcing himself to squeeze into a solid wall of burly, bewildered soldiers with knapsacks, kettles and kit bags. The women tried not to lag behind. Meanwhile, in the background, the solid, baying crowd continued flowing in over the shaking, bowing planks, packing the decks, holds and corridors in ever greater numbers . . .

Dawn slowly broke. From the thinning twilight emerged the steel-grey waters of the bay, with wooden barges, rowing boats and skiffs scattered throughout it. In the distance, through the morning mist, the town came into sight, the white colonnade of Grafskaya Pier[1] gleaming white, seeming so tiny from here. The dawn was of icy rose: the steel-grey waters, hazy with a cold, dingy mist.

Packed to the gunwales, the ship settled below the water-line, listing even more towards the shore. By the gangplanks, on which people were still clamouring aboard, stood armed sentries. From the decks one could see the crowd surging below, its arrival from the hill never ceasing, the low expanse of the shoreline increasingly taking on the aspect of some monstrous encampment, with unharnessed carts and unsaddled, wandering horses, their loads abandoned.

Suddenly someone cried out from the upper deck:

'Look, look! There's a horse swimming!'

Everyone turned around. Above the grey misty water, a horse's head could be seen craning. It was swimming apparently without knowing where it was going, borne by the current out towards the middle of the bay. At times it raised its head even higher, and then you could see the water washing over its dark, glossy back. Yet its strength was obviously running out: more and more it would sink, snort and, pinning its ears, stretch out its neck towards the shore, the ship, where it sensed people and from which it clearly expected help. The crowd suddenly fell quiet, forgetting itself, what was going on all around, and began watching it, exchanging hurried, hot observations:

'A Cossack horse . . . It's looking for its master . . .'

'Well, yes, after all, they were told not to take the horses . . .'

'Wait, I know that horse! It's Kunak.[2] It belongs to one of the men in our village, it has the same star on its forehead! It must have swum after him as soon as he had to abandon it . . .'

'It's no secret how a Cossack abandons his horse . . .'

'It will drown!'

'Look, look! A rowing boat, they're paddling towards it. They're going to save it!'

A lifeboat was fast making its way around the stern. It was

heading for the middle of the bay. By now strength had utterly deserted the horse, but on seeing the people it sensed, understood, that they were coming to its aid and it made a supreme effort to fight the current and suddenly turned and began swimming towards them quickly. Although it was unclear how they could save this great, heavy horse with their little lifeboat, everyone, with bated breath, forgetting everything else, waited tensely.

'Sternwards, you need to have the stern facing him!' someone in the crowd shouted from the deck.

'Get a rope under him!'

'Look, they've almost made it!'

The horse was already quite near to the lifeboat. Stretching out its fine bay head with a white star on its forehead, it gave out a glad, grateful neigh and with the last of its strength extended its slender, wet neck towards the people. The boat, slowing its course, turned its stern towards the horse. A man in a short Romanov sheepskin coat,[3] who had been sitting at the stern, bent forwards and, quickly drawing his hand from his belt, extended it towards the straining head with its pinned ears ... Suddenly a short, sharp sound lashed the air. A second and a third followed ... The people on the shore and those on the boat all gasped in horror and compassion.

The head jerked up sharply in the air, then plunged into the agitated grey water. A minute later it appeared again, but already much farther away from the lifeboat. It was clear that now the current was freely, and with terrible speed, bearing it away. It disappeared again, then reappeared ... until finally it vanished for ever in the quick-flowing water ...

The sun was rising. The bright, now vast bay was already aglitter with the sparkle of a mirror. In parts, there was still a fine light-blue mist; the town on the other bank was brightly illuminated, its tightly packed white buildings festively rising up against the mild, blue winter sky. In the east, the peaks of faraway mountains showed mournfully in their many colours, powdered overnight with snow.

The Murder of Valkovsky

NINA BERBEROVA

She knew that the man sitting before her was a scoundrel – it was enough just to look at him, to listen to him, to recall everything she knew about him; not for a moment did she forget that the man sitting before her was a scoundrel, and yet still she would smile long and tenderly at him with those moist lips, and in her gaze, directed at him, there was such devotion, rapture, a kind of sweet resolve, so much so that she came to her senses only after she had been called for the third time, came to her senses and understood that she mustn't stare like that, that her eyes mustn't light up at the sight of this man who was still a complete stranger, that it was ridiculous. Above all because he could have been her son, and, what was more, because he had already danced with her twice. He had held her so strongly and closely; she had covered the lapel of his dinner jacket with powder; she had felt beneath her arm his broad, burning shoulder, and in her hair, at her temple, his breath, which set her mind spinning.

It had been an astonishing revelation that nothing, it turned out, could be divined in this life, nothing could be averted or predicted. Everything that happened happened of its own accord. Even yesterday – as throughout all these long years – she had been calm and wholly satisfied with her serene, almost pure life with her husband, whereas now all that receded into the past – she could remember nothing, see nothing and kept trying to make predictions: if Valkovsky looked at her while sipping from his glass, it would mean that he had noticed her, and if he had, fate could go to blazes. He reaches for the glass and not only does he look at her but he says something to her, very slowly and quietly; he offers her a sip as well, and when she stands up and walks off he follows her with his eyes. Again she thinks avidly that if he gets up and goes after her . . . And so on all evening. As she leaves, he proffers her fur coat. The foyer is dark and crowded; she senses he is about to embrace her, she is struck with terror, her heart pounding so loudly that she can hear nothing but its beat. He slides both his hands down from her shoulders, from under her fur collar, towards her hands, and suddenly grips her fingers violently, all ten at once, and she responds to him just as violently and passionately. She wants to place his hand to her breast, so that he should know what is happening to her heart, she wants to place his hand to her left breast for a long time, for ever . . .

The following morning she awoke with a feeling of shame for the previous evening – she had behaved as though she were drunk, having had nothing to drink; it didn't at all become her. She had grown accustomed to discussing everything with her husband.

'I was beastly last night,' she said apprehensively. 'I don't know what came over me.'

'You were charming as always, quite charming,' replied Gustav Georgievich. 'Valkovsky was trying it on with you, but he's no fool.'

She was now standing in front of the mirror, half dressed, and suddenly she wanted to scream, to sob, to fall flat on the floor.

'Was he?' she asked. 'I didn't notice.'

Gustav Georgievich smiled and went through to the bathroom, from where, after a couple of minutes, through the half-open door, he said:

'But I did.'

There was only an affectionate teasing in his voice, which immediately set her at ease: she realized that he had no suspicions about what was taking place inside her.

For a whole long hour she remained calm. Then she glanced at the clock, and it occurred to her that Valkovsky might not call at all – not today, not tomorrow, not ever. She could meet him in the street two years hence, and they would have absolutely nothing to say to one another. The prospect made her whole body limp. She lay on the bed – on the wide, warm bed, where she had slept so peacefully in her husband's embrace for fifteen years – and fell into a reverie. It was the heavy, unwanted reverie of a person who has just woken after having slept fitfully throughout the night. The telephone rang. With her eyes still closed, still asleep, staggering and knocking into things, she ran into the dining room. It was her husband, calling to say that he would be late for lunch. She stayed by the telephone, cradling her head in her hands. For the first time in her life she reflected that there was one thing in the world that could not be overcome, that one had to endure: time, the time that would pass between today and that moment when she would be reunited with Valkovsky.

It was a mystery. But for now she didn't have to worry about that. However, she was harbouring a secret: she couldn't countenance the idea that someone might notice the changes in her. Today she would be afraid of appearing absurd, but tomorrow she thought the whole thing would appear absurd – what did it matter to her? For several days she was tormented by the idea that there was something dishonourable about her anxiety, about this anticipation. But this too passed: so what if it was dishonourable! A fortnight went by. No longer did she fear losing everything that she had ever possessed. Even her life? Even her life. And not a moment too soon.

Yet, invisibly to those around her, everything that she was gradually letting go, everything that was slowly but implacably turning tenderness to indifference, and at times even loathing, clung to her, perhaps for the sole reason that they had no inkling that she no longer had any need of them. Hers was the sort of life that every quiet person leads, when there is time to attend a concert, to read a book and in the evenings, by the lamplight, to talk with a companion about the most assorted, anodyne, inessential things, with a companion who for some reason, on account of some long-standing tenderness and intimacy, suddenly at night becomes an occasional lover, ever more bashful with each passing year.

This serene life had on occasion its own similarly benign,

peculiarly agreeable plights, coupled with a few little childish
joys: for her birthday her husband gave her a large blue lamp,
but a week later the lamp suddenly toppled over, and both of
them, having been in the room next door, were more astonished than distressed by this, as they picked up the shards and
swept away the silvery glass dust. Then a friend who had disappeared in America turned up; later some friends threw a
masked ball at their apartment, and her dress, hired from a
costume shop, suited her beautifully. Early spring brought the
funeral of a girlfriend, who had died while under the knife.
And so she went to see the coffin borne out, somehow convinced that she was sure to meet Valkovsky there (all through
the masked ball she had tormented herself, too, certain that he
would come). And so now, at the funeral, she was once again
consumed by the possibility.

Later, despite the vague terror of the days that followed, she
still found time to muse about what might have happened, had
she not met him on the day of the funeral, how much longer
she might have waited, and she realized that she would have
waited until he did come, meeting him one way or another,
that nothing inside her could be extinguished, that the desire
to take his hand and place it to her breast was stronger than
anything else, stronger than her very being, that from the very
outset she had been ready to pay the price for this.

The coffin was borne almost upright down the narrow staircase, placed into a hearse and covered with a wreath; the
mourners, who had been waiting outside on the pavement, got
into the vehicles that had been provided, looking just like a wedding congregation with their white roses, and the procession set
off through the city. Valkovsky did not sit beside her; he bowed
to her from a distance at the doorway. She told herself: 'It's
heart-breaking! Marusia – so young, too! And the children . . .'
But as she said this, her soul was soaring high above all the
words and tears, above all the black, somewhere up in the
rose-tinted sky, searching the gleaming windows of the city for
Valkovsky's eyes, his smile, invisible to all but her. Even at the
cemetery, she felt as though spring had come, although it was
only February, and the day before there had been frost.

'How lovely it is,' she said to him, forgetting why they were there, as he walked beside her. 'I think I could come here every day.'

He laughed. They lagged farther and farther behind. Her high-heeled shoes pinched; birds were singing; an empty van trotted past them. Later they stood in a circle and watched as the coffin was lowered on ropes. Taking a trowel, each person in turn threw in a mound of earth; when her turn came, she was in such a state of excitement that she strewed it all down her fur coat.

As they walked back, the crowd continued to thin out, as though the people had connived to leave them alone by and by. At first she had felt the need to latch on to someone (her husband was not there), but she was afraid it would look suspicious. And so they walked together about the city. Where did they go? To drink coffee, of course, to warm themselves up. After all, there had been frost yesterday . . .

She had no desire to talk to him. She was certain they had nothing to talk about, and, what was more, she would never be able to listen to him and answer him. She just wanted to sit beside him, to be near him, to watch him slavishly, waiting for the moment when he would want her. Without hiding behind enigmatic phrases or ambiguous glances, she barters all her self and her life for his desire. No one is leading anyone else. The game is being conducted in the open. His touch is the axis of her existence. Over a cup of coffee, she rests her pale face, still youthful and beautiful, on her hand.

His attack was sudden. What for her had been the first departure in life from that delightful, cunning charade that levelled her with every other woman in the universe, for him was a regular, customary pleasure. He found it slightly disappointing that she didn't put up any resistance, though her sensitivity and responsiveness were enrapturing. There was something within her that took him by surprise, exhausting him. On parting, he noticed that she was in a state of great agitation, that she was expecting something from him. So he told her to come to his apartment again tomorrow.

She had exhausted herself, too. Exhausted, mainly through

her bold physical unreserve. She returned home shaken, in a
kind of desperate joy, because for the first time in her life she
had not seen, did not see, did not want to see herself from
without.

'Did you go to the cemetery?'

'Yes,' she said, trying to recall how it had been. But instead,
she felt again the approach of avid excitement.

That evening she went to bed early, and Gustav Georgievich
came in to bid her goodnight – he still wanted to read awhile.
'Little one,' he said. 'Goodnight, my little one!'

She closed her eyes. The words had sounded so sad, so
lonely. But a minute later, she wanted to laugh malignly at him
and at the whole world. She clutched the pillow under her
cheek and gripped her knees. And her thoughts tripped lightly
and gaily back – to Valkovsky.

When the next day she arrived at his apartment, he was just
as silent and impassioned as he had been the day before. It was
still light in the room, but for some reason a lamp was on, and
it seemed to her that it was perhaps not dusk but daybreak.
Amid the silence, so effortless for him, there was something
that began to alarm her. He smoked in an armchair, while she
paced from the mirror to the table, powdering herself, brushing her hair, searching for her gloves and feeling that after a
brief hour of happiness something unbearable was commenc-
ing: some agonizing mix of fear, doubt and shame.

'I want you to come on Monday,' he said as she passed
behind him (it was Thursday). 'Promise me that you'll come.'

She dropped her bag, and her money, a compact and her key
scattered on the floor. Slowly she picked it all up.

'What a lot of unnecessary things you carry about,' he said,
smiling. He stood up and embraced her.

She pressed herself to him and heard some papers crumple
in the side pocket of his jacket. She reached out her arms and
embraced him. She felt something hard in his back trouser
pocket.

'And you don't?' she replied in alarm.

She was free right through until Monday . . .

She descended the flight of stairs, and this descent from

the fourth floor calmed her. All of a sudden she had arrived somewhere – somewhere where she would be alone, where there was still daylight, where it was clear that Valkovsky didn't love her. From those terrible, shaking heights, she had descended to terra firma.

'Why did I do that?' she asked herself. There was a ready reply to this: it was in her body, in her palpitating heart, in her weak, unruly knees, in her eyes that suddenly filled with tears.

'Because I wanted it. Because I needed it.'

Gustav Georgievich was already at home, and now they sat down to dinner. He was, as ever, cheery and equable, but she didn't notice him: to laugh at him was no longer what she wanted. She wanted to be left alone, neither to see nor hear him. That evening they were invited out, and so she went and chatted bravely with a smile. It was two o'clock in the morning when they went to bed and turned out the light; Gustav Georgievich fell silent straight away, and she thought he had fallen asleep. Then she began to think about him – not about Valkovsky, but about Gustav Georgievich – and the tears streamed down her cheeks, on to the pillow, into her hair. So it continued for a while: not a single sob, not a single sniff, she cried in silence. And suddenly Gustav Georgievich's great, dry hand covered her eyes.

'Little one,' he said barely audibly. 'Don't be afraid, come close.'

The darkness made her head spin, she was falling somewhere, speeding into an abyss, unconscious, like one possessed. And only his shoulder could save her from this fall.

'After all, we're together, the two of us, aren't we, little one?' he asked, firmly and chastely holding her to himself. 'The two of us? And we don't need anyone else?'

These simple words, uttered so many times over the course of their life together, now harboured some glad tidings, saving her in her despair. She pressed her lips to his hand. Yes, they were together, and there was no one else in the world. There was no one, nor would there be. He slowly and tenderly, ever more ardently with each passing moment, started to kiss her, taking charge of her, and she reciprocated until they fell silent in exhaustion.

They were together, and they should remain together, and Valkovsky had to be purged from life, otherwise it would be impossible to go on living – he was tertiary. 'I'll do it,' she told herself. 'It has to be done. It's what I want.' Now there was neither temptation nor excitement in her recollection of him. She had waited for an assignation with him, now she would wait for her liberation from him. Otherwise, neither she nor Gustav Georgievich could live.

The only thing she recalled from her most recent rendez-vous was that when she embraced him she had felt something like a revolver his back trouser pocket. The thought of the revolver kept returning to her; there was a tranquillity in this thought, a certainty that here lay the path to absolute freedom from Valkovsky. There was no fear, she wanted his death, just as these two months she had wanted the man himself.

Over these two months she had taught herself to guard her secrets and now she also learned to hide the fact that she had crossed from trepidation and greed to constancy and patient, cold expectation. 'On Monday,' she thought, enduring three long days and gradually realizing that if something unforeseen were to happen on Monday – an earthquake, a revolution – it would not save Valkovsky; she would find him, some day, as she had done before.

'Even her life? Even her life' – insomnia reminded her, poisoned days when she had been prepared so bounteously to pay for his love. Now she was prepared to pay for his death, and to answer for it, too, if necessary – that wouldn't stop her: prison had never stopped anyone who wanted to kill; it stopped only those who would have to kill to steal a purse. And when Valkovsky was no more, she would know that it was just the two of them in the world: Gustav Georgievich and she.

On the day when it happened, on the Monday, just after five o'clock, she entered the doorway of the building where he lived. Her face was luminous, bright, joyful, just as it had been a week ago when she had seen off the coffin of her dead friend. She entered the lift – no one saw her. She rang. But nobody opened the door. She rang a second time. Silence. She noticed a key sticking out of the door: Valkovsky must have run out for cigarettes or pastries . . . She went in. From the vestibule the door to his room was ajar, and for some reason it was completely dark inside, as if the shutters had not been opened since yesterday and the curtains had not been drawn back. She groped for the switch and turned on the light. Time had stopped: here it was still Sunday evening, late at night, supper not yet cleared away, a jacket hung on a chair, cigarette ends in an ashtray, bottles, and Valkovsky himself, lying in bed, very pale, covers drawn up to his chin, a hole in his temple, long cold, long dead.

Someone had taken revenge here yesterday, calmly and premeditatedly, aiming at the sleeping man.

She drew her hand across her face and shuddered. No, the revolver was no longer in his trouser pocket: the pocket had been turned inside out. Again she went over to the bed. By the bed head, on the rug, something sparkled: she picked up a long, thin crystal earring. Silence. Someone had been here before her. They had not finished drinking the bottle – two full glasses stood on the table – but they had managed to eat a chicken, picking at the bones to their hearts' content. Silence. The light had to be switched off. But how young he was! and truly, he might have been her son. Silence in the hallway, silence on the landing. We'll leave the key as it was. Silence below, in the lift. A gentleman and a lady come in from the street. Who could be frightened by that? The earring she placed in her handbag. 'What a lot of unnecessary things you carry about . . .'

And so she is left alone with Gustav Georgievich.

The Spy

GAITO GAZDANOV

The tall, sinewy gelding I had been riding for two and a half miles was killed by a bullet to its head as I veered right, crossing from the damp, sodden ploughland on to the hard road. The horse tumbled to the ground, and although I managed to free my feet from the stirrups I broke a spur in the fall. A few moments later, having recovered my senses, I was just able to make out the silhouettes of our soldiers already far in the distance. With all manner of cursing, and limping on my left leg, I set off after them. A few steps later I turned around.

A rider astride an enormous black horse was galloping slowly and heavily after me. I saw him throw a rifle over his shoulder and draw a sabre from its sheath. He was alone: there was no one behind him.

I extracted my revolver, a Parabellum of impressive dimensions, and, when around two dozen paces separated me from the rider, I fired: the horse lurched instantly to one side, and the rider was thrown from the saddle. Caught in the stirrup, his left leg impeded the fall. I walked up to the standing horse, disentangled the man and, laying him on the ground, stared at his face.

Beneath a soldier's peaked cap with its red star on the band I recognized Robert, a student whom I had known for about two years: he had always been famed for reckless bravery and had a reputation for being a good sort of fellow. He was a Frenchman by nationality.

Cavalrymen appeared on the horizon. Grabbing the saddle by the pommel, I took one final look at Robert. Blood was trickling from his mouth; he opened his eyes.

'*Vous n'avez pas de chance, Robert!*'[1] I said, leaning down to him.

The bedraggled soldiers of the White Army were traversing the wide expanses of southern Russia. Drunken ensigns crooned off-pitch arias from operettas; cavalry officers, having been snorting cocaine, swayed in their saddles; pimps and prostitutes, traders and profiteers followed on the heels of the attackers.

I met Robert once again, in a town that had been taken by the Whites. He was decked out in a Cossack officer's uniform, and his eyelids were red and swollen. He came up to me.

'I should alert you to the fact that my service in the Red Army was a mission that had been entrusted to me by my superiors. You mustn't draw any erroneous conclusions from it. I think we can consider the matter closed. I'm a patriot; we're saving the Motherland.'

'So, you recovered?' I replied, after a moment's deliberation.

That evening Robert showed up at my apartment. He was dressed in civilian attire and was wearing a false beard; there was a scar on his right temple. He told the maid that he was searching for a deserter by the name of Semyonov.

I came into the hallway and, flipping the light switch, recognized Robert at once. The maid looked at us both in amazement.

'What's the meaning of this, Robert?' I inquired in French.

'You're mistaken,' he said. 'You must have taken me for someone else. I'm afraid I don't speak French. I'm searching for the deserter, Semyonov. I'm an agent of . . .'

The front door opened and in shot a head wearing a green service cap, followed on by a second. Robert didn't finish the sentence and turned away.

'The bomb, Vaska, throw it!' shouted a desperate voice. 'To hell with him, let the ceiling cave in!'

The maid leapt aside in horror. Robert bolted for the door. That second, a bomb went off with an almighty bang.

We were left unscathed: Robert had vanished.

*

When all is said and done, the city of Sebastopol is not so bad. Homeless people first began appearing there in the closing year of the Civil War; hailing from every reach of southern Russia, this lot got by on theft, alms-begging and eating scraps of food.

I noticed one boy who was brighter than the rest. I recalled seeing him a couple of times throughout the city – turned out in pristine clothes, clean and looking entirely unlike his friends, who were going about in rags. One day I saw him talking to a French sailor, which surprised me.

I spotted his diminutive figure on another occasion: he had gone up to an Englishman, whom I recognized at once from the back of his head, on the Primorsky Boulevard. It was Robert.

'That one over there, in the hat,' said his voice. 'Just the address, nothing else.'

Robert then walked past me, keeping a straight face and pretending not to know me.

I let him pass.

I came across Robert again in that city: he was walking along the Nakhimovsky Prospect; a woman in a soiled under-shirt was running barefooted after him. Every five seconds she would cry, 'Murderer,' and stick out her tongue at him. He did not turn around.

'What's all this?' I asked a friend, who was walking with me. 'Who is that woman?'

'She's slow on the uptake,' he replied scornfully. 'Surely you must recognize her? It's Fenya, the Sebastopol madwoman. And that chap in the English uniform is a spy.'

The years passed by. I marked the unreality of it all: the combination of stringency and chaos, the change of scenery, the circus in which time juggles life, and life, human faces. Beyond the regular rhythms of day and the paroxysms of night I sought out the shrouded visages of hallucinations. I roamed about for some time, oblivious to my surroundings, and then, puzzled, I glanced back – this was somewhere on the outskirts of Paris – and entered a smoky little café. A drunken Serbian woman was dancing to the duet of a gramophone and an accordion;

neatly arranged bottles were clinking about; the diabolical scar-covered face of a man in a navy apron and a collarless shirt suddenly appeared before my eyes.

'*D'la bière, du pinard?*'[2] he shouted in my face.

'My usual,' I said in Russian. 'Black coffee.'

'*À la gare avec ça! J'suis pas obligé de connaître toutes les langues du monde. Qu'on parle français quand on est en France.*'[3]

'You mustn't work yourself up so much.' I paused for a second. 'For one, I can distinctly hear your accent, despite your nationality. Your French is tinged with Russian. Secondly, for God's sake, Robert, the only spy in here is you. You're quite free to speak Russian. You've become too used to the would-be tragic role of a man risking his life by the minute. I doubt anyone would give even a hundred francs for your head. I'm fed up of seeing your face, Robert. I'd have hanged myself from boredom by now if my mystique was limited to a false beard, ten suits, a dozen scars and a middling knowledge of three languages.'

'I prefer my line of work to yours,' replied Robert. 'You may have a dozen or so exercises in irony to ascribe to the vacuum that is your life, but you'll never know the meaning of danger, of fatality. You don't like to gamble because you're unable to fathom the excitement. You hate artists and prefer mad hacks. You know nothing of glory . . . If I were to tell you that my life consisted in a combination of inspiration and calculation, you naturally wouldn't believe me, because the concept is so inherently alien to you, as is a sense of duty to one's country, which I serve, and to war, to which I've devoted my whole life.'

'If I have time, I'll be sure to spare a thought for the philosophy of dilettantes engaged in espionage, I promise you,' I said. 'Right now, however, far be it from me to dish out advice. I'd merely like to remind you that soldiers are going out of fashion. We're living in the age of the civilian. Places are being reserved for people like you – heroes, soldiers in splints, saviours of the Motherland – in the fire brigade. *Voilà, mon vieux.*[4] The next time I meet you will doubtless be in Singapore, unless there's some radical change in your outlook and you relinquish that bothersome and entirely unnecessary profession of yours for the meagre trappings of a reporter.'

I fell silent, sipping my coffee slowly. Robert had always been a dreamer; he devoted his life to danger with the same ease as I would dedicate a story to a friend.

At one of the tables a painted woman in deep mourning suddenly caught my eye. Blood rushed to my face. The wail of the gramophone carried on in the background as the Serbian woman went about her wild, ridiculous dance – in this dilapidated, infernal joint. And, for the first time in my life, forgetting myself, the slippery beds for hire, the chilly abyss of the basement I lived in – for the first time understanding that the word sadness could be written without quotation marks – I said to this woman in mourning:

'Have you buried your profession, my dear? Or are you looking for a wealthy client with a penchant for originality?'

Her eyes met mine. How many times at Paris's misty crossroads had that scornful gaze slid away from me. I lifted my heavy eyelids. Despairingly I recalled the city I was born in, the deathly grandeur of St Petersburg.

Robert's smiling face appeared once again in my line of sight.

'Allow me to introduce you,' he said. 'This is Varvara Vladimirovna, my wife. In Russia she was a lady; now she works as a seamstress.'

'You've ruined my story, Robert.'

Turning to her:

'Shall we get acquainted, dear lady?'

I went home. The mulatto in the apartment next door, grinning with exertion, was playing his scales on the cello.

Black Swans

GAITO GAZDANOV

On 26 August of last year, I opened the morning paper and read that in the Bois de Boulogne, not far from the greater lake, was found the body of a Russian by the name of Pavlov. There were 150 francs in his wallet; there was also a note, addressed to his brother:

'Dear Fedya, life here is hard and dull. I wish you all the best. I have written to Mother that I have gone to Australia.'

I knew Pavlov very well and knew that precisely on 25 August he would shoot himself: the man never lied or exaggerated.

On the 10th of that very month I went to him for money: I needed to borrow 150 francs.

'When will you be able to repay it?'

'Shall we say on the twentieth, the twenty-fifth . . . ?'

'On the twenty-fourth.'

'Fine. Why the twenty-fourth exactly?'

'Because the twenty-fifth will be too late. On the twenty-fifth of August I'm going to shoot myself.'

'Are you in trouble?' I asked.

I shouldn't have been so laconic, had I not known that Pavlov never changed his mind and that to try to dissuade him would have been a complete waste of time.

'No, I'm not in any particular trouble. But the life I lead, as you're aware, is unsavoury enough; I foresee no change in the future, and I find it all very dull. I see no sense in going on like this, just eating and working as I do now.'

'But you have family . . .'

'Family?' he said. 'Yes, I do. They won't be much put out by it; that is to say, it will, of course, be unpleasant for a certain duration of time, but effectively none of them depends on me.'

'Well, fine,' I said. 'I think you're wrong, nonetheless. We'll talk about this again, if you like – completely objectively, of course. Are you at home in the evenings?'

'Yes, as always. Do come. Although I think I already know what you're going to say.'

'We'll see about that.'

'All right, goodbye,' he said, opening the door for me and flashing that strange, vexing, cold smile of his.

After this conversation, I had no doubt that Pavlov would shoot himself; I was as sure of it as I was that I would walk out the door and along the pavement. However, were anyone else to have told me of Pavlov's decision, I should have deemed it unlikely. Just then I recalled that two years ago a mutual acquaintance of ours had said to me:

'You'll see. He'll meet a bad end. Nothing is sacred to him any more. He'll throw himself under a bus or a train. You'll see . . .'

'My friend, you're letting your imagination run away with you,' I had replied.

Of all the men I knew, Pavlov was the most remarkable in many respects; and, without doubt, physically the most hardy. His body knew no fatigue; after eleven hours of hard graft he could go for a walk, and it seemed he never tired. He could live on bread alone for months on end and feel none the worse for it. He could work like no other, and was thus able to scrimp and save. He could go for days without sleep; ordinarily, he slept a mere five hours. I once met him in the street at half past three in the morning; he was walking unhurriedly along the boulevard, hands thrust in the pockets of his lightweight raincoat – it was winter, although apparently he was insensitive to the cold, too. I knew that he was working at a factory and that there were four hours left before the first siren.

'You're out late,' I said. 'You've got to be at work soon.'

'I have four hours left. What do you make of Saint-Simon?[1] A fascinating man, in my opinion.'

'Why Saint-Simon all of a sudden?'

'I have an exam in French political history,' he said, 'which figures, as you are aware, Saint-Simon. I'd been studying until just a short while ago since yesterday, so I decided to go out for a walk.'

'Aren't you working today?'

'Of course I am. Why shouldn't I be? Goodnight.'

'Goodnight.'

And so he sauntered on, just as leisurely down the boulevard. Yet his physical merits seemed almost immaterial and of no consequence beside his spiritual strength, which perished to no effect. Perhaps he himself could not determine how to employ his rare gifts: they remained without application. He would have made, I think, an indispensable captain of a ship, but only if catastrophe befell that ship unremittingly; he could have been a wonderful explorer of a city that had suffered an earthquake, or of a country in the clutches of a plague epidemic, or of a burning forest. But there was none of this – no plague, no forest, no ship, and so Pavlov lived in a wretched Parisian *pension* and worked like everyone else. One day it occurred to me that it was perhaps this innate strength of his, which had been searching for some outlet or application, that provoked him to suicide; he exploded like a stoppered bottle, from some terrible internal pressure. Yet whenever I tried to fathom the reasons for his voluntary demise, I was forced to abandon these ideas, for not one of those principles that determine a man's behaviour in the most diverse of circumstances applied to Pavlov, and as a result he always remained outside the entire framework of reason and conjecture: he stood apart from it, he was unlike anyone else.

He had a particular smile, which was unpleasant to begin with: it was a smile of superiority, and one sensed – almost everyone, even the most obtuse people did – that Pavlov had some sort of right to smile like that.

He never spoke untruths – which was utterly astonishing. Moreover, he never flattered, and indeed told each man what he thought of him: this was always distressing and awkward, and those who were among the most quick-witted would try to turn it into a joke and laugh; and he would laugh together with them – his peculiar, cold laughter. Only once in all my long acquaintance with him did I discern in his voice a fleeting softness – something I had assumed him incapable of. We had been discussing theft.

'Ah, it's a curious thing,' he said. 'You know, I used to be a thief, but then I decided that it wasn't worth it and stopped thieving. These days I wouldn't steal a thing.'

'You were a thief?' I replied in astonishment.

'What's so strange about that? The majority of people are thieves. If they don't steal, it's only out of fear or happenstance. But in his heart almost every man's a thief.'

'I've heard it said many a time. But I'd rather be inclined to agree that it's one of the most widespread misapprehensions. I don't think every man could be a thief.'

'But I do. I have a knack for sniffing out thieves. I can tell at once whether a man's able to steal or not.'

'Could I, for instance?'

'You could,' he said. 'You wouldn't steal a hundred francs. But for a woman you could steal, and if the temptation of more money were there, you might.'

'And Lyova?' I asked. Pavlov and I had studied together abroad; we had many friends in common – one of them was Lyova, a jolly, carefree and, for the most part, decent man.

'He would.'

'And Vasiliev?'

This was one of the best students – a glum and hopelessly conscientious chap, always unkempt, very diligent and boring.

'Him too,' said Pavlov unhesitatingly.

'Oh, come on! He's virtuous, hard-working, and he prays to God every day.'

'He's a coward first and foremost: everything else you mention is unimportant. But he's a thief – and a petty thief at that.'

'What about Seryozha?'

Seryozha was a friend of ours, an idler, a dreamer and a dilettante – but very able; he would lie on the grass for hours, thinking of impossible things, dreaming of Paris (we were living in Turkey back then), of the sea, and God knows what else; everything around him that was real was to him alien and indifferent. Once, on the eve of an important exam, I awoke in the night and saw Seryozha awake, smoking.

'What's the matter,' I asked. 'Are you nervous?'

'Yes, a little,' he said hesitantly. 'It's small beer.' 'Well, not entirely.' 'Are you afraid you might fail?' 'What on earth are you talking about?' he said in amazement. 'The exam, of course.' 'Oh, no, that's a bore. I was thinking about something else entirely.' 'What then?' 'I was thinking that a steam-powered yacht costs an awful lot, whereas one with sails wouldn't be worth it. But then I'd have no money left on a steam one,' he said with conviction. 'I'd have nothing to buy cigarettes with.' He was smoking – and threw the cigarette end away; it was dark, and I thought I saw the end fall on the blanket. 'Seryozha,' I said after a minute, 'I think your cigarette end fell on the blanket.' 'What of it?' he replied. 'Let it catch, then you'll know all about it.' 'More often than not they go out: the tobacco's damp.' And so he went to sleep, probably dreaming of his yacht.

'What about Seryozha,' I repeated.

And for the first time Pavlov's face took on a gentle expression that was uncustomary for him, and he smiled in a completely different way than he usually did – a strange and frank smile.

'No, Seryozha would never steal,' he said. 'Never.'

I was one of his few acquaintances; an ever-present curiosity drew me to him, and in conversation with him I would forget the usual necessity of proving myself via some particular means – by making a well-placed remark, by expressing some opinion unlike the rest: I would forget this rotten habit of mine, and only Pavlov's words would hold any interest for me. Most likely, it was the first instance in my life where my interest in a man refused to be dictated by selfish motives – that is, a desire somehow to define myself in yet another different set of circumstances. I could not say that I liked Pavlov, he was too alien to me – but then he never liked anyone, myself included. We both knew this only too well. I knew, moreover, that Pavlov would have felt no regret if some mishap were to have befallen me; had I ascertained that the possibility of such a regret did exist, I would have immediately rejected it.

I remembered how Pavlov had once told me about an acquaintance who asked him for money, giving his word of honour to return it the following day. For two weeks he didn't come back, then he showed up one evening and with tears in his eyes begged for forgiveness – and for another five francs into the bargain, since he had nothing to eat.

'What did you do?' I asked.

'I gave him the money. I wouldn't have given it to another man, but he was no man; I told him as much. He waited silently while I extracted the money from my pocket.'

He smiled and added:

'I gave him ten francs, as it happens.'

It was not spiritual compassion that he had, but logical compassion; I think it could be explained by the fact that he himself never asked for compassion from anyone at all. He was disliked by his acquaintances, and only the most simple-minded of people were kind to him: they didn't understand him and considered him slightly eccentric, but a wonderful person all the same. Perhaps this was true in a certain sense, just not in the one they believed. In any case, Pavlov was quite generous, and the money he earned from his ten or eleven hours at the factory he spent thriftily and frugally. He handed out a lot of money and had a great many debtors; he often helped strangers who would come up to him in the street. Once, as we were walking along a deserted Boulevard Arago – it was dark and fairly late and cold, the shutters in all the houses were tightly shut, the leafless trees in particular seemed to heighten the impression of desertedness and the cold – a shabbily dressed, thickset man came up to us and croaked that he had been discharged from hospital only the previous day, that he was a worker, that he had been left on the streets in the winter; could we not help him a little? '*Voilà mes papiers*,'[2] he said, knowing that no one looks at them. Pavlov took the documents, walked up to the street lamp and showed them to me; there was no mention of a hospital.

'See how he lies,' he said in Russian.

Then, turning to the vagrant, he burst out laughing and gave him a fifty-franc note.

Another time we met a Russian with a limp, who also asked
for money. I knew him already. One summer's day – this was
shortly after I arrived in Paris – as I was leaving the library and
crossing the street, engrossed in a book, I suddenly felt someone thrust a dry, cold hand over my book – and, raising my
eyes, I saw before me a man wearing a smart grey suit and a
fine hat; he was lame. With a casual gesture, he doffed his hat
to me and said, remarkably quickly:

'Are you Russian? I'm very glad to make your acquaintance.
Owing to my disability, as you can observe, and being deprived
of the opportunity, like others, to earn money in exile by hard
émigré labour, I'm compelled to turn to you in the capacity of
a former officer of the Volunteer Army and a final-year student
of the Faculty of History and Literature at Moscow Imperial
University, as a former hussar and irreconcilable political
enemy of the Bolshevist government, with a request to spare
me a moment of your attention and, putting yourself in my
position, to do what you can to assist me.'

He uttered all this without pausing, and I would never have
committed his long and incoherent dissertation to memory –
even more so because I had failed to comprehend half of it – had
I not the occasion subsequently to hear it again several times,
almost without variation; only sometimes he happened to be a
student not of Moscow, but of Kazan or Kharkov University,
and not a hussar, but an uhlan, or an artilleryman, or a lieutenant of the Black Sea fleet. He was a strange man; I happened
to see him one evening in a little garden near the church of
Saint-Germain-des-Prés – he was sitting next to an elderly,
melancholy-looking woman, hunched over with his head
bowed, and he had such an unhappy look about him that I
began to feel sorry for him. However, three days later, on the
Place d'Odéon, this same man could be found smoking a cigar
and sipping some lilac liquid in an especially tall glass, his
right arm with some made-up moll in its embrace.

That day, when he first approached me, I had only six francs
on me, and I said to him:

'Unfortunately I'm unable to help you; I have no money. I
can give you two francs, any more would be difficult.'

'Three-fifty, please,' he said.

I was amazed:

'Why three-fifty exactly?'

'Because, young man,' he replied almost didactically, 'three-fifty is the price of a meal in the Russian canteen.' Resuming his gracious air, he added: 'My thanks, friend.' He walked away, limping and leaning on his walking stick.

That was exactly how he addressed himself to Pavlov and me.

'Are you Russians? I'm very glad to make your acquaintance. Owing to my disability . . .'

'I already know all this,' said Pavlov. 'I'm well aware that you studied at the universities in Moscow and Kazan, that you were a hussar, an uhlan, an artilleryman and a sailor. Weren't you a submariner too, as it happens, didn't you also attend some theological academy?'

'Don't you know him?' he asked me. 'I've already given him money five times over.'

'I do know him,' I said. 'I think he's getting carried away with the Faculty of History and Literature. But he's a poor wretch all the same.'

'Next time ask someone else,' said Pavlov. 'All told, I've paid you fifty francs: I consider you unworthy of such a sum. Do not think that I say this to you to relish your unfortunate situation: if it were a bishop in your position, I should say the same to him. Here's some money for you.'

Pavlov lived in a very small room in one of the cheap *pensions* in Montparnasse. He had painted the walls himself, fitted shelves, set books on them, bought himself a paraffin stove, and when he had managed to save up a certain sum of money allowing him not to work for a period, he would spend whole months in this room, alone from morning till night, going out only to buy bread, or sausage, or tea.

'What do you do with yourself all that time?' I asked him during one of these periods.

'I think,' he replied.

At the time, I ascribed no significance to his words, but later I learned that Pavlov, this steadfast, unerring man, was a dreamer at heart. It seemed exceedingly strange and hardly at all like him, yet it was so. I suppose that, apart from me, no one would have suspected this, because no one ever tried to ask Pavlov what he thought about; it never occurred to anyone, all the more so because Pavlov himself was singularly uninteresting; he conducted experiments only on himself.

He had lived in Paris for four years, working from morning until night, seldom reading and taking little interest in anything. Then, all of a sudden, he took the decision to complete his higher education. It came about because someone had emphasized during a conversation with him that he was a university graduate.

'University, that's no great feat,' said Pavlov.

'But you never graduated.'

'Yes, but that was purely because of circumstance. At any rate, you've given me an idea: I'll finish my studies.'

And so he set to task: he enrolled in the philosophy department of the Faculty of History and Literature and studied in the evenings after work – which would have been beyond anyone else. Pavlov himself knew this well. He would say to me:

'They write about Russians who work on the railways by night and study by day. Such things remind me of war correspondents' reports; I recall reading in one newspaper about the preparations for war. There was a description of "the cannons standing menacingly with their trails pointed towards the enemy". It's obvious to any soldier, even to one who isn't an artilleryman, that this correspondent hadn't even the faintest notion of cannons, and had probably never seen one in his life. It's the same here: they'll talk to some reporter, and he'll make out as if they work at night and study by day. But just send a reporter like that to do night-time work, and he won't even manage to write up his articles, let alone do any serious work.'

He lapsed into thought; then he smiled, as always, and said:

'Still, it's just as well there are so many fools in the world.'

'Why does that give you pleasure?'

'I don't know. There's a comfort in the fact that regardless of how inferior or worthless one may be, there are still people far baser.'

This was the only instance where he expressed his strange

joie maligne[3] plainly; ordinarily he would never have said it. It was altogether difficult to judge him by what he said – difficult and complicated; many of those who knew him insufficiently well simply refused to believe him – which was understandable. Once he said:

'When I served in the White Army, I was an awful coward; I was terribly afraid for my life.'

This was inconceivable to me, and I asked one of his fellow soldiers, whom I happened to know, about his cowardice.

'Pavlov?' he said. 'The bravest man I ever set eyes on.'

I mentioned this to Pavlov.

'I didn't say,' he replied, 'that I ever shied away from danger. I was terribly afraid – and that was that. But it doesn't mean that I hid away. A comrade and I once attacked a platoon of machine-gunners, taking two rifles, although my horse was killed right under me. I went on counterintelligence missions – and could I have done any differently? But none of that stopped me being a coward. Only I knew of it, and when I told anyone else they wouldn't believe me.'

'By the way, how are your studies going?'

'In two years I'll have finished university.'

Two years later I was a witness to a conversation between Pavlov and that same acquaintance of his, with whom he had first spoken of university. They talked about various things, and at the end of the conversation Pavlov's companion asked:

'So, do you still think that a university education is all chance and small beer?'

'More so than ever.'

He shrugged his shoulders and set the conversation on a different track, making no mention of the fact that in the intervening years he had graduated from the Faculty of History and Literature at the Sorbonne.

His words left a strange impression: never in all that he said did I notice the desire to make even the slightest effort to pay a compliment, to say something kind or simply to remain silent about things that were unpleasant; that is why many shunned him. Once, finding himself in the company of several men, he casually mentioned that he had little money. Among us was a

certain Svistunov, a young man, always well dressed and rather
boastful: he had a lot of money, and whenever he spoke his
words would forever be accompanied by disparaging gestures:

'I don't understand, gentlemen. You simply don't know how
to live. I've never asked anyone for a loan, I live better than the
lot of you, and I've never suffered any indignity. I can only
imagine what a man must feel asking for a loan of money.'

And so this Svistunov, knowing that Pavlov was exceptionally punctilious and that he would risk nothing in offering him
his assistance, said that he would gladly give Pavlov however
much he wanted.

'No,' replied Pavlov. 'I won't take money from you.'

'Why not?'

'You're miserly,' said Pavlov. 'And what's more, I don't care
for your obligingness. I didn't ask you in the first place.'

Svistunov grew pale and stood there dumbstruck.

Pavlov neither knew nor liked women. At the factory where
he worked, his neighbour was a Frenchwoman of around
thirty-two, widowed not so long ago. She liked him a lot:
firstly, he was an excellent worker; secondly, she found him
physically attractive: she would spend long periods watching
the rapid, uniform movements of his arms, bared below the
elbow, the pink nape of his neck and his broad back. She was
just a worker and considered Pavlov one too: he almost never
spoke with his co-workers in the workshop, and she ascribed
this to his characteristic reserve, to the fact that he was a foreigner, and to other circumstances, in no way corresponding to
those reasons that really induced Pavlov to silence.

'Il est timide,'[4] she would say.

At last she succeeded. He spoke French in a slightly bookish
style – he never once used any argot. It was a strange conversation; and one could not imagine two more different people
than this worker and Pavlov.

'Listen,' she said. 'You're a young man and, I think,
unmarried?'

'Yes.'

'How do you cope without a woman?' she asked.

If they had anything at all in common, it was that they both called a spade a spade. Only they spoke and thought along different lines; and I think that the distance separating them was likely the greatest that could separate man and woman.

'You need a wife or a girlfriend,' she went on. '*Écoute, mon vieux*'⁵ – she was already on intimate terms with him – 'we could settle down together. I could teach you a lot of things, I see you're inexperienced. And then – you don't have a woman. What do you say?'

He looked at her and smiled. However insensitive she may have been, it dawned on her that she had made a first-rate blunder in approaching this man. There remained precious little hope of a successful exit to this conversation. Yet nonetheless – already mechanically – she asked him:

'Well, what do you say?'

'I haven't any need of you,' he replied.

He had yet another trait that was exceedingly rare: a peculiar freshness of perception, a peculiar independence of thought – and a total freedom from those prejudices that his milieu might have inculcated in him. He was *un déclassé*,⁶ like others: he was not a worker, not a student, not a soldier, not a peasant, not a nobleman – and he lived his life beyond any limitations of birth: all people of all classes were alien to him. But what seemed most surprising to me was that, not being graced with a very strong intellect, he could maintain such independence in everything that touched upon those areas where the weight of authority dominates – literature, sciences and art. His opinions in this regard were always unlike anything (or almost anything) else that I had until then had occasion to hear or read.

'What do you think of Dostoevsky, Pavlov?' inquired once a young poet who was very keen on philosophy, Russian tragic literature and Nietzsche.

'He was a villain, if you ask me,' said Pavlov.

'I beg your pardon, what did you say?'

'A villain,' he repeated. 'An hysteric who considered himself a man of genius, small-minded like a woman, a liar and a gambler at the expense of others. Had he been a bit better-looking, he might have been kept by some old merchant's wife.'

'But what about his literature?'

'That is of no interest to me,' said Pavlov. 'I've never managed to read a single one of his novels right to the end. You asked me what I thought of Dostoevsky. In every man there is one quality, the most fundamental to his nature – everything else is superfluous. With Dostoevsky, the main thing is that he was a villain.'

'You say such monstrous things.'

'I don't believe monstrous things exist at all,' said Pavlov.

I visited him on the 15th, drank some tea with him, and then I began to talk of suicide.

'You've got ten days left,' I began.

'Yes, more or less. Well, what grounds will you give to prove the irrationality of such an act? You may be utterly candid: you know it will change nothing.'

'Yes, I know. But I'd like to hear your reasons once again.'

'They're exceedingly simple,' he said. 'Judge for yourself: I work at a factory and live a fairly awful life. It's impossible to pretend otherwise: I had thought of making a journey, but now I think that if it failed to live up to my expectations, it would come as the most devastating blow for me. Next: absolutely no one depends on me. My mother has succeeded in forgetting me; as far as she's concerned, I died ten years ago. My sisters are married and do not keep up any correspondence with me. My brother, whom you know, that oaf of a twenty-five-year-old, will get by without me. I don't believe in God; there isn't a single woman whom I love. I'm bored of living: working and eating? Politics doesn't interest me – nor does art, or Russia's fate, or love: I'm simply bored. I shan't make a career for myself – but then no career would tempt me. Tell me, please: after all that, what sense is there in my continuing to live like this? Perhaps if I were still mistaken and thought I had some sort of talent. But I know that I have none. That's all.'

He was sitting across from me, smiling, and it was as if he were saying with his arrogant air: You see how simple it all is, yet I've realized this while you haven't, nor will you. I couldn't say that I pitied Pavlov, as I would have done a friend from whose hands, say, I snatched a revolver. Pavlov was somewhere beyond compassion: it was as if he were surrounded by some medium that the feelings of others were unable to penetrate, as rays of light cannot pass through an opaque screen; he was too cold and distant. However, I was sorry that after a certain time such a valuable, precious, irreplaceable human mechanism would cease to move and would disappear from life; and all his qualities – tirelessness, bravery and a terrible spiritual might – all this would dissolve into the ether and vanish, never to find any application for itself.

'Now tell me what you think of this,' said Pavlov.

'I think,' I replied, 'that you're wrong to search for some logical justification for everything: truly, it's a waste of time. You say you're bored and that there's no meaning in your life. How can such abstract ideas force you to commit any act – or, rather, I think the question is beside the point. Imagine that I work for fourteen hours without a break, I'm as tired as a dog and as hungry as if I hadn't eaten in three days. So I go to a restaurant, eat my fill, come home, lie down on the divan and light a cigarette. What the devil sense is there in that?'

He shrugged.

'Or another thing,' I continued. 'Imagine you've lived a year without a woman: I shouldn't have said this to you, but we haven't much time left to talk, so I don't have the time to find another example. You've spent a year without a woman – then you win the favour of a girl who becomes your mistress. Surely the sense in this would interest you?'

'These are all ephemeral things,' he said.

I was surprised that a physical love of life was not strong in this man. Had he been a sickly youth, it would have been understandable. But he was exceptionally strong and hardy; and such a consideration would likely have accounted for why fourteen hours of work did not exhaust him – but not for other things. Pavlov suffered nothing like despair or disillusionment. I had known this man for many years, I knew him better than other people and could only think as a result that before me had appeared and disappeared some mysterious apparition, to identify which I lacked the thoughts, the words, even an intuitive understanding. I could calm myself with the idea that

Pavlov and his suicide were as enigmatic for me as creatures living on the seabed that look just like plants, as the nocturnal sound of some anonymous incident, as a multitude of other inhuman phenomena. Yet I couldn't reconcile myself to this.

'Is there anything in the world that you love?' I asked. I expected a negative answer. However, Pavlov said:

'There is.'

'What is it then?'

And all of a sudden he began to talk. I remember how strange his admissions seemed to me that evening. He spoke without reservation, offering up terrible details, which at any other time would have grated on me: yet everything then seemed natural – and not for a moment could I forget that Pavlov was condemned to die and that no power could save him, and that his voice, with its power and modulations, would vanish without an echo, would die away in this body that was to become a corpse. He began far in the past and told me the story of his childhood, the long years of thieving, an astonishing hunt for a badger with a revolver, in Russia, in Vladimir Province – the little river, the boat he sailed in; he was visibly excited when he began talking about swans, which he termed the most beautiful birds in the world. 'Did you know,' he said, 'that in Australia they have black swans? At a certain time of year, tens of thousands of them appear on the inland lakes of the country.' Then he spoke of the sky, obscured by their powerful black wings. 'It's an alternative history of the world; it's a chance to understand everything in a way other than it exists,' he said. 'And I shall never see it.

'Black swans!' he repeated. 'When the mating season begins, the swans begin to call. It's difficult for them to do this, and so, to give out a stronger, clearer sound, the swan will lay its neck on the water at full stretch and then raise its head and call. On the inland lakes of Australia. To me, these words are better than music.'

He went on to talk at length about Australia and its black swans. He knew the many details of their lives; he had read everything that had been written about them, having devoted whole days to translating English and German texts, with a dictionary and a notebook to hand. Australia was this man's sole illusion. It united all the desires that had ever welled up within him, all his hopes and dreams. I fancied that if he were to invest the power of his feelings in a single glance and direct his eyes towards that island, then the water around it would suddenly begin to boil; and I saw in my mind's eye this fantastic scene that I might have witnessed in a dream: thousands of black wings covering the sky, and a cold, dead evening on a deserted shore, beside which the sea surged and boiled.

I sat with him almost until morning – and left tormented by strange feelings. 'All the best,' Pavlov said to me. 'Goodnight. I have to be at the factory in an hour.'

'What do you need to do that for now?' I inquired contrary to my will.

'Money, money. I shan't take it with me, of course, but I need to pay a few people. I'd hate to exploit my situation.'

I remained silent.

'Strictly speaking, I'm leaving for Australia.'

I walked out into the street; it was morning, and daily life had already begun; I looked at the people going past me and thought with rage that they would never understand the most essential things; it seemed to me that morning that I had only just heard and understood them, if this melancholy secret were made accessible to everyone, I should feel wretched and sorry for it. As always, I saw at first something indescribable in all that surrounded me – in the window of the cinema on the corner, in the parked lorry with its wheels turned in, somehow like a man frozen in an unnatural, crooked pose, in the woman selling vegetables, pushing her handcart – I saw in all this an incomprehensible and hidden meaning that I was unable to fathom; however, contrary to habit, the irritation and mute annoyance at this continued for a short while, because according to what I had just heard, everything had become unimportant and void, merely an optical impression – like dust floating over a road in the distance.

On 24 August I brought Pavlov the 150 francs.

'Thank you,' he said, offering me his hand.

I sat with him the whole evening; we talked about various

matters unrelated to his suicide. I was unsurprised by the fact that he maintained absolute calm: perhaps for the first time he found himself in such circumstances where his unspent spiritual strength might prove useful – circumstances in which he ought to have led his entire life. He walked with me to a square with a stone lion, where we parted. I gripped his hand firmly: I knew that this was our last meeting.

'*Au revoir*,' I said out of habit. '*Au revoir.*'

'All the best,' replied Pavlov.

I walked off, although I kept looking back. When I had made it almost as far as the middle of the square, I raised my hand and his calm, laughing voice reached me:

'Spare a thought some day for black swans!'

Princess Mary

GAITO GAZDANOV

There were four of them, three men and one woman. Once
every two or three days they would all gather at the same café,
not far from the racecourse, sit down at a table, order some red
wine and begin a game of cards. Because they were all rather
shabbily dressed, and because each of them had ceased long ago
to take any care over his appearance, it was difficult to guess
their ages. But they were all, more or less, of the same generation, and there could be no doubt that each of them was over
fifty. The woman who accompanied them – or whom they
accompanied – always wore the same sleek black dress. Gaunt
and dark-visaged, it was obvious that she had endured a number of devastating trials over the course of her life. She had a
deep, hoarse voice, and there was a strange expression of latent
impudence in her eyes, which now seemed entirely misplaced.
One of the men, a chap with salt-and-pepper stubble, which
always looked the same and so gave a rather strange impression
(one might have thought that he never shaved, that, rather, by
some astonishing freak of nature his stubble remained permanently the same length, like that of a dead man), seemed to have
been condemned forever to wear the same heavily soiled grey
raincoat – come winter, spring or summer. He never took off
his hat, which had most likely been acquired at the same time
as the rest. Opposite the woman sat a man sporting a cap, a
reddish-brown jacket and a pair of black trousers; he was the
only one of the four whose past was easy enough to distinguish,
judging by his broken nose and cauliflower ears, by his broad
shoulders and the fact that even now, in spite of all the years,
his movement retained a certain laboured precision. The last of

them was a shortish man with twitching cheeks and a peculiar expression on his face, at once anxious and trivial. He stood out from the others in that he owned a number of suits and two overcoats. However, as all these items were similarly thread-bare and worn beyond repair, and had been so for a long time, his evident predilection for playing dress-up was, by all accounts, a complete waste of time.

When the evening commenced, they would all sit in silence. I happened, through a series of coincidences, to come across them several times in that little café near the racecourse. On the first such occasion I had been compelled to leave soon after they showed up. But they immediately lodged themselves in my memory with that useless, automatic clarity that I find so difficult to escape, taxing as it does my mind with myriad wholly superfluous things. Some time later, finding an oppor-tunity to linger in the café until late one evening, I was able to listen in on their conversation as they played cards, and little by little I pieced together a rough plan of their complex net-work of interrelations. However deplorable and indecent (both in equal measure) it may have seemed, this woman was linked to each of her companions by what they termed 'love'. As far as I could make out, at the centre of these fraught emotions stood the woman and the man with the hat and raincoat. The other two, the ex-boxer and the fourth man, seemed to spend their time in constant anticipation of some stroke of good for-tune that would allow them to usurp her bestubbled favourite. It was difficult to tell what exactly they were counting on: the untimely death of their lucky rival, a chance lapse on the part of their heroine, a degree of intoxication that begets possibili-ties undreamed of in a state of sobriety. Whatever the case, they had managed thus far to avoid any unpleasantness on the matter.

Most surprising to me was that the chap with stubble and the hat that nothing could bring him to remove undoubtedly held the esteem of the woman and the other two men – the reason for which remained obscure to me for some time. Only much later did I learn why this was the case, from the details of a brief exchange immediately following a game of cards.

This was the first time I ever heard them argue. I noticed then
that the man with stubble, in contrast to his fellow players,
spoke in broken French, and with a strong Russian accent.
Defending him from an attack by the ex-boxer and the thin
man with twitching cheeks, the dark-visaged woman proclaimed in her hoarse voice that the other two could not hold
a candle to him and that they ought to recognize his indisput-
able superiority. Neither of them countered this, and it was
clear that they were both in agreement. Only, the man with the
anxious and trivial face answered that while he did, of course,
recognize this, he too was 'not just anyone', as he put it.

'Do not forget that I'm an actor,' he said. I was sure that he
would presently have cause to regret his words, for the woman
cut right in.

'An actor?' she said with extraordinary scorn in her voice.
'An actor!' She was so incensed that she began to use *vous*.
'You? An actor? What roles have you played? In which the-
atres? When?'

'I played ...' he began saying in a faltering voice. It was
clear that for him a catastrophic outcome of this argument was
a foregone conclusion.

'You played on the stage twenty-five years ago,' she said.
'And they got rid of you because you had no talent, monsieur.'

The boxer's face seemed to grow pale at the sound of the
word *monsieur*. The thin man fell silent, but the woman carried on speaking in that same disdainful tone. She first refuted
the very idea that the man with stubble had played poorly –
which was the accusation that his fellow players had levelled
against him. Secondly, according to her, even if he had in fact
played other than he might have done, they – the boxer and the
thin man – should never forget that, in deigning to sit with
them, he was doing them an honour, and they ought to appreciate that. No one contradicted her, and the argument drew
to a close.

Those two words – *monsieur* and *honneur* – might have
seemed unexpected from the lips of that woman. Yet I knew
that the law of hierarchical favour retained its power in almost
every sphere of human society. Among the pitiful and the

wretched, at the point in life separating them from death on
the street or in a prison infirmary, the concept of honour or
social advantage holds fast, despite its seeming to have lost
long ago whatever meaning it once held. I felt compelled to
understand the reason for this mysterious, and doubtless illu-
sory, advantage that the man with stubble held over his fellow
players – an advantage so incontrovertible that no one dared
to contest it. I inquired with the waiter. He told me everything
he knew about them. The man with stubble for some reason
went by the name of Marie. The ex-boxer was called Marcel,
and the gaunt-looking chap was Pierre. The woman's name
was Madeleine. In his time the thin man had in fact been an
actor, although only for a very short while. Marcel had indeed
been a boxer, and, when the waiter revealed his surname to
me, I recalled a few articles covering his matches, some fifteen or twenty years ago, which I had stumbled across one
day, rummaging around in the archives of a sports periodical.
Madeleine was a former dressmaker. The premature demise
of their respective careers could, according to the waiter, be
ascribed to the same attribute: a passion for gambling and red
wine. As to the matter of the man with the woman's name, the
waiter said something that struck me as highly improbable:
that the man called Marie was a famous Russian writer.

I saw them once again, a few days after my conversation
with the waiter. It was a cold winter's evening. Fine snow was
falling in the courtyard, and the streetlamps shone dimly
through a thin veil of mist. I do not know why everything
that evening appeared through this misty phantasm of snow,
lamplight and empty winter streets. I had been walking from
one end of the city to the other, and, as had happened many
times before, I lost all conception of where I was and when all
this was taking place. It might have been anywhere – London
or Amsterdam – the winter street scene, the lamps, the hazy
illumination of shop windows, the silent movement through
the snow, and the cold, the infidelity of what had happened
yesterday, the uncertainty of what would happen tomorrow,
the consciousness of my own existence slipping away from me,
a stranger's distant memories of St Petersburg haunting me

that evening, and those magic words – 'Night, a street, a lamp, a chemist's shop'[1] – that whole vanished world, which I had never known, yet which kept surfacing in my imagination with a potency that was lacking among all my memories of what had really transpired during the long years of my life, full of quiet despair and the expectation of something that was perhaps never fated to happen.

That evening I spotted them again in their usual café; I entered automatically, not even conscious that I was doing it. As ever, they were sitting at their table and, as ever, they were playing a game of cards. However, probably because I found myself in a strange state of mind, they seemed somehow different that night. Though the lighting in their corner of the café was no harsher or softer than it was every evening, they seemed to emerge in an almost Rembrandtesque twilight, out of the indeterminate past. I mused on how they all embodied elements of eternity: ever since the dawn of man, in every country and every age, those things that defined each of their lives had existed – wine, cards and poverty; then there were their professions – the dressmaker, the actor, the boxer or gladiator, and, last but not least, the writer. On a sudden, I distinctly seemed to catch a distant voice say in French:

'*Mais ils ne sont sortis de l'éternité que pour s'y perdre de nouveau.*'[2]

I stopped frequenting that quarter of Paris and only by chance did I later return to the café, almost two years after I last saw those people in it. They weren't there. A few days later, on my next visit, it was the same story. Eventually, I spotted Marie as I was arriving one day. He was alone. He was sitting at that same table, where previously the four of them had sat, in front of a glass of red wine, his eyes gazing fixedly ahead. Nothing, it seemed, had wielded the power to alter him – the same stubble, the same hat, the same raincoat. The same accent. I felt certain of this a few moments later, when some unpleasantness erupted between him and the waiter, who had refused to let him keep a tab open and was threatening to summon the police. I fancied that Fate was handing me a convenient pretext for an acquaintance, and so I settled his bill and asked him whether he would care for another glass of wine, which he accepted readily. I sat down opposite him, ordered myself a coffee and asked in Russian:

'Forgive me, but whatever happened to your friends?'

'Oh?' he said. 'Did you know them?'

'Yes, I used to see you all here together. That would have been around two years ago.'

'Yes, yes,' he said. 'Those were the days. A lot has changed since then. They both died – Marcel and Pierre, that is. Pierre came home one night having drunk a little too much and forgot to turn off the gas in the kitchen. Marcel died suddenly in the street – his heart. Madeleine is in hospital at the moment; she's been there for three months already. Why do you ask?'

Later, when he began to speak of literature, it became apparent that this was indeed absolutely central to his life. He did not reveal what exactly he was writing these days; he mentioned only that he was a contributor to one of the most widely read Russian periodicals, and that he had to work a great deal for a mere pittance. Then he began to talk of other things, of his earlier works and their woeful fate. He clearly suffered from some strange persecution complex, and a particularly acute one at that: he was a victim of envy, intrigue and a tacit literary conspiracy, which involved the most disparate array of people. Some envied his talent, others feared his competition, and this, he asserted, was the cause of his not being published anywhere. He said that in the old days he had been published in Russia 'to great acclaim'. It was possible to judge his naivety by this expression alone, just as it was by the rest of what he said to deduce his innocence, which not even the cruel external circumstances of his life or a multitude of other, no more auspicious, considerations had been able to remedy. He was little inclined to condemn even those who did everything in their power to deny him the possibility of being published abroad.

'You see, these people are just trying to hold on to their positions as editors. I understand this,' he said. 'The others, the younger ones, these modernists themselves, they'd sell their skin to come up with something new. Whereas I'm an artist. I write what I see – nothing more. Now that's real literature.'

Some time later I met him again in that same café, alone, as on the previous occasion. He was never well and truly drunk, but equally one could never say that he was sober; he was always somewhere between the two states, as though caught in some transitional, evolutionary stage of intoxication, which evaded any definitive categorization. He approached drunkenness, though was not drunk, and this contained something almost like a mathematical limitation, as in the theorem regarding the limits of inscribed and circumscribed polygons.

On this occasion he extracted from his pocket a typewritten manuscript and gave it to me to read through.

It was a fairly short novel, and I read it with a dreadful sense of embarrassment. It was written in the first person, and the protagonist was a woman. Despite the poor style in which it had been dashed off, the prodigious quantity of ellipses and exclamation marks and the abject poverty of the language, it was obvious that this book was the result of some colossal, fell effort of imagination. Each of the heroine's physical and mental states was described exhaustively. It was all utterly implausible, but it had been done with such an abundance of detail and such unwavering devotion to the plot, which itself did not even merit a dozen lines. Naturally the heroine was a very beautiful woman, although no one could ever appreciate her exceptional inner charm. She ended up committing suicide. The novel was titled *The Life of Antonina of Gaul*.

The day he gave me the manuscript – it was at the beginning of February – I saw him for the very last time. When I returned to the café a month or so later, the waiter told me that he had died of a liver complaint in hospital. The waiter handed me a note on some graph paper, the same paper on which the novel had been typed out. Written in poorly spelled French, it requested that I come to the café on such-and-such a day, at such-and-such a time. It was signed: Madeleine.

The meeting was set for the following day. Madeleine arrived in her black dress, as gaunt and dark-visaged as ever. But her dull eyes were sad, and they contained even more of that incongruous expression of impudence that had so struck me when I first saw her. Her speech was laboured, and she said little. She told me that he had died, that he was a famous Russian writer and that letters from female readers still arrived addressed to him. She asked me to go with her to collect his manuscripts. He had instructed her before dying that they were to be given to me, as I was the sole person who truly understood and appreciated him. Madeleine had been unable to bring them with her, as she had been in town since morning and had not had time to collect them. So we went together.

It took some time for us to climb the narrow stone staircase, past dimly lit doorways whose paint had long since peeled off. Above and below us, the cool, still air on the many floors was infused with smells of cooking, laundry, cabbage, onion and ash. The lingering waft of some foul, overpowering perfume hung in the air: a prostitute had clearly passed upstairs not long before, and a trace of her eau de Cologne permeated this vertical sequence of suffocating strata. On the landing at the very top of the stairwell Madeleine opened a door that had likely never been locked, and we entered a room almost identical to those one finds in cheap novels, whose descriptions had until then always seemed heavily exaggerated to me. It had a bare floor, two beds of rusted iron, a cracked mirror, a battered old washbasin, two stools, nails driven into the wall instead of hooks and a small narrow table on which stood a kerosene lamp with a tin reflector.

'We lived here by ourselves for many years,' said Madeleine. 'Sometimes our friends Pierre and Marcel would come to visit. They both died, just like he did. And it all happened so quickly, monsieur, so quickly.'

I listened to her disjointed speech and was suddenly struck by the strange expressiveness of her deep, hoarse voice. It was like an aural hallucination – that voice seemed to be the one that had uttered the phrase that no one ever said and only I heard:

'*Mais ils ne sont sortis de l'éternité que pour s'y perdre de nouveau.*'

I picked up the bundle of manuscripts. Madeleine said:

'Thank you, monsieur. He told me how kind you were to him. If I could be of any use to you, you may count on me.'

'If I could be of any use to you . . .' Those words contained a strange mix of meanings, so unnatural and almost sinister that for a brief moment I had a queer feeling. I thanked Madeleine and, in bidding her farewell, shook her coarse hand.

'He worked for *Paris Weekly*, the Russian magazine,' she said. 'I can't let you have the copies. I'm keeping them to remember him by.'

I said that I understood, and left.

That evening I began sorting through the manuscripts. I was alone in my apartment, and, after having seen Madeleine's, I felt a burden of shame owing to my own surroundings, which I had largely overlooked until now: wallpaper, rugs, coat hooks, a divan, an armchair, a bathtub, my books on the shelves. The first article I began to read surprised me. It bore the title 'A Woman at Forty' and began as follows:

'Time flies by unnoticed. Life weaves its thread. It seems that only yesterday you were twenty. Today you could be thirty-two. Just a little more and you'll be drawing near to the fatal forty. But you mustn't despair. If you're youthful and svelte, only your face will give away your age, and so you must pay attention to your make-up.'

Similar snippets of advice followed this – how to powder your face, what sort of cold creams to apply, and so on. 'Be careful in your choice of colour. Contrasting colours – avoid them! Smooth out any imperfections. Use sepia tones on the eyelids. Your mouth should be the only vibrantly coloured part of your face. It imparts a softness to the rest . . . Abstain from strong spirits . . . If you're always in good cheer and have a bright personality, you'll be the toast of those whom you love, and you'll remain young not only in spirit but also in body.'

The article was signed: 'Princess Mary'.[3] I read on – it was all much of the same thing. 'Civilized nations have long understood that facial massage not only does not hinder, but in fact aids inner cultivation. People wrote about this even in Roman times . . . Apply a good degree of pressure when massaging the chin. Do not be afraid, it is entirely safe, for you have a bone there . . . Avoid powdering your nose too heavily: this will only cause it to grow.'

'In polite society it is a must to display a demure glimmer of culture. Quote poetry. But not the lines that everyone knows by heart. Quote such lines, for example, as the ones printed in the previous issue of our magazine:

> All full of grace and swarthiness,
> She's cheerful and she's sly,
> A charming smile upon her lips,
> Cadiz's moraine passed by.

Then came descriptions of toilettes. 'Ensembles of black crêpe de Chine, while perhaps a little austere, are most elegant. Adorn the waist and the whole length of the manteaux trois-quarts with green leaves . . . Wear bright tones in the evening: cyclamen, heliotrope and lilac . . . A classically cut chemise gown . . .'

And everywhere that same signature: 'Princess Mary'. I laid the manuscripts aside. That evening I sensed the illusoriness of this man's existence with a peculiar clarity, which no effort of memory could ever subsequently reconstruct. Everything that had once seemed so wretchedly permanent and desperate in the life of this man was, ultimately, all irrelevant detail. Everything: his abject poverty, his unshaven face – swollen and inflamed because of the wine – his flaccid male body, his torn raincoat, his frayed trousers, his foul stench, his poor French, his lack of sophistication, his complete inability ever to be received at a 'society reception' where one had to quote lines of verse and display a demure glimmer of culture – all this was entirely incidental. For when this man was alone, in the world that was his sole reality, a miraculous and solemn transformation took over him. Everything was set in motion: muscles stirred, paths crossed, poetry and music rang out, electrified chandeliers glinted, and classic, austere ensembles of black crêpe de Chine floated on the air, mixing with impeccable French conversation – an evening reception at the British Ambassador's residence on rue du Faubourg Saint-Honoré.

And had my poor acquaintance, whose fate had so unexpect-edly crossed mine, wielded the strength for one last creative endeavour, then on the grey desert of a hospital bed, instead of the rigid corpse of this poor wretch, would have lain the youth-ful body of Princess Mary – in all her glory, triumphant over time, death and the impossible.

Requiem

GAITO GAZDANOV

It happened in the cruel and wretched period of the German occupation of Paris. Ever greater territories were being consumed by war. Hundreds of thousands were advancing along Russia's frozen roads; wars were being waged in Africa; bombs were exploding across Europe. In the evenings Paris was plunged into an icy darkness; no streetlamps were lit, and there were no lights in any of the windows. Only on a rare winter's night did the moon illuminate this frozen, almost spectral city, sprung out of someone's monstrous imagination and forgotten in the apocalyptic depths of time. An icy damp persisted in the tall buildings whose heating had been cut off long ago. In the evenings, inside apartments whose windows had been blacked out with curtains, the glass panel on the wireless would glow, and through the crackle of static a voice would proclaim: 'Ici Londres. Voici notre bulletin d'information . . .'[1]

The people were shabbily dressed; few now dared to go out into the streets, and the motor traffic had disappeared long ago. Many went about the city in horse-drawn carriages, and this only served to intensify the tragic surrealism in which the whole country had been living for a number of years.

It was during this time that one day I went to a little café in a suburb of Paris, where I had arranged to meet a casual acquaintance. It was evening, in the bitter winter of forty-two. The café was crowded. By the bar, well-dressed people – scarves, fur collars, pressed suits – were drinking cognac, liqueurs, coffee with rum and eating ham sandwiches, the likes of which I had not seen in a long time. I later discovered the reason for this ham, this cognac and all the rest: the regulars of the café in which I happened to find myself were Russians who traded on the black market. Before the war, in those peaceful, well-fed times, the majority of these people had been unemployed – not because they couldn't find work, but because they did not wish to work, on account of some incomprehensible, stubborn desire not to live as everyone else did: going to the factory, taking a room in some miserable hotel and drawing their wage once every fortnight. These people lived in a state of chronic and, more often than not, unconscious revolt against the European reality surrounding them. Many of them had spent nights in shacks knocked together from wooden planks, looming darkly in dilapidated, abandoned lots on the outskirts of the city. They had known all the doss-houses in Paris, the scant yellow lighting above the iron beds in the enormous dormitories, the dank chill of these unhappy spots and their permanent sour stench. They had known the Salvation Army, the dives and squalid cafés of Place Maubert, where the fag-end men gathered, torpid slumber on benches in the underground metro stations and endless wandering around Paris. Many had travelled farther afield, roaming the French provinces – Lyons, Nice, Marseilles, Toulouse, Lille.

Once the German army had occupied more than half the territory of France, an unusual change took place in the lives of these people. They were given a sudden, wonderful opportunity to get rich – without any especial effort and, essentially, almost without working. The German army and its affiliates would buy wholesale – no haggling – every item that was offered to them: boots and toothbrushes, soap and nails, gold and coal, clothes and axes, leads and machinery, cement and silk – everything. These Russians became intermediaries between the German buyers and the French merchants selling their wares. And so, as in an Arabian fairytale, yesterday's unemployed grew rich.

Now they lived in cosy apartments, which their previous owners had been forced to vacate, leaving behind paintings with obscure subjects, fine rugs and comfortable armchairs. They wore gold watches with gold wristbands, and their fingers were weighed down by rings with genuine precious stones. Behind each of them lay a difficult life – the cities, roads and streets of various countries, huge distances that had been traversed on foot – and here, now, they had arrived at what they had never before been able to dream of.

In the beginning I had come to know one of them – Grigory Timofeyevich, a wiry man past the first flush of youth, with deep-set eyes and a pointed chin. I had met him at a friend's house, a former singer, who in his time had performed in caba-rets and cafés. Though back then, when I knew him, all that was already a thing of the past. He had been taken seriously ill with consumption and rarely got out of bed. Every time I vis-ited him, however, lifting his thin hands, he would remove from the wall an enormous guitar that sounded like a piano and in his deep voice, which astonishingly bore no trace of his illness, he would sing all manner of romances and songs – and the richness of his repertoire truly amazed me. Grigory Timofeyevich had known him since childhood; both of them were originally from some village near Oryol.[2] Nobody, except for me, ever called Grigory Timofeyevich by his name and patronymic – he was always Grisha, or Grishka. No one, on the other hand, would ever call the singer by his given name alone – everyone called him Vasily Ivanovich.

'Vasily Ivanovich, I've bought myself a painting,' said Gri-sha. 'Oh, and I've brought you a roast chicken.'

'Thank you, Grisha,' said Vasily Ivanovich. 'What's the painting you've bought?'

'It's no ordinary painting, Vasily Ivanovich. I paid so much money for it, it doesn't bear thinking about. But the subject is just marvellous.'

'What's it a painting of?'

'It depicts, Vasily Ivanovich, a huge eagle; he's flying some-where, but on his back, you see, is a very young boy, whom he seems to be carrying away. I may not understand it entirely, but the eagle, I'm telling you, is the finest there is. I've looked at the painting so often – and every time I think the same thing. It's such an incredible painting, there's no denying it.'

'Who's the artist?'

'That, I don't know,' said Grisha. 'Someone very famous.

The vendor told me his name, but I've forgotten it. All I remember is that he said Repin couldn't hold a candle to him. He told me the title of the painting too, but, you see, I didn't even register it, so much had it taken my breath away.'

I saw this painting later in Grisha's apartment: it was a copy of Rubens' *The Rape of Ganymede*.

Still, all (or almost all) the clients of that café were buying up paintings back then, just as they would buy gold trinkets and coins. Within these people, who had never owned anything before, some brash, chaotic desire to acquire and possess had suddenly awoken, although it scarcely resembled the Western practice of mechanically amassing money. They would expend ever greater sums of money, paying without thought or necessity, with a sort of peculiar absurdity. I remember one of them, a tall, melancholy man with a black beard; his name was Spiridon Ivanovich. He had been standing in the café, drinking cognac. A glazier had been coming along the street, crying in his plaintive voice:

'*Vitrier! Vitrier!*'[3]

'I can't listen to that shouting,' said Spiridon Ivanovich. 'I just can't, my nerves won't cope. And anyway, he's no reason to shout like that. Who on earth needs him?'

His cry again reached us from the street.

'*Vitrier! Vitrier!*'

Spiridon Ivanovich ran out of the café, went up to the glazier and said to him in Russian:

'For Christ's sake, stop harrowing my soul with all your shouting. Shut up! How much do you want for all this junk?'

Then, suddenly remembering himself, he repeated his question in broken French. The glazier, amazed, hesitantly gave his reply. Spiridon Ivanovich extracted his wallet, paid however much the goods cost, waited for the glazier to leave and returned to the bar to finish his cognac, which somehow gurgled and burbled loudly in his throat and was accompanied by the motion of his pointed Adam's apple up and down.

'You slave away all day,' muttered Spiridon Ivanovich, 'nuisances from dawn, they haven't delivered this, the goods haven't turned up there, and then someone harrows your soul. The evening's the only time I get any peace and quiet. I come home, turn on the heating and lie in bed. I lie there and think: you've done it, Spiridon Ivanovich, you've finally made it. Well, chaps, it's time now to get some rest, not to have a go at glaziers, but to rest.'

'The next world's for resting, Spiridon Ivanovich,' said Volodya, an athletic man of forty and an expert in gold. 'I don't suppose there'll be any glaziers there. What glass have they? Just clouds and angels, nothing else.'

'There won't be any gold either,' said another of the patrons.

'Of that we cannot be certain,' said Volodya. 'I once went to Notre-Dame. They had a box there for donations. I took a closer look and saw that it bore an inscription: "For the souls in purgatory". Clearly some funds do get through.'

'That's their Catholic ways,' said Grigory Timofeyevich. 'Naturally, the money goes to the Church, so that they pray for the people they think are in purgatory. But you're right there. It's strange, of course, the inscription.'

For some reason, the day on which Spiridon Ivanovich delivered his monologue had remained curiously fixed in my memory: the hoarse sound of his voice, the motions of the Adam's apple on his long, thin neck, and those words – 'Well, chaps, it's time now to get some rest' – I recalled the expression in his weary, drunken eyes, the winter twilight and the mix of alcoholic smells in the café.

When Grigory Timofeyevich left, Volodya said to me:

'I should never have mentioned the hereafter, I ought to have kept my mouth shut. I worry about Grisha, we all pity him. He's a good fellow, but he's not long for this world. He's been ill for so long.'

Then Volodya began relating to me all his business affairs. His chat, as ever, was overflowing with jargon – percentages, alloys, carats, some or other cut of a stone. It was obvious that he had scarcely been able, in the brief period that had elapsed since the day the Germans marched into Paris, to master all these things. When I once asked him where he had managed to acquire all this knowledge, he told me that he had always been interested in everything to do with gold and jewellery. Before the war, he, like all his friends at the café, had been mostly unemployed and often homeless. But he had spent hours standing in front of jewellers' shop windows on rue de la Paix and reading technical books with the aid of a dictionary, learning the melting points of certain metals and which branches of industry used platinum – and so this formerly shabby, almost destitute man had been able to become an expert in the jewellery business. Before the war, however, his interest in all this had been of a completely abstract nature, and he had never imagined that the day would come when this inaccessible, shop-window gold would suddenly fall to his own hands. According to him, he had met his match only once: a Dutchman with a fair beard and light-blue eyes, a famous safe-cracker with whom Volodya had shared a cell for a few hours in the Central Paris Prison, where he had landed on the charge of vagrancy – that is, for having no money, nor any fixed address.

Looking at Volodya, I would often find myself thinking about how hypothetical so-called social distinction could be: this homeless man ought to have been the owner of a large jeweller's shop on rue du Faubourg Saint-Honoré.

Other patrons of the café, friends of Volodya and Grigory Timofeyevich, lacked such distinct individuality. They all knew how to drink, how to spend vast sums of money; the majority of them had wives or lovers of a very certain type – retouched photos on the covers of women's magazines, blondes in fur coats bought through a connection with some desperate Jew who had already packed off his family to a safe location and now, risking his own life, was selling off everything left in his fur shop. The café's clientele would spend whole days on the telephone, waiting for their next consignment, and in the evenings they played cards, chalking up vast sums of money.

Grigory Timofeyevich said to me:

'Of course, I live well these days. But I see now that I used to dream of all the wrong things. For example, I remember this one night in Lyons, in winter. I had no money, no work, no lodgings. I was sleeping on a building site – at least there was a roof to keep the rain off, if nothing else. It was cold, and I had nothing to cover myself with. I lay there, you know, on some wooden boards, unable to get to sleep – I had no way of getting warm. And so I dreamed. Here, I thought to myself, is an apartment for you, Grigory Timofeyevich, with central bloody heating, and a bed with sheets. And in the evening my wife would serve dinner: sausages, hors d'œuvres, steak. That would be the life.'

His eyes grew thoughtful.

'Though it turns out that all that was wrong. That isn't what matters in life. Or rather, it's not the only thing that matters. What does matter, I don't know – I just know it isn't this. Now I have all those things: the apartment, the dinner, the wife, and even a bathtub – I want for nothing. And yet, that's not quite true. Or so I'm now of the opinion. Say a man gets into difficulties, or finds himself destitute. The idiot will think that's his only problem. But for this poverty, everything would be fine. All right, then. Whisk him off, like in a fairytale, give him clothes, shoes, an apartment and all the rest, and tell him, "Right, then – now live, be merry!" But how do you give him happiness? In a bathtub? See here, I've got a Longines wrist-watch that I bought off Volodya. I paid more for it than I would have had to live on for half a year in the old days. I look at the hands on it, and what do they say? It's obvious what they're saying: we're counting down the hours for you, Grigory Timofeyevich. It was five o'clock, but now it's six. That's one hour less to live.'

Now he really did look at his watch.

'Seven o'clock? Another hour gone. But I'm not afraid. There's only one thing I regret: that I've lived for so many years without knowing where human happiness is to be found. Yes, it's all well and good that I've warmed myself, had a bite to eat and drunk my fill. But now what?'

A fortnight somehow passed without my visiting the café. Then, late one evening in February, I went there. Grigory Timofeyevich was nowhere to be seen, and when I asked where he was, I was told that he was ill, laid up in bed. I set off immediately for his apartment, as he lived nearby.

He was lying in bed, emaciated and unshaven, his eyes were bloodshot and sad. At the head of his bed, beneath the

light of the chandelier, the wings of Rubens's eagle shimmered
with their dark-blue light. I asked him how he felt. 'Not well,'
came the reply.

'The quilt feels heavy,' he said. 'It's the last sign. The end is
nigh. I'll die – and I still won't know what it was that my life
was missing.'

He died during the night, three days after my visit. Volodya
told me:

'Grigory Timofeyevich has passed away. He'll be buried
tomorrow. Will you come? There'll be a service at his apartment at four o'clock in the afternoon.'

Volodya had never called Grigory Timofeyevich anything
other than Grisha or Grishka; until that moment I had not even
been sure that he knew his patronymic. I now had the impression that while it was Grisha who had lived, it was someone else
who had died – Grigory Timofeyevich. The following day, as I
arrived, I witnessed Grigory Timofeyevich's entire apartment
overflowing with floral wreaths. Where Volodya had obtained
all these flowers, in the February of forty-three, in starving
Paris, and how much they had cost, I could scarcely imagine.
All the patrons of the café, friends of Grigory Timofeyevich's,
were already there, all with that same, uniform, almost indistinguishable face that people have in such circumstances.

'We're waiting for the priest,' whispered Volodya. The priest,
an elderly man with a voice hoarse from the cold, arrived a quarter of an hour later. He wore a threadbare cassock, and his
countenance was sad and weary. As he entered, he crossed himself, and his lips silently mouthed some phrase or other. In the
coffin, decked with flowers, lay the body of Grigory Timofeyevich,
in a black suit, his dead face, it seemed, looking towards the sky,
where the eagle soared, carrying off Ganymede.

'Where was the deceased from?' asked the priest.

Volodya replied: from such-and-such a district in Oryol
Province.

'A neighbour, so to speak,' said the priest. 'I'm from there-
abouts myself, not even thirty *versts* away. What a pity, I didn't
know I was coming to bury someone from those parts. What
was his name?'

'Grigory.'

The priest remained silent for some time. It was clear that this detail – that the deceased was from the same place as he was – had made a particularly deep impression on him. He might have been thinking, 'So this is what we've come to.' Then the priest sighed, crossed himself again and said:

'Were these different times, I'd have served the full requiem for him, like they do in the monasteries. But my voice is weak, and it would be difficult for me to sing it by myself, so may God grant that I make it through the shorter one. Perhaps one of you could help me by joining in, supporting me?'

I glanced at Volodya. The expression on his face was such that I should never have imagined – tragic and solemn.

'Serve it, Father, like you would have done in the monastery,' he said. 'We'll support you, we'll do it properly.'

He turned to his friends, raising both his arms aloft in what seemed like a commanding and familiar gesture – the priest looked on in astonishment – and began the requiem.

Nowhere and at no other time have I ever heard such a choir, either before or after that day. The entire stairwell of the building where Grigory Timofeyevich had lived was soon full of people who had come to listen to the singing. The choir, led by Volodya, sang the responses to the priest's gravelly and mournful voice.

'Truly, all is vanity, and life is but a shadow and a dream. For in vain doth every man born of this earth disquiet himself, as saith the Scripture. When we have acquired the world, then do we take up our dwelling in the grave, where kings and beggars are the same.'[4]

And then once again that merciless reminder:

'Such is this life of ours: verily, it is a flower, and smoke, and the morning dew. Come, therefore, and let us look upon the grave. Where is the beauty of the flesh? Where is youth? Where is the brightness of the eye, where the beauty of the complexion? Everything is withered like grass; everything is vanished.'

When I closed my eyes, it began to seem as if the mighty voice of one man were singing, now rising, now falling, and its sonorous swell filled the whole space around me. My gaze came to rest on the coffin, and at that moment the choir sang out:

'*I weep, and with tears I lament, when with understanding I think on death and see how in the grave there sleeps the beauty that was once fashioned in His Image, yet is now shapeless, ignoble and bare of all grace.*'

Never had I found the requiem so moving as I did on that gloomy winter's day in Paris. Never had I felt with such a convulsive jolt that human genius had perhaps never achieved such terrible perfection in anything as it had in this combination of searing, solemn words and in the swelling body of sound from which they emerged. Never before had I comprehended with such piercing hopelessness the irresistible approach of death for everyone whom I knew and loved, for whom the singing choir offered up that prayer:

'*With the Saints give rest . . .*'[5]

And I thought that in this terrible hour, which would grimly seek out even me, when everything for which it was worth living would cease to exist, no words and no sounds, apart from those I now heard, would be able to express that finality, beyond which there was no conception of what life was, nor any understanding of what death was. This was what mattered, and nothing else.

'*For everything will end and we all shall die: kings and princes, judges and potentates, the rich and the poor, and every kind of mortal man.*'

And these very words – searing like hot iron – will sound over the dead.

When the service was over I asked Volodya:

'What just happened? What miracle brought this about, where did you find such a choir?'

'It just happened,' he said. 'One of them used to sing in the opera, another at the musical comedy theatre, another in a bar. Everyone used to sing in choirs, of course. As for the liturgy, we all know it from childhood, just as we shall know it until our last breath.'

The coffin with the body of Grigory Timofeyevich was

covered, borne away, placed in a hearse and taken to a cemetery outside the city.

The February dusk fell, plunging Paris into the icy darkness
typical of this time of year, and night shrouded everything that
had just taken place. Afterwards, it began to seem as if none of
this had ever happened, as if it had all been an apparition,
eternity's brief intrusion into the historical reality in which we
just happened to live, uttering foreign words in a foreign
tongue, not knowing where we were headed, having forgotten
whence we had come.

The Tunnel

IRINA GUADANINI

As the sun set, by the same bench,
As in the days of my youth . . .[1]
Vladimir Sirin

Several years ago I came to a small town on the Riviera, where I
had happened to live at an early period. I rented the upper floor
of a villa which stood a few minutes' walk from the sea. There
was nobody that I knew, and I spent a lot of time on my own.

One day the owners of the villa, a middle-aged Italian and
his wife, invited me in.

They turned out to be very pleasant people, and I began to
drop in on them some evenings. Sitting in their small, scented
garden, which had a stone wall around it, we passed the time
in animated conversation.

My surname is a cosmopolitan one; I had been living abroad
for a long time, and not many people knew that I was Russian
by birth, as well as in spirit and upbringing. Nor did my hosts
know.

We talked about the most varied topics, including, of course,
politics, where our views largely coincided. It was these conversations about politics that led to them learning that I was
Russian.

'Before we bought this villa from friends,' said my host,
'there were Russians living here, too: a whole family, but we
never actually met them.'

'Do you remember what happened at the time?' his wife
remarked.

'What happened? I know what you're getting at, but that
was none of our business.'

'I assure you that people in town were saying they had seen them . . .'

'People say all sorts of things,' my host interrupted her brusquely.

'What did happen?' I asked, afraid I might hear something to the detriment of my compatriots.

I have written down what I heard, as I recall it. Probably this doesn't have a lot in common with reality; I wonder if it has anything in common at all.

I

> All this happened, happened, happened –
> The revolution of days is completed –
> What lies, and what force
> Will bring you, the past, back?[2]
>   Alexander Blok

If you leave the town centre and, before you get to the port, turn into a street on your right, soon, with a different name and continuing to climb uphill, the street turns into a highway that runs parallel to the sea, where there are fewer villas and the gardens are more extensive.

But almost immediately, after a large converted multi-storey villa with peeling paint, at a sharp angle to this street, there is a cul-de-sac, far lower than the ascending street. This cul-de-sac shelters two or three modest villas whose separate storeys are rented out to people who come here in the summer to bathe.

Relatively close by, but far higher up, a tunnel opens its black maw; the express that comes flying out of it with an exaggerated roar brings a sharp reminder of reality to the people who have surrendered to sweet relaxation and who are worn out by the sun.

The street, which is lined with trees on one side, passes at the height of the second storey of the houses in the cul-de-sac. A young woman who had arrived on the morning train and was now sitting on a bench opposite was staring fixedly at a window, where three bathing costumes were drying.

She had spent the night in a railway carriage and she felt that the train's wheels were still banging in her head. Or was it her blood pounding in her temples?

At this early hour the occupants of the second floor were still asleep. Time was passing infinitely slowly, but her heart froze at the thought of what would happen when it stopped passing.

Now, however, the window opened a few inches, and a woman's arm stretched out to retrieve two bathing costumes. There was not much longer to wait; her heart was racing like a racehorse's as it nears the finishing line, and her eyes dimmed.

Finally two persons opened the door and came out. A tall man was leading a small, wan little girl by the hand. Not suspecting that anyone was watching them, they meekly turned to the right and followed the narrow lane that led through a small municipal park to the sea.

It took only a minute to run downhill and follow them, her heels nervously and rapidly tapping the pavement. Suddenly she saw the man's head turn slightly, as if he was listening to the rhythm of her hurried running. After all, he had always found her quick, hasty gait amusing; he used to say, 'You always emerge, running like a puppy, from every corner of my thoughts!'

She caught up with them in the park, where the unnaturally large autumn leaves of the southern plants fell to the ground, slowly gliding through the air. When he saw her, the man stood still, astonished.

'You've come!' were his first words. 'But I . . .'

Her soul was quivering with the tension and the joy of meeting him, but instead of the words which she had meant to utter right now, she said sharply, 'Don't worry, I'm leaving tomorrow morning,' and turned as if to leave.

'Wait a bit, wait,' he said in a conciliatory tone. 'Where are you off to? You misunderstand me. We've got to see each other.'

· The little girl, displeased by this delay, tugged at her father's hand, but he ignored her. Now he had been noticed by passers-by who knew him:

'Come and see us this evening and bring your wife, as we agreed,' a tanned, short-legged lady called out cheerfully. 'The Shvesins are coming, too: a game of bridge is guaranteed!'

Unable to say anything in response, he merely bowed awkwardly. The little girl went on tugging at her father's hand, saying something as she did so.

'We've definitely got to see each other,' he spoke rapidly. 'What hotel are you staying in?'

'The Travellers' Hotel, no, the Foreigners',' she said, too upset to remember the name of the hotel where she had left her suitcase that morning. 'It's opposite the station.'

People could now be seen nodding to him. The child was acting up, whimpering and stamping her feet. The woman went ahead, without saying goodbye, and when she came to the sea, which was so bright that it dazzled her, she fell on to the still-cool sand. Soon, far off, by the water, she saw his tall figure.

Gradually the sun became baking hot, and soon a motley crowd occupied the beach. Coloured parasols were opened here and there. Children screamed as they paddled about in the water. Many people, aspiring to a slimmer figure, were doing purposeful gymnastic exercises. An ice-cream vendor's ringing voice warned of his approach. A moustachioed photographer, like a character from an operetta, was erecting his tripod.

A merry group of bathers, laden with colourful bags, inflatable rubber monsters and other beach equipment, joked and laughed as they approached the steps leading down to the sea. When they saw the man and the little girl, the passers-by welcomed them with a wave of the hand and headed towards them, stumbling over the friable sand.

Soon the new arrivals had an animated ball game in full swing. Then a big flowery ball, thrown too hard by someone's powerful hand, escaped the hands stretched out to catch it, spitefully bounced between a fat man's spread-out legs and, its multicoloured sides flashing by, rolled towards the woman lying on the sand.

'Come to the park at three,' a familiar voice suddenly pronounced over her head. She went on lying there motionless. But she suddenly felt a nauseous revulsion for the sea, the bright sun, which she had always loved so much. She felt like an actor who comes out on stage at the wrong time; so acutely aware was she of the dissonance of her presence on this southern sand that, getting quickly to her feet and not even looking around, she went off, not knowing where to hide or how to survive till the next day, when the early-morning train would take her far away from here.

The thought of the impending meeting gave her no joy.

2

I have known you for a long time, I foresaw it and
   could hear it,
I knew that you would come and smile at me.[3]

Dovid Knut

When she saw a trattoria on the road, one of its walls propped against a rock, she entered the dim, cool and almost empty room and sat down.

Her temples were still throbbing, fiery dots were floating in her eyes, but she pulled herself together and tried to be objective and consider the situation that had arisen. He was right: there was no reason for coming. She should have waited patiently and not irrupted into his life. Which of them was now suffering most? But how could she have forced herself to wait patiently when she sensed that every day, every minute that she lived was taking him further from her. This meeting had to be the decisive one.

They had met by chance in London, where she had come for a short time.

After spending a few hours in the National Gallery, she went back to look at Velázquez's *Venus and Cupid*[4] and sat down on the velvet bench. She sensed someone sitting down next to her and couldn't help looking round: she saw a tall, thin man, who suddenly addressed her with a question:

'Don't you find that Venus's face, reflected in the mirror, is disappointing? When you look at her elegant, I'd say "sophisticated", back, you can't help expecting something greater: no wonder that some experts doubt whether this painting is authentic.'

The suddenness of the question made her blush. But she detected a slight accent in his confident English, and the expression 'elegant back' led her to think that this man was not English; but she didn't know what country to place him in. Afraid of appearing impolite, she shyly replied:

'I was thinking very much the same just now: I don't think that the face in the mirror belongs to the same woman who posed for Venus.'

'True,' he went on, 'it's a round, flabby face which reminds me of the words of a Russian poet. Unfortunately, nobody so far has managed to translate him properly.'

As he said this he gave her an attentive look; a suppressed smile flashed in his eyes.

'You wouldn't happen to speak Russian by any chance?' he suddenly asked.

She nodded in the affirmative.

'So we're compatriots. I've been observing you for some time, the sense of purpose and the delighted enthusiasm when you move from one picture to the next; you don't notice anything around you, so I thought for some reason that you must be Russian, and that's why I decided to speak to you. But I'm sure you're very tired: there's nothing so tiring as museums, is there?' He added: 'Perhaps you'll agree to have a cup of tea with me somewhere near here?'

Embarrassed, she began to refuse, saying she didn't have the time.

'Please, let's go and have tea! I can see perfectly well that you're not used to meeting people this way, but we are, after all, both Russian and we could easily have met at the house of mutual friends. You may have heard my surname?' (He gave it.) 'My grandfather was a polar explorer and was famous . . .

Actually, it's of no importance what he was famous for: the only important thing,' he went on, with a smile, 'is whether you'll come and have a cup of tea with me or not. I can add that I've come to London for a congress and, as you see . . .' (He twisted the wedding ring on his finger.)

3

> Is it a storm from the sea? Or are heavenly Sirins
> Singing in the leaves? Or has time stood still?[5]
>   Alexander Blok

They chatted over tea like old friends, which they could, in fact, have been. Before the Revolution, their families had belonged to the same circle. Their fathers had the same careers and had probably met. They found that they themselves had many similar tastes and views.

They sat there so long that the waitress had by then walked the length and breadth of the tea rooms several times.

'Goodbye,' she said sadly, when they emerged on to the animated, darkened street, which seemed to her to be unreal. 'We're right opposite my bus stop.'

'No, no,' he protested. 'I don't want you to disappear completely: I'm so glad to have found you. And actually, why do you have to go? You yourself said that you are completely alone in London. Do you really have something urgent to do?'

'Nothing definite,' she admitted, as if she were in the wrong, but feeling as if she were tumbling into the abyss.

But at heart she knew that resistance was pointless: this was the meeting which she had, without knowing it, been waiting for all her life.

4

I've awoken . . . Happiness won't let me sleep![6]
Polyxena Solovyova-Allegro

A few days later she woke up early, and all of a sudden understood perfectly clearly that this unexpected meeting in a
museum had turned her life upside down and, as it were, erased
the years she had lived until then.

She began thinking over all the details of the last few days;
the more she thought, the more she was transfixed by horror.

They met every day. The evening before they had parted late,
having gone to have supper after a concert. When he saw her
home, he found every possible pretext not to let her walk away.

'Run for it, run for it, while I still can, while I can still make
myself run . . . What, apart from misery, will my feelings bring
me? This is all pointless.'

After thinking that she could still catch her train, she began
feverishly and chaotically throwing her things into a suitcase.
There was still plenty of time before meeting him as they had
agreed. Suddenly, someone knocked at the door.

'Someone downstairs is asking for you,' said the hotel servant.

'Who is it?' she asked in amazement.

'The gentleman wouldn't give his name: he said you
know him.'

She was overcome by mad joy. She ran down, jumping three
steps at a time; when his familiar slim figure got up from the
low armchair to meet her in the downstairs foyer, then only
the presence of strangers stopped her from throwing her arms
round his neck.

Without any spoken intentions, they quickly headed in
silence for the exit. They reached the gates just as silently, and
when they found themselves in a park, where it was too early
for anyone to be walking, he took her shoulders, turned her
towards him and began to kiss her eyes, her cheeks, her lips . . .

'You don't know,' he said between kisses, as he pressed her
closer, 'I haven't slept all night, I could barely wait for the time

I could come: I suddenly had this idea that you might melt away like a mirage and I would never find you again!'

'I was packing so as to catch the train,' she whispered. 'This is too serious for me . . . I have no right. I don't want . . .'

'Don't speak, don't speak, not yet: I'll explain everything to you later.'

5

> Like a swan, slowly gliding
> Over the mirror of the lake's waters,
> Like a falcon soaring in the clouds,
> My spectral, my unreal,
> My invented world is drifting . . .[7]
>
> Vladimir Smolensky

What next? Next came happiness . . .

Fate was protecting them. When he came to see her, he happened to say:

'What is this link that's joining my fate and yours? It's like some magic spell, my sorceress! Would you believe it? I've been asked to stay on here to do something.'

She had decided not to peer into the future; she was enjoying her fragile happiness.

They spent all their spare time together. The hours that they were apart were burdensome and dreary. Once, when he came back from a forced absence of several days, he embraced her and said:

'You should understand: you haven't been bringing me just nights and days, sweet nothings of time: you're with me in every minute!'

Everything they saw, heard, read together, the poetry they recalled: for her it all took on the colour of joy. Even if it was what she had known before, things now took on a different sense, a different significance. They laughed together so much, as if they were trying to save up a supply for the future. There was complete concord and harmony in their feelings and thoughts.

'What I especially love about you,' he once said, 'is the charm of your thoughts and this unerring assurance, which just frightens me, of every step you take towards me. It's so easy to walk side by side with you, and to think side by side, too.'

How could it be otherwise? Separated by Chronos in the Maeterlinck realm of unborn souls,[8] only now, after a long separation, were they together again, and their happiness was perfect.

6

> She confided to me all of her
> Whims, and dreams, and thoughts . . .[9]
>   Nikolai Gumilyov

He often read aloud to her.

Once, when he closed a book they had finished, she asked:

'Do you agree with what was said in it, that it's permissible to seek love by any means whatsoever? You remember, Ostap Bender talked about money which he wanted brought to him on a saucer with a blue decorated edge,[10] and that's what I say about love.'

'It's pride that makes you say that: after all, love always requires sacrifices, and, in any case, it doesn't come immediately, you have to know how to arouse it.'

'I don't deny it; self-interest is what I was talking about here.'

She was silent for a moment, then laughed and continued:

'I don't know why, but this is what I've just remembered: when I was at school I fell in love with a boy in my class. He was red-haired, freckled, and he had a long face, a bit like a grasshopper, if you like – can you imagine? He would help me with maths, and I collected stamps for him.'

'It was idyllic, was it?'

'Don't make fun of me; listen, although it was nothing special on the whole. Once we quarrelled over something unimportant. I don't remember now who was in the wrong, but neither of us would be the first to make up. After that I didn't see him for a long time: he was ill. Once I went to church, where there was an extraordinarily big crowd for someone's funeral: it was in that crowd that I saw him, my love, quite close to me. I was so embarrassed that I rushed out of the church and ran around the corner into the next street, where I waited. I thought he was bound to come and make up with me ... but it didn't happen. That was childish of me, wasn't it? But we never saw each other again, because he stopped coming to school. He may not have known that I'd been waiting for him, but I felt ashamed for a long time when I recalled it all.'

'Did he see you?'

'Yes.'

'But if you ran away in such a hurry, he might have thought you didn't want to meet him again, mightn't he?'

'Maybe, but I think that if that was real love and not just a childlike sympathy, then he must have felt it.'

'You expect too much of people: you idealize them.'

'Yes, that's true: I often think that the people I love are irreproachable or, at least, far closer to perfection than I am. I think that in olden times people also idealized those they loved. Take Botticelli, with his pictures portraying Simonetta Vespucci[11] as being so enchanting. But all today's artists want to do is to draw some hideous creature and then announce in the catalogue that it's a portrait of a woman they love.'

He laughed and said: 'But if the artist is famous, then they both equally deserve immortality, regardless: it depends on the artist's talent.'

'There are all sorts of immortality: the madman Herostratus[12] also won immortality, but what a shameful thing it was. It was even forbidden to speak his name in Asia Minor. But we've got away from the subject, and I wanted to say something else about love that is truly genuine. Could Levin have ever guessed what Kitty was writing on the table for him if he didn't genuinely love her? Well, take any letter, "l" for instance: it can conceal both the enchantment of "love" and the hell of "lies".[13] Do you agree?'

'I also want to tell you something about love,' he said, 'about our love, so you never forget it. The most important thing about our love is that we share the same reactions to and assessments of what is around us. If we were at opposite poles, or if you were in Nice or Chita, we would feel, understand and react just as we do now, to everything around us . . .'

7

We pay for love with our blood,
But a faithful soul stays faithful,
And we love with one love,
One love, like one death . . .[14]
                    Zinaida Hippius

Time was passing too quickly. They both knew that everything has an end. It was decided that when he left they would not even write to each other. She secretly crossed the fleeting days off in her pocket diary.

One evening, coming back from a concert, they sat on the soft green sofa that had over the last few days become a tame, domestic object. It was comfortable and peaceful. The stove was burning in a welcoming way.

'Do you agree that the performance was exceptionally brilliant: he played so marvellously,' she said, still absorbed by the melody of the violin concerto which they both especially loved. The sound was still ringing in her mind. 'The anguish in that theme is so typical of Tchaikovsky!'

He was silent for a while, as he gazed at the flames in the stove. Then he turned to her, took her hands firmly in his and squeezed them until they hurt, as if he wanted to stop her going; looking her straight in the eyes, he said in a muted voice:

'Meeting you has wrecked my whole life. Everything has been swept away and smashed. I never thought that so many years of my life could vanish as if they had never existed. Sometimes, when I wake up at night, I feel disembodied. Then I lose my sense of the reality of equilibrium. I feel horrified: that's how people must feel when they return after an earthquake to where their house used to stand. But there is a dazzling beam of happiness in this wreck of mine. The beam radiates from you, and there is such happiness actually creating my love for you that I haven't the strength to resent what has happened. I can no longer imagine life without you. Just be patient for a while: it is impossible for us not to be together.'

At first she couldn't utter a single word; then she slowly said: 'What you're doing frightens me. So far I'm not allowing myself to have any illusions. I know we have to part. I'll try to forget you, to stop loving you.' (She knew that she was talking nonsense and that she could neither forget nor stop.) 'But in any case, I hope to get through this. And if . . . if I were to believe you – don't misunderstand me – and I really believe what you say, and then you turn out to be unable, or you hesitate to keep your word, that will be a disaster for me. You and I have got into a labyrinth which has no way out . . .'

'No,' he interrupted her, 'we are now going through a dark tunnel, and we're groping to find our way, but at the end of every tunnel there is a point of light, an exit to the sun, to light and air . . . I don't know how I'll do it, but I can't go on living as I have been!'

8

Farewell – there is no sadder word,
Sadder and more tender . . .[15]
Vladimir Smolensky

For me your darling hands
Are like a bright memory of paradise . . .[16]
Anatoly Velichkovsky

She didn't go to the station to see him off on the day he left. She shut the door behind him and slowly went back to the room. The sofa's big cushion was hollowed out, a cigarette end was still smouldering in the ashtray . . .

She sat down, turned to stone, staring fixedly at one point. Gradually the sky clouded over with storm clouds: a thunderstorm was imminent, and it became darker and darker. So as to distract herself somehow from her thoughts, she began sorting and packing her things; suddenly she came across a necktie he had forgotten. Tears instantly poured from her eyes. She paced the room, repeating:

'Why, why did I let him go? I'll never ever see him again: everything's finished now!'

She sat on the floor in the middle of her scattered possessions, too weak to get up or to continue packing. The gathered clouds made it completely dark; there was a flash of lightning, and the downpour sounded more like an avalanche.

Despite the noise she heard a ring at the street door: not just any ring, but 'his ring'. Unable to believe what she thought, not understanding what it might mean, she ran down to open the door. Shaking off the raindrops, he was standing by the door, his face radiant:

'I told my colleagues who were travelling with me that I'd forgotten some essential papers in the hotel; they assured me that the papers were sure to be sent on, but I got a train back, and here I am . . .'

'I haven't seen any papers of yours,' she said in her bewilderment, while the tears would not stop flowing down her drawn face.

'I've still got them, they're in my briefcase,' he laughed as he squeezed her so hard that she gasped for breath. 'Don't cry, don't cry, my lovely! How agonizing it all is! My darling hands, so very cold,' he said, covering them with kisses. 'Never mind, it won't be long, just a little patience. Go home and wait for my letters.'

9

Je vous écris et je déchire mes lettres. Je relis les vôtres –
elles me paraissent toujours trop courtes.[17]

Julie de Lespinasse

Like a resumption of an unfinished conversation, like a pro-
tracted kiss, like a locked embrace, the letters, for a short
instant, similar to flashes of lightning, cut through the oppressive darkness of loneliness.

They were written on pages torn out of a notebook in the
light of a streetlamp at the corner of the road, or on a bright-
coloured postcard; they were written on the move, on his lap
in a stationery shop, in a tram, at a café table: the words of love
burned her and caused her to feel simultaneously happiness
and pain . . .

Being reread obsessively, until her head swam, the letters
became warm, alive, palpable; they filled the surrounding
emptiness and linked them with a fine, quivering, but unbreak-
able thread.

'I have such a desire to talk to you that, although I don't
have much time, I cannot stop myself writing to you, if only
a few words . . . I understand more and more that I cannot
share you with anybody, but I wonder if you can renounce
everything for my sake? Horror, despair . . . I love you so
much . . .'

Time was passing without bringing any changes. And gradually something alien and irrelevant became detectable in his
letters. The same words now began to sound dead and
false. The intervals grew longer and became indefinite; a lot of
reasons for postponement were suggested, and finally there
came a request: to put things off, to wait, to stop writing for
a while.

Not wishing to remain in a state of uncertainty, or to mis-
read the situation that had arisen, she made a journey to clarify
everything with a meeting in person.

10

Trembling, she whispered to me:
'Listen, let's run away!
We'll be as free as birds . . .'[18]
Yakov Polonsky

You were the most brilliant, faithful, and charming.
But do not curse me, do not curse![19]
Alexander Blok

After the calming coolness and the semi-darkness of the trattoria, the heat that hit her in the street seemed unbearable.
She went to the town park, which turned out to be surprisingly
close.

The big autumn leaves were circling just as slowly as before,
falling here and there. One of them, just like an improbably
large butterfly, trustingly fell on her knees when she sat down
near the entrance. The fountain's gentle flow was murmuring
something, as if to emphasize how quiet it was. There was
nobody about, except an old woman in mourning who was
dozing.

Very soon he came into the park; his steps were hurried
and light.

'Let's go somewhere else,' he said as he approached.

They walked along the embankment and passed by the little
port. There was a smell of tar and fish. Cheerful boats of many
different colours were dancing on the bright-blue water. Yachts
with alluring names promised the joy of distant voyages.

They walked in tense silence. Neither wanted to begin a
conversation that would decide things.

When they got to the bright-white lighthouse at the end
of the mole, they sat down on the parapet. The unhurried
tide ran up and smashed against the enormous pile of rocks
and suddenly showered them with refreshing splashes. The
closeness they were used to gave them a deceptive feeling of
peace. Their common tendency to observe things ironically

made them exchange a number of amusing comments. It seemed that only now had reality begun, and they had never been apart.

A hard-working little donkey was approaching along the mole; it was covered in little bells and wore a straw hat; its hooves had been painted red; it was pulling the ice-cream man's cart, with the sign: 'Freddy, Regina di Gelato'. That cheered them both up.

After a while she asked him reproachfully: 'Tell me, how could you ask me to stop writing, and, above all, why couldn't you write a few words?'

'It was completely impossible for me to do anything else. It's not worth talking about, but I was going through very difficult moments, when I was afraid . . .' he said, not finishing the sentence.

A wave of jealousy and despair flooded her whole being, but she restrained herself and said in a flat, indifferent voice: 'Did you not think what I must be going through? I lived just for your letters; for me, as I told you before, this is all too serious. I can't look at it as an amusing adventure. And I don't trust your reasons for giving me hope and making promises: I wasn't counting on anything, I never asked for anything.'

'You know very well that I loved you and still do. But at the moment . . .'

'If you really love me, then let's leave together immediately, today, tomorrow, wherever you like . . . I beg you . . . I . . . You know, don't you, how much I love you . . . I can't live without you . . . I . . .'

'Calm down, please, you understand yourself that it's completely impossible! How can I leave and slam the door behind me? Don't torment me.'

'If you don't come away with me right now, then you'll never slam the door behind you!'

'We have to wait a little . . . We will definitely be together . . . I'm sure of it.'

'Wait for what? After today I can see a lot of things clearly. I understand that it's hard to take a decisive step, but all you need is to want to and to dare.'

'We can meet in winter, I'll probably be coming.'

'Alone.'

'I don't know yet.'

'If you're not coming alone, I don't consider it possible.'

Very upset, she got to her feet. He also stood up. They walked off in silence. It began to get dark. Finally, he said reluctantly: 'I have to go.'

Those words were enough to make the feeling of anguish and despair, which seemed to have died down, hit her in the heart with renewed strength.

'You have to?! Go!'

And she ran away from him. He caught her up and seized her by the hand, but she tore herself free and ran even faster.

II

You are alone – and among them nobody
Is more defenceless and more invincible.[20]
Vladimir Smolensky

When she came to her senses, some distance from where they had parted, she slowly wended her way to the hotel, where she lay on the bed until it was dark, continuing the distressing discussion in her head and reproaching herself for what she had said and not said.

When the streetlamps came on, she got up and walked to the same house. She felt as if she had been through a whole eternity, not just one day. She was telling herself: 'I don't believe that he loves me. I'll just go now and say why I came, and then everything will be decided automatically. Why can't I act like that? All I need is a bit more determination. I have a right to defend my happiness.'

As she approached the house, she stopped. Only one window could be seen in the dark wall: an overhead lamp lit up a table, but there was nobody in the room. A few moments later the light was dimmed by the silhouette of a woman. Then she slowly turned around and walked off without looking round.

12

> ... And I left. And I entered the purifying circle
> Of loneliness, sadness, victory.[21]
>
> Dovid Knut

It seemed as if she had never in her life wept so much as she did in her room in the station hotel.

From under the window opposite, where there was an all-night bar, came the sound of loud drunken voices, women's shrieks and music. The same heartrending tune was repeated until it became annoying.

It was unbearably stuffy in the room, despite the window being wide open. It was nearly morning before she lost consciousness; when she woke up, she was horrified to realize that the only early train had already left. The thought that she had to spend another day here filled her with horror. Not knowing how to kill the time, once again she aimlessly went in the direction of the beach but, noticing the embankment over the railway line, she turned into a side street.

Wandering between modest houses and simple stalls, ending up in culs-de-sac and courtyards, she finally came across a path leading uphill and climbed up the stone steps at the end of it; then she crossed the railway tracks by a small metal bridge which hummed under her footsteps. She looked around when the path ended, and she began climbing higher and higher, making her way up a hill that was covered in thick, sunburned grass.

Her knees were beginning to sag, and her head was spinning. One and the same thought kept sucking, like a vicious insect, at her tired brain and then it seethed agonizingly: 'I have to get as high as I can, then I can see the whole beach and for the last, but last time see him ... he won't know.'

Still clambering up the almost vertical slope, she kept grabbing hold of any small bush in her path. Finally, she halted to get her breath back and turned round. The air was pure and light. The mountains behind her were like an amphitheatre.

Far below, merging with the horizon, lay the mottled colours of the deserted sea. Blocked by a series of lines, the beach was no longer visible.

'Higher, even higher, where that crag is. I can see everything from there. How slippery the grass is, I must try and clutch at these stones . . . They're rocking! Oh God! I think I'm falling, falling!'

That was her last conscious thought.

13

And you will hear the barely audible beat,
So familiar, of my heart . . .[22]
                                    Vladimir Smolensky

But don't dare to whisper spells to fate,
To stop me yearning for you.[23]
                                    Vladimir Sirin

Taking a seat at a little table in a café on the embankment, a customer said to the waiter when he approached: 'Have you heard, they say some woman has thrown herself under a train?'

'What happened? What woman? Where?' came several voices.

'Yes, I think it was over there, high up.'

A man on his way to the beach stopped, turned round sharply and suddenly ran off.

I ran,[24] panting for air, not knowing how to find the right way. The houses on my way were a hindrance; they blocked my path. Streets deliberately turned into culs-de-sac. The lanes ended up in workshops and garages. Children playing in the street made it impossible to run.

When, utterly exhausted, I finally asked a shopkeeper for guidance, it took him some time to understand what I actually wanted.

After searching for a long time, I found the path I needed and then the steps at the end that led to the metal bridge; by then I was no longer capable of running. As I got nearer, I saw that the crowd had begun to disperse: there were no visible signs of what had happened.

'Who was she? Where is this woman?' I kept approaching people with my pointless questions.

Nobody knew anything for sure. People were looking round at me dubiously, but I pushed my way through and saw a man in a workman's blouse, telling anyone who wanted to listen, evidently not for the first time:

'I came out of the workshop, you know, for a breath of air. I was standing, you know, and I suddenly see high up on the embankment something moving, and it was her, crawling higher and higher. Then I wondered how she got there, you're not allowed there, it's dangerous. And she keeps going even higher! Well, I thought, she's going to fall, she's sure to fall! And suddenly, I don't know if she got dizzy, but I see her trying to grab anything, and then she loses her grip. And then she just tumbled down!'

'What happened then, did she die?' asked several voices.

'I don't know about that. At least the express comes later. I ran to get help. When she was on the stretcher she looked dead, but perhaps she was just unconscious.'

'You're not likely to survive falling from such a height,' someone pointed out.

'Where's she been taken to?'

'They stopped a passing car to take her as fast as possible to hospital, but not to ours. They said it was too serious a case.'

I climbed up on to the narrow humming metal bridge and leaned over the railings. I was trying to imagine her, as she was so recently, lying on the tracks.

I leaned over lower and lower, my hands trembling as I clutched the metal railings. Like the entrance to hell, the black maw of the tunnel gaped before me. By bending over even more, I managed with difficulty to see at the other end of the tunnel a barely noticeable point of light. It began expanding and growing with extraordinary speed, turning more and more into a wheel of fire that roared as it revolved and bored into my head. The roar became ever louder and, enveloping me in puffs of caustic steam that smothered everything, the express train flew out of the tunnel like a tornado, the moving air almost knocking me off my feet.

When I came to my senses, I had trouble unclenching my swollen fingers. I bent down once more: at the end of the space that lay before my eyes there was an unmistakable light from a small, clear point.

They Called Her Russia

VASILY YANOVSKY

> The rusty buffers taught me once,
> As they traversed the Urals,
> A certain kind of wordless song
> More powerful than sorrow.[1]
>
> Nikolai Otsup

The wagons were knocking, ringing, staggering along. Their couplings kept rattling, now pulled tight, now sagging to the ground in knots. The armoured platforms were strewn with sawdust, empty boxes; one-and-a-half-inch planks lay scattered about like carrion. Gun shields glared from the parted doors of heated goods vans, and the gullets of barrels groped the steppe with dark eyes.

The locomotive sustained an ill-tempered, melancholy howl. It was tired, very tired. Like a cow galled with pain, it lowed: 'ooooooooo . . .'

Only from time to time would it cast a powerful, furious roar into the night, along with a tail of smoke and a funnel of sparks. Shaking, hissing with rage and wrath, it would suddenly roar – fiercely, cruelly. And then the soldiers sleeping on the tender would feel that it had a metal throat, cast-iron lungs and a steel tongue. But soon the locomotive would again commence its weary squeal, shaking and lowing balefully.

The talk on the tender was that the partisans were tightening their encirclement, that coal and water were harder and harder to come by, that any day now the commandant was going to lose it altogether: he's hopping mad, searching for dirty tarts at every stop; and the artillery lieutenant's afraid to go to sleep, afraid of even sniffing ether, because the commandant is jealous on account of Zinaida and keeps taking potshots at him.

The engine-driver offered to find a way through to the Reds; the stoker tried to persuade them to join the partisans and appoint the sailor *ataman*.[2]

There was a card game in the officers' wagon. It was listless, dull: money had lost all meaning. The armoured train was going round and round in a closed, cut-off circle. Money had no value. Only the sailor played with a measure of skill, with gusto. He had slyly hopped on to the platform at one of the halts, started gabbing in clever rhymes and just stayed on . . .

The sailor kept winning and winning, spouting jokes and sayings. A seasoned fellow.

Zinaida – a bedraggled woman with a dark, sallow face – sits frozen, her neck crooked at an awkward angle: for a long instant she just can't remember whether it's the commandant or the lieutenant she's married to . . .

Shuddering, limping, the artillery lieutenant wanders from corner to corner. He nods off as he walks. Then he flinches, jumps aside, surveys the players with a half-open eye – the humming sailor, the commandant on the cot – and, swaying and shuddering, again drifts off as he walks. He's afraid to go to sleep. He's afraid of the commandant.

The commandant lies in his corner, half-covered by dirty underwear, gently stroking his Mauser and following the hobbling lieutenant closely with his eyes: the lieutenant walks to the left, and the commandant's head – dishevelled, swollen, surprised – turns to the left; the lieutenant walks to the right – and the commandant's head turns to the right. When the lieutenant crosses the wagon and approaches Zinaida, the commandant's face twitches into something that's not quite a grimace, not quite a grin.

From time to time the commandant fidgets and begins to lift the Mauser: he sees two lieutenants. He knows that one of them is a reflection in a large mirror. But which one?

There they are, simultaneously raising their right hands to their faces, a single thick thumb sticking out from each bent wrist. They eagerly press the wrist close, sniffing, licking the

hollow at the joint, vainly trying to recall the smell of long
gone cocaine.

Carefully aiming the revolver at one of the lieutenants, the
commandant squeezes the trigger. He doesn't hear the shot.
It's only thanks to the startled Zinaida that he knows he's
fired. Everything remains the same. He must have shot at the
mirror. As soon as he points the barrel at the second lieutenant, the man takes off and disappears into a compartment.

'Heh, heh, heh,' the commandant whispers.

After gingerly soaking a section of his towel in ether, he
drapes it over his face and ties its ends at the back of his head.

The first gulp of ether is stifling, heavy, incredibly frightening, but at its very bottom lie liberation, transformation.

Now the lieutenant is safe.

The commandant sees:

The desert. Sand piled up in waves. Night. The moon is a
cannonball, red-hot and sinister. It troubles, beckons, tempts
you off your track. The commandant stands beside a Turkmen, both of them frantically stretching their arms towards
the moon ... Snakes are dancing on the stone ruins of an
ancient temple. Hundreds of them, thousands, tens of thousands ... The whole area, as far as the eye can see, is swarming
with sharp, muscular bodies. Standing on their tails, they rock
softly, rhythmically from side to side; their gyrating forked
tongues reach prayerfully up towards the moon ...

Suddenly the commandant hears quiet jangling. That kind
of ringing comes only from bells with clappers of human
bones, which hang around camels' necks.

The commandant and Turkmen fall on the ground.

Camels pass in the distance. Skinny, dark, humped – they
run along silently. Only if one peers very closely can one make
out human figures draped across their humps. Corpses.
Dried-up, charred skeletons.

Suddenly the Turkmen springs up and, raising his carbine,
pierces the air with a wild shriek: 'Plague!'

He spreads his legs, shrieking and shooting point-blank at
the caravan running silently past them. The caravan slowly disappears.

Several camels collapse. They hit the ground heavily; then they fall quiet with a sigh.

The caravan heads off towards Russia.

'Plague!' the Turkmen shrieks, firing into the sandy distance.

The train speeds along. The buffers clang on the slopes. They're arguing on the foot plate. The stoker insists that people have forgotten God, that they're possessed, and that's the reason so much blood's being spilt: it's the times we're living in.

'He's one of them Stundists.'[3]

The old artilleryman, for his part, keeps brushing the stoker's words aside scornfully, making snide comments and grinning bitterly. He argues that things had always been this way, and that it wouldn't ever change: blood's always being spilled.

'Times haven't changed. It's always the same time,' he proclaims. Then, turning his face to the window, he pronounces slowly, as if spitting it out: 'Who hasn't spilled a woman's blood? . . .'

The soldiers sigh. They stare glumly at the unruly black earth.

The wheels clash with the road in their age-old argument. They tear space into shreds. They pounce on the dawning track like beasts, swallowing it, choking and rumbling. The earth lies grey, unruly.

'What a dream . . .' The commandant smiles as he stirs from his sleep and affably recounts what he saw.

'The camels with plague – they were there,' Zinaida observes. 'Poisoned the springs . . . But there weren't any snakes.'

'The camels – they were real?' the commandant asks, dumbfounded.

'Yes, when we were headed for Khiva.'

'For Khiva?' the commandant asks in surprise. 'But now we're in an armoured train . . . Looking for our own?' he implores, entreating.

'And the snakes – they were there, too!' the lieutenant adds giddily. 'The snakes were there tomorrow.'

'Tomorrow?' the commandant repeats and nods his head with satisfaction: he understands . . .

At the halts, where the soldiers stock up on water, the

workers reluctantly approach the machine-gun mounts. The old artilleryman runs up to the commandant.

'Dream or real?' asks the commandant, letting his red, purulent eyes rove.

'Real, real,' the old man persuades him.

'On with it.' Dangling his bare, yellow feet, the commandant pulls on his trousers and, bracing himself against the partitions, staggers out of his compartment.

If the fire gets too insistent, the engine-driver puts the locomotive in reverse and leads the train back: he'll return at night and switch to another track . . . The wheels sing joylessly.

In the dewy dawn hours the sky looks like an unmade bed. The clouds are like fluffed-up quilts without covers. And the crimson sun rises on the side, like a flea engorged with blood.

Grinning, the commandant walks up to the machine gun, grabs hold of the grips and raises the muzzle: at the sky, at the sun . . . He opens fire, and his soldiers follow him down the line.

'Ta-ta-ta . . .' the gun issues faithfully and joyfully. 'Scum! Mother! Shit!' the commandant echoes.

Smiling hesitantly, the soldiers go on firing. From a distance the armoured train is an impressive sight: clanging, cloaked in smoke and sparks, it moves back and forth along a short length of track, letting its next-to-last cartridges loose into the overhanging sky.

Drawing water that moonlit night, the soldiers notice a host of reptiles on the site of an ancient ruin. Standing on their tails, they are slowly, softly gyrating, entranced by the moon.

'My snakes. There they are!' the commandant rubs his hands excitedly.

'Why yours?' Zinaida asks in surprise.

'You know, from my dream,' he answers anxiously.

'What dream?'

'I told you all about it! Camels with plague, too, remember?' the commandant grows pale.

'That was a dream,' the lieutenant explains . . .

Seizing a few boxes of ammunition, water and coal at the station, the train switches to another track.

The commandant hurriedly lays himself down on a bunk with Zinaida.

Her head is thrown back, straining towards the window. She sees bright stars on the sky's blue velvet. Motionless, with the hard banging of the wheels in her ears, she thinks of what she won't forget even in the next world: this deep sky and these moist stars – high up; and herself down below, like this, with this stranger – an exhausted bull collapsed on the dark pillow beside her.

'It's nice out in the field 'round this time,' she whispers.

'You won't get away – won't get away now!' the commandant suddenly lifts himself above her and his gaze becomes meaningful, triumphant and cruel. 'Now you won't get away! . . .' But a minute later he falls back into delirium.

He keeps repeating a single word over and over again, every which way. He's forgotten what it means. It's written on the ceiling of his compartment in thick indelible pencil with a sprawling, uneven hand . . .

'Brest-Litovsk, Brest-Litovsk,'[4] the commander repeats, spellbound.

Heated goods vans stand on railway bridges. The river resounds with its night-time noise: 'Bug-god-bug.'[5]

There's General Hoffmann, tapping his iron-shod boot in response to a lengthy speech; and Ioffe, leaning close to the Austrian chancellor, says in a pleading, stubborn whisper: 'We'll manage, I assure you . . .' The spot against which a trembling piece of steel will press itself years later is not yet smoking on his forehead.

The overloaded wagons shove off.

Gloomy men ride along on shaggy horses at an October wind's gallop, kicking the earth this way and that in a game of odds or evens. The river resounds with its night-time noise: 'Bug-god-bug . . .'

'Brest-Litovsk, Brest-Litovsk,' the commandant whispers, enchanted. 'A-a-ah,' he suddenly says to Zinaida. 'Now you won't get away! No, now you won't get away!' He smiles cruelly and meaningfully.

Zinaida stands up and staggers out of the compartment barefoot. She'd had a child. Once.

'Kostya, Kostya,' she whispers deliriously. Someone's arms wrap around Zinaida, drag her across the floor, toss her down on to a bunk.

'Kostya, Kostya,' Zinaida keeps whispering, then is suddenly startled and falls silent.

The lieutenant's round, sleepy face looms in the darkness above her.

At midnight the commandant props himself up, lights a candle, slips down from his bunk, peers out of the compartment and, grinning, affectionately beckons the lieutenant over with his finger.

Carefully, cautiously, never taking his eyes off the commandant, the lieutenant follows him into the compartment.

The commandant lifts up his shirt and, coming close to the candle, points his little finger at something. Leaning over, the lieutenant peers for a long time into a small, uneven, dry wound.

'Heh, heh, heh,' the commandant says.

The lieutenant's round, sleepy face turns crimson, swells, trembles. Then it goes soft again, yellows.

After a brief silence, he spits out harshly: 'It's a dream,' and, turning on his heel, slowly steps out of the compartment, pressing his hand to his belly. The commandant lays himself down again ... Towards morning the old artilleryman wakes him with a frightened look on his face.

'Shot herself.'

'Dream or real?' the commandant inquires.

'Real. Shot herself,' the old man repeats. 'Zinaida's shot herself.'

'Where?' the commandant scrambles to get up.

The train is stopped in the steppe. It smells of hot steam and coal. The cruel, grey sky hugs the ground. Hummocks and hills rise up like wounds, like rashes all around ... young spruce trees are scattered about like bushes. A pillar from which the Imperial Eagle had been shot off shows black on a hilltop. Europe lies to the left, Asia to the right ...

At the edge of the railway bed, beneath two firs, the commander spots the dirty, dark lump of a corpse – Zinaida.

He runs up to it limping, fusses about, lifts it. With the artilleryman's help he carries the corpse into the wagon.

'In the stomach?' the lieutenant asks.

'Put her down!' the commandant orders.

'In the breast,' the soldier stutters.

'Let's go,' the old man searches for the commandant's gaze. The train jerks, staggers, creaks – moves off. The locomotive lows plaintively . . .

The lieutenant and the commandant – each in his own compartment – take out bottles of ether, pour some on to towels and eagerly raise the towels to their faces. They grope their way to their bunks.

The train jerks along, then stops again. The soldiers argue. The sailor urges everyone to join the partisans. The engine-driver refuses. The old artilleryman's on his side: they're afraid. They decide to break through up ahead: if not Whites, then Reds – whomever they meet.

The sailor puts on the lieutenant's and Zinaida's undergarments and two suits. Plump, broad, with pockets stuffed to the brim, he disappears as inconspicuously as he'd appeared, just rolls off the railway bed . . . A seasoned fellow.

The soldiers detach the rear wagons. The locomotive, towing a few armoured platforms, gives a whistle and moves off.

It increases the distance between itself and the abandoned train at an ever-greater rate; finally, it fades into the distance. And the look of the orphaned wagons, standing still in the middle of the gently sloping, hilly steppe, is pitiful and incomprehensible.

The commandant beholds . . .

He lies on his bunk – worried, troubled. His face is covered with a towel. Something beats against his consciousness with a hammer, summoning him: help, help . . . But his body won't obey.

So now he's splitting, sliding off to the side. His body remains in the bunk, but he's hurrying off to the inaudible summons. He's delirious. In the neighbouring compartment he finds the lieutenant suffocating. In his drugged sleep the lieutenant tries vainly to remove the towel from his face with his disobedient hands. But the towel is bound at the back of his head with tight knots; the lieutenant is choking on his own foam. The veins on his neck twitch like blue ropes.

The commandant knows that he can't untie the knots without his body. He guards the lonely wagons with the wind. In one of them, on a crate that had once held rusks, lies Zinaida's corpse ... He touches the corpse with something not fleshly, not of this world, presses against it, tugs at it forcefully.

Zinaida moves, fidgets. Malevolently, she lifts her face – which is mottled with round grey spots – and snarls ... Like a dog, like a tamed wolf.

The commandant whirls around her like a funnel, tugging.

Snarling, Zinaida slowly – ever so slowly – lifts herself up from the crate, walks over to the lieutenant and undoes the knot with black, unbending fingers. The lieutenant gasps for air, coughing.

Zinaida turns around, as if under hypnosis, and heads back. But she doesn't manage to crawl all the way to the crate, falls flat on her back and stiffens. Her upper lip remains curled, like the lip of a vicious but powerless snarling dog.

The commandant returns to his body; he removes the towel from his face with an uncertain hand and drifts off in his bunk.

When he awoke the sun was smouldering like a bonfire directly above the horizon.

'Dream or real?' he uttered listlessly.

Then he wondered whether this sun was setting or rising.

Barefoot, treading very softly, he left his compartment, carefully stepped around the corpse of his wife and peered into the peephole of the lieutenant's compartment. He immediately jumped aside with great force, as if pushed; his eyes had met the spying, colourlessly blue gaze of the lieutenant.

In a great hurry the commandant rushed back to his compartment and grabbed the Mauser.

'Was it you that moved Zinaida?' the lieutenant, who'd appeared in the doorway, asked in a whisper, looking around nervously.

The commandant decided that he should say something grand; after some thought, he pronounced: 'Get down and pray, scoundrel.'

'What for?' the lieutenant asked, taken aback.

The conversation wasn't going too well. The commandant slowly lifted the revolver.

Leaping behind the door, the lieutenant drew his Brauning with a decisive gesture. His face was cruel and sleepy . . . The railway bed was obscured by hills. One couldn't make out the wagons from the steppe right away. And the horses were short, thick-legged. The detachment rode up a hill.

'Fellas,' a broad man in a felt cloak shouted. 'An engine!' The rest hurried up and stared in silence.

Gun shields stuck out from the parted doors of heated goods vans; machine-gun mounts lay about like corpses on platforms that were strewn with sawdust.

Suddenly, the almost toy-like sound of a gunfight reached their ears.

'Number six,' the wide man in a felt cloak pronounced.

After a short wait the men resolutely grabbed hold of their old blackened, greasy saddles, jumped up on their horses with a whoop and swept down to the wagons like an avalanche.

O saddles with purulent spots and sabre scars, O Russian saddles! What a rotation of sweaty feet they'd seen during every pursuit, while tired riders, spilling their thick blood, sullenly turned either their faces or their backs to the firing line; and the horses beneath them silently bit their angry lips and collapsed, dying of ruptured hearts!

O saddles! O Russian saddles!

High above the railway bed, above the detachment racing at full gallop over hummocks and bushes, stood a pillar from which the Imperial Eagle had been shot off: Europe to the left, Asia to the right.

Russian Émigré Newspapers and Periodicals

The following list provides details of all Russian émigré newspapers and journals mentioned in this book.

Newspapers

Illiustrirovannaia Rossiia (alt. *La Russie illustrée*) [Illustrated Russia], Paris (1924–39)
Poslednie novosti [The Latest News], Paris (1920–40)
Rul' [The Rudder], Berlin (1920–31)
Segodnia [Today], Riga (1919–40)
Slovo [The Word], Riga (1925–9)
Vozrozhdenie (alt. *La Renaissance*) [The Rebirth], Paris (1925–40)
Zaria [The Dawn], Harbin (1920–43)

Magazines, Journals and Almanacs

Chisla [Numbers], Paris (1930–34)
Krug [Circle], Paris (1936–8)
Novosel'e [Housewarming], New York (1942–50) and Paris (1950)
Novyi korabl' (alt. *Le Vaisseau nouveau*) [The New Ship], Paris (1927–8)
Novyi zhurnal (alt. *The New Review*), New York (1942–)
Opyty (alt. *Experiments*), New York (1953–8)
Rubezh [Frontier], Harbin (1926–45)
Russkie zapiski (alt. *Annales russes*) [Russian Annals], Paris and Shanghai (1937–9)
Satirikon (alt. *Satyricon*), Paris (1931)*

---

* *Satirikon* was a popular weekly satirical magazine edited by Arkady Averchenko and published between 1908 and 1914. The journal's original publisher, Mikhail Kornfeld (1884–1978), emigrated and from 1920 lived in Paris; in 1931 he resurrected the magazine with the publicist Leonid 'Lolo'

Sovremennik [The Contemporary], Toronto (1960–80)
Sovremennye zapiski (alt. *Annales contemporaines*) [Contemporary Annals], Paris (1920–40)
Studencheskie gody [Student Years], Prague (1922–5)
Volia Rossii [The Will of Russia], Prague and Paris (1920–34)*
Vstrechi (alt. *Rencontres*) [Encounters], Paris (1934).
Zveno (alt. *Le Chaînon*) [The Link], Paris (1923–8)†

Munstein (1866–1947), but it ran for only twenty-eight issues across several months.
* First as a weekly newspaper (1920–22), then as a weekly magazine (1922–4), thereafter as a monthly journal (1924–32).
† First as a weekly literary supplement to *Poslednie novosti* (1923–5), then as a weekly magazine (1926–7), thereafter as a monthly journal (1927–8).

Author Biographies

GEORGY VIKTOROVICH ADAMOVICH (1892–1972) was a poet, prose writer, essayist, critic and translator. He was born in Moscow and came to prominence in Acmeist circles. Having escaped military draft during the Great War thanks to student exemption, Adamovich remained in Petrograd until after the 1917 October Revolution. Following a brief period working in Novorzhev, in the Pskov region, he returned to Petrograd in the spring of 1921, where he lived with Georgy Ivanov and Irina Odoevtseva. In 1923 he emigrated to Paris, where together with Ivanov he founded the influential Union of Young Poets and Writers in 1925. After the Second World War he lectured internationally on Russian literature, notably at Manchester and Oxford universities.

The émigré critic Wladimir Weidlé (1895–1979) described Adamovich as 'the most read and most influential critic of the Russian emigration'. He was the chief arbiter of the so-called 'Paris note', one of the emigration's major literary movements, which sought to combine the despair of exile with the modern age of anxiety. Noted for his highly subjective opinions, he was one of the emigration's most outspoken literary critics and polemicists.

MARK ALDANOV (1886–1957), born Mark Alexandrovich Landau, was a writer of historical and political novels. Raised in Kiev, he moved to Odessa in 1919, and then on to Constantinople and Paris. One of the Paris literary circle's most prominent figures, he was a frequent contributor to journals such as *Sovremennye zapiski* and *Russkie zapiski*, and newspapers such as *Poslednie novosti*, *Segodnia* and *Illiustrirovannaia Rossiia*. Following the establishment of the Vichy government, he withdrew to Nice and in 1941 emigrated to New York, where he founded the influential quarterly journal *Novyi zhurnal* with Mikhail Zetlin (1882–1945). He returned to France in 1947.

Aldanov was one of the most popular writers of his day, and much of his writing was translated into English, with some novels appearing in print even before their Russian original. Notable among Aldanov's works are his tetralogy of novels about the Napoleonic wars *The Thinker* (*Myslitel'*, 1923–7), *The Fifth Seal* (*Nachalo i konets*, 1939), *Nightmare and Dawn* (*Bred*, 1954) and *Suicide* (*Samoubiistvo*, 1957). Throughout his life, he maintained an extensive correspondence with several prominent émigré figures, including Ivan Bunin, Vladimir Nabokov and Alexander Kerensky.

DON AMINADO was the pen name of Aminodav Peysakhovich Shpolyansky (1888–1957). Born in Elizavetgrad in the Kherson Governorate of the Russian Empire, Shpolyansky studied law at Odessa and Kiev, later moving to Moscow. He saw action during the First World War but was discharged in 1915 after being wounded. In 1920 he emigrated via Constantinople to Paris, where he published regularly in the émigré press until the outbreak of the Second World War.

A writer of poems, feuilletons, short stories and aphorisms, Don Aminado was ranked alongside Teffi and Chorny as one of the leading émigré satirists. His first collection of verse published in emigration was *Smoke without the Fatherland* (*Dym bez otechestva*, 1921), and his first collection of satirical short stories, *Our Little Life* (*Nasha malen'kaia zhizn'*), came out in 1927. His work was introduced to Francophone audiences through a collaboration with the French journalist and author Maurice Dekobra (1885–1973), which led to the collection *Le Rire dans la steppe* (1927). He later also published in French a collection of aphorisms *Pointes de feu* (1939).

NINA NIKOLAEVNA BERBEROVA (1901–93) was a writer, poet, memoirist, translator and biographer. Born in St Petersburg, she initially welcomed the overthrow of Nicholas II. Following the October Revolution she moved to Moscow and then Rostov, where she studied literature at the Donskoy University. In 1921 she returned to Petrograd, where she became acquainted with many prominent literary figures of the Silver Age. In 1922, however, after the execution of poet Nikolai Gumilyov and because of the increasingly difficult circumstances faced by artists in Soviet Russia, she left for Germany with Vladislav Khodasevich. The couple lived with Maxim Gorky, first at Saarow (near Berlin), then at Marienbad, Czechoslovakia, and finally at Sorrento, Italy. In 1925, Berberova renounced her Soviet passport, causing a rift with Gorky, and moved to Paris. She left Khodasevich in 1932. Having spent the war in Occupied France, she eventually settled in America in 1950.

As a prose writer, Berberova is notable for her perceptive evocation of the fraught psychological and emotional world of her characters, drawn mainly from the Russian émigré milieu in Paris. Her provocative and controversial autobiography *The Italics Are Mine* (*Kursiv moi*, 1969), as well as her biographies *Tchaikovsky: A Life* (*Chaikovskii: istoriia odinokoi zhizni*, 1936) and *Moura: The Dangerous Life of the Baroness Budberg* (*Zheleznaia zhenshchina*, 1981), drew popular acclaim and critical ire in equal measure. Among her translations, Berberova notably rendered Choderlos de Laclos's *Les Liaisons dangereuses* as well as several works by Romain Rolland into Russian, and Dostoevsky's *The Eternal Husband* (*Vechnyi muzh*) into French.

IVAN ALEXEYEVICH BUNIN (1870–1953) was born to a family of impoverished landowners in Voronezh, a provincial capital some 300 miles south-east of Moscow. He began his career on the newspaper *Orlovskii vestnik*, and his first collection of poetry was published in 1891. A member of the *Sreda* literary circle, he garnered fame as a poet and short-prose writer in pre-Revolutionary Russia. In the wake of the 1917 October Revolution, Bunin and his wife travelled to Odessa, where they remained for almost two years. It was during this period that he wrote the diary *Cursed Days* (*Okaiannye dni*, 1935). In 1920 the Bunins boarded one of the last ships to leave Odessa for Constantinople, from where they travelled on to France via the Balkans. In France they rented a villa near Grasse, although they often wintered in Paris. In 1927 Bunin began an affair with Galina Kuznetsova, whom he invited to live at Grasse, and the group was later joined by the writer Leonid Zurov (1902–71) and Margarita Stepun (1895–1971). In 1933 he was awarded the Nobel Prize for literature and reputedly gave away 120,000 francs of the prize money to impoverished writers. His fortunes suffered with the outbreak of war and steadily declined in the postwar years. He died in Paris.

Bunin was one of the few poets of the Symbolist era to have shunned Symbolism in favour of neoclassicism. Descended in the literary line of Chekhov, he is widely regarded as the master of the Russian short story, which reached its pinnacle in his collection *Dark Avenues* (*Temnye allei*, 1943). Bunin's rich prose style exhibits a technical mastery that combines sharp, precise description with vivid poetic beauty.

BORIS VASILIEVICH BUTKEVICH (1895–1931) was a staff captain in the 5th Alexandrovsky Hussars and saw action in the First World War, and in the Russian Civil War on the side of the Whites. He published his first verses under the pseudonym 'Boris Beta' in the Vladivostok press. In 1921 he emigrated to Harbin and later moved to Shanghai. Making his way to Europe by ship, via Hong Kong, Saigon, Djibouti and Suez, he arrived in Marseilles in 1924 without documents and was interned in the Victor Hugo concentration camp. Thereafter he worked as a stevedore, a stoker, and a general labourer in the docks at Marseilles, while continuing to publish poetry and short prose. He died in abject poverty.

The fine lyric sensitivity of Butkevich's writing brought him to the attention of Vladislav Khodasevich and Nina Berberova, as well as Ivan Bunin and Zinaida Hippius. Butkevich's premature death was widely mourned in the émigré community, alongside the suicides of the novelist Ivan Boldyrev (1903–33) and the poet Boris Poplavsky (1903–35).

SASHA CHORNY (1880–1932) was the pen name of Alexander Mikhailovich Glickberg. A satirical poet, short-story writer and children's writer, he enjoyed immense popularity in pre-Revolutionary Russia and in emigration. His first collection of verse, *Sundry Motifs* (*Raznye motivy*), was published in 1906, and he contributed regularly to the journal *Satirikon* along with the likes of Teffi. He served at the Front during the First World War and was opposed to the 1917 October Revolution. In 1918 he and his wife left Russia for Lithuania. In spring 1920 they moved to Berlin. Following a brief stay in Rome in 1923, he moved to Paris, and in 1929 he purchased a plot in La Favière, where he spent the last years of his life. He died at Le Lavandou, in Var, after helping to put out a fire on a nearby farm.

Despite a ban on his works in the USSR, Chorny has remained hugely popular across generations in Russia. In his eulogy for Chorny, Vladimir Nabokov wrote, 'He left only a few books, and a quiet, beauteous shadow.'

YURY FELSEN (1894–1943) was born Nikolai Berngardovich Freuden-stein in St Petersburg. In the wake of the 1917 October Revolution, he emigrated with his family to Riga, where he remained until mid-1923. After a brief period in Berlin, he eventually settled in Paris later that year. Felsen's early journalistic writing was probably published in the Riga press under the pseudonym 'Fen', although the author would later claim that his first works were published only after his arrival in France. Felsen owed much of his acclaim to the support of Georgy Adamovich, who invited him to contribute to *Zveno*. Following the German occupation of France, Felsen tried to escape to Switzerland with his family; however, he was caught, arrested, and interned in Drancy concentration camp. He was deported in 1943. He died in the gas chambers at Auschwitz.

Throughout his literary career, Felsen worked on a great literary project, variously titled 'The Recurrence of Things Past' (*Povtorenie proidennogo*) and 'A Romance with an Author' (*Roman s pisatelem*). Comprising eight short stories and three novels, *Deceit* (*Obman*, 1930), *Happiness* (*Schast'e*, 1932) and *Letters about Lermontov* (*Pis'ma o Lermontove*, 1936), Felsen's neo-Proustian project traces the tormented love of his protagonist, as well as his artistic and philosophical evolution. Influenced by the great modernists such as Marcel Proust, James Joyce and Virginia Woolf, Felsen's writing was at the forefront of aesthetic and philosophical currents in contemporary European modernism.

GAITO (GEORGY IVANOVICH) GAZDANOV (1903–71) was a novelist, short-story writer, literary critic and radio journalist. He fought on the side of the Whites during the Civil War, and in 1920 he was evacuated from the Crimea along with the remnants of Baron Wrangel's army and interned in a camp at Gallipoli. After escaping to Constantinople and completing his studies in Shumen, Bulgaria, he made his way to Paris in 1923. Following a series of manual jobs and a period at the publisher Hachette, Gazdanov embarked on studies at the Sorbonne, funding himself through an income garnered from driving a taxi at night. In 1930 his debut novel, *An Evening with Claire* (*Vecher u Kler*), was published, bringing him wide critical acclaim from prominent figures such as Vladislav Khodasevich and Maxim Gorky. Despite an abortive attempt to return to the Soviet Union, Gazdanov ultimately remained in Paris, where he served as a member of the Resistance during the Nazi occupation, an experience he later recorded in *Je m'engage à défendre* (1946). After the war he gained financial independence through the international success of his novels *The Spectre of Alexander Wolf* (*Prizrak Aleksandra Vol'fa*,

1948) and *The Buddha's Return* (*Vozvrashchenie buddy*, 1949–50). In his final years he also worked as a radio correspondent and literary critic for Radio Liberty.

Gazdanov was one of the leading figures of the younger generation of émigré writers. His prose straddles his nineteenth-century Russian literary heritage and the innovations of twentieth-century French modernism. His works display a lifelong preoccupation with fatalism, as well as the metaphysics of life and death.

IRINA YURIEVNA GUADANINI (1905–76) was an émigrée poet and journalist. Born in Tambov, she emigrated to Paris, where throughout the 1930s she made a living as a dog-groomer. After the Second World War she worked for Radio Liberty. In 1962 a collection of her poetry, *Letters* (*Pis´ma*), was published in Munich. She died in tragic circumstances, alone, suffering from loss of memory and mental illness.

GEORGY VLADIMIROVICH IVANOV (1894–1958) was a poet, prose writer and memoirist. A member of the Acmeist school, he left the Soviet Union in 1922 on the pretext of creating a 'state repertoire for theatres' but never returned and spent most of his life thereafter in Paris. Having enjoyed relative luxury prior to the Second World War, Ivanov and his wife found themselves penniless by its end: the Soviet Union's annexation of Latvia cut off their main source of income, and their villa at Biarritz was destroyed during Allied bombing. Ivanov ended his days on the French Riviera, in a retirement home for stateless persons.

Ivanov's most significant contributions were written from the late 1920s onwards, and blend classical literary forms with French existentialism. Much of his work is distinguished by nostalgic retrospection, and his late verses, such as those in the collection *Portrait without Likeness* (*Portret bez skhodstva*, 1950), show both the keen wit and nihilistic despair typical of his literary milieu.

VLADISLAV FELITSIANOVICH KHODASEVICH (1886–1939) was a poet, critic and literary historian. He rose to prominence as a poet of Russia's Silver Age, publishing several critically acclaimed volumes of verse including *The Way of the Grain* (*Putem zerna*, 1920) and *The Heavy Lyre* (*Tiazhelaia lira*, 1922). In 1921 Khodasevich met Nina Berberova; the two became lovers and escaped the Soviet Union to

Berlin via Riga. In 1925, after living with Maxim Gorky in various countries throughout Europe, Khodasevich and Berberova moved to Paris, where he continued to publish poetry and criticism, principally as the literary editor for the émigré newspaper *Vozrozhdenie*. It was also in Paris that he worked on his monumental biography of the poet Gavrila Derzhavin (1743–1816), as well as *Necropolis* (*Nekropol'*, 1939), his collection of waspish, unashamedly partisan memoirs. He spent his final days in Paris, plagued by poverty and ill health.

A major poet of the Silver Age, Khodasevich's style falls outside the modish trends of the era, flaunting a distinct neoclassical bent. A scholar of Pushkin and eighteenth-century Russian poetry, he also edited and translated several volumes of Polish and Jewish verse, most notably the anthology *From the Jewish Poets* (*Iz evreiskikh poetov*, 1922), which he co-translated with Lev Yaffe (1875–1948). He was an ardent supporter of the young Vladimir Nabokov, who would later describe Khodasevich as the greatest Russian poet of the twentieth century.

DOVID KNUT (1900–1955) was born Duvid Mironovich (Meyerovich) Fiksman in the town of Orgeyev in the Russian Empire (now Orhei, Moldova). Following the union of Bessarabia with Romania in 1918, Knut and his family drifted westwards, eventually settling in the Latin Quarter of Paris in 1920. After graduating from the University of Caen in 1924 with a degree in chemical engineering, Knut entered gainful employment, which afforded him financial independence and the freedom to pursue his literary interests. In 1942, pursued by the Gestapo, he fled to Switzerland and returned to Paris in 1944 after its liberation by the Allies. He moved to Israel in 1949.

Aligned with the Russian and European avant-garde movements of the early 1920s, Knut's early verse appeared in Soviet journals such as *Nedra*, and not in the émigré press until 1925. His early collections of poetry such as *Of My Millennia* (*Moikh tysiacheletii*, 1925) blend avant-garde techniques with Jewish biblical and exilic themes. Scholar Leonid Livak has called him 'a rare example of a harmonious fusion of Russian and Jewish cultural heritages'.

GALINA NIKOLAEVNA KUZNETSOVA (1900–1976) was born in Kiev. In 1918 she married a White officer, with whom she left Russia during the evacuation of the Crimea. She departed on a boat for

Constantinople, then lived in Prague, studying there at the French Institute. Her literary career began in Prague in 1922, with the publication of her verse in the journal *Studencheskie gody* (*Student Years*). In 1924 she moved to Paris, and two years later she met Ivan Bunin through an acquaintance with the Russian literary historian Modest Hofman (1887–1959). She soon left her husband and took up with the Bunins at Grasse, where she was both lover and pupil of Bunin. In 1932 she began a love affair with the singer Margarita Stepun, the sister of the philosopher Fyodor Stepun (1884–1965). She left Bunin for good in 1942. During the war, she lived with Margarita Stepun at Cannes and in the immediate aftermath spent some time in postwar Germany. In 1949 she moved to the United States, where she worked for Voice of America and later the United Nations. She transferred to Geneva in 1959 and retired in Munich in 1962.

Kuznetsova's strongly autobiographical first collection, *Morning* (*Utro*), came out in 1930 and dealt mainly with the plight of White Russian officers and their families during the evacuation of the Crimea. This was soon followed by her novel *Prologue* (*Prolog*) in 1933. In 1937 she published a collection of verse written between 1923 and 1929, *The Olive Garden* (*Olivkovyi sad*), and her best-known work, *Grasse Diary* (*Grasskii dnevnik*), which details her life with the Bunins from 1927 to 1934, was published in 1967. Kuznetsova's writing is pervaded with themes of separation and loneliness, creating a lyric tension that underpins her work. Her modest, limpid style shows traces of Bunin's influence, but her work ultimately departs in its preponderance for the prosaics of daily life.

IVAN SOZONTOVICH LUKASH (1892–1940) was a poet and prose writer who wrote under the pseudonym Ivan Oredezh. Born in St Petersburg, Lukash published his first collection of poems *Poisonous Flowers* (*Tsvety iadovitye*) in 1910. During the Civil War, he fought on the side of the Whites in General Denikin's Volunteer Army. His experience of the war and his internment at Gallipoli formed the inspiration for his collection of short prose works *The Bare Field* (*Goloe pole*, 1922). He left Gallipoli via Constantinople and Sofia and settled in Western Europe, living in Berlin, Riga and Paris. From 1927 to 1928 he headed the literary desk of the newspaper *Slovo*, and later in Paris he worked on the editorial board of *Vozrozhdenie*. He died of tuberculosis in a hospital at Meudon.

Lukash's early poetry is closely aligned with the work of the Ego-Futurists, but from 1922 onwards he would turn ever more to prose writing, specifically to the historical fiction for which he is best known. He was a close friend of Nabokov throughout the 1920s and collaborated with him on several scripts for pantomimes and cabarets.

VLADIMIR VLADIMIROVICH NABOKOV (1899–1977) was a prose writer, poet, translator, critic and literary scholar. Born to a wealthy, influential family in St Petersburg, he began writing poetry in his adolescence, and the first volume of his work was published in 1916. In the wake of the 1917 October Revolution, Nabokov and his family fled to the Crimea, and in 1919 he embarked on his studies at Trinity College, Cambridge. In 1922 he rejoined his family in Berlin, where he proceeded to write prolifically in Russian under the pseudonym Sirin. Having fled Germany in 1937, Nabokov, along with his wife and son, lived in France for a while, but the family was forced to emigrate once again in 1940, this time to the United States. In America, Nabokov continued to write alongside teaching engagements at Wellesley, Harvard and Cornell. After switching his medium to English, the success of *Lolita* in 1955 brought him significant financial freedom and allowed him to return to Europe to devote himself to writing. He lived out his final years in Montreux, Switzerland.

IRINA VLADIMIROVNA ODOEVTSEVA (1895–1990) was born Iraida Heinike in Riga. A student of Nikolai Gumilyov (1886–1921), she moved in Acmeist circles in Petrograd and became a member of the Guild of Poets, which had been reinstituted by Gumilyov in 1920. She first began publishing poetry in post-Revolutionary Petrograd, and her first collection, *The Courtyard of Wonders* (*Dvor chudes*), came out in 1922. She married Georgy Ivanov in 1921 and, having obtained Latvian citizenship, was able to escape the Soviet Union under the guise of accompanying her husband on a business trip. They travelled to Paris via Berlin.

Much of Odoevtseva's early work is virulently anti-Bolshevik: exalting victims of the Red Terror and expressing ideals of love, freedom and anti-totalitarianism, her verse mixes elements of the fantastic with realist detail. Her first short story, 'Shooting Star' (*Paduchaia zvezda*), came out in *Zveno* in 1926, and the following year she published her first novel, *The Angel of Death* (*Angel smerti*). In 1955 Odoevtseva moved with Ivanov to a retirement home in Hyères, near Toulon. Following Ivanov's death in 1958, she returned to poetry and worked on her two volumes of memoirs, *On the Banks* of the Neva (*Na beregakh Nevy*, 1967) and *On the Banks of the Seine* (*Na beregakh Seny*, 1983). She returned to the Soviet Union in 1987 and died in Leningrad.

IVAN SERGEYEVICH SHMELYOV (1873–1950) was a prose writer, essayist and playwright. Born in Moscow's Zamoskvorechye district, he studied at Moscow University's Faculty of Law. Publishing his first short story in 1895, he became a celebrated author in pre-Revolutionary Russia and was a member of the influential literary group *Sreda*, which also numbered Ivan Bunin, Maxim Gorky and Alexander Kuprin among its ranks. Although Shmelyov at first welcomed the 1917 February Revolution, a journey to Siberia as a correspondent for the newspaper *Russkie vedomosti* brought swift disillusionment. In 1918 he moved temporarily to Alushta on the southern coast of the Crimea, and after briefly returning to Moscow he received permission, through the offices of Maxim Gorky, to travel abroad for medical treatment. He and his wife left Russia in February 1922 and settled in Berlin, where they soon learned of their son's execution at the hands of the Bolsheviks. The following year they moved to Paris.

Shmelyov aimed at being a national writer. His prose continues the Russian nineteenth-century realist tradition in the vein of Nikolai Leskov (1831–95), but also draws on modernist innovations, combining fragmented, non-linear narratives with cinematic descriptive techniques. His works are strongly pacifist and informed by a devout Russian Orthodox and Slavophilic sensibility. His finest works deal with the traumas of the Civil War, as in the novel *The Sun of the Dead* (*Solntse mertvykh*, 1923), and the émigré condition, as in the short-story collection *Arriving in Paris* (*V"ezd v Parizh*, 1929). He was twice nominated for the Nobel Prize for literature.

TEFFI was the pseudonym of the writer Nadezhda Alexandrovna Lokhvitskaya (1872–1952). Born in St Petersburg, she was one of the most popular writers in pre-Revolutionary Russia and a noted favourite of Tsar Nicholas II and Vladimir Lenin alike. Her first works were published in 1901 and consisted of poetry and short satirical sketches. As her popularity grew, she joined the staff of *Satirikon* in 1908. Fearing difficulties after the Revolution on account of her publications, she left for Kiev in 1918. As the Bolsheviks advanced on Kiev in the spring of the following year, she travelled on to Odessa and from there to Novorossiysk. Teffi left Russia in 1919, sailing for Constantinople. In 1920 she settled in Paris, where she would spend most of her life abroad. Her final years were marked by poverty, loneliness and ill health.

Teffi's output includes a novel, a memoir, countless feuilletons and a number of one-act plays, but it is for her satirical short stories that she is best remembered. Her humorous style is underpinned by an aptitude for acute observation and a flare for caricature; however, her oeuvre is also marked by a profoundly elegiac tone. Reflecting on the tragicomic nature of her writing, Teffi discerned in her own work, 'like the pediment of a Greek theatre, two faces: one laughing and one weeping'.

VASILY SEMYONOVICH YANOVSKY (1906–89) was a prose writer, critic and memoirist, who wrote under the pseudonyms Tseyanovsky and V. S. Mirny. Having borne the hardship of the Revolution and Civil War, Yanovsky and his family illegally crossed the Polish border in 1922 and settled in Warsaw, where he began to publish his first short stories. In 1926 he moved to Paris, where he studied medicine at the Sorbonne. During this time he continued to publish as part of the young generation of émigré writers and was actively involved in several newspapers and journals. Soon after the outbreak of war, Yanovsky left France, travelling first to Casablanca in 1940 and then to New York in 1942. He continued to write in America, publishing his novels *No Man's Time* (1967) and *Of Light and Sounding Brass* (1972) in English. He also co-founded the ecumenical journal *The Third Hour* with W. H. Auden.

Often dubbed 'the Russian Céline' because of his explicit, physiological poetics, Yanovsky's prose broke many conventions of contemporary writing. His memoir *Elysian Fields: A Book of Memory* (*Polia eliseiskie: kniga pamiati*, 1983) is regarded as one of the touchstone chronicles of the 'Russian Montparnasse' during the interwar years in Paris.

Notes

In Paris

translated by Robert Chandler

'In Paris' (*V Parizhe*) first published in *Novyi zhurnal* 1 (1942), pp. 17–27, and later republished in the collection *Temnye allei* (New York: Novaia zemlia, 1943). This translation is a slightly revised version of the one first published in *Russian Short Stories from Pushkin to Buida*, ed. Robert Chandler (London: Penguin, 2005).

1. *Rien n'est plus . . . de bien*: 'There's nothing harder than picking out a good melon or a decent woman' (French).
2. *zubrovka*: A spicy vodka.
3. *shashlyk à la Kars*: A shashlyk is much the same as a kebab. Kars is a town in Eastern Turkey.
4. *L'eau gâte le vin . . . l'âme*: 'Water spoils wine as a cart spoils a road and a woman, a man's soul' (French).
5. *rassolnik*: A meat or fish soup made with pickled cucumbers.
6. *C'est moi qui vous remercie*: 'It's I who should thank you' (French).
7. *Le bon Dieu . . . derrière*: 'The good Lord always sends trousers to those who have no bottom' (French).
8. *Qui se marie . . . mauvais jours*: 'He who marries for love enjoys good nights and bad days' (French).
9. *Patience – médecine des pauvres*: 'Patience – the medicine of the poor' (French).
10. *femme de ménage*: 'Cleaning lady' (French).
11. *L'amour fait danser les ânes*: 'Love makes even donkeys dance' (French).

Three Short Stories

translated by Maria Bloshteyn and Bryan Karetnyk

This trio of stories, '*Un petit accident*', 'In the Alps' (*V al'pakh*) and 'In such a night . . .' (*V takuiu noch'* . . .), dated 7 April 1949 and first published in *Novosel'e* 42–4 (1950), pp. 1–4. They were later included in the collection *Vesnoi, v Iudee. Roza Ierikhona* (1953), the last volume of Bunin's short stories to be published during the author's lifetime.

Throughout his life, but particularly in emigration, Bunin would return to the composition of laconic miniatures such as the three included here. In 1930 a series of these miniatures were published in *Poslednie novosti* under the titles *Brief Stories* (*Kratkie rasskazy*) and *The Far Away* (*Dalekoe*). Descended from the genre of the Decadent prose poem, these terse works range in length from a few lines to several paragraphs, or a couple of pages at most. Bunin noted that 'even with the greatest writers, there are only isolated good passages, and between them – water', and so these miniatures are an attempt to distil prose into its purest form. Thus condensed and stripped, like poetry, of all superfluous detail, Bunin's miniatures in many ways conceal the author's intent behind purely formal elements, inviting a mode of reading that rewards attention paid to the minutest of detail.

Un petit accident

1.   *Un petit accident*: 'A little accident' (French).

'In such a night . . .'

2.   *The moon shines bright: in such a night as this*: The lines here and throughout are taken from Shakespeare's *The Merchant of Venice*, Act V, Scene i, in which at Belmont Lorenzo and Jessica compare themselves to lovers of antiquity.

Thou Shalt Not Covet

translated by Rose France

'Thou Shalt Not Covet' (*Vizy, valiuty, kaiuty*) first published in *Poslednie novosti*, 25 July 1920, p. 2.

1.   *To forget so soon, good God*: The opening line of 'To forget so
     soon ...' (*Zabyt' tak skoro* ...), a song composed by Pyotr
     Tchaikovsky (1840–93) with lyrics by Alexei Apukhtin
     (1840–93).

Hedda Gabler

translated by Rose France

'Hedda Gabler' (*Gedda Gabler*) first published in the collection
Gorodok (Paris: N. P. Karbasnikov, 1927), pp. 43–8.

One of the most enduringly popular writers of the emigration, Teffi
is most renowned for her mordant depictions of émigré life in Paris.
The scholar Temira Pachmuss remarked of Teffi's work that its principal achievement is the fusing of 'irony with bitterness and criticism
with pity'. These tragicomic portrayals of émigré heroes and heroines
conjure up the tedium of life in emigration and its attendant 'little
tragedies', while her comic plots, such as that here in 'Hedda Gabler',
evoke the hollowness of the émigré condition and the attempts made
by individuals to seek escape though dreams and illusion.

1.   *Night*: The poem 'Night' ('*Noch*'') by Alexander Pushkin (1799–
     1837) was set to music by Anton Rubenstein (1829–94) and
     became a popular romance in the concert repertoire of the late
     nineteenth century. Here Madame 'd'Ivanova' is revealing a cer-
     tain lack of knowledge regarding the work's provenance.

2.   *Solovyov*: Vladimir Solovyov (1853–1900) was a *fin-de-siècle*
     religious philosopher much better known for his philosophical
     and mystical writings than his poetry. He is best known in the
     world of poetry for having influenced the Symbolist poet Alex-
     ander Blok (1880–1921).

3.   *Nekrasov and Nadson*: Nikolai Nekrasov (1821–78) and Semyon
     Nadson (1862–87). Nekrasov was a poet, writer and publisher,
     whose socially conscious verse won him admiration among lib-
     eral and radical circles of the Russian intelligentsia in the latter
     half of the nineteenth century. Nadson was a poet who published
     only one book of poetry before his early death from tuberculosis;
     in spite of this, he enjoyed significant popularity, which grew in
     the decades immediately preceding the Revolution.

A Conversation

translated by Rose France

'A Conversation' (*Razgovor*) first published in the collection *Gorodok* (Paris: N. P. Karbasnikov, 1927), pp. 38–42.

Teffi's story plays on the prevalent fear among émigrés regarding the decline of the Russian language abroad. Through the conversation of two protagonists, the author pokes gentle fun at the new mongrel language used by her fellow émigrés, who pepper their Russian with foreign words and have forgotten the finer points of the language, while the very examples they invoke – 'leave me in peace', 'he went out of his mind', 'he flung himself downstairs' – subtly hint at the bleak reality of émigré life.

1.   *bonne humeur*: 'Good humour' (French).
2.   *meublé*: 'Furnished accommodation' (French).
3.   *bezirks*: 'Boroughs' (German).
4.   *arrondissements*: 'Boroughs' (French).
5.   *bilieux*: 'Ill-tempered' (French).
6.   *dazu*: Here, 'included' (German).
7.   *cendrier-thingummies*: From *cendrier*, 'ashtray' (French).
8.   *echt*: 'Real' (German).
9.   *merin*: The Russian word *merin*, which recalls *shurin* (brother-in-law, specifically the wife's brother), means 'gelding'.

Moscow in Shame

translated by Bryan Karetnyk

'Moscow in Shame' (*Moskva v pozore*) first published in *Vozrozhdenie*, 2 September 1925, pp. 2–3, and later included in the collection *V″ezd v Parizh* (Belgrade: komissiia, 1929), pp. 58–61.

Shmelyov's apocalyptic story, set in revolutionary Moscow, invokes the myth of Kitezh to express ire at the inefficacy of the White resistance in the city. Contrasting the relative ease with which the Bolsheviks overcame Moscow with the miracle at Kitezh, in which the city was saved from the Golden Horde through divine intervention, Shmelyov's jeremiad fixes the blame on a lack of religious piety and zeal among Muscovites, while lamenting the loss of the city and prophesying its descent into the grip of demonic forces. The fragmented, disorienting lyric narrative is a hallmark of Shmelyov's postwar prose: longer works such as *That Which Happened* (*Eto bylo*, 1919) and *The Sun of the Dead* (*Solntse mertvykh*, 1923) combine this modernistic narrative technique with unswervingly grim depictions of the horrors of war and revolution.

The 'sunken city' theme was also used to great effect as an allegory for the émigré situation, notably in Khodasevich's 'Atlantis', included here.

1. *Holy Kitezh ... Svetloyar*: The legendary city of Kitezh was reputedly founded on the banks of Lake Svetloyar in today's Nizhny Novgorod Oblast. According to legend, upon reaching the city the Golden Horde, under Batu Khan, witnessed the city submerge into the lake, where the citizens, through their zealous religious devotion, were protected by God.

2. *Minin, Pozharsky*: Prince Dmitry Mikhailovich Pozharsky (1577–1642) and Kuzma Minin (*c.*1570–1612) were the leaders of a volunteer army raised to expel the forces of the Polish-Lithuanian Commonwealth from Moscow during the Time of Troubles, the interregnum period from 1598 to 1613 bridging the end of the Rurik dynasty and the start of the House of Romanov. A monument to the two men, cast in bronze, stands on Red Square, in front of St Basil's Cathedral.

3. *Khodynka*: A field lying to the north-west of Moscow, often used before 1917 as a venue for marking state occasions. On 18 May 1896, during festivities to mark the coronation of Nicholas II, the Khodynka was the site of a mass tragedy, in which 1,389 people were trampled to death and a further 1,300 were injured in a rush for food and coronation gifts.

4. *Kostomarov ... Minin, Pozharsky ... anointed*: Nikolai Ivanovich Kostomarov (1817–85), an influential historian and author who wrote a prominent history of Russia stretching into several volumes. He wrote on Minin and Pozharsky specifically within the context of the Time of Troubles, a period that has frequently drawn comparison with revolutionary events in the early twentieth century in Russia. The 'anointment' is a reference to the practice of anointing a new tsar on the occasion of his coronation; here, the reference casts doubt on the effect of the ceremony in the light of the events being narrated.

5. *Butikov factory*: The Butikov factory was a large textile mill backing on to the Prechistenskaya Embankment in Moscow's Khamovniki district.

6. *The Nikolsky Gate . . . Mikola watching the people*: A reference
   to the icon of Saint Mikola (alt. Saint Nicholas of Mozhaysk)
   that forms part of the tower wall above the Kremlin's Nikolsky
   Gate. The icon was damaged by artillery fire during the 1917
   October Revolution and was later plastered over by the Soviet
   authorities. According to Orthodox tradition, when the city of
   Mozhaysk, some 70 miles west of Moscow, was besieged by the
   Mongols in the fourteenth century, the citizens prayed to Saint
   Mikola, who appeared holding a sword in his right hand and the
   city of Mozhaysk in his left, causing the enemy to flee.

Russie

translated by Bryan Karetnyk

'*Russie*' first published in *Vozrozhdenie*, 1 October 1925, pp. 2–3,
and later included in the collection *V″ezd v Parizh* (Belgrade: Komissiia, 1929), pp. 62–9.

1. *Très joli*: 'Very nice' (French).
2. *mer sauvage*: 'Wild sea' (French).
3. *Non, portez ailleurs vos coquilles, là-bas*: A French proverb,
   punning on the cockles being collected by the woman and her
   children. Literally meaning 'take your shells elsewhere', the
   figurative meaning of *portez ailleurs vos coquilles* is along the
   lines of 'try another one'.
4. *Donnons bœuf – avons œuf*: Literally, 'we give an ox, we get an
   egg' (French). A play on the French proverb '*donner un œuf
   pour avoir un bœuf*', literally 'one has to know when to give an
   egg to get an ox'.
5. *Ne faites pas la bête*: 'Don't play the fool' (French).
6. *âme slave*: 'Russian soul' (French).

Shadows of Days

translated by Bryan Karetnyk

'Shadows of Days' (*Teni dnei*) first published in the collection *V″ezd
v Parizh* (Belgrade: Komissiia, 1929), pp. 26–44.

One of Shmelyov's finest short stories, 'Shadows of Days' is a phan-
tasmagorical stream-of-consciousness variation on the so-called

'nightmare of the return' theme that haunted the psyche of many Russian émigrés. The dream of returning to their beloved homeland had by the mid-1920s grimly metamorphosed into a nightmare, as many began to accept the fact of Soviet rule as more than a temporary phenomenon. Accounts from the period reveal many émigrés to have suffered recurring nightmares of being trapped in Soviet Russia and trying to escape, or else of returning to their cherished past only to find it disturbingly altered by Soviet reality. As such, the genre came to be paradigmatic of the émigré condition: caught between memories of the past and the reality of present, between the dream of Russia and the night terrors of the Soviet regime.

Another variation on the 'nightmare of the return' theme can be found in Nabokov's 'The Visit to the Museum'.

1. *Into the quiet . . . swell*: The closing lines of Fyodor Tyutchev's (1803–73) poem 'A Dream at Sea' (*Son na more*).
2. *Presnya*: A district in Moscow.
3. *Therefore is my spirit . . . long*: Excerpts from Psalms 143 (Russian Orthodox 142) and 38 (Russian Orthodox 37) respectively.
4. *Around the World*: An illustrated geographic magazine founded in Russia in 1861. Still published today, *Around the World* (*Vokrug sveta*) is the longest-running magazine in the Russian language.
5. *The Great Obelisk*: The Obelisk of Luxor, which stands at the centre of Paris's Place de la Concorde.
6. *Khodynka*: See note 3 to 'Moscow in Shame'.
7. *Marylands*: Launched in 1910, Maryland was one of the two original varieties of Gauloises cigarettes (the other being Caporal).
8. *Kuskovo*: A grand eighteenth-century summer estate built by the Sheremetev family. Originally situated a few miles outside Moscow, it has now been subsumed into the city's eastern Veshnyaki District.
9. *Vindavsky*: Now named Rizhsky (or Riga), the railway terminus opened in 1901, serving the Moscow–Vindava line. The station was renamed Baltiysky (or Baltic) in 1930, Rzhevsky (or Rzhev) in 1942 and Rizhsky in 1946.
10. *Sadovaya*: Moscow's Sadovaya Ulitsa, or literally 'garden street'.
11. *the Tsar Liberator with his topknot*: Shmelyov's reference is to the tradition within Russian imperial portraiture of depicting Alexander II (r. 1855–81) with a ceremonial plumed helmet.
12. *id est, momentum juris*: 'That is, the moment of truth' (Latin).

13. *Ergo: victores sumus*: 'Therefore, we are victorious' (Latin).
14. *Kamergersky*: Moscow's Kamergersky Lane, which since 1902 has been home to the Moscow Art Theatre.
15. *Marchand d'habits et peaux*: 'Rag-and-bone man' (French).

Spindleshanks

translated by Maria Bloshteyn

'Spindleshanks' (*Komarinye moshchi*) first published in *Zaria* on 1 January 1931. The story, one of Chorny's finest written in emigration, was published independently and not included in any of his later collections.

1. *Pushkin's Olga ... Pechorin*: Olga is the coquettish sister of Tatiana Larina, the epitome of Russian femininity presented in Pushkin's 'novel in verse' *Eugene Onegin* (1833). The Demon is the eponymous protagonist of Mikhail Lermontov's (1814–41) Romantic masterpiece, written between 1829 and 1839. Pechorin is the Byronic hero of Lermontov's novel of 1840 *A Hero of Our Time*.
2. *Kustodiev ... Venus*: Boris Mikhailovich Kustodiev (1878–1927), a Russian painter. The narrator's allusion here is to Kustodiev's *Russian Venus* (1925–6), which, along with several other prominent works including *The Merchant's Wife* (1918) and *The Beauty* (1915), depicts a model of ample figure.
3. *Pierre Loti*: The pseudonym of Louis Marie Julien Viaud (1850–1923), a novelist and officer in the French navy. Loti is one of the founders of French colonial literature, and his writing is particularly noted for its romantic evocations of the sea and its exotic depictions of the Orient.
4. *Chaliapin*: Fyodor Ivanovich Chaliapin (1873–1938), a Russian operatic bass. Chaliapin made regular international tours both before and after the Revolution; after 1921, however, he was no longer able to return to Russia. He emigrated first to Finland and later to France, where in 1934 he was made a commander of the *Légion d'honneur*.
5. *Salle Drouot*: The Parisian auction house Hôtel Drouot is situated at the corner of rue Drouot and rue Rossini in the city's 9th arrondissement.

Pompeii

translated by Bryan Karetnyk

This version of the text, originally titled 'Pompeian Terror' (*Pompei-skii uzhas*), was first published in *Poslednie novosti* on 10 May 1925. A later version, published under the title 'Pompeii' (*Pompeia*) and containing several minor textual alterations, came out in *Segodnia* on 23 June 1937. The fatidic date mentioned in the text, 13 April, comes only a few days before Khodasevich and Nina Berberova ended their six-month stay with Maxim Gorky at his villa in Sorrento; they left for Paris on 18 April 1925.

1. *But it was 13 April ... doubly onerous*: According to Russian superstition, Mondays are considered inauspicious for travelling.
2. *Parva domus, magna quies*: 'Little abode, great peace' (Latin).
3. *And when, sans strength ... every bound*: An inexact quotation from the poem 'The Pompeian Girl' (*Pompeianka*) by the Symbolist poet Valery Bryusov (1873–1924).
4. *Petronius' characters ... these very parts*: The *Satyricon* is a work of Latin Silver Age literature, most likely written by Gaius Petronius Arbiter (*c.*AD 27–66), an advisor to the emperor Nero. The work is picaresque in nature and recounts the adventures of the rhetor Encolpius and his companions, in racy and often ribald detail, as they travel around southern Italy, particularly in the environs of Cumae. While the work is now dated from AD 63 to 65, in the early twentieth century the dating of the work was still hotly contested, with claims ranging from the first century BC to the third century AD; this accounts for Khodasevich's erroneous comment that the novel postdates the eruption that destroyed Pompeii, which occurred in AD 79.
5. *pood*: A Russian unit of weight, equivalent to approximately thirty-six pounds.
6. *the wicked flame of earthly fire*: Words taken from Vladimir Solovyov's (1853–1900) poem 'All in azure today ...' (*Vse v lazuri segodnia iavilas´ ...*).

Atlantis

translated by Bryan Karetnyk

'Atlantis' (*Atlantida*) first published in Vladislav Khodasevich, *Sobranie sochinenii v chetyrekh tomakh* (Moscow: Soglasie, 1997), vol. 3, pp. 116–18. The manuscript, which was never published during Khodasevich's lifetime, was discovered in a notebook in the author's archive, which dates the story to 17–19 May 1938.

In 1904 Khodasevich entered Moscow University to study law, but then switched to literature. His studies were erratic because of financial problems, most likely arising from his passion for cards and drinking. His diaries are peppered especially with notes on his most beloved game: bridge. In Paris, Khodasevich would often play with the likes of Yury Felsen, Wladimir Weidlé, Georgy Adamovich and a young Vasily Yanovsky. In his memoirs, Yanovsky would cite bridge as Khodasevich's 'sole consolation' in emigration, recalling the games often played for high stakes in the basement of the Murat, a café near the Porte d'Auteuil. Such was its bearing on his life that after his funeral in 1939 several of Khodasevich's former bridge partners retired to the Murat for an impromptu remembrance.

A gambling theme runs throughout the Russian canon, having its origins in Pushkin's 'The Queen of Spades' (1834), and finding later expression most obviously in works such as Lermontov's *A Hero of Our Time* (1840) and Dostoevsky's *The Gambler* (1866). More than for mere psychological portraiture, however, Khodasevich's contribution to the tradition combines it with the image of the sunken city of Atlantis in order to draw a parallel with the Russian émigré world at the depths of Parisian society.

1.   *The Government Inspector*: A satirical play by Nikolai Gogol (1809–52). The reference is to the 'dumb' scene, in which the characters, literally petrified by the news that the real government inspector has arrived, freeze in various attitudes and hold the tableau for a minute and a half, after which the final curtain falls.
2.   *jeunesse dorée*: 'Gilded youth' (French).
3.   *piquentia ... knavish tricks*: Khodasevich's nomenclatorial punning on the names of playing cards, particularly their grotesque dog-Latin and mock-Greek forms, recalls that found in Part 1, Chapter 1 of Nikolai Gogol's *Dead Souls* (1842).

The Astrologist

translated by Bryan Karetnyk

'The Astrologist' (*Astrolog*) first published in *Novyi zhurnal* 16 (1947), pp. 5–41.

1. *Begleitkommando*: The Führer's Escort Unit.
2. *Reichssicherheitsdienst*: Reich Security Service, a branch of the SS.
3. *Kriminal Polizei*: Criminal Police.
4. *Thinking about this . . . incompatible appearance*: The reference is to Reich Minister of Propaganda Joseph Goebbels (1897–1945), who was noted for his keen intellect and skill in public speaking. The 'incompatible appearance' indicated by Aldanov is an allusion to a congenital deformity in Goebbels's right foot, which caused him to walk with a pronounced limp. Goebbels suffered from ill health since childhood and, having undergone surgery on his foot unsuccessfully, was forced to wear a metal brace and special orthopaedic shoe – a fact that was at odds with the Nazi doctrine of racial supremacy. He would ultimately succeed Hitler, serving as Reich Chancellor for one day before he too committed suicide in the Führerbunker.
5. *Dienststelle*: A governmental department.
6. *the Coué system . . . in every way*: Émile Coué de La Châtaigneraie (1857–1926), a French pharmacist and psychologist who developed the so-called 'Coué method', a means of auto-suggestion initially used as a complementary therapy to boost the efficacy of medication. The method, satirized here, centred on a routine repetition of the following expression according to a specified ritual: *Tous les jours à tous points de vue je vais de mieux en mieux* ('Every day, in every way, I'm getting better and better'). Coué's studies, much vaunted in their day, were the forerunners to later research on the placebo effect and positive psychology.
7. *Schicklgrubers*: A common story during the war and long after was that Hitler was born with the name Schicklgruber. Although this was indeed his grandmother's surname, the story that it was Hitler's original name is a myth, which no doubt gained purchase largely because it made him sound more ridiculous.
8. *Walküre bist du gewesen*: 'Thy Valkyriehood is over' (German). From Act III, Scene ii, of Wagner's *Die Walküre* (1870).

9. *Standing there ... washbasin*: A variant ending was published in the collection *A Night at the Airport* (New York: Charles Scribner's Sons, 1949). The final line reads: 'The Professor stood flabbergasted: the Gestapo man, the man with a scar, was trying to fix a false beard on his face with trembling hands.'

Auto-Suggestion

translated by Bryan Karetnyk

'Auto-Suggestion' (*Samovnushenie*) first published in the collection *Nasha malen'kaia zhizn'* (Paris: J. Povolozky and Co., 1927), pp. 80–83.

Our Little Life (*Nasha malen'kaia zhizn'*) was Don Aminado's first collection of short stories and feuilletons to explore the tragicomedy of émigré life in France. The bitter irony of the author's writing combines here with a satirical commentary on modish trends in the nascent field of psychotherapy and self-help. The story was also one among several included in a French-language collection of Russian comic short fiction, *Le Rire dans la steppe* (1927), which Don Aminado translated, and edited together with the popular French author Maurice Dekobra. The collection also presented works by Anton Chekhov, Vlas Doroshevich, Arkady Averchenko, Arkady Bukhov and Teffi.

1. *that Frenchman Coué*: See note 6 to 'The Astrologist'.
2. *Nansen passports*: Identity papers created for Russians who had become de facto stateless persons by the High Commissioner for Refugees of the League of Nations Fridtjof Nansen (1861–1930).

A Scattering of Stars

translated by Bryan Karetnyk

'A Scattering of Stars' (*Rossyp' zvezd*) written in Gallipoli in August–September 1921 and first published in the collection *Goloe pole: Kniga o Gallipoli, 1921 g.* (Sofia: Balkan, 1922), pp. 55–70.

Lukash's *The Bare Field* (*Goloe pole*) is one of the most remarkable collections of fiction to be written about the White Army's internment in Gallipoli following its evacuation from the Crimea. Rather than a plain documentary narrative, as the subtitle ('A book about Gallipoli, 1921') suggests, the work is a compendium of Old Russia, its military traditions and history, as well as a haunting portrayal of the aftermath of the Civil War. Despite being one of the earliest pieces included in this anthology, written during the very first days of emigration, at a time when most still believed that the Bolshevik regime would fall, 'A Scattering of Stars' is a striking lyric elegy that marks the passing of an era.

1. *General Kutepov*: General Alexander Pavlovich Kutepov (1882–1930), commander of the anti-Bolshevik Volunteer Army during the Civil War. After the defeat of the army in the Crimea, Kutepov and his men were evacuated to Gallipoli in November 1920. He moved to Bulgaria in 1921 following the disbandment of the Gallipoli camp and later moved to Paris, where in 1928 he succeeded Baron Wrangel as leader of the émigré Russian All-Military Union (ROVS). He died during an attempted kidnapping by Soviet agents in 1930.

2. *sazhen*: A Russian unit of measurement equivalent to seven feet.

3. *Zemgor*: An official body, the United Committee of the Union of Zemstvos and the Union of Towns. Created in 1915, it was officially disbanded four years later by the Bolsheviks; however, it was reconstituted in emigration as a conduit for the distribution of aid among White Russian refugees.

4. *Sergievsky men*: A reference to the men of the Sergievsky Artillery School. Based in Odessa, many of its men saw action during the First World War, and it served on the side of the Whites during the Civil War. In 1920 the school removed to the Crimea, and in November of the same year it was evacuated along with Baron Wrangel's troops to Gallipoli.

5. *'Tis evening, the linings of the clouds have darkened*: Taken from Pyotr Tchaikovsky's 1890 operatic adaptation of a short story of the same name by Alexander Pushkin (1799–1837), the line opens Liza and Polina's duet in Act I, Scene ii.

6. *der Garten ist grün*: 'The garden is green' (German).

7. *Ich bin, du bist, er, sie ist*: 'I am, you are, he, she is . . .' (German).

8. *Budyonny's men charged*: Semyon Mikhailovich Budyonny (1883–1973) was a Don Cossack who commanded the 1st Cavalry Army. The army, which was the subject of Isaac Babel's *Red Cavalry*, played a decisive role in repelling General Denikin's forces as they advanced on Moscow during the Civil War.

Budyonny's army was subsequently sent to fight Baron Wrangel's forces in the Ukraine and the Crimea. Budyonny joined the Bolshevik Party in 1919 and remained a close ally of Stalin in later years.

9. *Skobelev's men ... Paris's suburbs*: General Mikhail Dmitrievich Skobelev (1843–82) was a commander in various Russian campaigns in Central Asia, notably against the Khanate of Khiva in 1873, and the Khanate of Khoqand in 1875–6. Tashkent had been annexed to the Khanate of Khoqand in 1809. The Seven Years War (1756–63) was one of the defining geopolitical events in the later years of Empress Elizabeth's reign (r. 1741–62); the reference is to the Raid on Berlin, when Austrian and Russian forces briefly occupied the Prussian capital in October 1760. Alexander I (r. 1801–25) reigned throughout the Napoleonic Wars. Napoleon's troops were defeated by the forces of the Sixth Coalition during the Battle of Paris in March 1814, which saw fighting in the suburbs of Paris and ultimately resulted in Napoleon's abdication.

10. *the Kornilov Ice March*: Known also as the First Kuban Campaign, the Ice March (February–May 1918) saw General Lavr Georgievich Kornilov's (1870–1918) heavily outnumbered Volunteer Army retreat from Rostov under attack from the Red Army. Despite arduous winter conditions and heavy losses, Kornilov's army marched south into the Kuban's frozen steppelands, where it laid an ultimately abortive siege to Ekaterinodar, the capital of the recently established North Caucasian Soviet Republic. Kornilov was killed when a shell hit the army's makeshift headquarters outside Ekaterinodar.

11. *Milyutin's standardization and Vannovsky's numbered regiments*: Dmitri Alexeyevich Milyutin (1816–1912) and Pyotr Semyonovich Vannovsky (1822–1904) were ministers of war in the Russian Empire from 1861 to 1881 and from 1881 to 1898, respectively. Milyutin saw through wide-sweeping military reform under Alexander II following Russia's defeat in the Crimean War (1853–6). Vannovsky's reforms as minister of war saw significant change to the military administration as well as to the organization of troops.

12. *All the colours ... man*: A fragment from the Civil War song 'The Volunteer Crane' (*Dobrovol'cheskii zhuravl'*).

13. *Drozdovsky's*: General Mikhail Gordeyevich Drozdovsky (1881–1919) commanded the 3rd Infantry Division of the Volunteer Army. After his death from a battle wound in the vicinity of

Rostov, his troops, one of the 'coloured units', became known as the Drozdovsky Rifle Division.

14. *the actress Astrova ... Alexandrinsky's stage*: Maria Astrova-Lazareff (1878–1968) played at the Moscow Art Theatre, where she studied under Stanislasky, and later co-founded the Maxim Gorky Theatre in Moscow. In emigration she moved between Paris, Brussels and London before the outbreak of the Second World War, whereupon she emigrated again to the United States. Nadezhda Plevitskaya (1884–1940) was a popular singer, who toured throughout Europe during her years of emigration. She and her husband, General Nikolai Skoblin (1892–1938?), were recruited by Soviet intelligence and were implicated in the kidnapping of several White generals in Paris. Plevitskaya was arrested, tried and convicted for complicity in the kidnapping of General Miller (see notes to 'The Assistant Producer'); she died in prison at Rennes during the Nazi Occupation. Nina Grigorievna Kovalenskaya (1888–1993) made her stage debut in 1909 at the Alexandrinsky Theatre in Petersburg, where she went on to perform in several of Vsevolod Meyerhold's productions. After the Revolution, Kovalenskaya worked in theatres in Prague and Riga; after the war, she emigrated to San Francisco.

A Literary Studio

translated by Bryan Karetnyk

'A Literary Studio' (*Literaturnaia masterskaia*) first published in *Satirikon* 6 (1931), p. 4.

Adamovich's story satirizes the political and artistic quagmire in which many young émigré writers found themselves abroad, stylistically caught between various Russian literary traditions, French modernism and the new Soviet literature. While Adamovich's characters immediately set themselves in opposition to Soviet literature, as many émigré writers did on principle, their 'variations on a theme' demonstrate three of the major competing influences among the younger generation of émigré writers: respectively, the classical Chekhovian tradition (via Bunin); the French modernist stylization of Marcel Proust, representing the literary traditions of their host country; and the emigration's Silver Age legacy (via Symbolism), which was embodied by many among the older generation of émigré

writers. The second 'version' of the moonlit evening in spring may
also be seen as a parody of the Proustian vogue that developed among
young émigré writers such as Yury Felsen, who reworked Proust's
style in his literary project 'A Romance with an Author' (see 'The
Recurrence of Things Past').

1. *Krylov's 'Quartet'*: A popular poem by the Russian fabulist
    Ivan Krylov (1769–1844). The poem begins with a monkey, a
    donkey, a goat and a bear setting out to play a musical quartet.
    During the course of the poem the animals argue over where
    and how to sit to play their instruments correctly, only to be
    told by a nightingale that they 'will never be musicians'.
2. *the old spellings be observed*: A reference to the reforms in Rus-
    sian orthography enacted by the Soviet government in 1918 (see
    note 14 to the Introduction).
3. *this mix of French and Nizhny Novgorod*: A line from the
    influential satirical comedy *Woe from Wit* (*Gore ot uma*, 1825)
    by the playwright Alexander Griboedov (1795–1829). Many
    lines drawn from the play, including this one, have entered com-
    mon parlance in Russian.

Ramón Ortiz

translated by Anastasia Tolstoy

'Ramón Ortiz' (*Ramon Ortis*) first published in *Chisla* 5 (1931), pp.
32–43.

1. *And, perhaps … parting smile*: The final lines of Alexander
    Pushkin's 'Elegy' (*Elegiia*, 1830).

An Experiment

translated by Bryan Karetnyk

'An Experiment' (*Opyt*) first published in *Zveno* 228 (1927), pp. 7–8.

1. *fauché*: 'Stony-broke' (French).
2. *Échec*: 'Fail' (French).
3. *Pas une occasion, c'est une sensation*: 'Not just an occasion, it
    was a sensation' (French).
4. *Je veux …*: 'I want …' (French).

5. *Tiens, le café est arrosé*: 'Hang on, the coffee's boozy' (French).
6. *Je vous emmène*: 'I'll take you' (French).

The Recurrence of Things Past

translated by Ivan Juritz and Bryan Karetnyk

'The Recurrence of Things Past' (*Povtorenie proidennogo*) first published in *Krug* 3 (1938), pp. 75–96.

As reviews and memoirs of émigré writers such as Adamovich, Gazdanov and Yanovsky attest, Yury Felsen was widely regarded among the emigration as 'a writer's writer'. His style is a conscious recasting of Proust's psychoanalytic narrative technique and as such was one of the emigration's most concerted and overt attempts at an engagement with the literary heritage of its Western European host countries. More than mere imitation, however, Felsen's appropriation of this style is refashioned towards his own end, incorporating elaborate linguistic experimentation that exhibits a degree of outré syntactic and lexical manipulation in search of the *mot juste*. One of his final contributions to the 'Romance with an Author' project before his untimely demise in the gas chambers at Auschwitz, 'The Recurrence of Things Past' was widely thought to be Felsen's finest and most successful work to date.

1. *mauvais et beaux jours*: 'Good days and bad' (French).
2. *sécurité*: Here, 'material well-being' (French).
3. *Ah, ses couleurs ... moscovite*: 'Oh, his colours are so fiery. This little Muscovite is exquisite' (French).
4. *Vendu*: 'Sold' (French).
5. *charme slave*: 'Russian charm' (French); a play on the more common *âme slave*, or 'Russian soul'.
6. *ces russes ... chaudes*: 'These Russians! Ah, what fiery voices they have' (French).
7. *chaud*: 'fiery' (French).

Giselle

translated by Boris Dralyuk

'Giselle' (*Zhizel´*) first published in *Illiustrirovannaia Rossiia*, 5 January 1929. It was republished with slight alterations in *Segodnia* in 1933 under the title 'Ellis'.

Ivanov's story is inspired in part by the events of the Knyazev–Sudeykina affair, which scandalized St Petersburg's literary *beau monde* in the early 1910s. Vsevolod Gavrilovich Knyazev (1891–1913) was a young poet and Hussar who was taken under the wing of the Silver Age poet and novelist Mikhail Kuzmin (1872–1936). A love affair ensued between the two men but ended in the summer of 1912, when Knyazev embarked on a fateful romance with the dancer Olga Glebova-Sudeykina. Sudeykina was the wife of the painter Serge Soudeikine (Sergei Sudeykin, 1882–1946), who had himself carried on an affair with Kuzmin before his marriage in 1907. She soon ended her affair with Knyazev (the poet Alexander Blok was rumoured to be Knyazev's rival), and in May 1913, ostensibly despairing from his unrequited love, Knyazev shot himself in Riga. Anna Akhmatova, a close friend of Sudeykina's, would also later draw on the events in her *Poem without a Hero*.

1. *Fontanka*: A branch of the Neva River, so named for supplying water to the fountains of the Summer Garden.
2. *clear, merciless light of day*: Likely a misquotation of the Symbolist poet Alexander Blok's (1880–1921) 'At the Trial' (*Pered sudom*, 1915). The original line runs: 'in the harsh, incorruptible light of day'.
3. *Green star . . . his last*: A slight misquotation of Osip Mandelstam's (1891–1938) poem 'A wandering fire at a fearful height!' (*Na strashnoi vysote bluzhdaiushchii ogon'*, 1918).
4. *L'Origan, Guerlain*: L'Origan is a scent designed by François Coty in 1905. Guerlain is a French perfume house founded in 1828 by Pierre-François-Pascal Guerlain.
5. *I do not know . . . strange*: Lines from Fyodor Tyutchev's (1803–73) poem 'The joyous day was bustling still' (*Eshche shumel veselyi den'*, 1851).

The Atom Explodes

translated by Justin Doherty

'The Atom Explodes' (*Raspad atoma*) first published in Paris in 1938.

'The Atom Explodes' is regarded as the zenith of the émigré 'human document' experiment, a meta-literary genre that found its roots in French existentialism and was promulgated by the likes of Ivanov and Georgy Adamovich. The genre, with its pervasive air of anxiety and pessimism (the so-called 'Parisian note'), sought to make an art of reality, focalized through individual experience and the private self. While advocating for stylistic imperfection and 'sincerity' above all else, the genre was travestied by other artists such as Khodasevich and Nabokov. In his review of the piece, Khodasevich was bitingly critical of the genre, while according (albeit backhandedly) a degree of praise to Ivanov's work: 'Ivanov arranges his inelegant images so elegantly,' he began, that they 'seem somehow too smooth, too polished and, in the final analysis, almost beautiful.' The critic witheringly concluded that Ivanov's story 'could be taken for one of those "human documents" so fashionable nowadays, but this would be incorrect and unjust . . . it is too artificial and skilful to be ranked among that wretched type of literature.'

1. *sticky little buds*: A leitmotivic phrase used by Ivan Karamazov to represent his love of life in Fyodor Dostoevsky's (1821–81) *The Brothers Karamazov* (1880).

2. *Woe to the victors*: A play on the Latin phrase *vae victis*, 'woe to the vanquished'.

3. *Over the blue waves of the ocean*: The opening line of Mikhail Lermontov's (1814–41) adaptation of a poem by the Austrian poet Joseph Christian von Zedlitz (1790–1862), 'Geisterschiff', which was dedicated to Napoleon.

4. *his Commandeur's cross*: The cross of the Legion of Honour, awarded for both military and civil distinction.

5. *O thou, last love*: From the penultimate line of Fyodor Tyutchev's (1803–73) poem 'Last Love' (*Posledniaia liubov'*, 1852–4).

6. *a new Werther*: A reference to Johann Wolfgang von Goethe's (1749–1832) novel *The Sorrows of Young Werther* (1774).

7. *the fate of Anna . . . disgrace*: A reference to Leo Tolstoy's (1828–1910) *Anna Karenina* (1877), Part 5, Chapter 33.

8. *In his arms the child lay dead*: The final line from Goethe's ballad 'Erlkönig' (1782).

9. *Over Georgia's hills nocturnal darkness lay*: A misquotation of the opening line of one of the most celebrated lyric poems of Alexander Pushkin (1799–1837), 'Over Georgia's hills nocturnal darkness lies' (1829).

10. *dyr bu shchyl ubeshchur*: A misquotation of the opening of the Futurist poet Alexei Kruchenykh's (1886–1968) famous *zaum*, or 'beyonsense', poem 'Dyr bul shchyl . . .' (1913).

11. *There steps . . . swirl*: A line from Pushkin's poem 'City of lux-
     ury, city of want' (*Gorod pyshnyi, gorod bednyi*, 1828).
12. *It was so marvellous . . . death*: Tolstoy's diary entry for 25
     September 1862 (in fact, some time after the wedding itself)
     reads: 'At Yasnaya. Morning coffee – uneasy. Students puzzled.
     Walked with her and Seryozha. Lunch . . . Slept after lunch, she
     wrote. Incredible happiness. Again she is writing beside me. It
     cannot be that all this will end only with life itself.'
13. *Montherlant*: Henri de Montherlant (1895–1972), an influen-
     tial French author and dramatist.
14. *Man begins with sorrow*: A line from a poem by Alexei Eisner
     (1905–84), 'Autumn is drawing near. The shrubs are turning
     yellow . . .' (*Nadvigaetsia osen'. Zhelteiut kusty*, 1932).
15. *Life begins tomorrow*: The title of a work by Matilde Serao
     (1856–1927), a popular Greek-born Italian writer. The novel
     enjoyed widespread popularity in Russia at the beginning of the
     twentieth century.
16. *the same fearsome din . . . roars*: A parody of the second line in
     Pushkin's poem 'Over Georgia's hills nocturnal darkness lies'.
17. *Temple*: A district of Paris.
18. *the Lubyanka*: The headquarters of the Soviet secret police in
     Moscow.
19. *Akaky Akakievich . . . a new overcoat*: A reference to Nikolai
     Gogol's (1809–52) short story 'The Overcoat' (1842).
20. *He was a titular . . . daughter*: The opening lines of a poem by
     Pyotr Veinberg (1831–1908), which became popular after being
     set to music by the composer Alexander Dargomyzhsky
     (1813–69).
21. *paradise, such as is not found even in Heaven*: A quotation
     from Gogol's *Diary of a Madman* (1835).
22. *Stand firm, city of Peter, and resplendent*: A line from the
     opening passage of Pushkin's *The Bronze Horseman* (1837).
23. *his 'Don Juan list'*: A notorious document listing the names of
     all Pushkin's amorous conquests.
24. *D'Anthès will murder Pushkin . . . drop off*: Pushkin was killed
     in a duel by his brother-in-law, Baron Georges-Charles de Heeck-
     eren d'Anthès (1812–95). Ivan Sergeyevich Turgenev (1818–83)
     was a Russian writer most famous for his novel *Fathers and Sons*
     (1862).
25. *But of course . . . Your Wartship*: Ivanov originally planned a
     different ending. In a letter to Roman Gul dated 29 June 1955,
     he writes: 'The *Atom* was supposed to end differently: "Heil

Hitler – long live the father of nations, the Great Stalin – Britons never, never, never will be slaves!" I discarded it, and I regret doing so.'

Klasson and His Soul

translated by Bryan Karetnyk

'Klasson and His Soul' (*Klasson i ego dusha*) first published in *Novyi korabl'* 1 (1927), pp. 11–14.

1. *Munken Vendt*: A possible reference to the Norwegian writer Knut Hamsun's (1859–1952) verse play of 1902 *Munken Vendt*, whose eponymous protagonist, the eighteenth-century monk Vendt, is a wanderer in eternal revolt against both man and God.

The Life of Madame Duclos

translated by Irina Steinberg

'The Life of Madame Duclos' (*Zhizn' madam Diuklo*) first published in *Zveno* 6 (1927), pp. 336–60.

1. *And before my eyes ... clear gaze*: Lines from Ivan Bunin's poem 'Light Everlasting' (*Svet nezakatnyi*), dated 24 September 1917.
2. *ma tante! Merci!*: ' ... Auntie! Thank you!' (French).

The Visit to the Museum

translated by Dmitri Nabokov

'The Visit to the Museum' (*Poseshchenie muzeia*) first published in *Sovremennye zapiski* 68 (1939), pp. 76–87. It was later included in the short-story collection *Vesna v Fial'te* (New York: Chekhov Publishing House, 1956). The English translation, prepared by Dmitri Nabokov, first published in *Esquire* (March 1963), and later included in *Nabokov's Quartet* (New York: Phaedra, 1966) and *A Russian Beauty and Other Stories* (New York: McGraw-Hill, 1973). When published in *Esquire*, the title was supplemented with the commentary: 'The exile's lament confuses Time (the beloved past) with Space (the forbidden homeland).'

The Assistant Producer

'The Assistant Producer' first published in *Nabokov's Dozen* (New York: Doubleday, 1958).

Written *à clef*, Nabokov's story is based on the notorious kidnapping of General Evgeny Miller, chairman of the émigré Russian All-Military Union (ROVS), which took place in Paris on 22 September 1937. Details of La Slavska and General Golubkov are drawn directly from the lore surrounding the popular Russian singer Nadezhda Plevitskaya (1884–1940) and her husband Nikolai Skoblin (1892–1938?). Skoblin was indeed a triple agent, operating on behalf of ROVS (the true W.W.), as well as Soviet and German intelligence agencies. On 22 September 1937 Skoblin led Miller to a supposed meeting with two German Abwehr agents; in reality, however, Miller was delivered into the hands of the NKVD, who drugged him, smuggled him aboard a Soviet ship docked at Le Havre and dispatched him to Moscow, where he was interrogated, tortured, and summarily shot on 11 May 1939.

The affair was but one in a series of high-profile kidnappings of White generals by Soviet intelligence. Skoblin was immediately implicated in a note left by Miller, in which he voiced his suspicions regarding Skoblin. The triple agent then fled to Spain, where he disappeared, leaving his wife to face trial and arrest. In 1938 Plevitskaya, who had also been recruited by Soviet intelligence, was sentenced to twenty years in prison, but died two years later, shortly after the Nazi occupation. Nabokov's story served in part as the basis for Éric Rohmer's film of 2004, *Triple Agent*.

1. *Cavalleria Rusticana*: An opera in one act by Pietro Mascagni (1863–1945). Premiered in Rome in 1890, the opera notably played a key role in ushering in the verismo movement in Italian opera.
2. *pour un arbre abattu*: 'For a felled tree' (French).

The Lady from Monte Carlo

translated by Bryan Karetnyk

'The Lady from Monte Carlo' (*Dama iz Monte-Karlo*) first published in *Russkie zapiski* 12 (1938), pp. 83–95.

On the gambling theme in Russian literature, see the brief note to Khodasevich's 'Atlantis' (p. 402). Among Russian émigré works, Dovid Knut's 'The Lady from Monte Carlo' is the brightest continuation of this theme, transporting it to the French Riviera while providing a clear allusion to Pushkin's 'The Queen of Spades'.

1. *Tenez . . . les pauvres*: 'Just a moment, Mr Beggar, sir, here's a sou that my good mother gives me each week for the poor' (French).
2. *ça va*: 'That's fine' (French).
3. *J'ai tout vu, madame. Je suis témoin, madame*: 'I saw it all, madame. I am a witness, madame' (French).
4. *Allez-vous-en*: 'Get away from me!' (French).
5. *Des chauffards de cette espèce méritent une punition*: 'Drivers like that ought to be locked up' (French).
6. *Où voulez-vous rentrez, madam, chez vous ou à l'hôpital?*: 'Where would you like to go, madame? Home, or to hospital?' (French).
7. *Chez moi*: 'Home' (French).
8. *Vous pouvez nous conduire chez madame*: 'Could you take us to the lady's house?' (French).
9. *Rien de grave?*: 'Nothing serious?' (French).
10. *Ma carte, madame. Pour le constat*: 'My card, madame. For the official report' (French).
11. *Je vous remercie, monsieur*: 'Thank you, sir' (French).
12. *Vous pouvez venir me voir un de ces soirs*: 'You may pay me a visit one of these evenings' (French).

Kunak

translated by Bryan Karetnyk

'Kunak' (*Kunak*) first published in the collection *Utro* (Paris: Sovremennye zapiski, 1930).

Kuznetsova's strongly autobiographical collection of short stories met with wide critical acclaim upon publication, drawing particular praise for its feminine sensibility. The collection is particularly significant, being one of the few major literary accounts of the Civil War told from a female perspective.

1. *Grafskaya Pier*: A white colonnaded pier on the west bank of the Southern Bay at Sebastopol. Taking its name from Count (*Graf*) Marko Voinovich (1750–1807), an admiral of the Russian Imperial navy, the first pier was built in 1783. It was refashioned in its current form (a double row of Doric columns topped by an entablature) in 1846 by John Upton (*c.*1774–1851).
2. *Kunak*: From the Turkic *qonaq*, literally 'guest', the term in Russian has come to be used among Cossacks in the broader sense of 'friend'; used here as a name.
3. *Romanov sheepskin coat*: Under Peter I (r. 1682–1725) the town of Romanov (now Tutayev, Yaroslavl Oblast) grew into a centre of the wool trade, lending its name to a breed of domestic sheep common to the area. The coat in question is specifically associated with Cossacks of the Upper Volga region.

The Murder of Valkovsky

translated by Bryan Karetnyk

'The Murder of Valkovsky' (*Ubiistvo Val'kovskogo*) first published in *Vstrechi* 4 (1934), pp. 147–53.

The Spy

translated by Bryan Karetnyk

'The Spy' (*Shpion*) first published anonymously in *Zveno* 221 (1927), pp. 9–11.

Gazdanov entered this early work under the title 'The English Call Them Stormy Petrels' (*Anglichane nazyvaiut ikh stormy petrel*) in a short-story competition run by *Zveno*. Although the story did not ultimately win the competition, it was reviewed positively by the editors Georgy Adamovich, Konstantin Mochulsky and Nikolai Bakhtin (the brother of the literary theorist Mikhail Bakhtin).

Gazdanov would revisit the Civil War theme in much of his oeuvre, but readers will note in particular the striking similarities between the opening sequence of this short story and that found in his major novel of 1948, *The Spectre of Alexander Wolf* (*Prizrak Aleksandra Vol´fa*).

1. *Vous n'avez pas de chance, Robert*: 'You're out of luck, Robert!' (French).
2. *D'la bière, du pinard?*: 'Beer, wine?' (French).
3. *À la gare ... en France*: 'To hell with that! I can't be expected to know every language in the world. When in France, speak French' (French).
4. *Voilà, mon vieux*: 'There you are, old boy' (French).

Black Swans

translated by Bryan Karetnyk

'Black Swans' (*Chernye lebedi*) first published in *Volia Rossii* 9 (1930). A slightly different version of this translation first published in *Cardinal Points* 6 (2016), pp. 30–46.

1. *Saint-Simon*: Claude Henri de Rouvroy, comte de Saint-Simon (1760–1825), an influential French political, social and economic theorist.
2. *Voilà mes papiers*: 'Here are my papers' (French).
3. *joie maligne*: 'Schadenfreude' (French).
4. *Il est timide*: 'He's shy' (French).
5. *Écoute, mon vieux*: 'Listen here, my dear' (French).
6. *un déclassé*: 'An outcast' (French).

Princess Mary

translated by Bryan Karetnyk

'Princess Mary' (*Kniazhna Meri*) first published in *Opyty* 2 (1953), pp. 103–12.

1. *Night, a street, a lamp, a chemist's shop*: The opening line of the second poem in Alexander Blok's 1912 cycle 'Dances of Death' (*Pliaski smerti*).
2. *Mais ils ... de nouveau*: 'But they stepped out of eternity only to lose themselves in it again' (French).

3.   *Princess Mary*: A point of connection between life and fiction, one of the regular columnists for the fortnightly (and later weekly) Parisian émigré newspaper *Illiustrirovannaia Rossiia* did in fact sign articles and replies to readers' letters on the publication's women's page as 'Princess Mary'.

Requiem

translated by Bryan Karetnyk

'Requiem' (*Panikhida*) first published in *Novyi zhurnal* 59 (1960), pp. 9–19.

1.   *Ici Londres. Voici notre bulletin d'information*: 'This is London. Here is our news bulletin' (French).
2.   *Oryol*: A provincial city some 220 miles south-west of Moscow; its name in Russian literally means 'eagle'.
3.   *Vitrier*: 'Glazier' (French).
4.   *Truly, all is vanity . . . the same*: Here and later, the lines are drawn from the Stichera of the Last Kiss, a part of the Eastern Orthodox Order for the Burial of the Dead whose text is traditionally attributed to Saint John of Damascus. The lines are sung before the body is borne to the grave.
5.   *With the Saints give rest*: A fragment from the Kontakion of the Departed. The full line is as follows: 'With the Saints give rest, O Christ, to the soul of Thy servant, where sorrow and pain and sighing are no more; but where life everlasting abounds.'

The Tunnel

translated by Donald Rayfield

'The Tunnel' (*Tunnel´*) first published under the pseudonym 'Alyotrus' in *Sovremennik* 3 (1961). This pseudonym has been interpreted as Russian for 'Hello, coward', which is plausible, given that the story is based on the author's affair with Vladimir Nabokov, broken off at Véra Nabokov's insistence.

1.   *As the sun set . . . youth*: 'Vladimir Sirin' was the pen name of Vladimir Nabokov. The lines are taken from the poem 'At Sunset' (*Na zakate*, 1935), which was later included in the collection *Poems and Problems* (1969).

2. *All this happened . . . back*: The first lines of an untitled poem by Alexander Blok (1880–1921), dated August 1909 and included in his 1916 collection *Poems: Book Three (1905–1914)* (*Stikhotvoreniia. Kniga tret´ia*).

3. *I have known . . . at me*: Lines from Dovid Knut's poem 'Night' (*Noch´*), taken from the collection *Daily Love* (*Nasushchnaia liubov´*, 1938).

4. *Velázquez's Venus and Cupid*: Known also as 'The Toilet of Venus' and 'The Rokeby Venus', the painting was done by Velázquez in 1647–51. The work, which is the only surviving female nude by the artist, was acquired by the National Gallery in London in 1906.

5. *Is it a storm . . . stood still*: Lines from Blok's poem 'The Artist' (*Khudozhnik*), also included in the 1916 collection *Poems: Book Three*. The 'Sirins' – in Russian folklore, mythological creatures with the heads and chests of women but the bodies of birds – are here yet another allusion to Nabokov.

6. *I've awoken . . . Happiness won't let me sleep!*: Polyxena Sergeyevna Solovyova (1867–1924) was a Symbolist poet, playwright, translator and graphic artist, who worked under the pseudonym 'Allegro'. The epigraph is untraced.

7. *Like a swan . . . drifting*: The opening lines of an untitled work by the émigré poet Vladimir Smolensky (1901–61). The poem was the first in the writer's debut collection *Sunset* (*Zakat*, 1931).

8. *Separated by Chronos in the Maeterlinck realm of unborn souls*: A reference to Maurice Maeterlinck's (1862–1949) dream-play *The Blue Bird* (*L'Oiseau bleu*, 1908). At the end of Act III, unborn children wait for Time to call them before they descend to the earth. The play was premiered at the Moscow Art Theatre on 30 September 1908 under the direction of Konstantin Stanislavsky.

9. *She confided . . . thoughts*: A slightly misquoted extract from Nikolai Gumilyov's (1886–1921) poem of 1917 'A Stroll' (*Progulka*).

10. *Ostap Bender . . . edge*: Ostap Bender is the picaresque hero of Ilya Ilf (1897–1937) and Evgeny Petrov's (1903–42) comic novels *The Twelve Chairs* (*Dvenadtsat´ stul´ev*, 1928) and *The Little Golden Calf* (*Zolotoi telenok*, 1931). The reference here is to a scene in *The Little Golden Calf*, in which Bender believes that if he can find an underground Soviet millionaire, he will be able to trick the latter into offering up the 500,000 roubles he requires to emigrate to Rio de Janeiro.

11. *Simonetta Vespucci*: Simonetta Vespucci (née Cattaneo, *c*.1453–
     76) was a Genoese noblewoman. Renowned as the greatest
     beauty of her day and nicknamed 'la bella Simonetta', she served
     as the model for several of Botticelli's female figures.

12. *the madman Herostratus*: The Greek arsonist Herostratus
     (d. *c*.356 BC) sought fame by burning down the Temple of Arte-
     mis at Ephesus.

13. *Could Levin . . . 'lies'*: A reference to Part 4, Chapter 13, of
     Tolstoy's *Anna Karenina*, in which Levin, some time after Kit-
     ty's refusal to marry him, asks her a series of questions by
     writing the initials of the words in chalk on a baize-covered
     table. Kitty is portrayed to be so spiritually in touch with Levin
     that she is able to discern the words behind the initials.

14. *We pay for love . . . one death*: The final stanza of Zinaida Hip-
     pius's (1869–1945) poem of 1896 'Love Is One' (*Liubov' – odna*).

15. *Farewell . . . tender*: The opening lines from an untitled poem
     by Vladimir Smolensky included in his 1957 collection *Happi-
     ness (Schast'e)*.

16. *For me your darling hands . . . paradise*: The opening lines of
     the untitled first poem in émigré poet Anatoly Velichkovsky's
     (1901–81) collection of verse *Face to Face* (*Litsom k litsu*,
     1952).

17. *Je vous écris . . . trop courtes*: 'I write to you and tear up my
     letters. I reread yours – they always seem too brief' (French).
     The quotation, misattributed here by Guadanini to the French
     salonnière and sometime epistolist Jeanne Julie Éléonore de
     Lespinasse (1732–76), is in fact an inexact one from a letter by
     Ninon de l'Enclos (1620–1705) to the Marquis de Sévigné. The
     confusion may have resulted from Lespinasse's two tragic love
     affairs, with the Marquis de Mora and the Comte de Guibert,
     which are immortalized in her letters.

18. *Trembling . . . free as birds*: Lines from the poem 'The Hermit
     Maiden' (*Zatvornitsa*) by the Romantic poet Yakov Polonsky
     (1819–98). Polonsky was noted for his attempt to continue the
     Pushkinian tradition into the era of great Realism, when lyric
     and narrative poetry suffered a terrible decline in Russia at the
     hand of civic verse.

19. *You were the most brilliant . . . curse*: The opening lines of an
     untitled poem of 1914 by Alexander Blok. The poem, written in
     free ternary metre, is significant for its obvious thematic links
     with Guadanini's story and bears quoting in full:

You were more brilliant, faithful, and charming.
But do not curse me, do not curse!
My train flies, like a gypsy song,
Like those days that won't return . . .

What was once adored – passing by, passing by . . .
Ahead – the uncertain road . . .
Blessed it was, unforgettable,
Gone for ever . . . Forgive me!

Intriguingly, this poem was in fact one of those translated by Nabokov into English after his emigration to America. Nabokov's translation, originally left unpublished and dated 1948–51, was included in the recent collection of the author's verse translations, *Verses and Versions* (New York: Harcourt, 2008).

20. *You are alone . . . more invincible*: The final couplet from the opening poem of Vladimir Smolensky's 1938 collection *Tête-à-tête* (*Naedine*).

21. *And I left . . . victory*: A slight misquotation of the closing lines of Dovid Knut's poem 'Betrayal' (*Izmena*), from the 1938 collection *Daily Love* (*Nasushchnaia liubov'*). The final line in Knut's version reads: 'Of loneliness, sadness, freedom, victory.' Although the precise wording shows that Guadanini's epigraphs are drawn from the 1938 collection, it is perhaps noteworthy that both this and the previous poem by Knut (see note 3) appear to be linked, earlier versions of each having been published side by side in *Chisla* 7–8 (1933), pp. 12–13.

22. *And you will hear . . . heart*: Lines from Vladimir Smolensky's poem 'Heart' (*Serdtse*), included in the collection *Sunset*. The final line, which follows, reads: 'But people will hear nothing.'

23. *But don't dare . . . yearning for you*: Guadanini attributes these lines to Vladimir Nabokov, although they do not number among any of his published verse. It is perfectly feasible, however, that these are from one of the many poems he wrote but never published.

24. *I ran*: The narrative here switches to the masculine past tense, marking a discreet final shift in narrator, impossible to reflect in the English.

They Called Her Russia

translated by Boris Dralyuk

'They Called Her Russia' (*Ee zvali Rossiia*) first published in *Krug* 2 (1936), pp. 55–66.

1. *The rusty buffers ... sorrow*: The final quatrain of an untitled poem in Nikolai Otsup's (1894–1958) collection *In the Smoke* (*V dymu*, 1926).
2. *ataman*: A Cossack leader.
3. *Stundists*: The word Stundist (or Shtundist) is used to refer to members of a number of Evangelical Protestant sects that emerged in the south-western part of the Russian Empire, in what is now Ukraine, during the second half of the nineteenth century.
4. *Brest-Litovsk*: The Treaty of Brest-Litovsk was signed on 3 March 1918, in what is now Brest, Belarus, by the Bolsheviks and the Central Powers. It ended Russia's participation in the First World War. Two of the most important figures at the negotiations leading to the agreement were General Max Hoffmann (1869–1927), Chief of Staff of the German armies on the Eastern Front, and Adolf Ioffe (1883–1927), a Bolshevik politician of Karaite Jewish descent who was a close associate of Leon Trotsky. After Trotsky was expelled from the Communist Party in 1927, Ioffe, who suffered from a number of serious ailments and had been refused permission to seek medical treatment abroad, committed suicide.
5. *Bud-god-bug*: The Bug River runs for 480 miles through Poland, Belarus and Ukraine. The town of Brest is on the Bug.

Acknowledgements

1. *Texts and Translations*

Every effort has been made to trace the holders of internationally valid copyright on all of the material included in this book. The publisher and editor apologize for any errors or omissions in the list below and would be grateful if notified of any corrections that should be incorporated in future reprints or editions of this book.

'Literaturnaia masterskaia', by Georgy Adamovich, first published in the journal *Satirikon* (1931). Copyright 1931 by Georgy Adamovich.
'A Literary Studio' translation copyright © Bryan Karetnyk, 2017.

'Ramon Ortis', by Georgy Adamovich, first published in the journal *Chisla* (1931). Copyright 1931 by Georgy Adamovich.
'Ramón Ortiz' translation copyright © Anastasia Tolstoy, 2017.

'Astrolog', by Mark Aldanov, first published in the journal *Novyi zhurnal* (1947). Copyright 1947 by Mark Aldanov.
'The Astrologist' translation copyright © Bryan Karetnyk, 2017.

'Samovnushenie', by Don Aminado, first published in the collection *Nasha malen´kaia zhizn´* by J. Povolozky and Co. (1927). Copyright 1927 by Don Aminado (Aminodav Shpolyansky).
'Auto-Suggestion' translation copyright © Bryan Karetnyk, 2017.

'Ubiistvo Val´kovskogo', by Nina Berberova, first published in the journal *Vstrechi* (1934). Copyright © ACTES SUD / Nina Berberova, 1934.
'The Murder of Valkovsky' translation copyright © Bryan Karetnyk, 2017.

'V Parizhe', by Ivan Bunin, first published in the journal *Novyi zhurnal* (1942). Copyright 1943 by Ivan Bunin.

'In Paris' first published in the collection *Russian Short Stories from Pushkin to Buida* in Penguin Classics (2005), translation copyright © Robert Chandler, 2005. This revised translation copyright © Robert Chandler, 2017.

'*Un petit accident*', 'V al´pakh' and 'V takuiu noch´ . . .', by Ivan Bunin, all first published under the title 'Tri rasskaza' in the journal *Novosel´e* (1950). Copyright 1950 by Ivan Bunin.
'*Un petit accident*' first published in the journal *Chtenia* (Spring, 2014), translation copyright © Maria Bloshteyn, 2014. This revised translation copyright © Maria Bloshteyn, 2017.
'In the Alps' and 'In such a night . . .' translations copyright © Bryan Karetnyk, 2017.

'Klasson i ego dusha', by Boris Butkevich, first published in the journal *Novyi korabl´* (1927).
'Klasson and His Soul' translation copyright © Bryan Karetnyk, 2017.

'Komarinye moshchi', by Sasha Chorny, first published in the newspaper *Zaria* (1931).
'Spindleshanks' translation copyright © Maria Bloshteyn, 2017.

'Opyt', by Yury Felsen (Nikolai Freudenstein), first published in the magazine *Zveno* (1927).
'An Experiment' translation copyright © Bryan Karetnyk, 2017.

'Povtorenie proidennogo', by Yury Felsen (Nikolai Freudenstein), first published in the almanac *Krug* (1938).
'The Recurrence of Things Past' translation copyright © Ivan Juritz and Bryan Karetnyk, 2017.

'Shpion', by Gaito Gazdanov, first published anonymously, under the title 'Anglichane nazyvaiut ikh stormy petrel', in the magazine *Zveno* (1927). Copyright 1927 by Gaito Gazdanov.
'The Spy' translation copyright © Bryan Karetnyk, 2017.

'Chernye lebedi', by Gaito Gazdanov, first published in the journal *Volia Rossii* (1930). Copyright 1930 by Gaito Gazdanov.
'Black Swans' first published in the journal *Cardinal Points* (2016), translation copyright © Bryan Karetnyk, 2016. This revised translation copyright © Bryan Karetnyk, 2017.

'Kniazhna Meri', by Gaito Gazdanov, first published in the journal *Opyty* (1953). Copyright 1953 by Gaito Gazdanov.

'Princess Mary' translation copyright © Bryan Karetnyk, 2017.

'Panikhida' by Gaito Gazdanov, first published in the journal *Novyi zhurnal* (1960). Copyright © Gaito Gazdanov, 1960.
'Requiem' translation copyright © Bryan Karetnyk, 2017.

'Tunnel´', by Irina Guadanini, first published under a pseudonym, 'Alyotrus', in the journal *Sovremennik* (1961). Copyright © Irina Guadanini, 1961.
'The Tunnel' translation copyright © Donald Rayfield, 2017.

'Zhizel´', by Georgy Ivanov, first published in the newspaper *Illiustrirovannaia Rossiia* (1929). Copyright 1929 by Georgy Ivanov.
'Giselle' translation copyright © Boris Dralyuk, 2017.

'Raspad atoma', by Georgy Ivanov, first published in *Paris*, by Maison du Livre Étranger (1938). Copyright 1938 by Georgy Ivanov.
'The Atom Explodes' first published in the journal *Slavonica* (2002), translation copyright © Justin Doherty, 2002. This revised translation copyright © Justin Doherty, 2017.

'Pompeiskii uzhas', by Vladislav Khodasevich, first published in the newspaper *Poslednie novosti* (1925).
'Pompeii' translation copyright © Bryan Karetnyk, 2017.

'Atlantida', by Vladislav Khodasevich, first published in *Sobranie sochinenii v chetyrekh tomakh* by Soglasie, Moscow (1997).
'Atlantis' translation copyright © Bryan Karetnyk, 2017.

'Dama iz Monte-Karlo', by Dovid Knut, first published in the journal *Russkie zapiski* (1938). Copyright 1938 by Dovid Knut. Published with the permission of Yossi Knout.
'The Lady from Monte Carlo' translation copyright © Bryan Karetnyk, 2017.

'Kunak', by Galina Kuznetsova, first published in the collection *Utro*, published by Sovremennye zapiski (1930). Copyright 1930 by Galina Kuznetsova.
'Kunak' translation copyright © Bryan Karetnyk, 2017.

'Rossyp´ zvezd', by Ivan Lukash, first published in the collection *Goloe pole: Kniga o Gallipoli, 1921 g.* by Balkan, Sofia (1922).
'A Scattering of Stars' translation copyright © Bryan Karetnyk, 2017.

'Poseshchenie muzeia', by Vladimir Nabokov, first published in the journal *Sovremennye zapiski* (1939). Copyright © Article 3C under the will of Vladimir Nabokov, 1965, 1966.

'The Visit to the Museum' first published in the magazine *Esquire* (1963), translation copyright © Dmitri Nabokov, 1963.

'The Assistant Producer', by Vladimir Nabokov, first published in the collection *Nabokov's Dozen* by Doubleday (1958). Copyright © Article 3C under the will of Vladimir Nabokov, 1965, 1966.

'The Visit to the Museum' and 'The Assistant Producer', by Vladimir Nabokov, from *The Stories of Vladimir Nabokov* by Vladimir Nabokov, copyright © 1995 by Dmitri Nabokov. Used by permission of Alfred A. Knopf, an imprint of the Knopf Doubleday Publishing Group, a division of Penguin Random House LLC. All rights reserved.

'Zhizn´ madam Diuklo', by Irina Odoevtseva, first published in the journal *Zveno* (1927). Copyright 1927 by Irina Odoevtseva (Iraida Heinike). Published with the permission of Anna Golembiovskaja. 'The Life of Madame Duclos' translation copyright © Irina Steinberg, 2017.

'Moskva v pozore', by Ivan Shmelyov, first published in the newspaper *Vozrozhdenie* (1925). Copyright 1925 by Ivan Shmelyov. Published with the permission of Yves Gentilhomme-Koutyrine. 'Moscow in Shame' translation copyright © Bryan Karetnyk, 2017.

'*Russie*', by Ivan Shmelyov, first published in the newspaper *Vozrozhdenie* (1925). Copyright 1925 by Ivan Shmelyov. Published with the permission of Yves Gentilhomme-Koutyrine. '*Russie*' translation copyright © Bryan Karetnyk, 2017.

'Teni dnei', by Ivan Shmelyov, first published in the collection *V"ezd v Parizh* by Izdatel´skaia komissiia, Belgrade (1929). Copyright 1929 by Ivan Shmelyov. Published with the permission of Yves Gentilhomme-Koutyrine. 'Shadows of Days' translation copyright © Bryan Karetnyk, 2017.

'Vizy, valiuty, kaiuty', by Teffi, first published in the newspaper *Poslednie novosti* (1920). Copyright 1920 by Teffi (Nadezhda Lokhvitskaya). Published with the permission of Agnès Szydlowski. 'Thou Shalt Not Covet' translation copyright © Rose France, 2017.

'Gedda Gabler' and 'Razgovor', both by Teffi, first published in the collection *Gorodok* by N. P. Karbasnikov, Paris (1927). Copyright 1927 by Teffi (Nadezhda Lokhvitskaya). Published with the permission of Agnès Szydlowski.

'Hedda Gabler' and 'A Conversation' translations copyright © Rose France, 2017.

'Ee zvali Rossiia', by Vasily Yanovsky, first published in the almanac *Krug* (1936). Copyright 1936 by Vasily Yanovsky. Published with the permission of Alexis Levitin.
'They Called Her Russia' translation copyright © Boris Dralyuk, 2017.

2. *Editorial*

In any book of such a scale, there are inevitably many people whose help and assistance merit special acknowledgement. Scarcely, however, did I ever imagine when embarking on this book that not only would it take me (in correspondence at least) to every corner of the globe, but also that wherever I went I would meet with such generosity, kindness and enthusiasm. Many of the people listed below were unknown to me at the time of this project's inception; yet they have all been integral to its completion. To each of them, without exception, I owe a lasting debt of gratitude.

Thanks must go first to my commissioning editor at Penguin, Jessica Harrison, who supported this book from the very outset and who at every stage was ready with invaluable advice. I also owe a great debt to Anna Hervé, editorial manager of Penguin Classics, and to my copy editor, David Watson. Robert Chandler, one of the book's contributors, also deserves special mention for his kind willingness to share so much of his expertise and experience in managing such projects. Also of vital assistance was Richard Davies, of the Leeds Russian Archive, who gave so generously of his time in helping me to track down many of the descendants of the authors included in this volume; it is difficult to overstate the extent of his help.

The various translators who have contributed to this collection have been another source of support and inspiration, and I should like to take this opportunity to express my heartfelt thanks to them all for giving so much of their time and skill to every aspect of its compilation: Maria Bloshteyn, Robert Chandler, Justin Doherty, Boris Dralyuk, Rose France, Donald Rayfield, Irina Steinberg and Anastasia Tolstoy. Without their labours it would not have been possible.

The descendants and literary executors of several authors included in this collection also require special mention. Their guidance and input have been crucial to the book's compilation, and so I thank each of them individually: Yves Gentilhomme-Koutyrine, Anna

Golembiovskaja, Yossi Knout, Alexis Levitin and Agnès Szydlowski. I can only hope that this book will bring its authors, the people so dear to them, to new audiences, and in some measure accord them the recognition they have long deserved.

I have also benefited greatly from many emails, letters and conversations with Anna Aslanyan, Ben Dhooge (Ghent University), Julian Graffy (University College London), Thomas Karshan (University of East Anglia), Lyubov Khachaturian (RGALI), Vladimir Khazan (Hebrew University of Jerusalem), Oleg Korostelev (IMLI), Leonid Livak (University of Toronto), Rachel Morley (University College London), Ian O'Neal, Melissa Purkiss (University of Oxford), Ekaterina Rogatchevskaia (British Library), Andrei Rogatchevski (University of Tromsø), Maria Rubins (University College London), Stephanie Seegmuller, Jekaterina Shulga (University College London), Julia Sutton-Mattocks (University of Bristol) and Paul Williams. Their expertise and assistance have been truly invaluable. Many of them also gave generously of their time to scrutinize various drafts during the preparation of this book; needless to say, the responsibility for any remaining errors is mine and mine alone.

The final acknowledgement goes to the dedicatee of this book, the late Ivan Juritz, who was a constant source of inspiration and encouragement, a colleague of humbling talent and versatility, and a dear friend, still sorely missed.

                                                                                B.S.K.